ENCOUNTERING RIEL

ENCOUNTERING RIEL

a novel by
DAVID D. ORR

Stonehouse Publishing
www.stonehousepublishing.ca
Alberta, Canada

Stonehouse Publishing Inc is an independent publishing house,
incorporated in 2014.

Cover design and layout by Anne Brown
Printed in Canada

Stonehouse Publishing would like to thank and acknowledge
the support of the Alberta Government funding for the arts,
through the Alberta Media Fund.

Alberta
Government

National Library of Canada Cataloguing in Publication Data
David D. Orr
Encountering Riel
Novel
ISBN: 978-0-9950645-5-3 (paperback)
Second Edition

To Lynn

PART OF THE NORTH-WEST
TERRITORIES – 1885

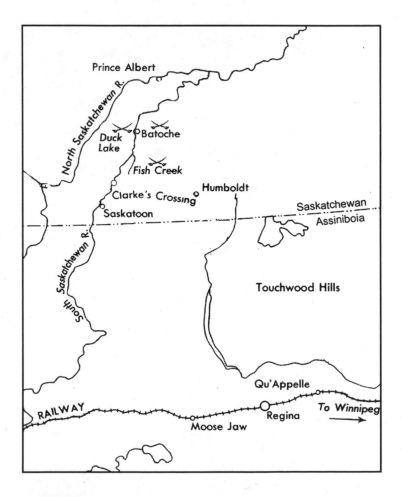

Map by Jessica Perry

PROLOGUE

I lay on my stomach, hunkering down desperately into the muddy ground of Tourond's Coulee. The wet, cold grass slapped against my cheek. Nolan's body was stretched out a few feet away. The dark red stain on the front of his scarlet tunic glistened in the greyish light.

Sanborn had been wounded too, and badly, as soon as we came over the lip of the coulee. But Roley was out there somewhere, or I prayed he was. My arm ached from the effort of holding the heavy revolver above the muddy ground. God help me if the barrel got jammed with mud.

Neither Roley nor I could hit much with our popgun revolvers. We were stalking a Métis rifleman hidden in his rifle pit, a man who could probably blow a crow's head off at five hundred yards. If we stood up, we'd be shot dead instantly by the riflemen farther up the coulee. So I pushed myself into the muddy grass and started pulling myself forward on my elbows.

Some cold rain splattered down the back of my neck, and an errant thought raced through my mind. I think I nearly smiled. What in God's name was a timid student of poetry from the University of Toronto doing in a place like this?

TORONTO
MARCH 28-30, 1885

I

There were crowds everywhere, that cool Saturday morning. The newspapers had sold out, but the storekeepers knew that people wanted to know about the fighting in the West. Shop windows displayed the front pages of the morning editions. Throngs of earnest-looking men and women stood in the slush, reading the dismal news.

The crowd in front of the Empire Tobacco and News, on Yonge Street, was huge. I wasn't strong, and under normal circumstances I could never have fought my way to the front of it. On this day, though, it parted respectfully in front of me, like the Red Sea.

I'll tell you why in a moment.

I was badly scared already, and when I got close enough to read the headlines, it got worse:

RIEL STARTS A NEW INSURRECTION
Mounted Police are routed in North-West Territories

THE TERRITORIES ARE ABLAZE
North-West Mounted Police & Volunteers
Slaughtered at Duck Lake

In the storefront window, between the posted sheets of paper, I could see myself. I hardly recognized what I saw. A short, slight twenty-one-year-old, a bespectacled stripling. That part was familiar. But the reflected "me" was wearing a navy blue wedge cap and a navy blue uniform overcoat. The top buttons were undone, and my red tunic blazed through. It sported the officer's shoulder-strap which marked a second lieutenant in Her Majesty's militia. In a flapped brown holster on my hip I was packing a .476 calibre double-action Enfield revolver.

God, no wonder all those people had parted for me. I actually looked like a *soldier*.

I read the newspaper columns. The details were worse than the headlines. Then I looked uneasily around me. I had the feeling that I was the centre of attention. A couple of feet away, a mature but still attractive matron gazed at me with a winsome, dreamy smile on her face. I started to push my way back through the crowd, and people patted me on the back; a couple of old men snapped to attention as I passed them.

Two overweight middle-aged businessmen were talking in the street. "Riel," one of them said. "God damn Riel. Riel and his pack of half-French halfbreeds. Why didn't we hang him in 1870, when he started the God damn uprising at Red River? When he murdered what's his name, a Canadian and a Protestant at that."

The other one laughed, and blew out a vast cloud of cigar smoke. "Getting absent-minded, are you, George?" he said. "It was Thomas Scott he killed. And we didn't hang Riel because we couldn't catch him. He flitted off to the States, like a bird, like a wraith. He became a Yankee citizen down there, did you know that? It's Riel having been down there that worries me. He met over and over with Ulysses S. Grant, right in the God damn White House. What did they talk about? What deals did they make? Now that Riel is back and killing Canadians, are the Americans going to intervene? Come over the border in their God damn blue coats to 'protect' our settlers? I'd never put it past them."

They both caught me looking at them and eavesdropping. If I'd looked like a student, as I usually did, one of them might have asked me what the hell I thought I was doing, and told me to be on my way.

But I wasn't dressed like a student. I was dressed in a soldier's red coat. One of the businessmen said, "God bless you, son. God keep you safe." The other one gave me a clumsy salute.

I looked around at the crowded, dirty street and its sidewalks, at the clattering horse-drawn buses and the hansom cabs. The street was full of my fellow militiamen. Laughing and smiling, in the red coats of the Royal Grenadiers and the green coats of the Queen's Own Rifles, they were walking and riding down the street, each the centre of the same worshipful attention I'd just experienced. Grinning, they saluted me; some of them unmilitarily clapped me on the back. The civilians beamed benignly.

I shook my head, like a baffled animal. My life had changed so fast in twenty-four hours that I hardly knew where I was. By now, the whole world knew that, two days earlier, far to the west, a column of the famous North-West Mounted Police had been ambushed, routed, by a ragtag force of Métis buffalo hunters and Indians. If the Mounties hadn't fled, they would have been annihilated. And now they were screaming for help.

Dead men in red coats, lying in bloody snowdrifts in the North-West Territories, had suddenly changed my life, as certainly as if some hurricane had uprooted me or some colossal wave were sweeping me away. The telegram calling Second Lieutenant of Militia William J. Lorimer up for "active service" was wadded in my back pocket. I'd be there to see Mr. Louis Riel and his lieutenant Gabriel Dumont, and very soon.

And the trouble was: we had sent all the British redcoats home. Canada didn't have a professional army. What it had was a militia—a collection of weekend warriors, Sunday soldiers, all wearing archaic (if splendid) uniforms, which each separate unit had designed for themselves. The militia hardly ever met to practice marksmanship, or tactics, or even to go on a route march. They were store clerks, bookkeepers, university students, farm boys, led

She was also a remarkably independent girl. Over her father's loud objections, she'd been one of the first girls to enter University College when it had opened its doors to females the previous year. She'd immediately become famous (or infamous) for advocating women's suffrage, in class, to old Professor Crosbie, whose views on women had evidently hardened sometime in the seventeenth century. It was said the poor old duffer had been forced to take three days off to recuperate. An astonished young man had pointed her out to me the next day as "the frightful Miss Niven."

Somehow, she hadn't looked frightful to me, so I had approached her, and she had greeted me with a smile. But I had never disagreed with her about anything. Not to her face, I mean.

Now, under the panes of glass, her blue eyes were filling with tears. "Oh, you fool," she said. "You indescribable fool. And if you do go, Riel will shoot you. You'd have a better chance with a firing squad. The Canadian militia couldn't hit the broad side of a barn. Riel's men actually know one end of a gun from the other, unlike you, Willie Lorimer, *you God damn fool!*" And then she hit me. Not very hard, I think she was capable of far more, but I felt it.

She got up and stormed across the room, keeping her back to me. I had never seen her in this mood before, and the courage I'd felt confronting her father had deserted me. I'd never even heard a woman curse before. I didn't know they could do it. I didn't know they could smack you one, either.

I could feel a little of the sweat from her palm on my cheek. This was the most intimate we'd ever been. "Alice, Alice dear," I said, forgetting how bright she was. "Nothing is going to happen to me. The Mounted Police will arrest all these so-called rebels. By the time we get there, it'll all be over. It will be just a jaunt."

She turned around, and faced me. She had stopped crying, and her face was set in a way that frightened me. "Yes," she said. "Just a jaunt. The Mounted Police will effortlessly defeat the primitives, just like they did at Duck Lake. Where the God Almighty Mounted Police all ran away, leaving dead men all over the place. And they had a *cannon, a cannon*! And all you have, Willie, is that ridiculous uniform and that stupid *revolver*."

I tried to speak; she silenced me by imperiously holding up her hand. "My father quotes Mr. Blake, the Liberal leader, all the time. Blake says Riel should have been negotiated with in 1870. Willie, you *know* the Métis are starving. You *know* the government won't recognize their titles to their land. They've been petitioning Ottawa for months. Mr. Blake believes that we can negotiate with them. Mr. Blake believes..."

"I wonder," I said, "if he believes his nephew, the lawyer Mr. Elliot of Prince Albert, is still alive. Because he isn't, you know. I saw it in a newspaper. The rebels shot Mr. Elliot. He bled to death in the snow. As dead as any chance that this thing is going to be solved by negotiations, even if it ever could have been."

She stared at me, white-faced. She said nothing. I took off my overcoat, threw it on a sofa, and sat down. Then I decided to throw caution to the wind, I don't know why. "I'll tell you something else, too, Alice," I said. She continued to stare into my eyes. "There are moments in history when we have to get past the elaborate arguments of fat little men with glasses, like Edward Blake. This is one of them. At moments like this, if you're worth the powder to blow you to hell, you decide what tribe you belong to. Riel apparently has. I know what tribe *I* belong to. That would be the tribe of the men in red coats, the English-speaking tribe, the Queen's tribe. Edward Blake doesn't know he *has* a tribe, and that's why he'll never be Prime Minister."

I don't know where all that Tory bombast had come from. Maybe I was tired of always agreeing with her. I half-expected her to throw me out of the house. But she said, "Willie, when you look at me, what do you see?"

"The woman I love," I said.

She smiled a little. "No," she said. "What you see is a bookish girl whom no man ever looked at before you did. My God, Willie, I read *books*. I have *opinions*. I wear *spectacles*. Men don't marry girls like that. Women like me, Willie, become teachers or governesses; or if their father's rich, like mine, they become rich old maids that everybody feels sorry for. 'Poor old Miss Niven, still living alone in her crumbling old mansion. Poor old thing. She must have been pretty once. Except for those awful glasses.' I'll tell you a secret, Willie. I don't want to be alone all my life. You're my only chance to have any kind of life. You'd better keep your stupid head down when they start shooting, because..." She was crying again.

"Look how short I am," I said, smiling. "They probably won't even see me." And I held out my arms to her. That did it. She ran over to me, threw my overcoat on the floor, and dissolved into my arms. I had never seen her cry before. She scarcely made a noise. I had never in my life seen anyone cry that hard before. She shook almost uncontrollably.

My reaction was completely perverse. I was delighted. I hadn't realized she cared for me a thousandth this much. But, after a while, I began to be seriously concerned, and so I sat her upright on the sofa. She pulled out her handkerchief and blew her nose violently. She stared at me so fiercely I did not know if it was love or fury at my seeing her weakness, or a mixture of both.

I touched her face gently with my hand, got up, and clumsily knelt on the floor in front of her. She stared at me incredulously. "It only gets worse," I said. "I'm asking you to marry me. I've been wanting to for ages, but I was afraid of your father, you, and myself. For some unknown reason, I'm not afraid, not right now, not today. So I'm asking you. Now you really *are* in trouble."

She was not a hesitant woman, not then, not ever. She reached down and, with surprising strength, dragged me by the collar back up on to the sofa. "Yes," she said, sniffling. "I will marry you. And that means you have to hide behind rocks and do whatever's necessary to come back to me."

"I promise," I said. "Alice, I'm no hero."

She put her hand over my mouth. Then she pulled me close, and took off my glasses. And, for the first time in our lives, we kissed.

I had never kissed a girl before. For the first few seconds, I expected something chaste and maidenly. But Alice pressed herself against me with every ounce of force in her muscular little body.

She covered my lips, my eyes, my face with passionate kisses, kisses so full of yearning that I wondered how I'd ever thought she might reject me. She was breathing hard. In a few seconds, I did not know where I was. I was sinking into a dark pit; my body was shaking with ecstasy. I heard myself moaning. My hands were clutching at her body, and the all-encompassing satin dress was maddening me. Then she pulled herself back gently. I opened my eyes, and found her dark blue eyes staring mischievously into mine. She had a grin on her face. "*Stop,*" she whispered.

"There, Willie," she said. "That's what life feels like. It feels better than death, I'll bet. Just remember that much better than that awaits you when you come back, when we're married. Which can only be accomplished if you come back alive and in one piece. So remember the last five minutes, and come back that way."

Then we just sat on the sofa and held each other. I sat quietly, with her head on my shoulder. The holstered Enfield dug painfully into my leg. Then the eternal restlessness which always seemed to flow through her asserted itself. She squirmed around, she seemed on the verge of speaking. Finally, I said, "I'm going to let you break the awful news of our engagement to your parents. Your father's not apoplectic, is he? I mean, not until he hears the news." She started to laugh.

And the doorbell rang.

I heard a maid's voice and a man's and then the lower, rumbling tones of Alice's father. Then Mr. Niven's heavy footsteps approached the door. I wondered if he'd have the courtesy to knock, and my opinion of him rose slightly when he did. Alice called for him to come in, and he opened the door. "Another officer has arrived," Mr. Niven said, in a slightly bewildered tone. "Apparently my home is to be a staging area for the invasion of the West. This one is called Captain Collison. He has come here looking for Lieutenant Lorimer, which I suppose is you, Willie. I've told him to come in. I trust that is all right." Without waiting to see if it was, he bowed slightly to someone behind him, and moved out of sight. "Go in, sir," he said.

Through the door came a man dressed like me: red tunic, sidearm and all. He picked up Alice's mood at once. "I think I've come at the wrong time," he said, in a steady but embarrassed voice. "I came here looking for Lieutenant William Lorimer. I went to his house, and his mother told me that she thought he'd be here." He stopped and looked down at the floor, reddening slightly. "I'm sorry," he said. "I'm Roland Collison."

Alice was a polite girl. She walked over to him and held out her hand. "That's all right, Mr. Collison," she said. "I've already had my tantrum over my fiancé's military career. I am Alice Niven, and this is your Lieutenant Lorimer, in the flesh."

And he gave her the most dazzling grin. This man was to play so gigantic a role in my life that I had might as well describe him as I saw him for the first time that day. He was, I later found, thirty-four at the time, but his black hair was beginning to go grey, and thinning very slightly in front, and this made him look more like forty. He had a trim, carefully-tended moustache. I am five feet seven, and he must have been four inches taller than me. He was a very handsome, powerfully-built man.

He took Alice's hand, politely, and shook it. "Call me Roley," he said. "Please."

"And I am Alice," she said, but her manner was a bit cooler than it had been, and I wondered why.

I walked over to him and shook his hand. "Lieutenant," he said. The grin flashed again. "Or should it be 'William'"?

"Willie," I said with a smile, gesturing him toward one of the sofas. Alice and I sat together on one facing him. "So," I said, "the Minister of Militia informed you that you were stuck with me as an officer?"

"Well, not 'stuck with,' I don't think," he said. "All the men are looking forward to meeting you. When I heard you were assigned to our unit, I went looking for you. I wanted to meet you and welcome you to the company. Willie, you're a perfect fit; even the uniform of your old University outfit is so much like ours. We're lucky to have you." For some reason, I sat taller beside Alice.

"Poor Tom McNaughton," he said, "who's normally second lieutenant of our company, is sick with typhoid. He'll never be able to go with us on Monday." Beside me, Alice gasped. He looked at her quite seriously. "Yes," he said. "They're sending six hundred men out right away to join General Middleton. The trains are actually waiting at the station, and we have to leave Monday morning."

"Middleton," Alice said, squeezing my arm with her soft hand. "Willie, we saw him, at the Dawson's Christmas party last year. That fat old man." She glanced at Roley Collison. "He fought in *Inja*," she said, "and against the Maori, don't you know. All the Empire's little wars."

It was clear that Captain Collison was troubled by her attitude, but he was obviously much too well-bred a man to argue with a lady. "They've sent him out there already?" I asked. "Has he got any soldiers with him?"

The captain turned to me with evident relief. "Yes," he said, "Macdonald and the government sent Middleton out to Winnipeg a few days ago, and there's a battalion called the Winnipeg Rifles there. They've now mobilized the eastern militia, and what few regulars we have. And the government wanted one more militia company from Toronto, and they asked our colonel who the best company in the Toronto Light Infantry was, and he said ours." He smiled with obvious pride. "Now that we've got you, Willie, we'll be invincible." He sounded like the coach of a baseball team. I felt myself turning red and smiling. He smiled back.

"Invincible," Alice said, a little dubiously. "What kind of men will Willie be serving with, Mr. Collison? Do *you* have any military experience?" She did not sound sarcastic now. She sounded like she wanted to be reassured.

Collison smiled, self-deprecatingly. "No," he said, lightly. "No, none of us do, Alice. Our whole regiment are store clerks, bookkeepers, salesmen, people like that. I own a little store on Bloor Street. We sell boys' clothing. 'Collison's Boys' Wear.' My wife helps me in the store. Maybe you've heard of it." Alice stared at him without saying anything. The captain looked around him at the splendour of the great Mr. Niven's library, the endless rows of leather books, the gigantic piano, and all at once I realized that he felt out of place, and a little humiliated. He smiled. "No, of course you haven't heard of it."

"'Childe Roland to the dark tower came,'" Alice suddenly said, with anger in her voice.

"He did? Who was he?" Roley Collison said with interest.

"He's a character in a poem," I said sharply. Suddenly I felt irritated with Alice, and her unconcealed hostility to this friendly, dapper man who was trying to welcome me to his company. I said, "Roley, when do you want me to report for duty?"

He looked relieved. "That's what I came to tell you," he said. "We're meeting at ten tomorrow, Sunday, at the Armoury. Bring your kit, Willie. I see you've got a sidearm. Thank God for that. Bring all the warm mittens and fur hats and long underwear you've got, because there are gaps in the C.P.R. line between here and the West. Bring your ammunition. You'll meet the men tomorrow." He stopped, and looked at us. Then he smiled again. "As for me, I'm happy. I've got a crackerjack second lieutenant for my unit, and I've just made two new friends." He held his hands up and made a square with his fingers in front of his eyes, like a man gazing at a picture in an art gallery. "I'll remember the both of you just like this, just like a photograph." I had gotten up and walked over to him, and he put his arm around my shoulders and gave me a quick squeeze, hard. He smiled at me. "Good to have you aboard, Willie," he said.

I suppose it was inevitable. I felt little for my cipher of a dad except boredom, and I genuinely loathed Alice's father. I was an only child. But all I knew at the time was that I felt humiliated by the unconcealed hostility and dismay on Alice's face. She was always so much quicker than I was, you see. She had seen at once what it would take me days to realize, which was that very soon, I would be ready to follow this storekeeper in a captain's uniform anywhere he chose to lead me, anywhere at all.

III

I was at the Armoury at precisely ten the next day, Sunday. The Royal Grenadiers and the Queen's Own Rifles militia were stomping up and down, getting issued rifles and ammunition and stores, getting shouted at by their officers, making noise to reassure themselves. I watched them for a few minutes. Then I heard my name called, and turned around to see Roley, waving at me and gesturing toward a corner of the big drill hall. Drawn up there were the ninety-one red-coated men of the Fourth Company, Toronto Light Infantry Regiment.

Roley actually introduced me to each of the men, who looked at me with indecipherable expressions, and shook my hand. Company Four had three officers: Roley, their commander; me, the second lieutenant and third-in-command; and, between us in the hierarchy, a man called First Lieutenant Jack Price. Lieutenant Price was a trim little man with a neatly trimmed moustache like Roley's, a pipe like Roley's, and a prematurely bald head under his neatly-fitted wedge cap. He watched Roley for his cues, and he laughed at Roley's jokes. I could see that the handsome captain was someone he'd like to be. Jack Price was a clerk in a shoe store. The senior non-com was Colour Sergeant Tom Quinn, a reassuringly military-looking, big, ruddy fellow with bristling, black Burnside whiskers. I thought for a giddy minute we might have an actual soldier on our side, but Quinn turned out to be a waiter in a Bloor Street restaurant.

The men were shouldering the rifles they'd just been issued. Our company, and most of the militia, carried the Snider-Enfield rifle.

It was actually a converted muzzle-loader, converted, that is, to a slow-firing, single-shot breech-loader. The Sniders were outmoded, heavy, cumbersome and inaccurate. They didn't even have an ejection lever. When you'd popped off your one shot, you had to tilt the thing to the side so the expended shell would fall out. That, in combat, made your head jerk up from behind the rock or log you were hiding behind; and we would find in the West that this was a very bad thing.

I asked Roley to come with me, and I led him across the vast, crowded, echoing hall, to a dark, empty corridor which led to a side entrance. "Captain," I said, "you mustn't have too much faith in me. I don't know *anything*. I mean, I've had no training at all. I've only fired this revolver six times. I've never even marched."

He started to laugh, then put his hand on my shoulder for a second. "God almighty, Willie," he said, "you'll fit right in. Do any of these fellows look much like soldiers to you? Do I? They all joined the militia for something to do, other than play baseball or football. Well, now we'll have something to do. We put on the red coat and now, unfortunately, there's going to be hell to pay. We have to ante up, or put our money where our mouths are, or some damn thing. And we will, and we'll win, too." He started to turn away, and then came back. "And don't worry about marching, either," he said. "You're an officer. You don't have to be in step. Just stroll along beside the men and watch them like you're looking for a misstep. I promise you, you'll look great. And we can really use you. Didn't you see the way the men looked at you? Most of these fellows only have grade nine or ten. Hell, I only have grade ten. To them, a university man is a higher form of life." He started to laugh again and punched my arm. I think he was serious.

* * *

And now it was Monday morning, the next day, and I strode out of a courtyard and onto King Street, as the bands blared, and the cheering of the crowds grew deafening. Our little company, rifles shouldered, was marching between the Grenadiers and the Queen's

Own. Roley led the way, Lieutenant Jack Price on one side of the little group, I on the other. A reviewing stand made of raw-looking pinewood, bedecked with Union Jacks, had been set up. It contained the mayor, his wife, and the great Adolphe Caron, the Minister of Militia, himself. Caron had a prodigious moustache, and wore a bright red sash.

I took Roley's advice and strolled insouciantly alongside the marching men, peering occasionally at them as if judging their marching quality. Roley looked over at me and smiled. For an instant he dropped out of step, and walked as I was, then, so fast it was a blur, he right-footed himself again, and fell back in step. He winked.

We marched, as if in a dream, down the familiar, wet, dirty street toward the familiar train station. But nothing was the same as it had been. A feeling of being utterly changed washed over me. The sidewalks were crowded with yelling, almost delirious men and women. Suspended over the street were gigantic banners, in red, white and blue: WE LOVE YOU, BOYS, and COME HOME SAFE. People shouted and waved from second-storey windows, from third-storey windows, from the roofs of buildings. Union Jacks and Canadian Red Ensigns were everywhere in the bright morning air, hanging from lamp posts, suspended from windows, held up by groups of excited little boys who had shoved their way to the sidewalk's front. The little boys jumped ecstatically up and down. The bands and the cheering were like waves sweeping over us. The men were in their Sunday best, with toppers and bowlers shining, and the ladies were bedecked in Easter finery. They roared their approval. The men yelled, "God save the Queen!" When they could, the women leaned out and patted our shoulders or touched our faces.

I could see that many in the crowd, men and women, were crying. It seemed to me that time slowed, and that for a long dreamy interval we passed down that avenue of cheering, weeping men and women, bathed in the roars of applause and encouragement, as in a vision. It occurred to me that there was something disproportionate about the scene—thirty thousand people wildly cheering six hundred young men, scarcely soldiers, in outdated uniforms, marching away to a war in a place most Canadians knew of only from newspapers or wild-west thrillers.

But I knew why. Canada was an infant country of eighteen years, and it had never been taken seriously, except by us. The British condescended to their "colonials." The Americans laughed at us. Now the Canadians had their first war. We were carrying the peoples' hopes and dreams on our slender shoulders to the West. The presence of those people on King Street was an affirmation. It was even a kind of prayer. We were a nation, and now we were going to prove it. No one would laugh at us, no one would patronize us, not after this.

On the sidewalk, looking at me and laughing, were two meltingly beautiful young blond girls, one in a dress of light blue satin with her overcoat unbuttoned to show it off, the other in a bright red hat. They were about sixteen, each waving a little Union Jack. Full of myself, I swept them a salute better than the one I'd given Caron, and they dissolved into each other with helpless giggles.

We swung smartly into the station. It was festooned with Union Jacks, and huge rosettes of red, white and blue. A giant red and white banner hung overhead: GOD SAVE THE QUEEN. The relatives and close friends of "the soon-to-be-departed," as Roley kept calling us, were waiting behind a red rope. The rope was lowered, and the folks moved forward to mill around with the militia, embracing them, caressing them, handing them last-minute gifts of cigarettes and chocolate.

I was introduced to Roley's wife and son. They weren't what I'd expected. His wife was a thin woman; she must have been pretty once, but now her face was anxious and lined with worry. The son was a bespectacled little fellow of eight or nine, with his mother's serious face. He clung tightly to her hand and seemed almost intimidated by his father's awkward attempts to embrace him. Alice held on tight to one of my arms and my mother to the other. My father smiled vaguely in the background. The more exclusive Mr. and Mrs. Niven had not, of course, dignified the vulgar and jingoistic spectacle with their presence. The previous night, I'd overheard Alice's father contemptuously calling us "toy soldiers."

Suddenly, one of the bands, which had been playing "The Maple Leaf Forever" and "The British Grenadiers" with metronomic regularity stopped dead, and then loudly started "Yankee Doodle." At the same moment, the crowds at the station entrance cheered wildly. I looked around, and at the same moment, Roley, forgetting for a moment that ladies were present, said, "Well, Jesus H. Jeremiah Christ. I'd heard about this, but I didn't really believe it."

Marching down the platform toward us was a youngish man in the familiar dark-blue tunic, light-blue trousers, and mashed-down blue kepi cap of the United States Army. Following this apparition came two huge, tarpaulin-covered carts husbanded along by soldiers in the blue and red uniforms and Glengarry caps of the regular Canadian artillery. Sanborn, one of the wits of our company, pointed south, and called out to the American in an affected accent, "Well, pardon me, suh, but Ah do believe that General Lee is down that-a-way."

The American grinned and clapped him on the back. "Not any more, he isn't," he said. He walked up to us and stuck out his hand to Roley. He had dark hair, a handlebar moustache, and the slightly weary, hollow, deeply-recessed eyes of the obsessive student. "Hello, Captain," he said. "Gentlemen, ladies." We just stared. "Second Lieutenant Arthur Howard," he said. It sounded a little like *Aathaa Hawadd*. "Connecticut National Guard. Although, strictly speaking, I'm not here representing Connecticut, or the U.S. armed forces. Informally I represent the Company, but at the base of it, I'm here as a friend of, and experimenter with, the gun."

"What gun?" my mother said.

Howard turned, doffed his cap, and gestured theatrically toward the huge carts. "Why," he said, "*that* gun, my dear lady. The guns in those wagons. The famous products of the brilliant mind of Dr. R.J. Gatling of Indianapolis." He seemed suddenly embarrassed by this Barnum and Bailey performance. "I'm sorry, Ma'am," he said. "I'm not usually this much of a show-off. It must be the occasion, or the music, or something. The Gatling gun is an artillery piece we call a machine gun. It can fire up to twelve hundred rounds per minute. Caron, your Minister of Militia, some days ago made arrangements to use two of the guns, if trouble erupted in your North-West. I took leave from the Guard, and brought them up here. It's taken me an eternity of trouble, but I'm here."

"Roley Collison," my captain said, taking his hand. "And the rest of these fellows?"

"Are troopers from your artillery school, assigned by Mr. Caron to help me," Howard said. "And very pleased to be in on this little adventure of yours, I am sure." He looked back at the patiently-waiting Canadian regulars. "We'd better get these Gatlings aboard and secured," he said. "I look forward to renewing our conversation on the train." He bowed slightly to the rest of us. "Ladies, gentlemen," he said, and he and his entourage passed on.

Jack Price said, "Good grief. Twenty-four hundred rounds per minute. How long would it take the whole of Company Four to fire twenty-four hundred rounds, Willie?" Apparently, I was deemed to be a mathematical prodigy.

"Twenty-four hundred *accurate* rounds?" I said. "About three weeks."

Roley dissolved into laughter, followed by a coughing fit. "Now, now," he said. "Enough of such negative thinking. We'll have Mr. Riel and his half-breeds winning the battle before it begins."

"Mr. Collison, they call themselves Métis," Alice said coolly.

Roley turned a little red, but he smiled. "All right, Alice," he said. "Matey. And so I shall call them, from this minute forth." I was proud of him. Then, with a smile, he turned and walked over to his waiting wife and son.

I looked behind me. The soldiers were starting to straggle onto the train. Conductors were bustling about, putting down wooden steps, helping the soldiers swing the long, cumbersome Snider-Enfields aboard. Suddenly, I felt a vaguely nauseous hollow in the pit of my stomach. I was just twenty-one years old, and I had never been away from my mother and father for more than one day in

my life. Now, God help me, I was going to be in a war. I felt Alice's
rather strong hands digging into my arm. She led me away a few
steps to an alcove where we could be more alone.

"You must say goodbye to your mother and father last," she said.
"It will kill your mother before the battle begins if you don't." Alice
was wearing a very modest little blue cap, an almost military little
cap, and her fair hair was ruthlessly brushed back beneath it, as if to
give the lie to anyone who made jokes about the frailty of women.
Her face was very red, and her blue eyes shone. Her gloved hands
held both of mine, tight. She looked straight into my eyes (we were
much of a height) and gave me a kiss of really startling ardour and
directness. When it finally ended, I looked around uneasily, thinking we might be arrested for an indecent public display, but everyone was too preoccupied to notice.

"Willie," Alice said, gripping me hard by the shoulder, "I know I
read too much, and talk too much, but I looked for over an hour last
night, because I knew that somewhere in Whitman he says what
I need to say to you. It's from 'When Lilacs Last in the Dooryard
Bloom'd.' He's talking about the American Civil War." I waited. She
pulled a little, worn red book out of her bag, and read from it:

> I saw battle-corpses, myriads of them,
> And the white skeletons of young men, I saw them,
> I saw the debris and debris of all the slain soldiers of the war,
> But I saw they were not as was thought,
> They themselves were fully at rest, they suffer'd not,
> The living remain'd and suffer'd, the mother suffer'd,
> And the wife and the child and the musing comrade suffer'd,
> And the armies that remain'd suffer'd.

"Willie," she said urgently, "*you have to come back to me*. You
have to. I can't live without you. I can't bear to spend the rest of my
life being one of those left behind who suffer. I'm not brave enough
for that." There were tears in her eyes. "So stay alive. Let that Yankee
win the stupid war with his stupid guns. He's just the man to do it.

Let your hero Roley perish, leading a charge waving a pistol, with his pipe in his mouth. He's just the man to do *that. But come back to me.*"

"I will," I said. I gave her the hardest hug I could, and then I just walked away toward the train. I knew if I hesitated much longer, I'd be there when the troops came back.

Shortly after I disentangled myself from my mother and father, the train pulled out of the station, followed by a second. They were going at a really unaccountable clip, as if to discourage anyone from having second thoughts. Alice had been wearing a very quiet, dark-blue coat, but I found I could see her for a long time as we pulled out of the station, and even after that, the way a bright flash of light lingers after it's gone, I found if I closed my eyes, I could still see her, as plain as day.

THE JOURNEY

I V

The two trains charged northward across the fields of Ontario. It was almost April. The snow was melting, and the dark, thick, muddy fallow was emerging everywhere. Everything had been swept off the tracks for us to pass, although the trains slowed in every village, because on every station platform there was a band, *("The Maple Leaf, our emblem dear, the Maple Leaf forever...")* and a crowd waving Union Jacks. There were old men, and some of them stood at attention, and saluted. There were women and girls, shouting excitedly, or just gazing at the train, with moist eyes. Children pressed up to the edges of the platforms, and we saluted *them,* and waved, and blew kisses to the little girls. There were signs: MAKE US PROUD OF YOU, BOYS, and CANADA IS PROUD OF ITS HEROES, and, more ominously, AVENGE THOMAS SCOTT. This reference to the Protestant executed by Riel in the '70 rebellion made Lieutenant Jack Price of Company Four nod solemnly. We did our best to project courage and indomitability.

We clattered onward, our backs and asses aching horribly on the wooden seats. Men sat on their bunched-up overcoats; when they got up they tripped over the huge Snider-Enfields protruding every which way into the aisle.

Roley had predicted that some idiot on the train would be carrying a loaded rifle. He was right. The idiot in question was in the Queen's Own militia. He somehow discharged his rifle in the middle of the first night, scaring everyone in his carriage shitless. They all woke up thinking that Gabriel Dumont was upon them, smoking six-shooter in hand. (The bullet went through the ceiling, which was lucky, considering we were already understrength.)

The trains sped on, stopping only briefly to attach fresh carriages carrying men from the regular schools of artillery. Combined with us, they would be the first contingent of the North-West Field Force to reach the North-West Territories from the East. Occasionally, we stopped and were fed huge meals that townswomen had cooked for us. They hugged us and called us "son," and insisted we were heroes. It was excruciating. After a day or so of this, we actually felt as if we were roughing it. We didn't know, then, that a couple of days after *that*, we would have been willing to sell our souls to get back on that train.

I watched Roley as he circulated among our men. He used every man's given name, and to every man, even the youngest private, he was "Roley," not "Captain." He cracked jokes, he inquired about wives and children, he promised to try to ensure that no one would find himself unemployed after he came home. He flashed his grin and patted backs and shared tobacco, and I saw that he was not only respected but nearly loved.

The American Lieutenant Arthur Howard watched all this with obvious approval. "That's the way to do it," he said. "That's the *only* way to do it."

There were a number of newspaper correspondents aboard, young men representing the big Toronto and Montreal dailies. On the first day, we came upon one of these journalists, surrounded by a crowd of wide-eyed Company Four men. The reporter was regaling them with horror stories about the slaughtered Seventh Cavalry at the Little Bighorn, and the disembowelled redcoats at Isandlwana. "They were veterans," he said. "How much chance do you amateurs really have?" Our troopers were gazing at him like terrified little boys being told ghost stories around a campfire.

Roley put a gentle hand on his shoulder. "Sir," he said, "you're demoralizing our men."

"Kiss my ass," the reporter said. Roley hoisted him out of his seat with one arm. I heard the seams in the journalist's coat rip. Roley dragged him down the aisle. At the far end of the car, he spoke to the white-faced young man for about thirty seconds, in an urgent undertone, punctuating his remarks with sharp jabs in the chest.

I don't know what he said, but that reporter never came near a Company Four trooper again.

That night, a Lieutenant Colonel Portman talked to us. He was said to be an intimate friend of the Prime Minister's. Portman had a plump face, pomaded black hair, moist blue eyes, and an ingratiating manner. He told us that three thousand men would be transported to the West. General Middleton would use the legendary North-West Mounted Police, "as auxiliaries, only." We were bound for Batoche, on the South Saskatchewan, the home area of the Métis. Trouble might erupt, as well, to the west of there, around Battleford on the North Saskatchewan, a stronghold of the Cree, and in the District of Alberta.

Portman kept using the phrase, "At the Queen's pleasure." Roley Collison watched him steadily, puffing his pipe, without changing expression. But I noticed the left side of Roley's mouth curling up, in a slight grimace which I was to learn invariably meant that he found what he was seeing or hearing distasteful. After Portman used that phrase for the third time, Roley interrupted him. "Can we assume, sir," he asked, "that Queen Victoria is *personally* directing this campaign?"

Portman turned a bright red. "Of...of course not," he said, angrily. "What an absurd thing to say. It's...it's a political expression. It simply means at the pleasure of the government."

"Oh," Roley said. "Oh, I see. Well, I suppose the government will get a lot more pleasure out of it all than these poor bastards," and he waved his hand at the sprawling militiamen around us.

Portman turned even redder. "It will be useful, Captain Collison," he said, "for you and your men to acquire habits of respect for your superiors. No war can be fought without that."

"I meant no disrespect, sir," Roley said. Portman glared at him for a few seconds, then pulled himself to his feet, and marched away.

"That's the stuff, Roley," Lieutenant Jack Price said, with a smile.

"Make the colonel mad at us, right off the bat."

Roley turned a bit red, but smiled. "Nuts," he said, succinctly.

As the train ground on into growing darkness, Roley, Jack Price, the Yankee Lieutenant Arthur Howard, and I sat and smoked. Roley and Jack puffed calmly on pipes. Arthur Howard smoked long, foul-smelling black cigars which made him look even more like a fugitive from Gettysburg. I puffed on my cigarettes. I had resolved, once we reached Winnipeg, to buy a pipe exactly like Roley's. He smoked a beautiful Irish Peterson pipe, with a silver band on the stem.

We all wanted to know why an American officer was on that train. Arthur Howard was a voluble, friendly man, and in his flat New England accent he told us about his love affair with the Gatling gun. He'd served five years in the U.S. Cavalry, fighting Indians, sometimes using a Gatling. This, of course, made him the only man in the entire North-West Field Force who knew anything at all about frontier fighting.

After his stint in the Long Knives, Arthur had come back to New Haven and made a living manufacturing cartridges. But he was in love with the Gatling gun. He'd gone out morning after morning in the dewy Connecticut dawn, to a farm near the town, and fired thousands of rounds from his Gatling into two-inch spruce planks. "I checked the penetration and the spiral scratches on the bullets," Arthur said. "I adjusted the sights and computed the ranges." He blew a huge smoke ring in my direction, and then, grinning, he blew a smaller one through the middle of it. "I want to be the greatest expert there is on the machine gun, and what it can do for the U.S. Army. I need to test it in actual battle conditions. I need reliable data about the ratio of rounds expended to numbers of the enemy incapacitated. I need data about effective ranges and gun performance under extreme stress. There is no such data; I'll be the first.

"That's why when your government wanted Gatlings, I volunteered. I got leave from the National Guard. And I came. I've been solemnly ordered not to pass myself off as a representative of the United States government. I represent the manufacturer. I represent Dr. Gatling, but he telegraphed me to just describe myself as a 'friend of the gun.' So that's what I am, I guess; the best friend a machine gun ever had."

I can still see his thin, eager face. It was the face of a perpetual student, wreathed in cigar smoke as he talked about his beloved gun.

All that day and night, and all the next day, the trains plowed relentlessly north and west. The terrain grew wilder, the towns vanished, the dark forests encroached more and more closely, the farms grew ruder, and the fields more wooded and rocky, and at last houses and fields disappeared altogether. Every Canadian knew that the Canadian Pacific Railway wasn't completed. Few of us had realized that in the wilderness of northern Ontario, there were huge gaps in the line before the track began again and pushed on through Manitoba and into the Territories. The closer we got to those gaps, the less confident we felt.

At suppertime of the second day, the train slowed down to a crawl. Presently, Lieutenant Colonel Portman came through the cars to explain. Over a hundred miles of track lay ahead of us where no ballast yet lay between the ties, and the trains were going to crawl along at less than ten miles per hour. That night, I got a better night's sleep, because the slow, gentle motion of the train didn't jolt or sway. I remember thinking about Alice as I drifted off in the crowded car that smelled of heavy uniforms, sweat, strong coffee, and tobacco. What was she doing? Was she thinking of me?

When I woke up, it was still as black as soot. It took me a minute to realize that the gentle motion of the train had stopped. Men, officers and sergeants, were out in the snow yelling orders, and I could hear militiamen grunting and coughing as they disembarked from the train, the snow crunching beneath their boots. Lights were flashing around out there. For a few surreal moments, the men of Company Four continued to sit, awake but motionless in the darkened carriage. I was warm and comfortable, wrapped up in blankets, and the childish thought flashed through my mind *Maybe they'll forget about us, and I can go back to sleep.* Then the door of the carriage opened, and a major from the Queen's Own, carrying a coal-oil lamp, came in. "Captain Collison?" he said. Roley, still wrapped in a blanket, his morning pipe not even lit, struggled to his feet and saluted. "Dog Lake. End of the line, Captain," the major said. "We're all boarding sleighs. Get your men up and moving; we're not waiting." He turned away, and then came back. "And get all their warm clothes on them. It's colder than a witch's tit out there. The conductor told me this is unheard-of cold for early April. Well, we could God damn well have counted on *that,* now couldn't we?"

Roley was already struggling into his tunic, while making for the next carriage to get the rest of our men moving. It was then that I realized what was different about the carriage. It was hellishly cold in there as well. And the windows were no longer clear; they were covered with thick, snowy frost. A journey of a few miles, and the elapsing of a few hours, and the seasons in Canada can pounce on you. It had been almost spring where we had come from, but up here the winter still held, hard. Arthur Howard was tracing a pattern on the frozen window with his finger. He looked a little scared. "Jesus Christ, Willie," he said. "I was so busy packing my guns and shipping them that I didn't bring the right clothes. I've got uniforms for a Connecticut April."

I started to laugh. "Are all you Yankee scientific geniuses this impractical?" I said. "Fortunately for Dr. Gatling and his guns, my mother and my fiancé made me bring enough warm clothes for twelve people. Or at least two." I was already tearing open my ridiculously over-stuffed knapsack. I handed him a brown fur hat. It would clash with his uniform. I gave him mittens, and some extra socks. By now, Roley had come back. He told Arthur to take one of the C.P.R. blankets and cut holes in it for his head and his arms, and put it on under his blue Yankee overcoat. Then he stopped, thought for a minute, and told me to tell all our men to take their railroad blankets with them.

Jack Price had a slight smile on his face. "C.P.R. property, Roley," he said.

"To hell with the C.P.R.," Roley said. "They have been farting around forever with their damn railroad. They should have had it ready when the Canadian Army needed it. Anyway, they can bill Macdonald for the blankets. Or Caron."

We piled off the train, the clumsy Snider-Enfields clanging against the doors. It was snowing, hard. The sharp, stinging cold hit me in the face like a blow. There was no wind, but the air had that frightening, unforgiving crispness that tells you that you could quite literally freeze to death, and that damned quickly. Underfoot, the thick snow didn't have the soft coziness of Christmas snow, but the crunching dryness of extreme cold.

The tracks simply stopped, and the huffing trains were pulled up a few yards short of the terminus. The Queen's Own were wading down the snowy embankment of the track to the plain below, where endless lines of horse-drawn sleighs were waiting for us. Coal-oil lamps flared at the front of each sleigh. The teamsters huddled into their overcoats, their huge horses snorting, plumes of steam pouring from their nostrils into the iron dark. The regular gunners from Quebec and Kingston had already unloaded horses and cannons, and headed out. The militia sergeants had stopped shouting. The men quietly loaded themselves into the sleighs, ten men to each.

The Grenadiers weren't embarking, because their sleighs weren't ready yet. They would remain on the trains and embark later. A Grenadier sergeant told us that Portman and other senior officers would have a sleigh to themselves, "with extra God damn blankets," and Roley started laughing.

Ahead of us, I could dimly see a long white avenue reaching away into the blackness, dark trees overhanging it on either side, tendrils of snow drifting downward like fog. The marks left by the gunners and their horses and gun-carriages already were being filled in by the falling snow. The enlisted men of Company Four got into the last nine sleighs. Arthur Howard had somehow informally become one of the Toronto Light Infantry. He, I, Roley, Jack Price, and Colour Sergeant Quinn got into the very last sleigh, with the five artillery regulars that Caron had assigned to Howard. Arthur's precious Gatlings had a whole sleigh to themselves. He insisted that the sleigh with his guns be in front of us, so he could watch over it like an anxious father. The trainmen came out and yelled, and waved to us. The army was on the move.

V

There are no words in English which can describe that transit of northern Ontario which the North-West Field Force made. If the Métis and Indians had never fired a shot at us, that journey should have been enough to earn the gratitude of Canada. If it wouldn't, then to hell with Canada.

If there was a jingle-bells aspect to our mass sleigh ride, it evaporated after ten minutes. The wind picked up, although the snowfall did not abate. The wind howled down the long avenue of snow along which we traveled, hurling drifts of frozen sleet into our faces. Sometimes even the rear of the sleigh in front of us became invisible. Our faces got cold, then they stung, then they became carved into rictuses of frozen agony; then they grew numb and we found we couldn't move our lips, that we had to press our mouths shut with our hands as the terrible air froze our tongues; that our eyelids froze open, or froze shut, and we had to bang in a frenzy at our eyes, terrified that they'd freeze shut forever, or that the exposed eyeballs would freeze like marbles, and we'd go blind. We saw with horror that our neighbours' faces were fish-belly white in places. At first, we mutely just pointed in terror at these frozen patches. After a time, and without apology or shame, we reached out and rubbed the faces of other men as they rubbed ours. We knew that disfigurement or even death were the alternatives to this strange intimacy. We huddled together, we embraced one another like children. We got into postures, in the extremity of our need to escape that awful cold, which would have scandalized Mr. Oscar Wilde and his friends over in London, had they been there to see.

Jammed ten men to a sleigh, we could not flex or stretch our arms or legs. Within hours, the pain and cramping in them became terrible. We flexed our fingers, which even inside heavy mittens were becoming numb. Inside our shoddy boots, stuffed with layers of the heavy socks our mothers, wives, and sweethearts had made for us, our feet, immobilized by the sardine-tin conditions inside the sleighs, gave no pain. That, too, was frightening. What if they were frozen solid? What if they snapped off when we finally tried to stand up? And if something snapped off, and one didn't want to dwell on all the somethings that might, would one bleed to death? Of course not, the blood would freeze. It was freezing, anyway. So we stomped our feet, like drunken spectators at some soccer game, stomped them until I thought the matchwood floor of that accursed sleigh would give way, and dump us into the snow. We cursed God, we cursed our leaders, we cursed ourselves for being stupid enough to be here. We damned Louis Riel to the most colourful part of whatever Hell Papists descended to. Of course, this was in the privacy of our own minds. We did not speak in that awful cold, we couldn't. We could only croak with a frozen larynx and a frozen tongue.

But Arthur Howard kept muttering the same thing to himself. "Jesus, Jesus," he kept saying. "Not even in the God damn Dakotas."

We had forty-two miles to travel before the track commenced again. It took sixteen hours. That long avenue of snow, which had looked almost inviting from beside the trains, was the graded embankment on which the tracks would be laid. But it kept giving out, and then the sleighs had to traverse rough tracks through the woods. Under these were huge potholes, and every so often a sleigh would overturn, dumping men and rifles into the snowdrifts. That was funny, until the fourth sleigh overturned. We heard screaming coming from ahead of us, like the screaming of a terrified woman, then becoming more like that of an injured animal. With a curse, Roley pulled himself out and hobbled toward the sound, and I followed him. A sergeant from the Queen's Own had broken his arm on a huge rock which protruded up through the snow. His friends were stripping off his overcoat and tunic, even in that savage cold, to try to find out what ailed him. I almost fainted when I saw his dead-white arm. The bones in his forearm were sticking out through the skin. Thin blood was running. His sergeant-major took one look at him, and hit the screaming man in the side of the head with the butt of his rifle. "Have to be amputated," he said. "There's a camp up ahead, maybe some half-assed doctor there."

They loaded the moaning, semi-conscious sergeant back into the sleigh. There was a strong smell of vomit. One of the young Q.O.R. privates had thrown up all over his overcoat and was making ineffectual, helpless efforts to wipe it all off. The North-West Field Force had its first casualty.

Onward we struggled, through the thick snow. Half-way through the journey, we stopped at a construction camp. There they fed us a vile meal of rancid butter, unsweetened tea, salt pork and biscuits. The regular artillery, incredibly, had already been there and departed. The militiamen crowded pathetically around gigantic fires, which looked like the flames of Hell. Yet they scarcely seemed to ease the pain in our arms and legs. I did not get too close. My legs were trembling so badly that I feared I might topple in.

Roley was circulating among our men, encouraging them, handing out pipe tobacco and cigarettes, making jokes. Jack Price was imitating him. After a few minutes, it dawned on me that I was an officer, too. I timidly approached a little group of our company, huddled around a fire. These men all were older than I was. I was a virtual stranger to them, and I knew less than a child about soldiering. And, thus far, our great adventure wasn't going very well. I wouldn't have been surprised if they'd laughed at me, spat on me, or even assaulted me. I needn't have worried. I had reckoned without the hierarchical strain in men which emerges in crisis, and which is as necessary to the making of war as the flags, the bands and the pretty girls. I was a lieutenant, that was all they knew, a lieutenant because God or the Queen or somebody had made me one. Therefore I had their respect, until I did something to forfeit it. This was the other side of the coin from Arthur Howard's dictum that men will only follow an officer they respect.

The men straightened up as I approached; some even saluted. They actually saluted me. "Well, boys," I said, with fraudulent jocularity, "all we need is bloody Saint Nick, and we'll have a proper bloody Christmas." They roared with laughter, and one of them grabbed my hand and shook it. The new lieutenant had made a joke. The next day, I heard some of our fellows repeating that foolish line, as if it were the wittiest thing ever said. Roley looked around to see what was so funny, and then grinned and gave me the thumbs-up.

After that, I, too, circulated around, reassuring our men. They all smiled at me, and called me "Lieutenant," or "sir." Something was happening to me, too. Before this, I had vaguely resented these men. They weren't educated. They would laugh at me, I thought, as a stripling, or a sissy escaped from some library. Certainly, they had nothing in common with me, nor I with them. Now, suddenly, I felt that there could be no finer, nobler group of men on the planet, nor any more worth fighting beside, and for.

If ever there were an army of civilians in uniform, it was us. I watched our men as they tried to adjust to the sudden brutalization of their lives. These store clerks and office secretaries stood shuddering with cold in their shoddy, inadequate overcoats, and I saw with a rush of affection that they were performing the reassuring, familiar rituals of their civilian lives. One man compulsively polished and re-polished his spectacles. Another took out his pocket watch and solemnly consulted it, as if the time of day in that monstrous place were significant, and then carefully wound it up. Sanborn, the amateur wit who'd mocked Arthur Howard at the train station in Toronto, stumbled around in the snow telling appalling jokes at which the men laughed with a kind of desperation. They smiled a lot, more than men generally would under comfortable conditions, and they pounded each other on the back and told each other things would be fine, just fine.

I stumbled past a lieutenant and a sergeant of the Queen's Own, who were laughing like hyenas, and pounding their arms against their sides to keep warm. One of them had left the gas burning in his office. The other had an overdue book from the Public Library— *Around the World in Eighty Days*—and he would pay three cents a day until Louis Riel surrendered. Or until we all perished, one or the other.

The injured sergeant was dragged out of his sleigh, drooling, still stunned, his head lolling ignominiously like that of a sick, white-faced doll. I could see blood on his coat. It had frozen, slick and shiny on the stiffened green cloth. Some of the Queen's Own, looking sick and scared, lugged him into a large tent. The red-faced camp "doctor," stinking of drink, his face and hands black with dirt, brushed past me and swaggered into the tent. Minutes later, more screaming came from that tent. Compared to this, what I'd heard from the sergeant on the trail sounded like the happy, playful shrieks of little girls at play in the lane behind our house in Toronto. This was so awful that I saw Jack Price clap his hands over his ears. Seconds later, the screaming stopped. A few minutes later, a big construction worker came out of the tent, shaking his head, and laughing. He had blood on the arms of his overcoat. He walked over to us. "Didn't have no liquor to give him," he said. "That dumb quack never even give him anything to bite down on. One of his pals knocked him cold again with a rifle butt. Anyways, his right arm's off, and it ain't gonna grow back. He'll haveta learn to wipe his ass with his left hand." He started to turn away and then said over his shoulder, "Leastways, less'n his friends knock *all* his brains out, to spare him the pain, before his first shit."

The teamsters who drove the sleighs all were civilians. The eleven sleighs which transported our Company Four and Arthur Howard's beloved guns were under the command of a red-haired, red-bearded, red-faced colossus named Hannigan, a man of six feet five or six. He was gigantically massive under his heavy coat. On the trail, I had seen him bawling curses at his men, manhandling them, and whipping and kicking the horses, and beating them in their faces, like a crazy man. I saw this man deep in violent argument with the man who seemed to be the boss teamster. I heard voices raised and made out curses, but what they were shouting about, I couldn't tell.

We were back on the trail within an hour. When the orders to board the sleighs were given, I thought for a moment that the men would disobey them. I *hoped* they would, so that I could stay for all eternity close to one of those gigantic bonfires. But no such luck. The men were still game, and although they couldn't walk properly, they hobbled back to the sleighs. Shouting with laughter, they pulled and pushed and lugged and booted each other back into those damn wooden boxes.

One heartening thing happened, though. Our friend Colonel Portman had brought a large wooden box with him, and I'd had a brief look inside it when they'd resealed it a few minutes before. It was filled with neatly packed bottles of Scotch, each with the yellow label that showed it was the best that could be had.

Now I heard Portman bellowing at somebody, "I'll require an explanation! Bastards! I'll require an explanation!" I moved toward his voice. A lance corporal and two privates of the Queen's Own had "accidentally" dropped the box containing all Portman's Scotch, shattering every bottle.

"Imbeciles! Imbeciles!" Portman was shrieking.

The lance corporal went past me and winked broadly. "Just between you and me, Lieutenant," he said, "what's an imbecile?"

"In this context," I said, "someone who won't do what he's told."

He winked again. "Oh, that's the Queen's Own," he said. "Born imbeciles, every one of us."

Laughing, if but for a moment, I went back to Company Four, and, five minutes later, we got underway. I had learned a little about how to ride the sleighs by now. I had learned to hide my head under my arm, almost bird-like, to burrow into the coat of the man beside me, even to jam my face into my own crotch like a schoolboy pervert. The wind died down, and was replaced with an even thicker snowfall, so thick it was almost dreamlike. The sleighs filled up with snow. Snow blanketed our overcoats, it buried our equipment and the Gatlings, it muffled all sound. And eventually, I did something I would have previously bet was impossible: I fell asleep.

I was walking with Alice down a long path with overhanging green branches just above our heads. There was a lake beside us, and I was becoming more and more sexually excited. Somehow I knew that today Alice would give herself to me, although we were not married yet. I was very cold, though. Alice murmured my name, and she took my hand. We turned down a narrow path between beech trees.

I was being shaken. I looked up and saw Jack Price's narrow, overly serious face glaring down at me. The snowfall had increased; it was almost suffocating. "God damn it, Willie, wake up," Jack said. "There's something wrong. We've got to help Roley."

Jack pulled me out of the sleigh. When my legs hit the ground, I thought that I would simply pitch over into the snow. My legs were cramped; it felt like knives were sticking into them. But Jack held me up and shoved me forward. We were following faint tracks in the snow. I could dimly see the sleighs filled with men, drawn up, motionless, in line. We were moving toward the front of the procession of sleighs, I could see that, but where were the teamsters? And when we got to the front of the line, I had counted only ten more sleighs. There were faint tracks ahead of us in the snow, already rapidly being wiped out by the heavy fall. Company Four of the Toronto Light Infantry was now on its own. The rest of the column, the Queen's Own troopers in their multitude of sleighs, was gone, just gone.

Hannigan, the huge boss teamster, was standing, looming, red-faced, over Roley. Roley was leaning against the lead sleigh, and I could see from the way he was standing, or trying to stand, that his legs were as numb and contorted as mine. The American Arthur Howard was standing a few yards away, watching, with an odd look of cold detachment on his face. There were two teamsters for each sleigh, which made twenty-two of them. They were all standing in a semi-circle around Roley and the red-bearded teamster. Their seats allowed their legs to be stretched out, not cramped in confinement like the sleigh passengers. The teamsters and their leader looked infinitely spryer than I, or apparently Roley, felt. I looked at Roley's face, and I saw that he was frustrated, confused, and abysmally weary.

"I'll say it again," Roley said. "You contracted with the army to haul all of us up to the beginning of track, at this Camp Desolation place. How far away did you say it was, again?"

One of the teamsters laughed. Their red-haired leader, Hannigan, smirked. "I think maybe you ain't too well, General," he said. "I already tole you that, twice. Fifteen more miles; and I've decided we ain't going any further. I tried to talk it out back at the construction camp with that piss-ant Ferguson, calls hisself a teamster. Calls hisself my boss. I tole him we ain't goin' all the way to Camp Desolation without we get paid double, not in this weather. I tole him clear. He tole *me*, go to hell, that I agreed to these terms. Well, to hell with him, instead. And to hell with the Canadian army. Like I already tole you, General, I been thinkin' it over, while we rode along, and like I already tole you, *General*, I decided I was right all along. I just slowed down the lead sleigh, and the rest of them assholes of Ferguson's, and all them other soldiers, just pulled out of sight. In this snow, they could barely see us anyway. Them fools still think we're right behind 'em. And your soldier-boys didn't notice a thing.

"Happens I don't give a shit what I agreed to. Snow's heavier than I counted on, and sooner or later one of my sleighs is gonna get wrecked, pullin' you toy soldiers up to Desolation. So God damn Ferguson, and God damn *you*. We're goin' back to the construction camp. You and your assholes are comin' with us. Or, if you're so bloody anxious to get to Camp Desolation, you can march. That's what you do, isn't it? March?" There was laughter from his men.

Roley looked down at the snow and at the avenue leading away from us. The tracks left by the Queen's Own as they pulled away from us had completely disappeared. The snow came down in clouds. I turned, and found I could not even see the third or fourth sleigh in line. Roley looked at the big teamster and shook his head. "We'd never make it," he said, reasonably. "The track keeps giving out, and we don't know the shortcuts. The men are all crippled up with the cold. We'd die."

There was more laughter. "That's right, General," said Hannigan. "You would. Now, I've had enough of this bullshit. I ain't in any army. You don't tell me, or any of my men, what to do. This ain't Russia. I'm a free Canadian citizen, and I don't work less'n I want to. *And I don't want to.*"

Roley shook his head again, as if bewildered, and I saw the teamsters grinning. "One last time," Roley said, almost pleadingly. "It's really important that we get to this Fort Desolation…"

"*Camp*, not Fort, you asshole," Hannigan said.

"*Camp* Desolation," Roley said. "Like I said, I'll make a request that you get double pay for the last lap of the trip. I'm telling you…"

"You ain't telling me nothing," said Hannigan. "I had enough of your whinin'. Truth is, *General*, you ain't really no army at all. What youse are is a bunch of toy soldiers in silly uniforms, playin' at bein' an army. None of youse could hit the broad side of a barn. I'm doin' you a favour, takin' you back. Riel woulda killed you all in ten seconds, anyways." He spat, copiously, and the spit landed on Roley's boot. The teamsters laughed again.

Roley looked over at me. Through his awful exhaustion, he looked strangely calm, and somehow resigned. "Well, Willie," he said, "I actually do know one line of poetry after all. It's from a silly poem my wife likes to read out loud to the boy and me." He looked at the grinning, incredulous boss teamster. "I've told you three times that we need to get to this Desolation place, and you have to take us there. I've told you why. And, like the poem says, what I tell you three times is true." With a sudden, fluid motion, Roley unsnapped his flapped holster and produced the American Colt revolver he carried in it. He pointed it directly at the red face of the boss teamster, and with equal grace, cocked it. At the last second, he pulled the gun slightly to the right. "Shut your eyes," he said, and Hannigan did. Roley pulled the trigger.

In the close interval between the trees, amidst the thick falling snow, the pistol sounded like a cannon going off. Hannigan rocked back and forth, but he did not fall. His face was now as black as coal from the gunpowder gushing out. If he hadn't shut his eyes he would have lost his sight. His eyelashes had been burned off. The slug going past his head had torn off a small chunk of his left ear, and blood was spattering down on his shoulder. It was becoming increasingly apparent that he had shit his pants.

"All right," Roley said, in a soft voice, but it carried, "several things. One is, these pips on my shoulder-strap make me a captain, not a general. Another thing is, you're going to take us on to Desolation right now. I get any more argument out of you, I'll blow your God damn head off." He moved the Colt slightly back to the left, so that it pointed right at the teamster's nose. "And," Roley said, "I'll personally execute any man who doesn't obey my orders."

"That would be murder," one of the teamsters said, but his voice lacked conviction.

"I'm not a lawyer," Roley said. "I'm a captain." He cocked the pistol again. In that snow-shrouded silence, the little *click* was incredibly loud.

Several of the teamsters had pulled out pistols from under their overcoats. Several more had Bowie knives. I saw that Arthur and Jack had pulled their sidearms; then I looked down and saw to my wonderment that I had the Enfield revolver in my hand. I'd cocked it, too. You don't have to cock a double action, so I must have been imitating Roley. It occurred to me that I was a hell of a long way from Mr. Niven's book-lined library.

If we'd been alone, I don't know what kind of OK Corral gunfight might have erupted, but of course, we weren't alone. The silence behind me was suddenly broken by the loud metallic noises of the men in the first two sleighs opening the breeches of their Snider-Enfields, chambering cartridges, slamming the breeches shut again with the palms of their gloved hands. I saw one of the teamsters smile and shake his head. I suppose the absurdity of getting into a gunfight with an entire company of light infantry had occurred to him.

"Jack, Willie, Arthur," Roley said. "Take some men and disarm all these bastards. I want all their guns and knives thrown in a snowdrift. Ammunition, too. I don't want them armed while they drive us, or when we get to Desolation." Some of the men from the sleighs were hobbling out. They were doing a pretty good job of keeping their rifles aimed at the teamsters though. Hannigan said nothing. Having part of his face shot off and his pants filled with shit seemed to have made him mute. We disarmed all the teamsters, and none of them said a word. They didn't even look at us, just stared down at the snow. I personally threw all the pistols and knives as far into the woods as I could. If any of them turn up before Judgment Day, it really will be a miracle.

I finally clambered back into the rearmost sleigh with Roley. Jack Price and I had given orders for the men to keep their rifles on each teamster as they drove, and to "shoot them if there was any funny business." I had invented that phrase. I suspected my professors would have condemned it as vague and excessively vernacular. But it seemed to have a magical effect on the teamsters. I had voyaged quite a way from the dear old U. of T. Roley was sitting in the sleigh, staring down at his boots. He turned, and smiled briefly and ruefully at me. "That big ape might've had a point about our marksmanship," he said. "I was trying to miss his head completely."

* * *

We made the rest of the journey to Camp Desolation without incident. When we got there, I was expecting trouble from the teamsters, but they just filed away from the sleighs. Indeed, I never saw any of them again. I suspect that they had had enough of us and of their red-bearded leader as well. That gentleman, however, had recovered his voice and his bad temper. He soon found the commanding officer at Desolation, a lieutenant colonel. I could hear Hannigan from the other end of the camp, ranting and raving and screaming bloody murder about the "piss-ant bastard in a red coat" who'd shot his ear off. I went over to listen to this conversation, and to intervene if necessary. The big bastard's ear was actually still almost intact, although a long, glistening red icicle of blood now depended from it almost to his shoulder. He finally ran down, and glared at the colonel. "Now what the hell are you going to do about this?" he said.

The colonel was a small, prim man with a prissy moustache and spectacles. I had seen him several times on the train. Then, he'd looked like the principal of an elementary school, and that, or something like it, was no doubt precisely what he had been, only a few days ago. Now, he looked like a refugee from Dante's *Inferno*, the cold part of it. His little moustache was coated in ice, as were the bottoms of his nostrils. His beet-red face was streaked with dirt, and with frozen sweat. His hair stuck up in frosty tangles. His eyes were as red as cherries. He looked utterly exhausted, and a little insane. "What am I going to do about it?" he said. Hannigan grunted. The colonel had a high, carrying voice, and it kept getting louder and louder. "I'll tell you what I'm going to do about it. It sounds to me like you were trying to abandon our men in the snow, or at least prevent them from reaching the fighting front. That would be high treason. The penalty for high treason is death. I should be having you shot, but there's an ammunition shortage. So I'll just tell you, if you don't shut up about this right now, I *will* have you shot, *and if I ever hear you brought this up again to any living soul I will have you hunted down and executed at bloody sunrise!*" His face had, improbably, gotten redder. He turned on his heel, and stalked away.

I could see that the erstwhile boss teamster had been entirely cowed by this extravagant and slightly irrational threat. His shoulders slumped, and he turned to go. Then he looked in my direction. The American, Arthur Howard, had joined me. "Well, you Yankee bastard," said the teamster, almost jovially, "what you think of this?"

"I'll tell you," Arthur said. "I think it's a great opportunity to learn a valuable lesson in successful living." Arthur's face had that cold look of scientific detachment again. He was staring at the teamster with the expression of a laboratory researcher who has just spotted a relatively familiar and not-very-interesting specimen. "And here's the lesson," Arthur said. "Never contest anything of importance with a man when you know he's in the right, and *he* knows he's in the right. Even more, don't insult him, don't mock him, and in particular don't spit on his boot. And, most of all, don't do these things when he's carrying a gun and isn't afraid to use it." He turned and started to walk away. Then he came back. "I learned that lesson by observing some events one night in a bar in Abilene, in the state of Kansas," he said. "And now you've learned it, too, right here in the middle of God damn nowhere."

*　*　*

I wish I could say that reaching Camp Desolation was the end of that nightmare. In fact, it was scarcely the beginning. At the camp, we ate another disgusting meal, consisting this time mostly of half-frozen potatoes. We had finally caught up with the regular artillery and their horse-drawn gun carriages. The exhausted gunners and their sagging horses looked even worse than we did. The good news was that the tracks began again here, and we all promptly got on the train. The bad news was that all that could be provided for us were flatcars, with hastily-made wooden sides which only came up to about the waists of the seated men.

We huddled on hard wooden seats which still bled sticky pine sap, gluing the asses of our coats down, as we endured the worst ordeal we had faced yet. On these flatcars, forty or fifty men were crushed together. The howling wind had risen, and the temperatures had dropped to at least thirty below. Now we knew real misery, at last.

The engineers of that train had been told by the damned C.P.R. and Ministry of Militia to cover the next one hundred miles of track quickly, and they certainly tried. Fortunately for the survival of the North-West Field Force, on that winding and half-built track they could make only perhaps twelve miles per hour. But twelve miles per hour is too fast. It's too fast when the arctic wind screams directly into your face at another thirty miles per hour.

The plight of the artillery horses was worse than that of any human. They had already endured the same trek that *we* had made on sleighs. Some of them had hauled nine-pounder cannons behind them, cajoled and lashed forward through the snow by desperate men. Nine-pounder cannons are not called that because they weigh nine pounds, but because they fire shells that weigh that much. And other horses had to haul hundreds of those shells.

We'd watched at Camp Desolation as the cursing gunners forced the horses onto the flatcars. The men had hauled the nine-pounders aboard by main force. Two of the artillerymen had collapsed, groaning, having herniated themselves lifting the heavy cannons. Now, as the train clattered through the deadly night, the terrified, exhausted animals screamed in pain. They were shitting, and foaming at the mouths. They bucked, heaved and smashed their hooves into the wooden sides of the flatcars, reducing them to kindling. The gunners, standing in the same filthy flatcars as the horses, fought, cursing and pleading, to calm them, dodging wildly around to avoid being crushed against the flimsy walls or thrown out into the snow.

The car immediately in front of that carrying much of Company Four, including its officers, was filled with horses and their keepers. A couple of hours after we started, one of the wildly heaving horses in that car broke its leg. It fell, and immediately started screaming. This was worse than the wounded sergeant, worse than anything I had yet heard in my life. The horse shrieked; its voice broke. It clattered its unbroken legs against the bottom of the car as the frantic gunners crowded around it. It screamed again and again, like a woman in extreme pain, or a demon in a nightmare.

The gunners had no sidearms. One of them shouted to Roley to shoot the horse. At first, Roley refused. The soldiers would be firing forward, in the direction of other cars filled with men, in the dark, surrounded by wreaths of snow and smoke from the train. And our light infantry were terrible shots. Their arms and hands were almost frozen. But the gunnery sergeant of regulars was not taking "no" for an answer. "God damn you, you bastard!" he roared. "I don't care if you are a officer, you bastard, if you don't put this animal out of its misery, I'll catch you and bust your head. Do it! DO IT!"

Finally, the shrieks of the horse were more than Roley could bear. He gave the order. Two of our men loaded their Snider-Enfields, rested the long, clumsy barrels on the wildly clattering front of the flatcar, gestured to the gunners to get out of the way, and fired. It took four shots. Roley sank down on his seat and muttered to me, "God help us if we hit anyone in the forward carriages." By sheer luck, we had not.

When we reached the end of track, many of the men had to be lifted out of the flatcars by the C.P.R. men. There was now a gap of eighteen miles to cover by forced march. We covered it by forced march, the men staggering on exhausted legs, shouldering their rifles with arms that shook with fatigue and pain.

When we had covered the eighteen miles, we boarded more flatcars, and clattered onward to another frozen encampment. There we were at last allowed to sleep, some of us in an old warehouse, some in a half-sunken schooner frozen into the ice of Lake Superior.

By the time we got up, the Royal Grenadiers had caught up to us. One of them promptly went mad. All around us, there were huge bonfires. The poor Grenadier suddenly pulled off all his clothes. I was standing nearby, struggling to light one of my cigarettes. For a moment, as I saw him stripping, I silently applauded what I took to be the ultimate in black comedy, the last word in sardonic comments about our plight. But the noises he was making drove everything from my mind except pity and horror. Howling like a banshee, he rushed straight toward the bonfire. At the last moment, some of his comrades came to, and they grabbed his white, skinny body and thrust him down into the snow. They shouted with laughter, and sat astride the naked madman as he thrashed, shrieked and kicked. I saw a corporal push the lunatic's head into the snow. "Now, there, Jim," he said. "No point in burning your nuts off. Not when they'll just drop off, like everybody else's."

Then we marched twenty-six miles across the frozen lake, and got in more open flatcars for a ride to another camp. There was a C.P.R. hospital there, and the amputation cases were at last hauled away on stretchers. I felt a momentary and irrational envy of these men, soon to be missing hands, arms or legs. At least the buggers would be sleeping soon in warm beds.

After that, we did fifty more miles in the flatcars, and then we marched nine miles. By now, the men were at the last extremity of their strength. For days, they had eaten almost nothing, drunk almost nothing, slept hardly at all, and endured cold which would have daunted a polar bear. Some of the men were snow-blind by now, including Lieutenant Colonel Otter, who had given away his snow goggles to a young private who had lost his. Otter was a stalwart soldier. But I saw him crying like a child at the awful pain in his temporarily-blinded eyes.

During that last trek, I saw Roley, staggering with exhaustion, endlessly moving up and down the ranks of Company Four. He was patting the men on the back, murmuring encouragement, muttering silly little jokes, saying and doing anything he knew to keep these worn-out, starving, frightened store clerks and office workers on their feet. As he passed me for the fifteenth time, I looked at his face. It was contorted with pain and exhaustion. Roley was weeping, he was so tired. Drool came out of his mouth. "Just a few more miles," he was mumbling. "Just a few more miles, boys, then warmth and food and rest."

At the end of this last trek, we staggered on rubbery legs through a sleeping village, gasping, choking, shaking, dragging our rifles in the snow, heaving air into our exhausted lungs. At the end of the street there was a railway station. Standing there, chuffing, glowing, golden-lit, inviting in the darkness, was a long, long train of Pullman cars. We were going to ride in Pullman cars for the last stretch to Winnipeg. *Pullman cars*! I staggered toward the warm, steaming train, and I remember thinking that I quite literally could not have made half a mile further.

Arthur Howard was walking, or rather staggering, along beside me. He looked like a Union soldier who had just been released from Hell. His face was blotched, red, grimy and exhausted. But he had jammed his jaunty Yankee's cap back on his head, and he solemnly handed my father's brown fur hat back to me. "I know you people worry about us coming up here and trying to conquer this place," he said. "But you can stop worrying. I am going to write the Secretary of War and tell him it's a bad idea. I am going to suggest we turn our national attention southward to a warmer climate, maybe toward Cuba. I wouldn't want to be responsible for the deaths of men like these men who've made this trip with us." Then he lowered his voice. "Besides," he said, "if we invaded Canada, most of the U.S. Army would be frozen stiffer than mackerels, before they advanced twenty miles."

Alice

Long after every light in the house went out, I sat up in my bed and thought about Willie and me. I arranged on the blanket in front of me everything I have of him.

It isn't much. A photograph in a gold frame, of Willie sitting in a chair looking contemplatively at a book of poetry—Browning in fact, his favourite. He always made fun of the picture, saying he looked like "an old woman in pants."

I thought he looked very handsome.

And there are some books. One that he gave me for my birthday, Browning, of course. And my Christmas present, Whitman, after he discovered that I preferred him. The inscription says, "Here is the barbaric yawp you love so much. Affectionately, W. Lorimer."

"Affectionately, W. Lorimer." Willie, is that the best you could do?

I kept looking at the picture, and paging restlessly through the books. This is all I have. All I have.

He is going to a war. Father forbade me to read the stories about Duck Lake in the newspapers, but I read them anyway. They shot the Mounted Police and the civilian volunteers down like rabbits. The snow was all red.

Oh, please let him come back.

VI

Still wearing my snow-covered overcoat and my boots, I collapsed into the upper berth of one of the Pullman cars. I fell asleep the second my body hit the mattress.

I slept for fifteen dreamless hours.

When I woke, I climbed down from the upper berth. In most of the berths, the dark-green curtains were open, and the sheets were filthy and disordered. In some, snoring from behind closed curtains told me that some of the boys were still sleeping it off. I paced through another Pullman car, and then I discovered the dining car. It was half-full of men, it blazed with light, and it smelled of tobacco, coffee and bacon. Near the entrance, Roley, Arthur Howard, and Jack Price were slouched in armchairs around a table with a shining, white cloth. They were puffing clouds of tobacco smoke, with empty, egg-smeared, carelessly shoved-aside plates, and coffee cups in front of them. They had somehow acquired a bottle of whiskey.

"He's alive! He's alive!" Arthur cried, waving his black cigar. "The rumours of his death were false! The North-West Field Force is saved!" Jack grinned at me. As I sat down beside him, Roley thumped me on the back. A waiter in a white coat—*a waiter*—came over to take my order. He asked me if bacon and eggs and coffee would be sufficient, as it was all they had. I allowed as how it would.

"Same helpings as we had, please," Roley said. That turned out to be eight eggs, twelve pieces of toast, a full pot of coffee, and twenty slices of bacon.

I looked out the window into the blackness. The dark firs of northern Ontario were rolling by, but there was much less snow. It was a lot warmer.

The waiter put the coffeepot and a cup in front of me. Arthur leaned over and poured a little whiskey from the bottle into my cup. I drank greedily. A few minutes later, the three plates, one laden with toast, the second with sizzling bacon, the third with eggs, landed in front of me. For twenty minutes, I guzzled it with the ecstasy of an animal.

When I emerged from this, they all had left the table. So I got up and headed back toward my Pullman car. In the first coupling space between the cars, I found Roley, smoking, leaning against the door. He greeted me with a smile, and I stood beside him. We stood quietly for several minutes. "I'm wondering what on earth I'm doing here," he finally said. "You?"

I thought about saying something heroic. Eventually, I said, "I'm here because I forgot to resign my commission. It never occurred to me that there'd ever be a war. I'm no hero, Roley. I want to keep my head down and get through this. If I'm forced into a situation where I have to do the honourable thing, I guess I'll do it. But I am really hoping that I'll be fast asleep when the opportunity to be brave presents itself."

Roley laughed. He didn't seem as scandalized by this as I'd thought he might be. He blew out another mouthful of smoke. "My reasons are even more ridiculous than that," he said. "But I'll tell you what they are. Inasmuch as I understand them myself. Maybe, as an educated man, you won't laugh. *Maybe*. Willie, I joined the militia because I thought maybe it would give me a chance to be something—I don't know—something bigger than my own skin. A chance for an adventure, but something more than an adventure. Do you see?"

Roley looked for a few seconds out the jouncing window of the coupling space. Then he looked at me very directly. I think he had decided to trust me. "Every day I wait on people in my store. The customer is always right, have you heard that? Well, they are. You can't run a store any other way. Rich women—you know, influential—come sweeping down the street, with a lot of maids and sometimes manservants, like a big—you know, there's some French word for it."

"Entourage," I said.

"Yes," he said. "Trust you to know the right word. The rich women like to show off by abusing merchants. They say, the garment you sold me shrank. I tell them, you didn't wash it the way I told you. I know I did; I always tell them the right way, or Vera does. They never washed anything in their lives; some servant does it for them. They don't listen to a word I say. They demand their money back. On occasion, I argue. 'Oh,' I can see them saying to themselves, 'here is a tradesman who doesn't know his place. Here is a tradesman who doesn't know what my husband does in this city. And he thinks he will not refund my money. He is not yet in possession of all the *facts*.' And, you know, in the end I give the money back, while the maids giggle and the manservants smirk, because if you don't, your store gets a bad reputation. Sometimes their husbands come in with them, and sometimes they're rude to me, to show off in front of their wives and servants. That's the hardest part. I used to box, a little, and occasionally I've wanted to invite the husband to step outside, but I don't. I have to make the store pay, for my wife and my son. Then at the end of the day, I go home."

He stopped and looked at me quietly for a few seconds. "I hope you don't find this out, you and Alice, but home life sometimes isn't all you'd hoped for. I married a woman a lot like my mother. I think a lot of men do that. Like my mother, Vera thinks being a storekeeper isn't much of a thing. She teaches my son Donald to look down on me, and what I do. He's good at school. I wasn't. I dropped out at sixteen, to work for my father in the store. Donald will be an important man, some day, and he won't be grateful for all the shit his old man took for him." He looked searchingly into my face, as if challenging me to laugh at him. "I think sometimes—this can't be all there is to my life." He stopped again, as if searching for something. "Not by bread alone, you know. I guess I thought maybe, just once, a man like me could be what my mother was always reading about, and talking about," he said. "You know—a knight in shining armour, or something like it."

"It sounds right to me," I said.

"Well," he said, "you didn't laugh, at least not in my face." He walked into the Pullman car, and left me standing there, alone.

* * *

Not far east of Winnipeg, the fir trees and lakes come to an end, and the prairie begins. Rather suddenly, the huge, coarse rocks protruding through the thin soil end; the rivulets and creeks end. And there, stretching to the horizon, is the flatland. Of course, east of Winnipeg, it was already domesticated. Farms, barns and granaries, and half-melted fields rattled past the windows of our train. The conductors came up and down the aisles of the cars, saying that Winnipeg was just ahead. The sergeants bellowed, and the officers bustled around giving instructions, and then we were there.

We reached Winnipeg on the morning of April 7. In a huge tent beside the railway station, we ate a gigantic hot breakfast—more eggs and bacon, more oceans of hot coffee, but who cared?—and then we marched through more streets of cheering citizens, to a tent encampment beside the Presbyterian college on Portage Avenue.

There was an officers' meeting that morning, and at it we discovered our fate. Middleton had already marched north from Qu'Appelle toward Batoche, Riel's capital, with his Winnipeg Ninetieth Rifles, a battery of guns, and some irregular cavalry called French's Scouts.

When we got to Qu'Appelle, our Company Four, the Grenadiers, about forty infantry regulars, and an artillery battery would disembark and march off after Middleton. Another artillery battery, the Queen's Own and the rest of the infantry regulars, under the command of Colonel Otter, would voyage hundreds of miles to the west, to Swift Current. When the situation in the West was under control, Otter and his command would head eastward for Batoche, by steamboats, on the South Saskatchewan River.

Only one thing was wrong. Arthur Howard, his gunners and his miraculous Gatlings were leaving us, and voyaging to Swift Current.

"Just when I was getting used to you, you Yankee rascal," Roley said to the grinning American.

* * *

The whole force was going on to Qu'Appelle the next morning. That night, we decided to explore Winnipeg. Jack refused to come with us, and Roley, Arthur and I went walking down the wooden sidewalks of Portage Avenue, looking, as Arthur put it, "for civilized U.S. whiskey." It wasn't hard to find. We sat for a while in a big, brilliantly-lit bar filled with red and green-coated troopers, and Arthur drank, with cold efficiency, glass after glass of Bourbon. The first couple of times, he insisted we drink to the United States cavalry, and after that, he just drank, silently, unemotionally and without much visible effect. I had the odd feeling that he was reverting, almost before my eyes, to the hard-bitten cavalryman he had been before he went back East to raise a family, and fall in love with the Gatling gun.

Roley was moody and silent, seemingly almost angry. That, too, was familiar to me, because it was a frequent mood of every man in our family, except for me. Roley drank little. I had never drunk anything before, except for some beer at a university party. After I had two glasses of Bourbon, Roley put his open palm over my glass. "Be careful, Willie," he said. "It's easy to get sick, if you're not used to it." So I puffed solemnly on the brand-new pipe I had bought that afternoon in Winnipeg's best tobacco shop. The pipe was identical to Roley's.

Suddenly, Arthur stood up and announced that he wanted to keep walking. We started down Main. The night air was getting colder. There was a faint moon, and thin clouds raced against it. I smelled for the first time in my life the unforgettable smell of the early spring prairie, as the icy wind blew across it, and rushed through the town. There was the smell of soil emerging from beneath the snow, of cold water, and of wet vegetation.

There were still numbers of half-drunken troopers in their greatcoats, thumping up and down the boarded walks, but their numbers kept diminishing. The occasional war-whoops and catcalls from soldiers in the neighbouring streets were rapidly diminishing, too. It reminded me of something, and for the longest time I couldn't think what it was. Then I had it. It was like the later hours of Hallowe'en, when the children in their unlikely costumes start to vanish into their brightly-lit houses, leaving the streets alone and darkened to whatever real bogeymen there might be.

Roley dropped farther and farther behind us, dawdling, and staring darkly into store windows. I kept looking back at him. "He's all right," Arthur said. He clapped his arm around my shoulders. We stopped at the entrance to an alley, leading off Main. There were lights burning at the far end, and we heard the sounds of doors slamming, and glass breaking. "A low joint, an establishment of ill repute," Arthur said, happily. "The first I have scented since I left the West for New Haven. I didn't think you Canucks were capable of such a place. Come on, Willie."

We entered through a low, ill-fitting door. The place stunk of alcohol, tobacco, sweat, and cheap scent. There was another smell, too, which I didn't recognize. Somehow, though, I knew it had to do with the three overweight, blowzy-looking women who sprawled on chairs, legs sticking aggressively out, near the door. There were a couple of drunks huddled, almost comatose, over their glasses. The bartender was hugely fat. Beside the bar, with a proprietary air, stood two men in fancy, satin robin's-egg-blue vests. One was short and bald, with a huge moustache. The second was a big man, with long, lank, greasy hair and a clean-shaven, sullen face.

The big man let out a howl of laughter when we walked in. "Well, Jesus on the cross," he said. "Carl, look at Billy Yank, in his blue monkey-suit." Then he walked over to Arthur. "Billy, what you doin' up here in this ice box?"

"Same as you, Johnny Reb," Arthur said, equably. "Just trying to get by."

"Just trying to get by," the big man repeated, as if looking for an insult embedded in it. He couldn't find one, and brightened. "What you and the kid want to drink, Yank?" he asked. Arthur told him.

"Tom, you going to *wait on* a damn Yankee?" the little bald man called Carl said.

"Sure, sure," said the bigger one, Tom. "War's over." He slammed down two glasses of Bourbon in front of us, so hard that drops of whiskey spattered on my red tunic, and Arthur's blue one. But Arthur only smiled, and lit another of his awful-smelling cigars. "What's yore unit, Yank?" Tom asked.

"Connecticut National Guard," Arthur said.

"Connecticut!" said Tom. "I kilt a lot of Connecticut boys in the war."

"Well," Arthur said, reasonably, "*someone* sure did."

"*Someone* did," Tom sputtered. He giggled. It wasn't pleasant. "*Someone* did! Well, damn me! A *humorous* damn Yank!" He went back to the bar and stood by his friend, Carl, but neither stopped staring at us. They talked to each other in an undertone, they smiled, occasionally, but they watched us every minute. Arthur drank his drink, with a funny half-smile on his face. He did not look at me, or at the Johnny Rebs at the bar. Arthur, Roley and I had left our sidearms back at the camp. I was badly scared of those two men, and I wanted to get out of there. I kept directing shying half-glances at Arthur, but he ignored me, and puffed his cigar, and sipped his drink, and stared into space. It occurred to me quite suddenly that Arthur was enjoying this very much.

Suddenly, one of the three women heaved herself to her feet with a grunt. She came over to our table. She must have been about forty, with a fat, red, scowling face, and straggling blond hair. She was wearing a green dress, cut lower than I had ever seen in my life, and she stunk of alcohol, cheap perfume, and sweat. "Hello, sweetheart," she said to me in a raspy rumble. Then, to my amazement, she hopped onto my lap. Without thinking, I put an arm around her fat shoulders to steady her. At once, with a quick darting motion, she pushed her face toward mine and planted a wet kiss on my lips. Her tongue immediately started prying at my mouth, like a grub. Despite my disgust at the hot, sweaty body sprawled on me, I felt myself getting hard, in spite of myself. Her underarms were slimy with perspiration. My hand kept getting wet, brushing against one of her armpits, as she balanced on my lap.

The two ex-Confederates were laughing. "Give it to him, Lizzie," the one called Carl said. "Show the little shit the ropes."

Lizzie laughed, spraying spit all over me. "I'll show him his first pussy," she said, and the two men laughed, again. I was trying to pry her off, but she was much too heavy. I was too much of a gentleman to hit her, or shove her. Now, I found to my horror that she had my fly-button open, and was pressing on me with her wet fingers. I was getting harder and harder, and closer and closer to throwing up. Arthur did not look amused any more, but he was not doing anything to help me, either. "Come on, kid," Lizzie whispered urgently. "We got a couple of little rooms, just in back."

The door banged. I looked around, and Roley was standing there. He stood motionless for a long minute, just staring at the men at the bar, the drunken whores, and Lizzie flopping around on top of me. Then he came over to my table. "Leave the boy alone," he said.

Lizzie laughed, and spat on the floor. "Your boyfriend, is he?" she said. Tom and Carl laughed again. Roley reached out and took her by the forearm, and then with a heave he pulled her to her feet, with one arm, and gave her a mighty shove. Lizzie gave a scream, and landed with a resounding thwack! on her ass on the floor. I expected a torrent of fishwife abuse from her, but she did not make a sound. I looked at Roley, and saw the reason why. He had the same angry, slightly exalted look on his face that he'd had when he'd shot part of Hannigan's ear off. Roley clearly meant business in a way that Lizzie recognized, although Hannigan had been too dumb or too self-confident to see it.

"Here, now," Carl said. "No way to treat a lady."

Roley turned and faced him. "No," he said. "But the right way to treat a cheap whore." He turned back to us and jerked his thumb toward the door. "Willie, Arthur, outside," he said. He walked swiftly out into the alley. I did not even think of disobeying him. Arthur got up as well, with a faintly embarrassed look on his face.

"Yore keeper, is he, Yank?" Tom said. He was staring darkly at Lizzie, still flat on her ass on the floor. She had started whimpering. "Git the hell out," Tom said. Arthur said nothing, and we went out into the darkness.

Roley was waiting for us. He walked over to Arthur, and the American stepped back a pace. "Arthur, you son of a bitch," Roley said. He was shaking with anger. "What in hell is wrong with you, taking Willie into a place like that? He's engaged to be married. I met his girl. Did the U.S. Cavalry drive you out of your God damn mind?"

Arthur looked into his face for a few seconds. "Yes, a little, I think," he said, finally. "I've seen things…"

"Arthur, I'll tell you what you will see," Roley said, evenly, although he was still shaking. "If you don't take care of the boys in my unit, you'll see my fist in your face."

Arthur did not seem to grasp what was happening, and I realized how drunk he actually was. "Come on," I said. I put my arm around him, to steady him, and we walked out of the alley and headed back toward the camp. Roley stormed along beside us for a block or two, and then, with a dark look on his face, he again dropped behind us.

I struggled on, hanging on to Arthur. He had lost his cool air of scientific playfulness. He stumbled along, muttering to himself, leaning heavily on me. I could think only of getting back to the camp, which was at least a mile away. It was midnight, and the dark streets were deserted. The moon was going down. I kept looking behind me for Roley, but he had disappeared again.

Behind us, I heard a crash, but when I stared over my shoulder, there was nothing there. Suddenly, Arthur punched my shoulder. "In here, Willie," he said, gesturing to another alley. "Going to puke. Goddamned schoolboy. Disgrace to cavalry. Shit." He grabbed my arm, painfully, and half-steered, half-dragged me into the darkened lane.

It was murky in there. Arthur stumbled over to a wall, and stood bent-over, groaning. I watched him, but he did not vomit. Finally, he straightened up and spat on the ground. "Okay," he said. "Temporary weakness gone. 'Sget out of here." Relieved, I turned around, and found myself facing two men who were between us and the entrance to the alleyway. A shaft of moonlight showed me that it was the two Johnny Rebs from the bar, Tom and Carl. Tom had a huge Bowie knife in his hand. Carl had a revolver, and it was aimed right at my face.

Tom, the big one, started to laugh. "Surprise, asshole," he said. "You think we let a Yankee and some little shit redcoat come in our place and rough up one of our girls and just go home? No way. No *God damn way.*"

"We didn't..." I started to say, and Tom backhanded me across the face so hard I almost fell down.

"Speak when you're spoke to," Tom said. "And not before. I know. It was yore other friend hit Lizzie. We'll find him, too. He hurt my girl. And, right here, we got you two sons of bitches with no guns. A Yankee trooper. And you, yuh little cocksucker. I got sick a long while back of that ugly red coat. God damn p'lice on their big horses. So," and he smiled an almost radiant smile, "yore about to find yore guts in yore hands. And yore nuts rollin' on the ground. Like the Yank, there. Wrong place, wrong time, young fella." He was tossing the Bowie knife from hand to hand, so fast I couldn't see it. It was a blur, punctuated by an ugly thwap! each time the leather-covered handle hit one of his meaty hands. He was about two feet away, and I knew he would stick me if I lunged at him. I was too scared to move, anyway.

I looked at Arthur. He was dead-white, swaying on his feet. He was too drunk to do anything. He sighed, and caught my eye. "Jesus, Willie," he said. "I'm sorry. I really am."

"Ain't that sweet?" said Carl, the little one with the gun. "He's sorry." Carl stood nearer the alley entrance, and in the moonlight I could see him better. He knew what he was doing. He had me and

Arthur covered, without any chance of Tom getting between us and him. It occurred to me that they'd done this before, maybe many times.

"Not as sorry as soon will be," Tom said, and he and Carl laughed.

I was cringing into myself in panic. All that I could do was to stare, mesmerized, at the flying, silver blade. I could feel what it would be like when it tore into my stomach. It would be as cold as ice for a moment, and then it would be drowned in warmth and wet and stink, as my hot viscera spilled out over my pants. I kept trying to bend over to protect myself, but my back was as stiff as a steel rod with fear. My balls were trying to crawl up into my stomach. A little gasping wheeze of indignation escaped my lips, the last squeak of a cornered animal.

A shadow came over the moon, and Carl began to turn around. Roley was standing there. He hit Carl in the face with his clenched fist, with a crunching impact which echoed through the alleyway. The little man started to fall. Roley took the gun out of his hand. Tom turned to face him and began to lunge forward with the knife, even as I began to move toward Tom from behind. Roley hit Tom in the side of the head with the barrel of the gun. The big man collapsed, the knife flying out of his hand.

By now, Carl was sitting up, cursing, with an astonishing amount of blood pouring out of his nose. From somewhere, he had produced another Bowie knife. "Gut yuh," he said, matter-of-factly. He started to get up. Roley turned and quite coolly and deliberately stepped back a pace, like a footballer; then he kicked Carl in the forehead, hard. Carl toppled over, and lay as still as death.

"Willie," Roley said, "I followed you. I thought we might see these bastards again." He picked up both knives and handed me Carl's gun. "Hold this gun on this man. If he hurts me, or tries to, shoot him." Tom was groaning and sitting up with his legs out in front of him, like the whores in the bar. I pointed the pistol at Tom, making sure Roley wasn't in the way. Roley went down on his haunches and started patting Tom all over, to see if he had another weapon.

"Didn't really do anythin," Tom said. "No harm, friend. No harm. Just our little joke, that's all. Let us go."

Roley stopped and stared at him. "Keep still," Roley said, "and nobody needs to get hurt any more."

"Screw you," Tom said. Quick as a weasel, his right hand vanished into his left sleeve, and I saw a flash of brightest silver in the dim moonlight of the alley. I started to cry out, but the noise stuck in my throat. I forgot that the revolver was even in my hand. Roley hurled himself backward, and the blade of the straight razor missed his throat by inches. Tom over-balanced and toppled over on his side. He dropped the razor. "God damn head off," he said, and pulled himself upright again.

I cocked and aimed the pistol, now, and Roley said, calmly, "No, Willie." He reached up, and grabbed the gun from me. Tom had hold of the razor again, and his arm shot back for another swing with it.

Roley hit Tom full in the mouth with the butt of the gun. The razor went flying. Blood came shooting out of Tom's mouth, mixed with white objects which I knew were fragments of his teeth. He was groveling, now, on the ground in front of us.

Roley looked down at him. Roley was breathing far harder than his economical motions thus far would justify. His face was wet with sweat. "I am going to give you some advice," he said. His voice was getting louder and louder. "Here it is. Go back down there and tell them, when they come up here, and somebody in a red coat tells them to do something, don't say 'screw you,' *because it's the wrong God damn answer!*"

Suddenly, Roley seemed to realize where he was and what he was doing. He stopped shouting and stared, seemingly dumbstruck, for a few seconds at the pistol in his hand. Then he quickly handed it to me. "Holy God, Willie," he said. "What am I doing? Get rid of that. Get Arthur back to the camp." He pointed to Arthur, who was still standing, swaying. "We've got to get out of here."

Roley did not move. Tom was staring up at him. His voice was mushy, but it was steady, and very cold. "'Fore you leave this town,"

Tom said. "All three of yuh are dead. I'll find yuh, and kill yuh like dogs, 'fore the sun rises. Or git yuh when you git on your train, tomorrow. But I'll do it. Don't matter what happens to me after that."

Roley looked down at him. "But we don't want any trouble," Roley said, in a puzzled way, as if he were seeing something he had never dreamed could exist. "We're not looking for trouble. We never were. And you'd still come after us and kill us?"

"Sometimes trouble looks for *you*," Tom muttered. "*Damn* right, I'll kill all of yuh."

"No," Roley said. He stepped back in that same graceful movement, and kicked Tom in the side, very hard. I heard the ribs crack. Roley stepped over Tom, who was now retching on the floor of the alley. He finished patting him down, carefully side-stepping when the infuriated man tried to spit blood on him. Then Roley went over to Carl, who was starting to stir, and patted him for weapons as well. Roley had the two knives and the razor. I had the gun.

I hauled Arthur out of the alley. Roley strode on in front of us, and I knew better than to try to catch him, or speak to him. Arthur and I stumbled along, leaning on each other, he drunk, me terrified and shaking. A few blocks from the alley, I threw Carl's gun into a ditch full of water. I suspect that Roley had tossed the other weapons in there, too.

By the time we neared the encampment, Arthur was starting to sober up, fast. He lit a cigar. He had stopped staggering. "Jesus Christ," he said, suddenly. "That was quite something, wasn't it?"

I thought that was the understatement of the nineteenth century. I felt sick. "Holy God, Arthur. You ever see anything like that?" I said.

"Oh, yes," Arthur said. He stopped on the sidewalk and faced me. "Such occurrences are not unknown in the American West. This reminded me of somebody, though."

"Who was that?" I said.

"George Armstrong Custer," Arthur said. He took several deep lungfuls of cold, night air, and stared up for a minute at the coldly shining stars, as if for inspiration. "I saw him once at Camp Supply. Some commissary sergeant had gotten dead drunk. There must have been something more than normally poisonous about the home-made hooch he'd drunk, because it had sent him right off his head. He had a huge knife in his hand. He was yelling and screaming, something about Antietam. I guess he'd been there. And daring us to come on and get him. He was boxed up in a little space at the end of a warehouse, with troopers blocking his exit. He kept leaping from side to side of it, like an ape, and swinging the knife, each time almost taking somebody's head off. The men would shy away from him like girls afraid of a mouse, and then press up again. He'd stabbed his corporal, and the poor fellow had crawled away a few feet, bleeding, and he kept yelling, 'Shoot him! Shoot him!'

"Some of us had revolvers, and had pulled them—*I* had. Irresolute as hell, we *were* all starting to think of shooting him. Then Custer walked in. He pulled his sidearm. We all sort of stepped out of the way. He was that kind of man, the kind of man you step aside for. Custer just walked up to the drunken sergeant. The crazy bastard was watching Custer, his head screwed to one side, like a God damn weasel. 'I'll gut you, mister,' he kept saying. 'I'll gut you, mister.' I remember Custer just laughed. 'You'll have to get in line,' he said. He walked right up to the crazy man, like you'd walk over to a bar for a beer, and hit him in the side of the head with his pistol, with a thud I can hear yet. Then, with the erstwhile frightening sergeant lying there out cold at his feet, he turned on us, and said, 'Bunch of lily-livers. My Libbie could have managed this.'" Arthur laughed. "She *could* have, too. I met the lady."

"Custer," I said.

"Yes," Arthur said, with his former cheerfulness. "Brevet Major General George A. Custer. In the flesh." We walked along for a time in silence. "Let's be realistic about what just happened," he said. "Those men would have done just what they said. Disembowelled us, cut our balls off, then killed us, because they couldn't really leave us flopping around after all that, could they? Shot us if we resisted. Been back in their saloon before the police knew a thing. Roley saved us both." We walked a little farther. Then he said,

"Still and all. Man with that disposition, he can be a hero. Roley probably didn't know he had that character in him, but sometimes the army releases the real you. Often it does. Man with Roley's disposition can be a hero, make heroes of others. Or, he can get all his men killed, deader than shit." He looked at me, and blew some cigar smoke into my face. "Or both at the same time, just like good old General George A."

Alice

All I can think about tonight is Willie. I let him down. That ridiculous scene at the station, right out of a third-rate play. Little Alice, spectacles shining, declaiming poetry to a man I may never see again.

It's Mother's and Father's fault. Easy to say, but oh, yes, it's partly true. From the moment Father found out we were engaged, to never let us be alone, not for one minute. What a dirty trick. And the things they said. All right, I eavesdropped. I refuse to feel guilty about it. "Quite unsuitable. A family of nobodies. The dowdy life of a professor's wife, if he can even manage that."

Yes, and "We'll make sure it doesn't happen." Try, Father. Just let's see you try.

I feel so strange about what I did with Willie to try to make sure he comes back to me. I felt dirty. I've heard about things like that. According to my mother, bad women do them. I did that to manipulate Willie, but to do it for that reason only would be wicked, indeed.

The fact is, I wanted to, as well. And really, the more I think about it, I don't feel dirty at all.

Well, is my mother the model, then? She's beautiful. She flirts with men; she giggles, she caresses their hands. My father, mostly, but not only him. To get what she wants. And only for that reason, it would appear. Twice she's told me how disgusting being in bed with a man is. "Repulsive," that's the word she used.

I don't think Willie repulses me.

One thing I know for sure: even if, God forbid, I do not marry

Willie, I am leaving this house. I will not stay in this overfurnished menagerie, this trap for people. Not with those two. Is it a sin to start to despise your own parents?

God, my own banality disgusts me. Listen to me, sitting in my asinine flounced petticoats, in my overheated bedroom, toasting my plump little pink feet—which Willie will think so adorable if he lives to see them—before the fire. Thinking my rosewater-scented female thoughts. And soon the man I love will be out there in the desperate cold and emptiness of that wilderness. In danger. And him so small and frail, so weak and unprepared. Nearly blind without his glasses. His wrists and hands are as small and weak as mine. And he doesn't know anything. He thinks his absurd poems and books are reality.

And so does his commander, that Collison. He hasn't read anything, of course, but impressive-looking as he is, he's nothing but a storekeeper, stuffed full of ridiculous, patriotic, "manly" clichés out of the Sunday paper.

Two innocents with pistols.

I wish I could be there. Funny to think of. Me in my little pink country overcoat, and adorable pink hat, lugging Willie's ammunition and his knapsack. Ducking bullets. Except you don't hear them coming, so you can't duck.

I'd learn how to shoot the pistol. Yes, men would laugh. And they'd be right about many girls. Their cute little knees would quiver, and their delicate wrists would flutter, and they'd shoot off their own big toe.

But not me. I'll use a phrase Father uses about his business enemies when he thinks no woman is listening.

If any son of a bitch tried to hurt Willie, I'd blow his brains all over the Saskatchewan prairie.

And not turn a hair.

THE CHILDREN'S CRUSADE

VII

When we headed west from Winnipeg, the track ran for a while longer through tamed Manitoba prairies, with tidy, new farmhouses and big, red wooden barns. We did not pay much attention. We knew that the real West still lay ahead of us. We reached it when we crossed the invisible boundary into the District of Assiniboia. This was the North-West Territories, which stretched from the American border to the North Pole, and all the way out to British Columbia: an empty expanse of grassland, parkland, mountains, firs, tundra, water and ice, with room for fifty Englands, for ten of the states of Texas the Yankees were always bragging about. Canada had bought it sixteen years earlier from the Hudson's Bay Company, but Canada had made no imprint on it. It remained what a writer had called it, "the great lone land." The Indians waited uneasily for the long-promised flood of settlers, which had not yet come. The tiny detachments of North-West Mounted Police, Union Jacks fluttering on spindly flagpoles, huddled with what dignity they could in the immensity. The handful of European settlers stared around themselves in something like frightened awe. The half-Indian Métis looked fearfully over their shoulders at Manitoba, and wondered if *les Anglais* would do them dirt again, as they had in '70, when Riel led the Métis before. The scorching summer sun shone down on a Canadian empire which had not yet come to be. The killing winds of winter howled down from the Pole across untouched immensity, lashing the flatlands, billowing against mountains which made the Alps look like molehills, as the winds had blown for unrecorded millennia, as they might blow forever.

I was staring out the train window at the flatness stretching away to an ending which I could not imagine. Very occasionally, I saw a settler's hardscrabble shack. Most of the land was empty, as empty as the day Columbus had landed. I knew that the Indians had wandered it, until we herded them onto reserves where they sometimes refused to stay, but there was almost no sign of any human presence. Shoals of melting snow alternated with mudbanks of dark-brown soil. The horizon was vague, almost a blur in the soft light of early spring. The huge semi-circle of sky, streaked with stringy grey clouds, seemed to stretch upward to infinite heights.

The train was slowing, as it approached a water tower. I wondered vaguely what had become of Carl and Tom, and was for some reason elated to find that I didn't give a damn.

Roley, characteristically, had wanted, upon arising the next morning, to go straight to the Mounted Police, to explain the whole incident. It had taken Arthur Howard forty-five minutes to convince him that he should do no such thing, that we would never hear anything about the incident again, and that he, Roley, had done the world in general and Winnipeg in particular an enormous favour by the thrashing he had given those two bastards.

Roley had looked dubious but he had gone along.

My backside ached from the hard wooden back and seat of the train. I pulled out a little golden locket which I kept around my neck under my tunic. Alice had surprised me with it the night before we embarked. It contained a tiny profile photograph of her. She had a slight smile on her face, and was glancing ever-so-slightly toward the photographer. When she'd given the locket to me, I'd realized with a rush of affection that she must have had the photograph taken, and arranged it inside the locket, months before, in the hope that I'd eventually get up the nerve to propose to her. As I sat on that cold, worn wooden seat, I could feel the warmth of her, her yellow hair brushing my cheek. I remembered what we'd done on the sofa in her father's library. I felt myself getting warmer, thinking about it.

It occurred to me that it must have taken an immense amount

of nerve for her to do that. Alice was a terribly smart girl, much smarter than I. She had used every weapon she had to get her hooks into me, so that those hooks would pull me back from some suicidal encounter with a Métis rifleman. It couldn't have been done any better. And I was glad of it, and I took a vow to do what she wanted and hide behind every rock. I didn't know then that it was a vow I was to break over and over again in the next few weeks.

I glanced around me at some of the men of Company Four of the Toronto Light Infantry. They had tossed the heavy red tunics over the backs of seats, and in their grey under-tunics sprawled in unlikely poses on the rock-hard wooden benches.

They had not recovered from that God-awful march north of Superior. But they already looked harder, and wiser. Some of them still thought they were off "to fight the French," and some still thought they were going "Indian-fighting."

But not so many of them thought they were off on a jaunt.

Arthur Howard sat alert and slightly forward in his seat. He was staring out the window at the bald prairie with an abstracted half-smile, like a man who had come home again. Jack Price frowned, and fidgeted, and rubbed the skin on the back of one hand with the fingers of the other, and irritably lit and relit his pipe. Roley sat and gazed out, smoking calmly, apparently placid. But I had learned to distrust these reflective moods. They would be replaced, almost instantaneously, by restless, almost angry frames of mind, where he was not good company. Much as I liked him, I was learning not to break into his solitudes, but to wait for him to break into mine.

After the episode in the alley, the man intrigued me even more. His need for privacy was great. But when he was in a good mood, and he often was, he talked very freely. "Talk your ear off," Jack had said affectionately, and on occasion it was true. He was always poking fun at himself, at his lack of education, at his store. He sometimes talked about his mother, her endless reading about romance, her fascination with King Arthur and the Round Table, her addiction to her beloved books. But I was beginning to know the man. God help the stranger, or even the friend, who made fun of his store, his wife, or his son. Or his mother, come to that.

Roley Collison was a wonderful example of the Irish Protestant Ulsterman he'd told me his ancestors were: the courage, warmth, humour, and hair-trigger quickness to take offence, coupled with dark Puritanism, sudden red anger, and the deepest and most inexplicable sudden fits of melancholy. No, you did not break into the solitude of a man like that. But if you were me, and fascinated by him, you constantly wanted him to break into yours.

Suddenly, he did just that. Roley touched my arm. "Come and look," he said. The men were staring out the opposite windows. I went across and saw, on a slight rise, silhouetted against the grey sky, three men on grey horses. They were Mounties, rifles slung over their shoulders, red tunics faded by weather as ours were not. The famous golden bands on their pillbox caps glowed palely in the pale sunlight of early spring. They resented us, the North-West Mounted Police, I had heard in Winnipeg, for coming west to do the job they had failed to do at Duck Lake. But their sergeant gravely saluted us, and I saluted back.

"Willie," Roley abruptly said. "You're an educated man. Who are these Matey people?"

It was Arthur Howard who answered him. "Jesus H. Christ," he said. "Don't you people know your own history? Well, why should you, when the American people don't know theirs?"

We all stared at him in surprise. "Look," he said. "The French explorers and fur traders were the most amazing people in the history of our West, or yours. Or maybe the second-most amazing, after their half-caste children, the Métis. Listen. While the British and their American colonists were hugging the Atlantic seashore like drowning men clinging to a mast, and there weren't yet any Canadians who spoke English, and the Hudson's Bay Company was huddling on the edge of the Bay, it was Frenchmen who were running all over the West. Exploring it, mapping it, when Lewis and Clark's grandparents were just gleams in their fathers' eyes."

He made an expansive gesture at the train window. "It fascinated me, when I was in the Cavalry. The early West. I carried books about it around with me. The other boys thought I was crazy. Look. In 1724, *1724,* a Frenchman named de Veniard was in Kansas, meeting with some western tribe, maybe the Comanche, maybe even the Apache. In the early 1740's some French explorer named La Vérendrye was in Wyoming. *Wyoming!* He was the first white man to see the northern Rockies. Twenty-five years after that, Daniel Boone thought he was being intrepid by pushing into eastern Kentucky."

He started fumbling in his pocket for a cigar. "And everywhere they went, those Frenchmen made marriages with Indian women, real marriages, see? And the Métis people, Catholic, half-French, half-Indian, were the result. The very word means something like 'mixed together,' an old Frenchman told me. There were Métis with de Veniard.

"And later on, when the Canadian fur traders from Montreal pushed out into the West, they used Frenchmen from Quebec as boatmen, and those men made more and more marriages with the Indian girls. Sometimes the British and English Canadian fur trader bosses made marriages too, and so there's a minority of English-speaking, Protestant half-breeds. Who are largely on your side in this mess.

"Anyway, the Métis grew and prospered. They were even more intrepid than their white fathers and their Indian mothers. They were everywhere in the old Canadian and American West, trapping, fur-trading, exploring, hunting buffalo, fighting Indians, raising hell. And seventy-five years ago they had made their biggest settlement back where we just were, on the Red River, at Winnipeg. They beat the shit out of the British when they tried to displace them." He stopped, and looked a little dubiously at us, as if noticing our British red coats for the first time.

"And then along came 1870, and Louis Riel. Your country had just bought your West from the Hudson's Bay Company. There was no Canadian authority out there at all. I know for a fact that people in Chicago, important people, wanted U.S. Grant to just seize the Canadian West. One can argue that Riel stopped that. He was the one educated man the Métis had. He set up a government, he pressured your government into making Manitoba a province. And then he killed some nuisance of a Canadian who objected to his authority."

"I resent that," Jack said, coolly. "The man he murdered wasn't 'some nuisance.' He was a great Canadian patriot and Protestant martyr named Thomas Scott."

Arthur looked at him with something like disappointment. "All right, Jack," he said. "I know a lot of Canadians feel strongly about it. I won't argue the point."

"Good," Jack said, biting down on his pipe.

"Anyway," Arthur said, "killing Scott tore it. An army of British redcoats struggled out to Red River. Riel had to skedaddle. He fled to the States, and he wound up an American citizen. I heard he was meeting with old U.S. Grant himself. If I was a Britisher or a Canadian, that would have scared me. A lot. What in hell was Riel thinking? What was he doing down there? You don't want to underestimate Louis Riel. His people weren't the only ones to think he was a great man, a hell of a great man. Did he bear a grudge against the Canadians and the English? Americans who knew about him thought he had every right to.

"Last I heard, from a fellow I knew in the Cavalry, Riel was teaching school in Montana. And I guess he came home to Canada. And then it was in the New Haven newspaper. Riel and Gabriel Dumont, his lieutenant, had shot a column of the North-West Mounted Police to pieces. He'd declared some kind of self-government, and the Mounted Police went out with Union Jacks flying and red coats gleaming to confront him, and he crushed them. And the next thing I knew, I had a telegram from good old Dr. Gatling. The Canadians were sending their militia out to fight Riel. And how would I like to go along?"

"Yes," I said. "Well said. After Riel killed Scott, and the British chased him out of Winnipeg, the Métis moved away from Red River, up to Batoche on the South Saskatchewan. They had ten years or so of good times. And by that time Canada was creeping up on them again. And the buffalo died out. All those mighty animals were killed off, which was a catastrophe for those people. And their farms failed, and the federal government wouldn't give them title to those farms, or some such thing, and they invited Riel back from Montana to save them. Last year. And now the damned fool has started a revolution."

"What do you think Prime Minister Macdonald will do with Riel, if we beat them?" Roley said.

"If he wants Ontario's votes, hang him," Jack said.

Roley said, "And lose Quebec if he does? God, I'll bet the Prime Minister hates Riel." Then he turned to Arthur Howard. "And what about the Indians?"

We had been hearing that some of the Indians had joined Riel but most were, thus far, loyal or neutral. "The Indians, ah, the Indians," Arthur said. "I once saw quite a lot of your Indians. They sent me up to Dakota, toward the end of my hitch. We used to come up here, across the Medicine Line. The U.S. Cavalry. To show the Great White Mother over in London that Uncle Sam wasn't afraid of being turned over her knee.

"Crees, mostly, some Assiniboine, which are Nakota Sioux, a few of Sitting Bull's accursed Lakota, who didn't go back when he did. Some Santee, some Ojibwa. Lots of Indians. God help us if they join Riel."

Now the train, slowly picking up speed as it headed west toward Qu'Appelle, turned a corner, through some scrub brush. Suddenly, there was a collective intake of breath all over the carriage, and all the men rushed to look out one side of the train. I walked over and stared out. "Speak of the devil," Arthur said.

Riding alongside the train, as fast as their sinewy, mottled horses would carry them, were seven or eight Indians, several brandishing Winchester carbines (whose rate of fire vastly exceeded the clumsy Snider-Enfields we carried). They wore buckskin breeches. Some of them had shirts made of the same stuff; some wore bright flannel shirts of red or blue. The lead one let out a whoop, aimed his carbine at the sky and fired a shot. The men laughed, and cheered, and waved at them. Then we were past them.

"Theatrical as ever," Arthur said. "Those fellows are Assiniboines, by God! Off their reservations, or reserves, or whatever you people call 'em."

The train was rounding a bend, and so we could still see the Indians, racing madly alongside the rear train cars, still yelling, still firing in the air. It was all irony, of course. They were having fun with the gaping eastern tenderfeet, laughing at us, really. Putting on their own, ironic Wild West show, for the red-coated idiots on the train. But the men gazed as if in a trance. Nobody made a sound. Every Canadian had read about the West. Every Canadian boy had at least one yellow-backed penny-dreadful about the West. Now, as I looked at our men, staring in fascination at the receding figures, I thought that, for us at least, the West was more than a place. It was more, even, than the myth the Americans had made of it. It was an idea, and, more than that: it was a dream.

Except for Arthur, we all craned our necks, staring behind us, and pressed our faces harder and harder against the window glass, and watched the dwindling figures of the Assiniboines, until they had vanished into the blue-grey blur of the prairie.

* * *

When the train stopped, shouting sergeants and officers quickly separated into two halves what there was of the North-West Field Force. As I watched half the infantry regulars, the Grenadiers, our own Company Four and one artillery battery form up beside the train, I thought I remembered that Caesar (or somebody) had cautioned against dividing your forces. I *knew* Custer had divided his at the Little Bighorn. Did our leaders know what the hell they were doing?

Roley and Jack had already shaken Arthur Howard's hand and bidden him goodbye. I walked over to him. He smiled at me. "Willie," he said, "I'm still shaking about what almost happened in Winnipeg."

"Me, too," I said. "But no harm done. Except to Tom and Carl, of course." Arthur laughed. "Look, Arthur," I said, "you must have some opinion about what's going to happen. To our column, I mean. You've fought Indians. Just how ready are we?"

Arthur looked down at his boots for a minute. "I haven't said anything," he finally replied. "No point in undermining morale. But maybe I owe you the truth. Fact is, Willie, these are the greenest soldiers I've ever seen. The rawest recruit we got in the U.S. Cavalry was better trained than most of these men. Christ, most of them have scarcely ever fired those out-dated blunderbusses they're carrying. They're townsmen, all of them, never until now spent a night outdoors, never missed a meal. This is a children's crusade. The men are *not* ready, and Jesus, I hope this General Middleton of yours doesn't try to use them like British generals love to do, marching them in a straight line at the enemy. Because they'll be shot down like rabbits, and they'll crack and run."

He lit one of his cigars and looked around reflectively. "Stupid, God damn Custer," he said, finally. "He refused to wait for the Gatlings. It would have changed everything, if he'd waited for the Gatlings. And now Middleton's separated his main force from *my* Gatlings. Idiot."

I thought about that. "Arthur," I said, "you said you knew our Indians. What about the Métis? You ever meet any of them?"

He looked at me. "Ah, of course I met them," he said. "Everybody in Montana and the Dakotas knew them. I even saw this Gabriel Dumont, once. He was a legend. He could drink all night and all the next day; he was unbeatable at poker; he could shoot birds out of the sky with his Winchester. So was Riel a legend, and a more frightening one, because Riel was a medicine man. He was educated at the white man's schools. He had made fools of the British and Canadians at Red River. You see, Willie, the Indian is the best irregular soldier in the world, the fastest, the most improvisational, the most deadly. But Indians are emotional, swayed by the spirit. That gives them a short attention span in a battle or a war. White men are the opposite: all rational as hell, determined, armed to the teeth with fancy weapons. But they're clumsy; their instincts are blunted. They don't recognize danger when it's right in front of them. They make all kinds of stupid mistakes, like Custer, or me back in Winnipeg. But the Métis in battle have all the best qualities of both peoples and not a single one of the worst. And so I pray for your boys. I really do."

He got on the train, and the train pulled away, with Arthur, his two Gatlings, an artillery battery, half our tiny force of regulars, and the Queen's Own, west toward Swift Current. Those of us who'd disembarked gave three loud cheers. Then we marched off toward the tent city which glistened whitely on the edge of the little town of Qu'Appelle. I don't know about the rest of them, but I already felt a lot lonelier than I had an hour before.

Alice

This afternoon, the butler came in and told me that my father "required" me in his study. I was afraid, I don't know why. Summoning people in a regal fashion is very much his manner, and I am used to it.

But there was something different about this time.

He has his desk up against the west window, and the light hurts your eyes when you walk in and take your seat in front of him. My mother was sitting off to the right side, and she gave me a smile that she apparently meant to be encouraging. But it wasn't.

My father gave me a wintry smile. "Alice," he said, without any throat-clearings or protestations of fatherly affection (he was in his authoritative mode). "Alice, thank you for coming so promptly. Your mother and I wish to convey something to you. You have apparently chosen to marry this Lorimer boy."

"Yes," I said.

"Well," and he tilted his head upward in the commanding way he has, "we will discuss that further. I can assure you of that. A girl of your tender age does not get to make such decisions without the guidance of her parents. It was quite wrong of you to have told Willie that you would marry him. Quite wrong. A girl does does not have the

right to make any such commitment without parental approval."

I said nothing.

"But that," he said loudly, "is not why I have asked you here. We will discuss your marriage further. I wish to inform you that I do not wish you to attend any more university classes."

"No, please," I said. "Father, it means so much to me. It makes me feel alive."

"You are alive, Alice," he said, wearily. "Too lively for my liking, as a matter of fact. No. I forbid it. Higher education is quite unsuitable for women. They do not benefit from it. They do not have the intellectual or spiritual capacity for it. It does nothing but fill up their heads with ideas that they are emotionally incapable of handling. Like your asinine notion, so often expressed in my hearing, that women should be allowed to vote."

I said, "I thought you were a Radical, Father."

"And so I am, and proud to be," Father said. "One of these days this country will be placed in the hands of men like me, believers in Science and Reason, not sentimental fools and militarists like Macdonald and his followers. In any event, your remark simply shows that you are incapable of logic. Your unsuitability for university has nothing to do with my political opinions. Nothing. And this discussion is over. Closed. You are forbidden to attend any more classes at that place. You are going to start searching for a husband—one who is appropriate for your social class, and ours. And that isn't Willie Lorimer."

On other occasions, I would have burst into tears and pleaded with him. But I knew from the flinty look on his face that this wouldn't work. And, frankly, I am sick of abasing myself.

I ran up to my room and sat on the bed. But I didn't cry. I shook all over, and it took me a little while to realize that I was shaking with rage.

VIII

Early the next morning, our column was to head north from Qu'Appelle. General Middleton and his Winnipeg militia, with an artillery battery, and French's Scouts, his irregular cavalry, had marched out of there toward Batoche several days earlier. Batoche, two hundred miles away to the north-west, on the South Saskatchewan River—Batoche, the home settlement of the Métis, the capital of Riel's Provisional Government. Now we were going to follow in Middleton's footsteps. His column was said to be deliberately going slowly, waiting for us to reinforce him.

We wondered if we might be attacked as we marched north. In my imagination, our terrified column hastily formed ragged squares of British scarlet, as the screaming Indians and Métis suddenly swooped down on us out of nowhere. The squares blossomed clouds of grey-white smoke, as the frightened men fired in volleys. Then the image mercifully petered out.

These visions were still in front of my eyes as we dragged ourselves up the north crest of the valley the next day. The valley hillcrests were still covered with snow, and the empty plains into which we were marching were only half-melted. Ahead of us stretched a crude, half-visible prairie trail, winding to the horizon. The trail was half-snow, half-dirt. When the temperature dropped below the freezing point, the dirt was hard, rutted, yet sticky. When the feeble sun of early spring showed itself, the packed dirt turned to mud the consistency of glue.

We stepped smartly northward away from the semi-domesticated slopes of the Qu'Appelle Valley. Around us stretched to the grey-blue, cloudy horizons a long, rolling expanse of icy, glistening soil. Last year's withered grasses waved from the knolls, and receding from them lay long banks of soft-looking, dirty, melting ice and snow. The rank, vital smell of early spring was stronger now.

There was no sign of life besides our gaudy caravan, except for occasional hawks, soaring in the high, grey sky. No living figures marred the land, except for the struggling horses and riders of our Scouts, as they returned to the column. At first, they were tiny fluttering dots. Finally, as they neared us, the dots resolved themselves into sweating, exhausted horses and slumping men.

The land didn't need us. It didn't even notice us. Our clattering, self-important expedition passed over it and was gone, and things were as they had always been.

In the midst of the column were the precious nine-pounder cannons of battery "A," shone to a glow by their proud, spit-and-polish regular gunners. The artillery horses whinnied and plunged and sometimes fell, on the rough and rutted trail. The gunners cajoled them, and shouted and cursed, and raced to control the occasionally rearing animals, so that they would not overturn and smash the cannons' fragile carriages. The oxen pulling the heaviest carts plodded patiently through the muck.

Company Four of the Toronto Light Infantry was third in the column, just behind "A" battery. Roley marched at the head of our little band, beside the flag-bearer. Our Union Jack, kept carefully wrapped until then, snapped harshly back and forth in the icy wind. Jack ranged up and down one side of the struggling, sweating men, I up and down the other.

The men soon lost their good cheer as the cold wind bit through cheap overcoats and shoddy uniforms, already ripped and frayed by the awful trek north of Superior. Many of them, used to office chairs or leaning on a store counter, not yet recovered from our awful ordeal in the snow, were visibly in trouble. Their faces were wet with sweat. Their eyes stared; their shoulders slumped. They visibly struggled to stay in step. As I'd pass by, they'd look guiltily at me, as if they were letting down the side. They were shamefaced at their bad performance, as if I was going to report their lack of soldierliness directly to Queen Victoria herself.

The fact was, I couldn't blame them a bit. The Snider-Enfield was four feet long and weighed nearly nine pounds. The bayonet made it a foot longer, and (when it was mounted on the rifle) you stood a good chance of putting another man's eye out if you didn't hold it right. The packs weighed another ninety. Each man also carried two hundred rounds of ammunition, and the Snider fired immense .577 calibre bullets. Roley had told me that their last route march with packs had been the previous spring, for three miles around Lake Ontario. *Three miles!* Two men twisted their ankles in the rutty trail and could no longer walk. They had to be supported, struggling and cursing, by increasingly exhausted men, as we struggled toward the pale and ever-receding north-west horizon.

If I'd had to carry a nine-pound rifle and a ninety-pound pack, I'd have fallen face-first into the mud after one mile. Officer's packs were lighter, and I had no armament except for my revolver. Thank God light infantry officers didn't have swords. But I was soaked in sweat after a mile or two, sweat that pooled under my armpits and in my groin, sweat that saturated my tunic so I smelled like a horse, sweat that froze when I unbuttoned my overcoat. I staggered rather than walked.

Every so often, a man would plunge to his waist in muddy, freezing water which had been hidden by the dirty crust of ice covering it. Cursing, he'd be fished out, and his rifle retrieved from the muck. Then he'd be dried off, lest he freeze stiff. The poor bastard would strip in the icy cold, while laughing and jeering troopers wrung out his clothes. The victim, growing as blue as the artillerymen's coats, would frantically towel himself with whatever fragments of dry cloth we could find. Then he'd put his filthy, soaked uniform back on. Groaning, despairing loudly and profanely of the future workability of his private parts, he'd resume his march.

After a time, Roley stopped marching at the head of the column like a British officer in a lithograph. He started ranging freely up and down both sides of the column, doing what he was so good at. He cracked jokes that were worse than awful. He told the men that we'd stop soon for food. He loudly and profanely proclaimed that when we'd finally hung Riel, he personally was going to sleep for a week. He'd take the Snider away from a man when that man started to reel and shoulder it himself for a mile or two. And then shoulder another and another and another. "Maybe we should make you the captain, Charlie, (or Bill, or Sid)," he'd say. "Look how natural I look with this God damn thing over my shoulder. And look how natural *you* look, with that inborn air of command, there. Why, old Middleton ought to turn the God damn army over to you, right here and now." And the recipients of this nonsense would laugh until there were tears in their eyes. Their comrades would grin and straighten up, and shoulder their rifles, and march straight ahead into whatever future they had.

A couple of times that first dismal morning, Roley fell into step beside me. He would walk quietly beside me for a time. Then he'd say, "A penny for your thoughts." Tired and apprehensive as I was, I didn't respond with the hearty enthusiasm he no doubt wanted to see. But he was undaunted. After a while, he would slap me on the back. "Attaboy, Willie," he would say. "You're the one who'll write the history of this when it's over," or "Make sure you spell 'Roland' right when your book comes out."

And I felt heartened and warmed. Which was, of course, the aim of the exercise.

There were war correspondents from Canadian and American newspapers with us. They were terrible riders. They bumbled along, floundering on their saddles, scribbling occasionally with pencils in little notebooks, trying to record their impressions of this terrifying emptiness, so that they could telegraph their eastern readers sooner or later and tell them what it was like.

But nobody can tell what it was like.

As I struggled along, I wondered what we would look like to a man in a hot air balloon, soaring overhead. A straggling, frayed and stumbling serpent-like monster of red and blue, toiling over vastnesses, with drab little dots on horseback breaking away and returning, with shiny little toy cannons drawn by toy horses, all of it fumbling, struggling, labouring toward some fate we could not imagine.

The children's crusade.

When we finally stopped for lunch, we found that there was no firewood for cooking and barely enough for warmth. The crucial shortage of the North-West Field Force—apart from trained soldiers, of course—was horses. The half-frozen plains of early spring offered no forage for the horses we did have, so that what wagons we had were piled to the bursting point with feed for the horses themselves. And then there was our food, huge barrels of fresh drinking water, our extra rifle ammunition, hundreds of spare horseshoes, thousands of horseshoe nails, hundreds of nine-pound shells for the clattering cannons. There weren't enough horses, enough wagons or enough teamsters to bring fuel for cooking. There were no proper trees, only scrubby wet brush. I had not seen the men angry before, but they were now. There would be no hot coffee, no tea, no beef stew. We would live on cold bully beef, cold biscuits, and ice-cold water.

That day, the exhausted, dispirited men made only eighteen miles. At nightfall, we had to use hammers to pound our tent-pegs into the frozen ground. The fires were sparse; the cold food made me gag, starving as I was.

Roley and Jack and I remained around our little fire, smoking, and shivering in the darkness. Jack suddenly brought up a topic which until then had seemed taboo. "Roley," he asked, "are these men going to be able to perform in battle? Are we?"

"Perform?" Roley said, and laughed. "Jesus, Jack, you make it sound like wedding night jitters."

"I suppose the wedding night and the first taste of combat are the two great anxieties of a man's existence," I said.

Roley looked at me, laughed, and blew a mouthful of smoke in my direction. "Jesus," he said, shaking his head. "We've got a philosopher on our hands. That's what I get for having a college man as a second lieutenant. I should have known better."

Jack hunched his shoulders down, his face dark. "No," he said. "But seriously, it's an important question."

Roley said, abruptly, "Of course it is. And I don't know the answer. The men have fired a few rounds with those damn Sniders at paper targets. They've learned how to fire by volleys, front rank kneeling, rear rank standing. Present, aim, fire, reload. That won't be much use unless the Mateys come rushing at us like Zulus. Which they won't. The men've learned how to use the bayonet. *That* won't be much use unless the Mateys walk right up to us and punch us in the nose. The men're going to have to learn how to use cover and fire from it. I suspect you learn that in a damn big hurry once the bullets start to fly. And for the rest? Nobody knows how men are going to perform in combat. But I'll tell you one thing. Because these men are so green, how they'll do depends on how we'll do. Experienced troops can operate by instinct in a battle, but these men are going to be looking to us to tell them what to do and how to do it." He blew out some more smoke. "And I'll bet the enemy knows that, and will try as hard as they can to shoot the officers first."

Jack did not look very reassured. Since I realized that I knew nothing about being an officer, I didn't feel reassured either. We sat a while longer, in silence. Then Roley said, "I don't like what I heard at Qu'Appelle. That all the French volunteers from Quebec are being sent on to Alberta, where there's no fighting. Because Middleton doesn't trust them to fight against French Catholics like Riel and his men. I don't like that at all. I felt really happy when I heard the Frenchmen were volunteering. I thought, Canada works, and this proves it."

"I agree," I said.

"No," Jack said. "We can't trust the French. We can't trust the Catholics. That's my view."

"Oh, Jack," Roley said.

"Now, damn it, Roley," Jack said, stubbornly. "I've had it explained to me and explained to me. Down at the lodge. The Catholics aren't really Christians at all. They worship old relics, and marble statues. They're not loyal subjects of the Empire. They're subjects of the Pope."

Roley shook his head. "All right, sure, Jack," he said. "But are they really so bad? One time when I was small, I went into one of the Catholic churches, a couple of blocks away from where we lived. Just out of curiosity. All my friends told me, if you went in there they put you in some kind of booth, and you never came out again. Like Sweeney Todd, only with candles and incense, I guess.

"So I marched right in, and the old priest came and sat beside me and asked if I was a Catholic. Then he gave me tea and short-bread cookies. He invited me to come back any time. And I got out alive. I'll be damned if I see what's so dangerous about them."

He looked at Jack. "But, Jack, your lodgemates are always worked up about the Frenchmen, too, aren't they? And Riel and his men are a sort of Frenchmen. Nobody ever shuts up about it. Didn't we start Canada up to put all that shit behind us? Why can't everybody just get over it? Do Frenchmen have two heads? Do we? We're all human. We all want the same basic things. Well, *don't* we, for Christ's sake?"

I could see that this was an old argument, and that Jack did not like not being taken seriously. "All right, then," he said, irritably. "If everything is so wonderful, why are you here, Roley? I know why I'm here."

"Oh shit," Roley said, laughing again. "I made this speech on the train. Willie has already been subjected to this." He paused, and again that dreamy look I'd seen before came over his face. He hesitated for a little longer, and then, at last, he spoke. "Sometimes, I think most of what they tell us is nonsense. All the stuff your Mom and Dad insist is true. Because their Mom and Dad said it was, and so on, back to Adam and Eve, I guess. So much nonsense poured down your throat at school with a funnel. A lot of school was completely meaningless to me. I was always embarrassed about it. I felt so stupid. I guess I *was* stupid. I dropped out, as soon as I could, to work in the store. I thought you were a man if you worked and made money.

"Immediately, they start in with the dignity of work, and the sanctity of the marriage bed, and the joys of family life. I looked forward so much to all those things. And every mile farther you get, it's not what you'd hoped it would be. I mean, it's not *bad*, oh, no, and it's much better than nothing, but it's not what you dreamed of. If you even knew exactly what you were dreaming of." He stopped, and looked out at the blackness for a minute. The dreaming, dancing look in his eyes had grown brighter. "When you were little, on cold nights like this, did you ever lie awake in bed when you knew you should have been asleep? And listen to the train whistles, vanishing into the night? I did, all the time. I used to think, if I could only be on that train. I wonder where it's going. I wonder where it's been. And I'd feel so much yearning, for God knows what, and God *damn* it, I still feel like that. I still want more than I have, more than my life has in it. And that's why I joined the militia. I believe I always knew something like this"—he gestured out at the sleeping camp—"would happen to me sooner or later."

He stopped again and laboriously relit his pipe. I often suspected that he used this as a way of collecting his thoughts. "I have to say it means a lot to me that I have friends here I can rely on. Jack and Willie. Willie and Jack. You'll never let me down, and I'll never let you down. That's what we have here. That's all we have." He started to laugh. "Oh, Christ," he said. "You've just listened to a long speech by a man permanently stuck at the age of twelve."

"Hell of a good speech, though," Jack said. He was smiling, and it occurred to me that I never could dislike him, no matter how bad his opinions were.

"Meanwhile," Roley said, "the only educated man here says not a word. What about you, Willie?"

I liked these men so much I decided to throw caution to the winds. "Mostly," I said, "I'm here because of some federal regulations."

"Regulations?" Jack said.

I stared for a minute at the two of them. "Laws," I said. "The regulations say that if you have an active militia commission, and they call you up, you have to go, or they can court-martial you. You see, I was commissioned a second lieutenant in an outfit called the Toronto University Volunteers. And that regiment was disbanded in less than four months, because the fellows wanted to sit around and drink beer, and talk about girls, instead of marching around in the rain. I kept meaning to resign the commission, but I forgot to. And for some God damn reason, they called me up."

I think I expected them to beat me up, or at least turn their backs on me, but they immediately burst into laughter and slapped me violently on the back.

"Wonderful," Roley said. "When we're all killed by Riel, Jack's tombstone will read, 'Here lies John Price, who died for the Protestant religion.' Mine will say, 'Here lies Roland Collison, who died because he wanted to be a hero.' And yours, Willie, will read, 'Here lies William Lorimer, who couldn't find a loophole in the federal regulations.'"

At twelve midnight, after an hour's fitful sleep wrapped in all the blankets I had, I got up to make the rounds of our sentries. It was a task which I had to alternate with Roley, Jack and Colour Sergeant Quinn all night, every night. The first sentry on my round was a man named Nolan, a little, bandy-legged, red-haired, freckled Irishman who always had a pipe stuck in his mouth. Arthur Howard had said he looked like a leprechaun. I could see him in the dark by the glowing bowl of his pipe, but would he see me? Or would he be startled and turn around and shoot me or bayonet me? I made a discreet coughing noise as I approached. Nolan yelled, "Jesus!" and swung around, hauling his Snider up so that the barrel pointed straight at me.

"For Christ's sake, Liam," I hissed, "it's me. Lieutenant Lorimer!"

"Oh, shit," he said, moving the barrel away. Then he gestured to me. "Come here, Lieutenant," he whispered. He went down on one knee and I with him. He pointed. I stared out into the void. A black, low, shapeless mass lay thirty feet or so beyond us at the top of a slight rise, barely visible in the cold starlight. "Look at that black thing out there," Nolan said. "That looks like a man, don't it? A man just lying prone, just waiting?"

I stared out into the pitch blackness. The blackness was almost total, but somehow it seemed to move and shimmer. The stillness was absolute. I stared until pinwheels began to form in front of my eyes. It *did* look like a God damn man, just lying there. "It *does* look like a God damn man," I whispered.

"I swear to God it wasn't there five minutes ago," he whispered. "I swear to God. Could they be creeping up on us? I was thinking of challenging it, or firing a shot at it, or giving the alarm, or something. What should I have done, Lieutenant?"

"I don't know," I said. He looked at me. That was obviously the wrong answer. "I mean, you did exactly right, Liam. Kept your eye on it, see if it moved. If it moved, you would have fired at it."

"Yeah, I would," he said.

"I know you would," I said. I knew that this was my first command crisis. I couldn't just wander off and leave Nolan peering out at what might be a Métis scout creeping up to slit a throat or two. I searched my mind for ideas and the only one I found which didn't involve waking up the whole camp was one I didn't like at all. I searched some more. Nolan looked at me. I could see he believed I knew what I was doing. I wondered how many men in wars had died because their officers felt the need to do something, anything, to justify their men's faith in them.

Finally, I straightened my shoulders. "I'm going out there and see what the hell it is," I whispered. He nodded. I thought, and then added, because it sounded good, "You cover me." He nodded, again. I don't know what on earth *that* meant, but it sounded right.

I pulled out my revolver, swallowed twice, and stepped out briskly into the darkness, keeping low. About three seconds later, an obvious thought occurred to me, and I turned and went straight back to Nolan. "You go around to all the sentry posts that have this for their field of fire," I said. "You don't; somebody will see me out there and they *will* fire. At me."

He saluted. "Sir," he said and tore off into the dark. I crouched there in the dreadful cold, watching that stupid, unmoving, but scary black mass. It shimmered in the darkness, it seemed to gather itself up to spring forward. And yet, I had almost relaxed, indeed I was beginning to feel sleepy, when Nolan almost frightened the shit out of me by putting his hand on my shoulder and whispering, "It's done."

"Good man," I said, in a strangled voice, and I moved out again. I could hear Nolan fumbling around behind me, shifting his position, trying to distinguish me from the black bastard of a thing I was stalking. Or which was stalking *me*. During that very short walk, I learned something new about soldiering. Really brave men may be able to move slowly and cautiously in battle, but ordinary men like me can do brave things only if they do them so fast they don't have time to think. Which, if you consider it, probably explains why so many ordinary men die in combat.

So I stopped creeping and moving low. My back was starting to hurt. The freezing wind scored my face. So I levelled the revolver and walked straight up to the God damn thing, making a tremendous amount of noise. If it had been a Métis buffalo hunter, I'd have been dead, of course, ten times over. At the last extremity, I started to run, cocked the revolver, and threw myself with a yell at the black son of a bitch of a thing.

It wasn't a Métis. It was a bush. A Saskatoon bush.

I turned my back on that infernal bush and started walking back to Nolan. Halfway there, I heard the marrow-freezing sound of the breech of a Snider being slammed shut. "Who goes there?" cried a voice.

"Me," I screamed. "Lieutenant Lorimer! *Don't shoot.*"

There was a silence, during which I again nearly shat myself. Then the voice asked, pleasantly enough, "Having a late crap, Lieutenant? And shouting with glee when it turned out all right?" There was laughter as the men began to wake up.

I strode back to Nolan. I was opening my mouth to speak when Roley appeared out of the blackness, smiling, pipe glowing, wedge cap a-tilt. He looked as if he'd just emerged from the Toronto armoury. "What in the name of Christ are you fellows up to?" he said.

"Nolan and I saw something," I said. "I went out to check it out. It was a bush."

Roley started to laugh, then to shake, and then to howl with laughter. "But was it," he said, struggling, "but was it…an *armed* bush?" This did not seem very funny to me. He went into another of his coughing fits.

"*God damn it,*" a voice roared out of the darkness. "*Will you God damn laughing hyenas shut the hell up?*" A boot flew out of the darkness, and hit me, painfully, on the leg.

Roley straightened up, coughing, with eyes streaming, clapped Nolan on the back and started leading me back to our tents. "You'd better sleep for a while," he said. "An encounter with an enemy bush is enough to exhaust a young fellow your age."

"Jesus, Roley," I said. "It's not funny. I've made a God damn fool of myself."

He looked at me with a smile. "On the contrary," he said. "Nolan will tell everybody how brave the new lieutenant is. You wait and see."

I rolled myself back up in my blankets. I felt like the biggest fool in the North-West Field Force. I thought my humiliation wouldn't let me sleep, but exhaustion soon dragged me down. Roley and Jack were kind men. They let me sleep for several hours. After a while, I dreamed. Alice came to me, whispering softly in my ear. She held my hand. Her hand was small, plump, and a little sweaty, as it had been on the sofa in her father's house. She had a very firm grip. She was whispering, and whispering in my ear. I could feel the warmth of her breath, although I could not make out a word. I kept getting more and more excited.

Roley was shaking me. "Rise and shine, Lieutenant," he said. I looked down, embarrassed, at my blankets. He ignored this. "I took two of your turns," he said. "Time for me to get some sleep."

I got up and went out into the raw dark. I wondered if Roley had guessed correctly about my misadventure with the Saskatoon bush. Would the idea get around that I was unusually brave instead of just unusually stupid?

As it turned out, he was right. I wish he hadn't been. God, do I ever wish that.

* * *

The next day, we passed out of the rolling prairies and began to pass the gravelly Touchwood Hills. We started to see signs of Middleton's column, which had passed this way a few days before. Here and there was the wrecked kindling of wagons that had managed to break their axles. Just off the trail, sinking into the mud, were the half-frozen corpses of horses, that had broken their legs and had to be shot. The unforgiving prairie was swiftly claiming this debris, and I found myself thinking of the graves we would leave behind us when this work was done, and how quickly the men in them would be obliterated in the cold dirt.

I found myself walking more easily. The grey look of exhaustion on the men's faces was being replaced by something more purposeful. Making tired and out-of-shape men march is a good way to get them in shape—if it doesn't kill them first.

* * *

Several days out of Qu'Appelle, we passed over a bleak salt plain where melting snow and toxic alkaline mud made a clay-like slush. Around us, there were the skeletons of aspens, willows and poplars. The alkali bubbled up around our feet. The salt burned the horses' hooves; it ate away at the shabby leather of our boots.

The next day, we started marching through more heavily wooded "parkland," and we started to fear ambush. We were in the District of Saskatchewan now. Middleton's column had halted for a time at the settlement of Humboldt. We would join them there in a few days, or catch them up just north of the town.

After supper that night, with the sky darkening, and the men huddling around the scanty campfires, I decided to walk a half-mile to a nearby low hill overlooking our campsite. I wanted to see what it looked like from up there. Roley was sitting quietly, cross-legged before our fire, smoking his pipe. I asked him if he wanted to come

with me. "Jesus Christ," he said. "No, my boy, I don't. It must be
wonderful to be of an age where, after you've tramped across half
the God damn Territories, you want to put in some recreational
walking. No, you go ahead, and don't fall in a bog or anything."
I looked at him, and saw the dark smudges under his eyes. It occurred to me, as it had when he faced down Hannigan the teamster,
that despite his strength and grace, underneath it all his constitu-
tion was not made for endurance.

I slowly walked over the prairie. Above me there was a sliver of
moon, and one bright planet, Jupiter, I thought, shining near the
curve of its crescent. In an hour or so, the whole magnificent Milky
Way would be visible. The first night on the trail, I'd seen our town-
bred infantry looking up at it in awe. Huddling in my overcoat, I
climbed the hill, puffing on my new pipe, turning now and again
to stare down at our campsite. The sentries, little stick-figures in
the growing gloom, were strolling slowly back and forth. I could
see flickering fires, and hear the whinnying of tired horses and the
murmur of conversation. The cold wind blew.

Then I heard from just behind me, much louder, the answering
whinny of a horse. I spun around with a smile, thinking that one
of our scouts was there. And I found myself staring at a very dark,
bearded man in a black coat astride a tough-looking, runty grey. He
had a sweat-stained slouch hat pulled down almost over his eyes
and a long, antique-looking rifle cradled in his arms. I saw his high
cheekbones, I looked into his expressionless black eyes, and I realized that I was in the presence of the enemy.

I pulled open my overcoat and started fumbling at my flapped
holster. He brought the rifle barrel up with a swift fluid motion so
that it pointed right at my heart. He shook his head, almost imperceptibly. *No.* I raised my hands in the universal symbol of surrender. For a couple of minutes we stood like that, my hands raised,
him looking right past me at the peaceful encampment. His lips
moved occasionally, and I realized that he was memorizing all that
he could see. His horse swayed in the wind, and made whickering noises. Used to getting treats, it stretched its head inquisitively

out to me. Its rider pulled it back with one hand on the reins and muttered something in French. I wanted to plead for my life but, in my terror, all my schoolboy French had deserted me. What was "please," in French? *Merci beaucoup.* No, that was "thanks a lot." But what was "please?" *S'il vous plaît.* That sounded like something you said when you wanted the salt shaker. What did you say to plead with a man not to blow a hole through your chest?

Then he gathered up the reins with one hand. The rifle barrel still pointed at my heart. I knew that it was likely that I was going to die right there and then. The horseman looked at me for a few seconds. I tried to say something, but only a whisper, like that of a baby, came out of my mouth. Then he smiled, and winked, and swung his horse rapidly away from me and over the crest of the hill.

I stood there like an idiot for about fifteen seconds—as he'd known I would--and then I yanked my revolver out of its holster and ran after him. On the other side of the hill, three coulees choked with brush ran away to the north, east and south. There was still light, but he had vanished. Coming from somewhere, I could hear the diminishing sound of his horse's scrambling hooves. I thought for a second of firing a shot down each coulee—God knows what good that would have done—and then it occurred to me that the result of *that* would be that about sixty Snider-Enfield rounds would be fired at me the instant I walked back over the hillcrest. About fifty-eight of them would miss, of course, but I was in no mood for further adventures. I walked back to the camp, like a man strolling through a Toronto park, but with my useless revolver still clutched in my hand.

I reported what I'd seen to Roley, who ran off to inform our cavalry scouts that the enemy was watching us. I doubted they'd be surprised. I also suspected that if they'd pursued my black-bearded friend, they'd have caught nothing but pneumonia, from the icy prairie wind.

Alice

I wanted to talk to my mother, about my feelings for Willie, how I missed him. We were in her bedroom, which has two overstuffed pale pink satin armchairs, side by side. It was late, and her lamps made strange patterns on the carpet, on the walls.

"Mama," I said, "I've never felt this way before."

She reached out and touched my hand. "Talk about it, sweetie," she said. "That always helps, if the one who's listening loves you."

I couldn't stop thinking about that cold-blooded spectacle at the station. I'd read him a poem, like some idiot of a schoolteacher, instead of hugging him so hard he couldn't breathe. Whining about what I wanted, what I needed. Every time I thought about it, I shuddered. It might be the last time I ever saw him. He had needed my love; he had needed my encouragement.

"Oh, Mama," I said. "Have you ever made a mistake so huge you want to hide from everybody? That's what I've done. I'm so stupid."

She put her arms around me and pulled me out of my chair and onto hers. I started to cry, like a little girl, and she held me, and for just a few moments, all my pain went away. It was as if I were nine again, and in pain and misery, and Mama would make it all right.

I finally stopped crying, but she still held me. "It's all right," she said. I pulled away from her and looked into her face. She really is very beautiful. Her hair is so dark and lustrous, and there is not a grey hair in it, although she is forty-one. "It's all right," she said again, and I looked into her eyes, and for the first time I saw something wrong in them, something evasive.

"It's all right," she said for the third time. "I have been hoping that you would come to me." I did not speak. All of a sudden, I felt deadly cold. "I have been hoping and trusting that you would begin to see what a mistake you are making."

She pulled back from me a little more. "We women have to be so careful," she said. "That's what you don't know. I learned that, younger than you. Men control everything, and they think they're gods." She shook her head, as if exasperated, and started again. "You have to make a good marriage. Mother drummed that into my head every day from when I began to...you know. I was very remiss in not drumming it into yours. But you were always such an odd child, with your books and your curious ways. And those awful spectacles." She shuddered; I actually felt it.

"But nevertheless we can do so much better for you than Willie Lorimer. I know we can. The Campbells have a young son, and they are so promising a family..." She looked off into space, with a curious, tense expression. Finally she looked at me again, and her face was hard, as hard as flint. "You've got a lot of silly ideas, sweetie," she said. "You have to get rid of them, or they'll destroy you." Her fingers gripped my shoulder, so hard it hurt. "You have to learn to do what men want. You have to. I don't care what silly ideas they teach you in that college, or what's in your books. Men know what they want. And you do, too, if you have your wits about you, and...you learn to give them what they want. All they want. Understand? Because if you don't, you're finished. You won't have any money, you won't have any comfort. You'll be a joke." Her mouth twisted a little in a way I had never seen before. "There are ways of humiliating any woman who forgets her place. Believe me, there are."

There was another pause. "Your father and I will help you get rid of him, when he comes back beaming like a fool, with his stupid uniform," she said. "Of course, if he comes back at all."

I went back and sat in the other armchair. She was sitting, staring into space, and occasionally her mouth moved. Once, for just a moment, I thought she started to cry, but then her face abruptly changed, and she smiled serenely. After a few minutes I just got up and walked away.

It was as if she'd forgotten I was even there.

I X

We marched straight down the main street of Humboldt—the only street, for that matter—and just kept going. Ten miles west of the village, we caught up to Middleton's column. They had spent two days at Humboldt, dawdling, waiting for us, and they had made an early camp, and dawdled still—almost as if they did not want to get any closer to Riel without reinforcements.

Still, we got a great reception. The Ninetieth Rifles of Winnipeg, resplendent in coats so dark green they were almost black, gave us three loud "hurrahs!" Boulton's Scouts, irregular cavalry who'd joined Middleton while he rested in Humboldt, waved their hats. One gun of the Winnipeg Field Battery fired a ten-shot salute. It was the first time I'd heard one of the nine-pounder cannons fired. The result was not completely reassuring. In that empty immensity, the report sounded like the pop of a child's corked rifle, and the answering echoes were mean and derisory.

This was also our first chance to see our commander, the English Major General Frederick Middleton. He spent hours walking around and speaking personally to the men of our column. In some ways, he was a figure of comedy: a tired-looking old man with a drooping white moustache, and a pendulous belly. In person, though, he was curiously reassuring to our inexperienced, apprehensive men. His uniform was a simple one of blue, with a fur hat. His voice was low and calm; he looked you in the eye steadily when he spoke to you. His manner was one of painstaking, slow-moving courtesy. He had lived a considerable time in Canada. Indeed, he was married to a much younger French-Canadian girl. He had learned that Canadians wanted to be spoken to as equals, and Middleton was good at it. He courteously asked Roley "what kind of things" he sold in his store, and made a little joke about his not being able to shop for his daughter in a boys' store. He asked me about my studies and told me that his mother had met Wordsworth.

I knew that Middleton had been commandant of Sandhurst. Probably this set of reassuring mannerisms is the first thing taught there to aspiring young officers, but it worked. Our men were visibly calmer and more optimistic after the old man had passed by.

Trotting along at Middleton's heels, wearing a snow-white African explorer's pith helmet, was handsome, dark-moustached young Gilbert John Elliot-Murray-Kynynmound, more properly known as Lord Melgund, military secretary to the Governor General. He looked like someone's dream of an imperial officer. Melgund lacked the old general's common touch, but the presence of an authentic British lord, right there with the rest of us in the middle of nowhere, cheered all us little imperialists up no end. "If we're all killed," Roley said, cheerfully puffing his pipe, "at least you and I'll die with the quality."

The combined number of our column was now over seven hundred men. That night, there was an officers' meeting. Middleton told us that we were going to march forthwith straight west to Clarke's Crossing on the South Saskatchewan, thirty miles southwest of Riel's little capital of Batoche. Roley told the story of my encounter with the Métis scout, and Middleton gravely replied that he was aware that our every move was being watched by the enemy. The loyalty of some of our teamsters was suspect. The enemy's strength was reported to be great. We were short of fodder for the horses, and steamboats were trying to get down the river from the west with ample supplies of the stuff. We would halt "for a prudent period" at Clarke's Crossing.

On the way back to the tent, Roley put his hand on my shoulder. "The old man's worried," he said. "He knows how green we are. He's delaying the battle. But for what? We'll stay just as green as we are until somebody fires a shot at us. After that, only God knows what will happen."

The next day, the column set out for Clarke's Crossing. We were marching through more wooded country, where our strung-out column could be attacked at many points by the Métis cavalry. French's and Boulton's Scouts, lean, tanned prairie farmers on rangy horses, in drab, loose-fitting work clothes and slouch hats, repeating carbines slung beside their saddles, ranged around the column. Yet, three times we saw the dark figures of Métis scouts on distant rises, watching us. Each time the cursing cavalrymen went rushing out to intercept them. Each time, the distant horseman simply wheeled away, and vanished into the misty horizon of early spring. The Scouts would come busily clattering back, horses sweating and exhausted. Their riders avoided our gazes. "Bastards," I heard one of them say to another. "Bastards. Like catching puffs of smoke."

Clarke's Crossing nestles on the bank of the South Saskatchewan. From there, the river flows roughly northward. Thirty miles or so north, and slightly east of us was Batoche, the rebel capital. The river is wide, a thousand feet, and the low, grey water of mid-April still held huge chunks of ice.

We no sooner got to Clarke's Crossing than Middleton announced that we were going to ferry half the force across the wide Saskatchewan. One half of our column would advance up the east bank of the river toward Batoche, while the other half advanced up the west bank. Rumours swept the camp that some of the senior officers, notably Lord Melgund, were horrified by the plan to divide a green, half-trained army.

But Middleton was adamant. The force from Swift Current would soon be joining us. Then we'd have over thirteen hundred men. There was no telling which side of the river the Métis would choose to finally meet us in force. This way, we'd "envelop" them.

Middleton now believed that rebel strength had been greatly over-rated. They might not even fight at all. This belief was strengthened when Lord Melgund and some of his men captured three Sioux scouts on April 18. The Sioux said they'd been coerced into joining the rebellion, and that there were no more than two hundred and fifty fighters to oppose us.

We were to wait until Colonel Otter brought the Queen's Own, and "B" battery, and half the regulars, and Arthur and his Gatlings back to us from the west, via steamboats on the rolling Saskatchewan.

So, the tired, grumbling militia hurled itself into a new task— ferrying half our number across the river. There was only one leaky old scow at the Crossing, and we borrowed another from nearby Saskatoon. We had to rig a wire cable across the Saskatchewan, cut oars, build platforms, and make a pathway down the steep side of the river, past huge chunks of ice, to the water's edge.

As we divided our army, we heard endless rumours about Riel's new provisional government at Batoche: a council governed. Riel claimed to be the prophet of a new religion, a purified form of Catholicism for the half-caste peoples of the North-West. The Métis council had first appealed to the white settlers of Saskatchewan, then to the Indians, but received little offer of help from either. Now they were hunkering down to defend Riel's capital from the invading *Anglais*.

This all sounded like the weirdest kind of madness to us town-bred, English-speaking militiamen. The legendary Riel, the infamous, ingenious bogeyman of the Manitoba rebellion of '70, had decided that he was the prophet of a new religion. It sounded like the most lurid kind of Yankee penny-dreadful about crackpot medicine men stirring up the natives against civilization. As this impression grew, the men began to relax a little. General Middleton and Lord Melgund had told us that we were going to be liberating the innocent, ignorant people of Batoche from the rule of a crazed tyrant. Certainly this could not be a serious rebellion by serious frontiersmen we were facing.

Could it?

On the evening of April 22, Jack and I were sitting in our tent about eight at night, puffing our pipes. The tent flap opened, and Roley came in. He had been at a meeting of senior officers. His face was as dark as a prairie thunder-cloud. He stood looking down at us. "You won't believe this," he said. He picked up a bootbrush which was lying there and hurled it back down on the ground with all his force. We looked back at him. "Otter isn't coming," he said. "He's not bringing his men down river from the west on steamboats to join us before we advance on Batoche. Remember the Queen's Own and all the rest? Try to, because you may never see the buggers again. Otter's not bringing Arthur and his Gatlings back to us. There's been a slaughter of civilians away out west at some place called Frog Lake. The Indians are besieging Battleford. Otter's marching straight north to Battleford to relieve the town. I suppose Arthur and the Gatlings are going along on this sideshow. I think our wonderful God damn commander has known this for days. But guess what? *It hasn't changed his mind about his tactics.* We are *still* going to leave half our force on the other side of the river. A force that's only half as big as Middleton originally expected it to be. The Royal Grenadiers, and the Winnipeg Field Battery, and French's Scouts, and His Lordship Lord Melgund and all the rest of them are going to be on the west bank of the river as we advance on Batoche. Only a thousand feet away, if we should chance to need them. If we should chance to be having our asses shot off. Only it's a thousand feet of freezing water. As we advance on Batoche." He glared at both of us, his face red and perspiring. "Which, by the God damn way, we do tomorrow morning at eight a.m." He turned and stalked out of the tent. Jack went rushing after him to try to calm him down. I sat there, just thinking, for a very long time.

* * *

Our march toward Batoche the next day was different from any earlier march. It started auspiciously enough, with British military idiocy. Each column of our divided force gave the other three cheers across the Saskatchewan. The artillery batteries on either side of the river fired a ten-gun salute with lots of smoke (and further cheering). "Just in case," Jack said darkly, "the French don't otherwise hear us coming."

But after that, things got serious. We were in treed country now, with wooded bluffs overlooking our line of march. Occasionally, we saw an abandoned settler's cabin. There were shallow, densely brushed coulees, surrounding little springs that rushed down to pour their ice-cold spring runoff into the South Saskatchewan. Through these we straggled, our cavalry busily charging, splashing through the cold water. The horses struggled; their gunners cursed. We shivered in our wet uniforms, and we shot shying glances around us at every tree and bluff. We all knew that one or two of the enemy could get close enough for a sharpshooter's shot.

It's been reported that the men were over-confident. That's a lie. I found myself mentally bracing over and over again for a buffalo-rifle bullet to slam into my chest, and I doubt I was the only one.

As if in obedience to the general feeling that something was going to happen, and soon, we halted our march early that day, a few miles south-west of a place the Scouts said was Tourond's Coulee. There was a settler's farm at Tourond's Coulee. This was the home country of the Métis. They would fight for it, as surely as we would fight for ours.

That night, Roley, Jack and I sat around a fire with one of Boulton's Scouts, a leathery man called Sutter, with a faint Scottish accent. He had been out here, he told us, since '66, when he came out with the Bay Company. He was cursing Middleton's English arrogance in refusing to use the Mounted Police. "They wanted to attack Batoche from the north while we came at them from the south," Sutter said. "And Middleton said no. The *Mounted Police!* The best cavalry in the West! Except for the enemy, of course."

I asked him why the Métis hadn't attacked us. "Many say it's because Riel shrinks from violence," Sutter said, "and is restraining Dumont, and that's true, like enough. For what it's worth. Except, you have to know the Métis, as I do. Their whole tradition is defensive fighting. They've won their biggest battles that way. At Seven Oaks in Manitoba, against the Bay Company and the Scots settlers. Or at the Grand Coteau in the fifties, when the Sioux attacked them during the buffalo hunt. At Grand Coteau, the 'breeds built elaborate rifle pits around the camp where the women and children were. They slaughtered the Sioux with their buffalo guns. It may be wise or it may be unwise, but I'll bet you they are digging elaborate rifle pits for us, right this minute. Besides, whatever nonsense Riel is feeding them right now, they are devout Christians. They believe it is against God's law to fight unless you are defending your home ground, or yourself, or your women and kids. Anything else is murder. If they attacked Prince Albert, or Saskatoon, or Qu'Appelle, it would mean killing women and children. They could never do that. I knew Dumont. He could never do that. Killing women and children would be dishonourable, unmanly, un-Christian. It would be every damn bad thing to them. They'd think God would punish any people that did things like that."

After a few minutes, Sutter got up and left us. Jack walked moodily away into the darkness. Roley puffed on his pipe and stared darkly into the fire. "Are you happy, Willie?" he finally said. I did not answer. "I am," he said. "I guess this is what I wanted. An adventure. When you start wondering what it will be like when a bullet hits you, Willie, I'm pretty sure you're having an adventure." Then he was silent for a couple of minutes. "Killing the innocent," he finally said. "Well, Jesus Christ. I'll just be happy if I get through with my soul and body in one piece, so I can take them back to Vera and Donald. And of course, I want the same thing for my friends." He put one arm around my shoulder and gave me a brief, hard hug. "Of whom you are definitely one," he said, and then he got up and walked into our tent.

Alice

Damn my weakness. Another bad word Father doesn't know I know. Damn my weakness. Damn it, damn it, damn it.

It's past three in the morning. You can't wander anywhere in this over-furnished monstrosity of a house without hearing the clocks chime. I have been prowling for hours.

I can't sleep. I can barely breathe. The newspapers say the column is nearing Batoche. There is some coulee with a French name, and they should have reached it by now. And "resistance is expected soon," so say the correspondents.

Men trying to kill my boy. Big men, with beards, who sleep with guns next to them, men who could break Willie's back over their knee.

God, women are such ninnies.

No, they are not. Men make us this way, society does. I dare to think that, although I could never say it out loud. Not even to Willie, who is quite a comic little Tory, in his way. But, me. Tonight. First, I was sitting up in my bed, thinking of Willie (where is he sleeping, and is he eating right, and is he safe, and is the enemy drawing near?), and then I was crying, and saying out loud, "They will kill him," and then I was kneeling, crying, on the floor, and then finally, in my desperation, I was trying to crawl under the bed like a little girl, crying and crying, lashing out with my fists, and saying over and over, "They will kill him. They will kill him."

Here is the sofa on which he proposed to me. A good excuse to start wailing again, but I won't. It would wake the servants. Father would come down the stairs in his night gown, and command me to stop acting like a child, and to go to bed.

And then I'd brain him with something.

Well, I'm quite the little warrior. In my dreams. But your day is done, Father. In my life, that is. You can take your "radical" philosophy—which always involves your getting richer and richer, not more and more equal to, say, the butler—and you can stick it...

Another awful phrase, which Willie taught me. On this very sofa. I laughed so hard I nearly disgraced myself.

It is time to go to bed. But, over there. The various carafes of fancy wine Father serves his more sophisticated male guests. Women are not permitted to have any. Well, I am going to try a glass. They say it helps you sleep. I hope I don't fall in a drunken stupor down the stairs. The first casualty of the war.

It doesn't work. Wandering the house, pretending I'm formidable, tossing down a glass of wine like a woman of ill repute. It doesn't make the fear go away.

Please let him come back safe. Please, please, please.

X

I was too excited to sleep. Eventually, I wandered to the edge of the camp to watch the sun come up. At first, the darkness reigned absolutely. Shoals of stars shone coldly down on me. There were no sounds, except for the whickering of the horses and the trudging footsteps of the sentries. Then, so slowly that at first I thought I was imagining it, dim, pale light began to brighten the eastern horizon. For the longest time, it seemed that the world held its breath. Then the silvering of the east became unmistakable. Just as it did, from here and there beyond our camp came the jaunty, artless, repetitive song of early meadowlarks. The light in the east was white, not silver, now. Gaping up, I saw that the stars were vanishing. Only the morning star shone on, dimmed but still visible.

Now, pink clouds were visible on the eastern horizon, brightest at the point where the emerging sun began to show. Shot through with darker gleams, they stretched farther and farther toward the edges of the eastern horizon, and farther and farther above it. The morning star was gone. Even overhead, the sky was lightening, and around me the camp began to come to life. The trumpeter, ten minutes late at least, blared his off-key sunrise call. The early-morning grunts and mutterings of the soldiers rose, mingled with a louder whinnying and clattering from the tethered horses. There were soothing tones from the gunners coming to them with their early morning fodder. Men cursed, pans rattled, and the eternal hoarse shouting of the sergeants began again. I stayed on the edge of the camp for a while longer, though, and I found that if I tried hard enough, I could make the multi-noted calls of the meadowlarks almost drown out the clattering of the camp.

I strolled back to our tent. Roley and Jack were awake, and carefully shaving. I followed their example. I had the sense that today it was important that formalities be followed. We made a fire and cooked some eggs that Jack had stolen from a chicken coop at Clarke's Crossing just before we left. We had hunks of unbuttered bread with it, and coffee, and this homely meal made me think of home, and how far I was from it.

After breakfast, for once, Roley did not light his pipe. He and Jack and I strolled across the meadow to where Company Four was sprawled around its dying campfires, smoking, chewing tobacco, and grumbling. Colour Sergeant Quinn saw us coming and shouted, "Attention! Company Four!" The men got up, quicker, I thought, than they ever had before, and formed a slightly ragged line, shouldering the Snider-Enfields and coming to attention.

Roley walked ahead of Jack and me, smiling at each man and pausing to say something to each group of two or three. Each time he did that, the men laughed, and Roley laughed with them. A wave of trust and affection washed from them over Roley, a wave of *belief* that I could feel. When you are marching into danger, you have to believe in your commander. Jack and I said nothing and we remained serious.

I saw the way men looked at Roley—and at Jack and me—and I realized that Roley had been right about them. They were civilians in uniform and, on a normal day, they would have refused to accept any discipline they didn't want. But today, when they looked at us, I could see that they wanted reassurance. More than that, they wanted us to tell them what to do. Something was in the air. At nightfall that day, none of us would be the same ever again, and all of us knew it.

As I walked past Nolan, erect as a banty rooster in the line, he winked at me. I grinned at him. Whatever lay in store for us today, it was no Saskatoon bush.

Roley walked back to a position in front of the middle of the line. The men stood, expectant, waiting for him. These were down-to-earth fellows. They were not rough men, not even outdoor men, but higher education and flowery sentiments meant nothing to them. Under any ordinary circumstances, they would have reacted very impatiently to anybody making a speech or trying to say some high-flown thing. Men who acted like that were damn fools.

But this day was different. This was special. They *wanted* Roley to say something.

And he did. Perhaps he had composed it beforehand, written it on a scrap of paper, and laboriously practiced saying it aloud. I think so. He looked at the men for a moment. "We are going into battle for Canada in a little while," he said, in a quiet voice. "Nobody's ever done that before."

He pulled at the gold watch chain which ran across the front of his red tunic and consulted his pocket watch. "Six-forty-five, Colour Sergeant," he said to Quinn. "The column will be forming. March the men to their place, behind Battery 'A.' And unfurl our Union Jack *and* the red Ensign. I want them flying today."

The column formed up fast, and with all our flags fluttering we stepped out toward Tourond's Coulee. Boulton's Scouts rode hard past us on either side of the column, dust flying, and took the lead. Behind them came Middleton and his staff officers, mounted on beautiful horses. The old man looked tired. Sergeant Quinn had told me that the general had made the rounds of the sentries the night before, encouraging them quietly, making sure they knew their jobs, sharing his cigarettes with them.

Behind the mounted staff officers marched the main column. First came the forty infantry regulars, their red tunics shining, the white cross-belts over their left shoulder pipeclayed to a gleam. The dark coats of the Winnipeg Ninetieth Rifles came after, then "A" battery, then our own Company Four. Our men's scarlet tunics were faded now, and the men lean and sun-tanned.

I was almost strolling along, right beside Roley and Jack, staring at the wreckage of what I later was told was an English-speaking settler's house. Its windows were smashed in, its doors off their hinges. The sun was getting hotter and I was already starting to sweat. I could still hear the meadowlarks. The air was sweet and incredibly pure. Suddenly, two rifle shots, spaced about ten seconds apart, came from in front of us and to the left. The column ahead of us halted, and Roley put up his hand to stop our part of it. "It's those idiots across the river," Jack said. "Lord Melgund saluting us or some damn fool thing."

"No, it's too close," Roley said. Then a fusillade of shots, shockingly loud, rang out, from the same place. "Shit," Roley said. "Colour Sergeant Quinn, the men stand fast! Come on." He, Jack and I ran to the front of the column, past the restless, apprehensive artillery horses, and the scared-looking Winnipeg militia, standing in place. The Winnipeg officers were also heading at a run toward Middleton. I bumped against Lieutenant Hugh John Macdonald as we tore along. He grinned at me. If there was to be a fight, the Prime Minister's son would be there to see it.

When we reached the staff officers, Middleton smiled at us and said, "Let us be calm, gentlemen." He produced a pipe from his capacious tunic and calmly, puffingly, lit it. Then he produced a little tin, opened it, put the match inside, and put the tin back. He smiled again. We waited. No one said a word. The horses whickered. The birds sang.

From ahead of us came a deafening volley of fire, followed by a second. It sounded like Waterloo crossed with Gettysburg. Three minutes later, from ahead of us, came Major Boulton himself, racing toward us on his lathered horse. He pulled it up and gave Middleton a sporty, civilian's salute. His green, flannel shirt was soaked through with sweat. "Sir," he said, gasping for breath, "I beg to report we have contacted the enemy."

"I suspected that," said Middleton, smiling again. "Report, please."

Boulton was still wheezing. "Yes, sir," he said. "A bunch of 'em, mounted, were waiting for us in a grove of trees up there to the left. One of our fellows spotted them, because there are no leaves on the poplars. They chased him, trying to bring him down without shooting. Trying not to alert us. But he got away. Then they all opened fire and rode like hell toward Fish Creek. That's in Tourond's Coulee, just ahead. Two of our boys were hit." He stopped, and looked out over the meadow, toward the east. "There must have been about twenty of them. They rode down into the coulee. When we tried to follow, a large body of the enemy, concealed in the coulee, opened fire on us. Two volleys. Our men are dismounted and are returning their fire."

"Describe the coulee and the enemy's disposition," Middleton said.

"Yes, sir," Boulton said. "Tourond's Coulee is about fifteen hundred feet from the South Saskatchewan. At the bottom of the coulee is Fish Creek, which drains into the river. The main trail to Batoche runs right through the coulee. Our line of march lay straight through the coulee, across Fish Creek."

"It was an ambush," Middleton said.

"Yes, General, it was," Boulton said, mopping his sweaty face with his bandana. "And a God damn good one, too. The sons of bitches have dug themselves rifle pits on both the north and south sides of the creek, under the edge of the coulee. There's thick willow brush in there. They're completely invisible until they fire. They were going to wait until we were descending the coulee and fording the stream, and then massacre us from ambush. Those twenty men we encountered first would have closed the trap behind us. Anybody who tried to retreat back the way we came would have been shot down. We'd never have gotten out of there. It's a buffalo pound, General, a slaughter ground, but for the army, not animals. Thank God it's early spring. Thank God there's no leaves on the poplars. I recognized Dumont; he was leading the twenty."

"The number of the enemy?" Middleton asked.

"I don't know," Boulton said. "Couple of hundred, maybe. One of my boys told me he thought it was 'breeds on our right, Sioux and Cree on our left. I think the main firing was coming from our right. That's where my men are, on the right, firing down into the coulee."

"Are the enemy retreating now?" Middleton said.

Boulton stared at him. The sound of rifle fire from ahead of us was continuous. "No, sir," he finally said. "They most certainly are not."

Middleton sat his horse silently for a minute. "Very well, then," he said. He took off his fur cap and looked around at us. "These are my orders. The column will advance to the edge of the coulee but not beyond it. The infantry regulars will advance on our left. The Winnipeg Rifles will occupy our left-centre and right-centre. Company Four of the Light Infantry"—he looked at Roley—"will occupy the extreme right of our position, to the right of Major Boulton's men. Battery 'A' will be deployed once we get a clearer idea of the enemy's disposition. Eventually, our column across the river will come to our aid. But they are two miles away, with a thousand feet of river between us, and one scow to ferry them across. Effectively, we are on our own. Now, order to advance."

The whole column quick marched northward, toward the coulee. We were off the trail now, and the artillery battery and the ammunition carts jounced and lurched wildly across the prairie. The sound of firing grew louder, and I could now hear war-whoops and yells coming from in front of us. Our company halted for a minute while some of us helped pull out a cart which had gotten bogged in mud. While we halted, the infantry regulars and the Winnipeg militia had apparently reached the coulee. The noise of firing increased, and now I could hear the heavy boomings of the Sniders over the sharper reports of the Scouts' repeating American carbines, and the rebel gunfire.

As we neared the coulee, we passed a clump of leafless poplars on our right. There were frightened-looking, sweaty horses tethered there, and other cavalrymen were leading more horses back from the direction of the coulee. Four or five men were kneeling beside four wounded Boulton's Scouts, who lay sprawled on the muddy, sparsely-grassed ground. One of them lay motionless, and the ground around him was red with blood. One of the wounded men raised his head, and shouted something to us as we clattered by.

"The enemy's disposition appears to be downright grouchy," Jack said, and Roley laughed.

I could see to our far left the red coats of the infantry regulars as they efficiently deployed along the ragged, muddy bank of the coulee. Ahead of us, the dark-coated Winnipeg militia milled in a disorganized mass. Their officers and sergeants were yelling ferociously, as they tried to impose order and arrange their men along the lip of the coulee. Roley shouted an order for our company to halt. He told Jack to stay with the men, and then banged my arm, and said, "Come on. I want to see what the hell's going on."

We raced forward, to the right of the Winnipeg men. The air was already thick with clouds of acrid, choking, grey gunsmoke. On our right, a few score of Boulton's men lay prone, a few feet back from the edge of the gully. Some of them were crawling to the coulee's edge, firing quickly, and then crawling back a few steps. The one closest to us was a giant of a man in a red flannel shirt and broad-brimmed white hat. He had blood on his bearded face. He shook his fist at Roley and me, and shouted, "Keep low, you bastards! Don't give 'em a target! Or you'll end up like those!"

He was pointing to three troopers of the Winnipeg Rifles. Two of them were crawling, moaning, away from the lip of the coulee. One of them was holding his hand under his belly, grunting in agony. I could see blood on his hand, and more blood spattering into the dried-up yellow grass. Several Winnipeg men, cursing and shouting words of encouragement, were kneeling, getting hold of these men, and dragging them away toward the rear. In front of them, perhaps three feet from the edge, lay another Winnipegger. Roley crawled past him. We were both on our hands and knees. My red tunic was already getting sticky with mud.

I stopped and looked at the sprawled militiaman. A bright smear of deepest scarlet lay over the breast of his dark tunic. His head was toward me, his long blond hair fluttering in the breeze. His cap had fallen off. I could see the pink of his scalp, where his hair had been thinning at the crown. His bright blue eyes were open, staring vacantly at the grey sky. His right leg was bent under him at an impossible angle. He had clearly died the second the bullet hit him and dropped headlong. The broken leg was a nasty injury, but he was never going to care.

I was fascinated. I pulled myself around to look down into his face, and that absent blue gaze bored into me. Was there a hint of accusation? *Why should you have breath, and I have none?* "I'm sorry," I muttered, absurdly.

Roley was at the lip of the coulee, flat on his stomach. He beckoned impatiently to me without turning around. I felt a surge of anger. For Christ's sake, hadn't he seen the dead man? Hadn't he heard the Scout, warning us? Roley beckoned again, and I dragged myself forward on my stomach until I was beside him. "Look down there," he said.

I made myself take a quick glance into the coulee. Then, since I hadn't died, I decided to take another. The ravine was not deep. Its sides and floor were choked with thick brush. The banks closest to the top were steep; then it flattened a little. Narrow, grey Fish Creek meandered along its bottom. The creek, just to our left, wandered out southward, in the direction of our advancing force, then back to the north again and then again proceeded roughly westward toward the Saskatchewan. The trail to Batoche was barely visible to my left. Now I realized that from where I was, I couldn't see the infantry regulars on the left, or even the Winnipeg Rifles, who were dropping into place just to the regulars' right. On the other side of Tourond's Coulee, perhaps eight hundred yards away, lay a neat little farm with a white house, outbuildings, a big barn, and a fenced corral in front of it.

There were dozens, maybe hundreds, of enemy riflemen concealed in that ravine. And I had not seen the slightest sign of them.

As if in acknowledgement of this, Roley put his head over the edge of the gully again, and I did the same. Immediately, a huge plume of greyish smoke billowed out from the bank immediately below us, maybe thirty feet away. At the same moment I heard the crash of a rifle shot, and mud splattered into Roley's face and mine, as the bullet struck between us, not an inch from my head. The man who had shot at us yelled something in French. Something in his angry tone reminded me of the Scout who'd warned us to stay low.

"Shit!" Roley yelled, pulling back from the lip of the ravine and dragging me with him. "Christ! All right! We'll get away from your God damn coulee!" We rose to our hands and knees and backed away as fast as we could. My boot hit the dead Winnipegger in the shoulder. "So they sometimes miss," Roley said. "Damn good thing."

"He missed because he was shooting almost straight upward," I said. Roley didn't hear me. He had gotten up and was running back to our waiting company. I wondered if my legs would work. I doubted that they would, but experimentally, I tried to get up. Amazingly, I did. I started running, and pretty easily too, although with a slightly dreamlike, running-on-air sensation. My stomach felt a little sick, but not much. The rest of me felt loose, exhilarated. *I'll be God damned,* I thought. *I've been shot at.*

I ran back to the waiting company. They were gathered around Roley in an anxious semi-circle, more like a crowd listening to a lecture than an infantry company. Roley was gesturing. "...fall in there, in a line, to the right of the Scouts," he was saying. "Six feet from the coulee's edge. *Do not go peering into the God damn ravine!*" He gestured at me. "The brave Lieutenant Lorimer did that, and that dirt on his face is from where the bullet hit half an inch from his over-educated head." Some of the men grinned at me. I was getting an entirely undeserved reputation as a fire-eater.

Jack started herding the men into line safely this side of the coulee's rim. They were to the right of the Scouts, who had suffered more wounded, and were now hanging back from the gully's edge. Roley and I walked toward our men. "No God damn way are we going to start firing over the rim of the coulee," he said, quietly. "The enemy are completely invisible in there. They'll shoot us, one by one. It'll just be a slower version of the ambush they planned for us."

Three of the newspaper correspondents were walking toward the coulee. "Get away from there!" Roley roared. "If you want to live to write your stories, don't stick your heads out over that coulee!" They scuttled back.

The gunners prepared to fire one of their cannons. One of the officers was shouting. The cannon went off with a satisfying roar, and the shell exploded close to the top of the coulee. The gunners depressed the barrel and fired again. This time, I could actually see the shrapnel and debris flying into the ravine.

But the gun could not be depressed any further. It would have been convenient if it could have been fired to the side, so that the shells would burst down in the ravine, amongst the enemy, some distance to the west. But that was impossible, because the coulee endlessly curved and twisted.

And so, with a new volley of frantic commands, the gunners began bombarding the white house and barn across the coulee, perhaps half a mile away. Boards hurtled through the smoke of the shellbursts. Geysers of mud, shit and chicken feathers rose into the air. It was all utterly futile. Beside me, Roley put his head in his hands.

But it wasn't all in vain. To our right, horsemen suddenly came charging up the other side of the coulee and started tearing away from us across the meadow. The horses must have been tethered in the bush. The rider in the rear had a bright blue bandana tied around his head. Company Four started firing at them, and I saw four horses topple over. Three of the riders got back on their comrades' horses. The one with the blue bandana never got up.

We ran forward to our waiting men, some of whom were still kneeling and firing formally at the disappearing horsemen. "Spooked by the cannons!" Roley yelled. Some of the men nodded. "But that's only some of them," Roley shouted. "Be careful."

Roley and Jack started walking toward the west, past Boulton's Scouts, all of whom were now hanging back from the lip of the ravine. I followed. To our left, the officers of the Winnipeg militia were herding their men toward the coulee's edge. I watched, through Jack's field glasses. They were exactly where Roley and I had been before. They were actually going to fire by volley. The officers lined about eighty men up at the edge of the ravine, and on command, the men aimed their Sniders down toward the enemy. The Métis had stopped firing, and the battleground was more silent than it had been since I'd first come rushing up. I could hear the Winnipeg officers shouting. The soldiers had to lean over the lip of the gully to fire. There was a thunderous crash of rifle shots, and plumes of grey smoke billowed out over the coulee's edge.

The Winnipeggers fired three volleys—God knows what they were aiming at—and were leaning over the edge to deliver a fourth. Suddenly a horde of invisible insects seemed to come boiling out of the ravine and begin eating at them. I saw three or four men flung backwards, their rifles flying away from them. One soldier simply toppled like a sack of grain over the edge and out of sight. The officers were yelling louder than ever, and those who had swords had taken them out and were waving them.

On command, the troopers leaned over the coulee's edge again. Again, the invisible insects came tearing at them. Several more fell over. Another fell limply into the coulee. Most of the men were only wounded, and were dragging themselves away from that awful swarm. One of them had been hit in the artery of his left arm. Through the field glasses, I saw the bright blood splashing over his spiffy dark green tunic, and then he was obscured by a crowd of his friends, as they tore off the tunic and frantically tried to staunch the bleeding. The Winnipeg officers were still yelling, still waving their swords, but the men were falling back from the top of the coulee. "I should God damn well hope so," Roley said, from behind me. We started walking back toward our men.

The intermittent roaring of the cannons had stopped. The farm across the coulee was now in flames. Huge clouds of white smoke shot up into the grey, now-overcast sky.

A staff officer came riding up to us. He was almost a boy, but imperious-looking and red-faced in his peaked officer's cap. "Captain Collison!" he said. "Colonel Portman wants to know why your men are not engaging the enemy."

Roley looked disgustedly at him. "Lieutenant," he said, "I think that's obvious. I don't want my boys slaughtered firing down at an enemy they can't see. Look what just happened to the Winnipeg

Rifles. I haven't seen Colonel Portman up here all morning. Let him come up and stick his fat face over the edge, and maybe he'll see the light."

The lieutenant looked scandalized. "You can't want me to say that to him."

Roley's face was hard with anger. "Yes, I do, though," he said. "Word for word." Looking a bit stunned, the lieutenant spurred his horse away.

Minutes later, Major Buchan of the Winnipeg Rifles rode forward from the staff officers huddled behind us. He spurred his horse toward us and jumped off. "Roley," Buchan said, "what the hell did you say to Portman? He's on the verge of soiling his pants."

Roley grinned. "Declined to get my men massacred, Larry."

"Well," Buchan said, "you were right, of course. And Middleton made it worse by saying as much to Portman. Sticking our heads out over the ravine doesn't make sense. Neither does what the regulars just did, making a little unsupported bayonet charge into the coulee. They got chased right back out." Buchan paused, and lit a cigarette. He was a big man, with a balding head, with what hair he had brushed forward, and magnificent Burnside whiskers. His little eyes and jutting chin gave him a supercilious look. But he was a good officer. "Things got away from the staff, a bit. But now, Middleton's coming down here," he said. "And he's given orders for a general advance against the enemy positions, here on the right and on the left-centre. Most of the Winnipeg Rifles, some regulars, and fifty of your boys. Supported by the artillery. They're going to wheel one of the cannons to the coulee's edge and fire down."

"Jesus," I said. "Can they do that?"

"Possibly," Buchan said, a bit doubtfully. "We'll soon find out. Anyway, here's some things we *can't* do. We can't get in the ravine on either side of them and advance from there. In various places, the coulee's choked almost from side to side with mud and brush. The creek is running through heaped-up mud. Our boys would be hung up and slaughtered at leisure. We can't send men across the ravine and surround them. No matter how far to the left or right, when we show ourselves, we attract the proverbial God damn hail of lead from down there. And they may have more men the other side of that burning farm, and if our chaps go over there, the 'breeds will come swooping down on them on horseback. Get fifty of your best men over to the Rifles' position. Now." He mounted his horse and rode back up the hill toward Middleton, who was advancing with the staff officers.

"I'll take one more officer and fifty men," Roley said. "And leave one officer and Quinn with the rest at the coulee's edge." I tried hard to look like someone who could be left with the rest at the coulee's edge. The truth was that I did not want to charge into that murderous ravine. I kept thinking about the wounded Scout lying in the grass, about the dead militiaman with the waving blond hair, about the arterial blood boiling out of the Winnipegger's arm. I never felt more like a poetry student and less like a soldier.

"Come on, Willie," Roley said. "You'll go with me, won't you?"

"Yes," I said.

The worst part of it was how disappointed Jack looked. He wanted to go with his idol.

Middleton was walking along the crest of the coulee now, with an aide-de-camp on either side of him. This was British gallantry as I'd read about it, suicidally insane. They were all trying to keep low, although the old man was too fat to do it effectively. The men gave a ragged cheer. A rattle of gunfire came from out of the ravine, and one of the aides toppled, his right hand clutching his left arm. Some of our men dragged him away from the edge. Middleton turned and said something to the wounded man, and then he and the other officer carried on calmly. The general pointed something out to the other aide-de-camp. There was another rattle of gunshots from below us. Middleton flinched, and I shuddered, thinking he'd been hit. Then he pulled off his tall fur cap, and exuberantly waved it, with one finger poking through the hole a rebel bullet had just made. The men cheered again more lustily.

Over a hundred of the Winnipeg militia were bunched together on the right-centre of the line. Roley selected his men, and then he and I marched them over to join the Winnipeg Rifles. To our left were another hundred or so of the Winnipeggers. Our rush was going to be led by Buchan, the group to the left by Boswell, another Winnipeg major. Middleton and his remaining aide were walking around, speaking calmly to the men, helping the sweating, shouting Winnipeg officers get their men into position. The Manitoba men were wet with perspiration, and many of them had dark red smears on their green tunics from helping the wounded. Mostly, they just looked furious. They'd been shot to pieces all morning. Now they wanted to pay back the debt.

I got out the locket and looked at Alice's picture. Then I said a prayer that I would get back to her.

Buchan banged me and Roley on the arm. "Come on," he said. "Enough diversions. Captain, Lieutenants, our group is going to try to establish a foothold, then fan out to the right and drive them up and out of the coulee. Boswell's men will fan out to the left." He walked closer to the coulee and waved his sword. Then he glanced over at Major Boswell to make sure the two of them were acting in concert and roared "Charge!"

The men cheered, and we went rushing straight for the gully's edge. Waving his revolver, Roley tore over the side with me right behind him, our troopers crashing behind us. Instantly, the gully erupted with puffs of grey-white smoke, as the Métis fired in unison. Some of the gunshots were coming at point-blank range from directly in front of us. There were even a couple of men standing in the creek, firing carefully. To my left, four or five dark-coated Winnipeg men went down, and two of our men toppled past me down the slope and thudded against the bushes just below us.

I should have been terrified, but I wasn't. I felt that I was slightly outside my body, watching it, willing it to act. Yelling like a wild man, I looked down at one of our wounded as I rushed past him. He was a private named Potter. The right side of his red tunic was wet with blood. He looked up at me, smiled and winked, and gave me the thumbs-up. But he did not try to get up.

In front of me, Roley had stopped, and was emptying his revolver with great deliberation at two Métis in dark coats who were pulling themselves out of their rifle pits and running toward the creek. They were too far away, and he missed with each shot.

The volume of firing from the Métis across the creek was not letting up. A cannon shell burst directly at the top of the bank on that side, showering them with mud, water, and shrapnel. Our men were no longer rushing forward but were taking cover behind bushes, banks of earth, or in the abandoned rifle pits themselves. There was no more volley firing. They were blazing away thunderously at every bush where a puff of smoke showed an enemy.

There was some kind of ramshackle log shack in the ravine beside the Batoche trail, I now saw. The rebels were firing from behind it. The clever devils had been ready for us again. They had made a series of wooden barricades by piling fallen trees and brushwood between boulders. Now that we had burst into the gully, they were abandoning the nearer rifle pits. They were taking refuge behind these wooden walls, which faced any enemy trying to get at them from above.

I felt a *zing!* of something, rifle bullet or pellet, go by my cheek. My rush of adrenaline was replaced by the realization that only a flimsy red tunic lay between me and the flying lead. The air was choked with gunsmoke. I looked around and saw one of the abandoned rifle pits. I dived into it. One more second, and I was knocked flat on my face into the mud by a body landing on me. Choking, I pushed myself upward, and found myself looking at one of our troopers, Lance Corporal Stuart.

He grinned. "Better you than me on the bottom—sir," he said. Stuart turned, and fired his Snider at one of the wooden barricades not fifty feet away. I rubbed the muck off my face, edged round beside him, and stared out. The rebels behind the barricade were incredibly good soldiers. I saw nothing at first; then there was a grey-white blur as one of them momentarily popped his head above the wooden wall. A split-second later, there was the crash of his weapon. I heard the weird *beeyow!* of a ricochet. His bullet had struck a small rock not two inches from my head, and the rock splinters showered over Stuart and me. I realized that the Métis had taken off his hat, because he wanted to show as little of himself as he could. It was a good idea. I stuffed my wedge cap under my epaulet and motioned to Stuart to do the same.

Then I waited, trying to arrange myself so that only one eye peeped out. It was still too much; somebody else fired at me, and a shower of mud burst into my face again. Patiently, with water from my canteen, and my handkerchief, I rubbed it all off. There was no military point in this. I was simply sick of getting filth all over myself. It occurred to me that if I were killed, I wanted to look like a soldier, not a chimney sweep.

I decided to emulate the rebels. I hadn't fired a shot yet, and I wanted to. I darted my head up, looked, and brought it down. Nothing. I did it again. Nothing. I did it again, and there was a dark rebel face, and a shotgun coming up. I brought my revolver up and fired, faster than I would have thought possible. I missed, but I amazed myself. Brown splinters flew up not two inches from his head, and I had the satisfaction of seeing him duck. The next second, Stuart dragged me down. "Good work!" he yelled into my ear. "But don't stand around admiring it!"

He fired his Snider again. Another drawback of the antiquated, God damn things was that they were so long and heavy. You had to elaborately raise, level and steady them, exposing yourself every time you did it. The rebels, with their light, short Winchesters and shotguns, had no such problem.

I looked around behind me. Our men had taken shelter everywhere, lying prone, crammed behind miserable bushes that wouldn't deflect a rubber arrow, jammed in behind rocks that wouldn't make a doorstop. They were directing a heavy, steady fire at our almost-invisible enemies. Another shell went off with a thunderous roar, even farther down the far coulee wall. I ducked, because the shrapnel was zinging all around me. *They've lowered the God damn barrel as much as they can,* I thought. But the rifle pits were lower still.

I crawled back to the edge of the rifle pit facing the rebels' barricade. A cloud of shotgun pellets hit the dirt above my head, showering me with filth once more. I waited for about ten seconds, then popped up again like a wild turkey. The same dark face was visible, and the barrel of his gun. I snapped off two fast shots at him, and the splinters flew atop the barricade again. Fear had turned me into a marksman of sorts.

I immediately ducked down, and found to my horror Stuart rising beside me for a look. The rebel's shotgun went off. Stuart gave a scream and toppled over into the rifle pit beside me. I bent down over him. He was moaning, and holding his handkerchief to his temple, where some of the pellets had grazed him. "You'll have a romantic scar," I said. I tried to sound reassuring, the way I thought Roley would. "Nothing more. The girls will love you."

"Then I really am in shit," he said, smiling. "I'm married."

"Got to get you back up the bank," I said. I looked around again, at our position, and that of Boswell's men. Dark green and scarlet-coated bodies lay everywhere. At least thirty men had been hit, and militiamen were carrying the dead and wounded up the bank. Our men were keeping the Métis heads down by a remarkable volume of fire. Smoke billowed from the Sniders; the noise was like thunder. But I got the impression that the enemy wasn't firing at the wounded or their bearers. Suddenly Buchan and Roley appeared out of the smoke, farther down the bank. Roley saw me, and gestured toward the top of the coulee. Buchan roared, "Retreat! Retreat!" Off to the left, Boswell was leading his men up the bank, too.

Our whole force began scrambling up the hill, slithering in the wet grass and mud. The enemy fired a volley at us, and several men toppled back down the slope. I had my arm around Stuart's shoulder, but he was moving very fast on his own, still holding that handkerchief to his head, kicking at the leaves of the bushes that flapped around our knees and impeded our way.

I heaved myself and Stuart over the bank, and fell on my face, shaking and gasping for breath. Several other men stumbled over me. One of them kicked at me, so I rolled out of the way. I fumbled on my hands and knees until I was ten feet from the lip of the ravine. All around me lay wounded men and a larger number of unharmed refugees from the relentless rebel fire, pale, sweaty and looking as shocked as I felt. Several gunners were sprawled on the wet grass. They were either gravely wounded, or dead. They'd been sitting ducks for the sharpshooters, when they'd pushed their cannon to the edge of the ravine. Middleton himself was standing a few feet from me, supporting his other aide-de-camp. The aide had been shot in the foot, and was cursing violently. He was limping along on his general's shoulder, with one dripping boot hanging off the ground.

Roley and Buchan came over to me. "Christ, lad," Buchan said. "Are you hit? You're covered in bloody offal."

"Good," I said. "I *feel* bloody awful."

"Jesus," Roley said. "First Jack and now you. I didn't know being shot at turned people into comedians."

"Proves the boy's a Scot," Buchan said. "Foreigners don't like being shot at. The English, Irish and Welsh don't mind. But only the Scots actually enjoy it." He smiled slightly as he recited this mess-hall joke, but his face showed no amusement at all. He was staring at the mass of moaning, wounded men who were gradually being carried away to the ambulance area in the rear. "Anyway, this is the end of it. I am going to tell Middleton that the rebels can't be dislodged from that damnable ravine. Can't and shouldn't be. What are they going to do, stay down there till they starve? Their ambush failed; that's the long and short of it." He stopped and looked at us. "And we've learned something from this engagement. What might that be, do you suppose?"

"That they're damned tough," Roley said.

"No, we knew that," Buchan said. "We've had a lot of men hit, but relatively few killed. What we have are many really awful, jagged wounds. That means they're low on ammunition. They're using shotguns. Or, they're using muzzleloaders, jamming them full of rusty nails, pieces of chain, anything they can find. They've got lots of powder, but they're low even on old-fashioned ball ammunition. And repeater ammunition. And they're conserving what they've got for the defence of Batoche."

Buchan went off to talk to Middleton. Roley went back to the ambulance area to see after our men. I returned with the unwounded ones to Company Four's original position on the extreme right of the line. During the engagement, Jack Price had done something which should have earned him a medal but was never going to. He had roamed down the lip of the coulee to the east, farther than most of the rebel positions, farther than Boulton's Scouts had explored, and he'd discovered something. Tethered in plain view on the other side of the coulee were dozens of the rebels' horses. Jack had taken Quinn and thirty men, and they'd fired three very fast volleys at the wretched animals, killing them all. They'd suffered from the surprised enemy skirmishers, in return, only two minor wounds. They were beautiful horses—I saw the corpses later—and among the most cherished possessions of the Métis. And more: their loss gravely impaired the mobility of these incomparable light cavalrymen.

I sat in the soaking grass. The seat of my pants had gotten wet, but I did not want to get up. I looked down at my hands. They were shaking, uncontrollably. I wasn't sure that I *could* get up. "Jesus, Jesus Christ," I kept whispering to myself.

What I wanted was to go home. "I want to go home," I said, out loud. I tried to light my pipe. My hands were shaking so badly that I could not. Jack abruptly sat down beside me, took the pipe out of my hand, put it in my mouth, and held the match while I sucked in smoke. "Thanks," I said.

"My pleasure," he said.

Somebody down in the coulee started yelling, monotonously, in a high, clear voice. "*Maudits cochons,*" he shouted, over and over. "*Maudits cochons, bandes de cochons!*"

"What's that mean?" Jack said.

"Pigs," I said. "Damn pigs, bunch of pigs."

Jack's face turned red. "Well, *God damn you,*" he shouted. The veins in his thin neck stood out. "*Pigs* right back at you, you bastard!"

One of Boulton's Scouts looked over wearily at him. He was a youngish man of thirty-five or so, with a lined face and a heavy black moustache. "Lieutenant," he said, "please."

Roley slapped me on the arm. He had come up silently, from behind us. "What are you fellows shouting about?" he said. "Anyway, nine. Nine Fourth Company men back at the medical tents. Six bad wounds: Fraser, Dixon, Potter, Shavers, MacKenzie, and Sanderson, but the doctor says they're all going to make it. Stuart, Jones and Pemberton have flesh wounds. No amputations. And no dead in our company. That's just about a miracle. Thank God."

"How many wounded do we have in all?" Jack said.

"Fifty or so," Roley said. "Ugly wounds, like Buchan said. Nine or ten dead. That's less than I thought."

The battle had settled down to a stalemate. Our men lay a few feet from the ravine and occasionally fired, knocking a branch down on the rebels below, but hitting nothing. The rebels did not fire. The occasional sound of hooves told us that they were starting to slip away, but most of them were still in the ravine. I used up most of the rest of my water cleaning myself up again. "Like an offended cat," Roley said with a smile. A light rain started, and stopped again.

Suddenly, down in the ravine, a rather good tenor voice began to sing in French, and one by one the rebels joined in. Somebody down there had a flute, and played it well. My French was not good enough to understand it, but it had something to do with the nineteenth of June. I caught the phrase *bois-brûlés,* "the burnt-wood people," which I knew meant the Métis. The song ended, and then the same voice started singing a song I knew, to a tune everybody knows, and again they all joined in:

> *Malbrough s'en va-t-en guerre*
> *Mironton, mironton, mirontaine*
> *Malbrough s'en va-t-en guerre*
> *Malbrough s'en va-t-en guerre*
> *Ne sait quand reviendra*
> *Ne sait quand reviendra*

Malbrough s'en va-t-en guerre
Malbrough s'en va-t-en guerre
Malbrough s'en va-t-en guerre
Ne sait quand reviendra

The men were staring at each other with bewilderment. Roley shook his head. "What are the damn French singing about now?" he said, wearily. *"Who's* a jolly good fellow?"

"Nobody is," I said. "Same tune, but different words. They taught us this in history. It's a song the French made up to make fun of a famous English general two hundred years ago. It's where the tune we use comes from."

Roley turned, and looked at me searchingly. "The French in France?" he said.

"Yes," I said. "Why?"

"Oh," he said, carelessly, "nothing. Only, it's odd. His Lordship Lord Melgund was telling me only the other day that we are fighting savages. Odd that savages would know a song made up two hundred years ago in France to make fun of a British general, and sing it to taunt us today."

We were tired, that is the only thing I can say to excuse it. Tired, and since we knew the rebels wouldn't come up out of the ravine, careless. From the corner of my eye, I saw a sudden movement. It was one of the ambulance attendants, a scrawny red-haired kid in a red tunic, years younger than me. He had not been near the fighting. Nobody had told him a thing about it. Now the poor bastard had come up to the line to see what he could see, and maybe to find a souvenir to show his friends back home. Seeing hundreds of tired, dispirited men lying or sitting quietly a few feet from the coulee, he had assumed that there was nothing to fear. He sauntered casually between our position and the Scouts. I saw two of the Scouts staring at him, too amazed by his temerity to say a word. The kid wandered right over to the edge of the coulee before I found my voice. "Hey, you!" I screamed. "Get the hell away from there!"

He looked over his shoulder at me, with all the sublime bravado of youth on his face, ready to tell me off. Two rifles went off in the coulee, and the boy simply fell over the edge and vanished, like a magic trick, or as if he were playing a game with me. I started to get up, and Roley slammed me back down again with his powerful arm. "No, it's too late," he said in a choked voice. "God damn it, God *damn* it!" Then he crawled over to the edge and stuck his head over for an instant. He pulled it back and, writhing on the wet ground, he pulled out his revolver. He reared up for an instant over the lip of the ravine and fired a shot downward. At once, two rifles went off, and two geysers of dirt shot up inches from Roley. He darted backward like a cat, and then picked himself up, a safe distance from the coulee, and walked over to me. "Nothing we can do," he said, but he did not sound like he meant it. "He's away down near the bottom. He's hit in the chest, I think." There was dirt on Roley's face. It was wet with sweat. He looked like he had in the alley in Winnipeg.

Then the boy started to moan. I did not want to hear that awful voice. He was not speaking very loud, and he had to be dying, but I could make out every word. "Momma, Momma," the boy called. "Momma, where are you? It's so dark. It hurts. I'm scared."

A jeering voice came out of the ravine. *"Il appelle sa mère. Pauvre petit. L'agneau perdu cherche sa mère."*

He wants his mommy. Poor baby. The lost lamb wants his mommy.

Somebody else bellowed at him, *"Pour l'amour de Dieu, tais-toi!"* Another man, with a voice like a fog-horn, roared, *"Laisse-le mourir en paix!"*

For God's sake, shut up! Let him die in peace!

There was no more shouting from the enemy. I could barely hear the wounded boy now. He was coughing and still crying for his mother.

Roley made a choking noise. I looked over at him. He was crying. He glanced at me and wiped the tears away with a furious motion of his arm. "Look, Willie," he said. "We can't save that boy, but I've had enough of this shit. We've been sitting here all day while they murdered us. The creek winds just down there. There's a kind of ridge of mud down there. It separates the bottom of this part of the coulee from the rest. There's just one rebel dug in on this side of it. I saw the son of a bitch and shot at him, too far for a pistol shot, and he waved. Waved at me, the filthy bastard! If we can get down to the bottom of the coulee, the sharpshooters up-coulee can't shoot at us. That ridge'll be in the way. We can kill that man. Pay them back."

"Yeah, but the boy was shot at twice," I said.

"I know, I know," Roley said, impatiently. "That's what I said. When we get to the bottom of the ravine, that ridge of mud'll protect us from the sharpshooters upstream. Those bastards that were jeering. The man that waved at me will be on our side of the ridge. But we have to get to the bottom first."

This was horrible. I had just been so scared, in the coulee, that I had nearly pissed myself. Now he was talking about going back down there again. I looked into his face. I knew that there was no talking to him about this. He had the same exalted look on his face that he'd had when he dealt with Hannigan, Lizzie the whore, and the two rebs, Tom and Carl.

I knew that I could refuse to go with him. Roley would have been the last man on earth to hold it against me. Jack would be eager for some glory. Buchan had said it was pointless to try to dislodge the enemy from the ravine. I never needed to go down into that coulee again, as long as I lived. Roley looked searchingly into my face. His eyes still looked watery from his tears. His face was red and running with perspiration. His greying hair was matted with it. I saw now that he was *not* as he had been in the alley in Winnipeg. He was badly scared this time. But there was no question of his own turning back. "Willie," he said, "I need you. Will you help me?"

"Yes," I said.

"Good boy," he said, "thank God for that," and he squeezed my shoulder. At that moment, I would have followed him into hell, and he knew it. "Get two volunteers," he said. "Make *sure* they're volunteers. And bring Jack back with you as well."

I went over to the men, who were sitting fifty yards away, talking and smoking, and eating scraps of food they'd carried. They all looked angry. They had seen the ambulance attendant die. They'd heard him die. My feelings had changed utterly. Now I wanted to make an appeal that would stir up the men to volunteer. I knew Roley wanted me to, and that knowledge overwhelmed the abject fear I'd felt one minute earlier.

"Now look, boys," I said, loudly, trying to act more confident than I felt. "You all saw that kid get shot and fall into the coulee. You all heard the Frogs"—God help me, I said that, because I knew it would stir them up—"you all heard the Frogs laughing at him while he died. Captain Collison wants two volunteers. The captain and I are going down there to kill one of those sons of bitches, one that's just beneath us here and isolated from the rest." I raised my voice a notch. This was a bravura performance. "*Who's with us?*"

I had done my job. Dozens of hands went up. One belonged to Liam Nolan, the little red-haired mick who'd been with me on the night of the Saskatoon bush. "Take me, Lieutenant," he said. "Take me." As if he were a little boy wanting to be picked for a ball team. He looked around proudly at the other men. "Lieutenant Lorimer's a brave man," he said. "I seen it." Other men nodded.

This was great stuff. "All right, Nolan," I said. "You're coming with us." I looked around. Just beyond Nolan, actually stretching his arm up into the air with eagerness, more like a child on a playground even than the Irishman, was Sanborn, the company clown, the fellow who'd made fun of Arthur Howard at the station in Toronto. He had a huge grin on his smooth, pimpled, beardless face. He couldn't have been over nineteen. "And you, Private Sanborn," I said. "Think of the fund of stories you'll have after this." He grinned more largely, and some of the other men laughed.

I led the two of them over to Roley, along with Jack Price. Jack had a dark, disappointed look on his face. Roley saw it. He walked over to Jack, and put his arm around his shoulders. "Look, Jack," he said. "I'd like nothing better than to take you down there with me. But if any of us is going to come back, I need somebody up here who's an experienced commander. You've got to spread them out at the lip of the coulee. They've got to cover us, at your command. Got to keep the heads of the enemy down while we kill that man down beneath us. We are going to need a volley when we go over the edge of the coulee. We'll need your men to fire at everything that moves when we're down there. And when we come back up, we'll need all the covering fire you can give. Got it?"

Jack nodded. "All right," Roley said. "Now, Jack, Willie, Nolan, Sanborn, crawl over there and stick one careful eye over the edge. The man we are going to kill is hidden behind that big set of bushes immediately below our position. I got the briefest look at him. He's wearing a light-coloured coat. But he's not going to show himself when we go down there. To the left, about thirty feet from his hiding hole, is a big ridge of mud. It will protect us from the fire of the other sharpshooters *once we get down there*. I saw the puffs of smoke from their positions when I fired over the edge. All of them are up-coulee, to the left of the ridge. Three of them, at least. Only the one light-coated one is on our side of the mud ridge."

No one thought to say, *Are you really, really sure, Roley?*

We all crawled over and carefully darted a glance down. We knew enough now to take off our blue caps before we did that. And we knew better than to show any more than our eyes, or to look into the coulee for more than a second or two before pulling back. Roley had described it well. Fish Creek turned down there. In front of us, between us and the creek, was the big bush he had described. That was where the light-coated sharpshooter had shown himself. To the right was much more open ground, where concealment would be much harder. I saw the red of the medical orderly's tunic over there, half-concealed in the scrubby bush. To the left of the big bush was one of the glistening ridges of mud running from side to side of the ravine, which Buchan had described. There was no easy way in (or out) in that direction, except the narrow and mud-dammed waters of the creek itself. To the left of the mud ridge, the coulee meandered away to the west, toward the main group of the enemy. In the clumps of willow to the left of that ridge lay several invisible sharpshooters. When we got to the floor of the coulee, the mud ridge would protect us from fire coming from our left. But only when we got to the bottom.

When I looked to the left, I was looking into the face of death. They would all be firing at us the instant we came over the top. Before we could get the shelter of the ridge, the four of us would have to traverse at least fifty feet of treacherous, descending ground, muddy, slippery ground covered with wet tussocks of last year's grass. Ground where the easiest thing in the world would be to fall down, and as you struggled to get up, a bullet would blow out your brains, or blow off your balls, or tear out your heart.

As this thought flashed through my head, the lot of them fired at us. I saw three plumes of greyish smoke billow out from the left of the ridge and another from the very middle of the big bush right beneath us. The bullets hit just beneath us, splattering more filth into our faces. None of us was hit. Sanborn actually laughed. Jack spat out a mouthful of mud. "*Thank* you," he said. "I now know exactly where you are. The first stupid thing I've seen you sons of bitches do all this long day."

We crawled back over to Roley. "We've seen it," I said. "Jack knows where the other ones are."

"Good," Roley said. "Jack, you go and explain what the men need to do. Try to explain where the enemy positions are." He turned to me, Nolan and Sanborn. "Look," he said. "The longer I talk, the harder this is going to be. You saw where the man right below us is hid?" We nodded. "Good," he said. "We are going to go over the top real, real fast. It will be Lieutenant Price and his men's job to keep their heads down with covering fire while we get to the bottom. Lieutenant Price knows now where the other sharpshooters are. When we're at the bottom of the ravine, Willie, you and Sanborn go to the right of that bush. Nolan and I will go to the left. Keep down, and that ridge of mud will protect us from his friends. Crawl toward the bush, toward his rifle pit. The bastard has to rear up and aim that long rifle of his. When he does, one of us will see him, or we all will, and we'll kill him. Then up we go again with Lieutenant Price and all our friends covering us." He smiled, because we all needed steadying, including Roley himself. "All right?"

"Yes, sir," we all said in unison, and we all saluted.

In a few minutes, Jack came back to us. "Ready as we'll ever be," he said, darkly.

All the remaining men of Company Four were placed alongside the gully's edge, a foot or two from the lip. Boulton's Scouts, huddled, half-defeated and smoking furiously, stared at us from our left in bewilderment. Roley and I reloaded our revolvers. Sanborn and Nolan put a live round in their Sniders, and put ten more rounds in the breast pockets of their tunics. Jack was motioning the men forward now. They were putting their barrels over the edge of the ravine. Roley, Nolan, Sanborn and I moved forward.

Nolan was muttering to himself. I moved closer to him, so that I could hear: "Hail Mary, full of grace. The Lord is with thee. Blessed art thou amongst women, and blessed is the fruit of thy womb, Jesus. Holy Mary, Mother of God, pray for us sinners, now and at the hour of our death. Amen." *Of course*, I thought. *Of course, Nolan's a Dogan. What else would a red-haired, freckled Irishman be, for Christ's sake?* I wondered how much it cost him to keep his mouth shut while the aggressive Protestants in our ranks ranted and raved.

I needed a prayer of my own. Hadn't the Presbyterian Church taught me one? Finally, I thought of it. I looked at the edge of the ravine. *Yea, though I walk through the valley of the shadow of death, I will fear no evil. For thou art with me, thy rod and thy staff they comfort me.* I couldn't remember any more of it, and anyway, Roley was now talking, urgently.

"Come on," he said. "If we don't do this now, we never will. Jack, we're going over on the count of ten. Give us all the covering fire you can 'till we reach the bottom." Roley and I still had our revolvers holstered. There was too much chance of dropping the damned things on the way down. Nolan and Sanborn had to go down carrying the heavy Snider-Enfields in both hands, while desperately trying to go so fast that the Métis riflemen could not draw a bead.

But I had noticed something. When Roley had fired down at the rifleman just below us, they'd shot at him. When Jack, Nolan, Sanborn and I had peeped carefully over the ravine's edge, just minutes before, they'd shot at *us*. Now, all that remained of Company Four was perched on the coulee's edge, with their rifle barrels pointing down, and no shots were coming from below.

The enemy riflemen were conserving their ammunition. That was because they'd realized that somebody was coming down into the coulee, and they wanted to save their ammunition for big, fat targets. For us.

"Three, two, one, zero, *go!*" Roley roared, and we went over the top. I was prepared for the thunderous roar of Four Company's rifles. But I nearly shat myself when Sanborn shrieked a gleeful war-whoop as he plunged down the slope. I was too frightened to look at the dark brush to the left of us. But I still saw three deadly grey plumes of gunsmoke burst out from the scrub to the left of the ridge, and another from the massive set of bushes at which we were charging. At once, Nolan fell over and went plunging ass over tea-kettle down the slope, past Roley, who was scrambling like a monkey toward the bottom, his arms held out for balance. Something in Nolan's rubbery, bouncing, boneless fall told me that he was dead.

At the same moment, Sanborn gave another shriek, this time of fear and pain, and he fell, his rifle clattering down the slope. As I rushed past him, I looked down. There was bright blood on both his trouser legs, on each leg above the knee. He looked up at me, his face contorted with pain. I wanted to stop and help him. I will swear that to my dying day. But it was no part of our mission to help him, not then. And that was just as well, because otherwise I would have been shot.

Roley had scrambled almost to the bottom. He'd looked like an exuberant boy. I was far behind. I cursed myself. How many times had other boys laughed at me for coming down a steep hill "like a girl" or "like an old lady," because I put one slow, careful foot splayed in front of the other instead of plunging fearlessly ahead? Now my lack of athleticism was going to kill me. I needed another technique. I took a giant leap straight ahead. At once, the inevitable happened. I simply soared head-first into mid-air. As I sailed downward, I thought, *They won't shoot me. I'll break my neck.* I actually heard, over the roar of the Sniders, one of the Métis riflemen over the ridge laughing at my clumsiness. Then I hit the ground with my shoulder and rolled down the rest of the way, landing winded and half-stunned. As I landed, I saw a small geyser of dirt erupt fifteen feet above me, where my body had been two seconds earlier.

I lay there on my back, my mind doing a lazy, confused half-turn in mid-air. The grass was wet and soft, and part of me wanted to lie there, quite still. Wouldn't the people who wanted to hurt me just go away if I hid in the grass? Then sanity started to trickle back. I looked around me. Lying companionably in the soaking grass, right beside me, was a figure which looked just like me. I shook my head desperately, and I saw that it was Nolan. He looked so normal that for an instant I wanted to wake him up and tell him that we had work to do. Then I saw the splash of wetter red on the chest of his tunic. He hadn't even lost his wedge cap. His pale blue eyes stared vacantly up at the vacant sky. His freckles were almost black against the pallor of his face.

Then full consciousness came rushing back into my brain. Where was I? In wet grass, last year's yellow grass, nearly two feet high. That was good. To the right of the bush where the light-coated enemy sharpshooter lay concealed, and between the bush and the slope down which I'd come. Where I was supposed to be. Where was Roley? If he'd made it to the bottom without being shot, on the other side of that bush. Roley had been right: the ridge of mud shielded me completely from fire from beyond the ridge.

I glanced over my shoulder and found that I could dimly see the red outlines of our men shrouded in clouds of grey gunsmoke, as they leaned over to give us covering fire. I doubted that they could see me, but they knew I'd reached the bottom. The covering fire was slackening. Some of our boys, bless them, had come over the edge into the ravine. They were dragging Sanborn over the lip of the coulee. His legs dragged uselessly behind him.

Then I suddenly realized what I should be doing. I stared straight into the depths of that dark bit of underbrush, where there was a man I had come to kill. For an instant, I thought I saw a rifle barrel pointing straight out of the underbrush, straight at me, and my heart nearly shot out of my chest. The next moment, I realized that it was nothing but the shifting, mocking shadows of the wet, endlessly moving branches.

I wriggled around on the wet ground and pulled out my revolver. Cursing, whimpering under my breath, I began to pull myself forward on my elbows. They slipped and slithered in the mud. I held the Enfield revolver up high; God help me if its barrel got choked with dirt. I was moving around the mass of bushes, to its right, away from the slope, away from our men. I was moving downward, too, into a depression in the ground that I hadn't known was there. I realized that in a moment Jack and his men would not be able to see me at all. All the time, my eyes stared at that bush. It felt as though they would pop out of my head. Back and forth, back and forth, my eyes raced, until the muscles ached with the effort. Would he have to stand up or sit up to shoot me? Wouldn't he at the least have to level the long rifle barrel, so that I'd see it? Or was he at that second sighting on me, effortlessly, perfectly hidden, before he turned his attention to Roley? At that range, the rifle bullet would split my head like a pumpkin. There'd be blood and brains all over me. I'd really be a mess. But all I'd feel was the beginning of a hard blow. Over and over this thought raced through my mind. Over and over I violently shook my head to make it go away.

I stopped for a moment, and glanced over my shoulder. I could no longer see any of our men on top of the coulee, and they couldn't see me. Roley (if he was still alive) and I were alone with the enemy now. A poetry student who had once fired a revolver at some pieces of paper, a boys' clothing merchant who had shot off part of a man's ear at a range of three feet while meaning not to, and a Métis rifleman who could probably blow off a crow's head at five hundred yards.

Suddenly, with shocking loudness, over the dwindling rifle fire, came a loud, confident voice. *"Jeannot, Jeannot, il reste deux de ces maudits chiens. Deux officiers, armés de pistolets."*

Johnny, Johnny, there are two of the damned dogs left. Two officers with pistols.

For an insane second, I thought it was the man I was stalking, speaking to me. I was so frightened that I wanted to jump up and say, *Here I am! Don't shoot! Let's be friends with each other!* Then I realized that it was one of the sharpshooters from the other side of the ridge, trying to coach his friend. He was trying to encourage the boy by using his nickname, just as Roley would have done. At that point, for some reason, I started to think more coolly, more like Roley. It was good that Jean should know that two of the damned dogs were stalking him. It would scare him, and make him less likely to actively come stalking *us*. No, he would be more likely to hide in his hole, and surely then either Roley or I would see him, and kill him, before he could kill us.

I decided that the odds were on our side after all, and like a fool, I relaxed a bit. I also looked down for an instant, while continuing to drag myself forward on my elbows. When I looked up again, I saw to my horror that I could see scarlet to my left through the branches of the underbrush. It was Roley. Jesus, had we circled the bush on either side without seeing the bastard, snug in his rifle pit? That meant he was now *behind* us, and it meant that he would in the next second or two shoot one or both of us in the back, before we could get ourselves turned around.

One second later, I saw a blur of grey to my left, between me and Roley's red tunic. It was the Métis, hauling himself up and out of his gun pit. To level his long rifle barrel at Roley, he had to step up so that his head was above me. I got up on one knee to aim. He saw me out of the corner of his eye, and whirled around to shoot me first. He was hardly more than a boy, thin-faced, with a straggling beard. He was dressed in a grey woolen coat. It was deeply stained with the mud amidst which he'd lain all day, and the left arm was badly torn. *His mom won't be too thrilled by that*, I thought.

The boy, panicked, was staring straight into my eyes. Even in the extremity of my own fear, I knew that was a bad mistake. He whirled the rifle barrel around toward me. It collided with a thick branch with a loud thump. It stopped dead. He looked down, perplexed and scared. His eyes flickered back to mine, and a moment of human recognition passed between us. His gaze showed annoyance, and a boy's embarrassment at his own clumsiness. For an instant, civilized instinct took over. I found myself waiting courteously for the other fellow to get over his frustration and go first. Then he pulled the rifle barrel back toward himself, to avoid the branch. He began to swing the barrel toward me, and I shot him.

A puff of dust spurted out of the left side of his coat, about four inches below his collarbone. He looked down at it, and then his eyes met mine. His eyes were still full of intelligence. He knew what was happening to him. Then his face went utterly blank, and he fell over, very lightly, like a straw man. He landed in the thick branches, which cushioned him. I stood up to see if he was still moving. Instantly I was hit from the right by a tremendous blow which knocked me flat. I thought, in a fraction of an instant, *I'm shot. I forgot, and stood up so I could be seen over the ridge. Fool.*

Then I realized that there was a heavy body on top of me, one that smelled of tobacco and sweat. There was a muddy red tunic in front of my nose. At that instant, I heard three rifles go off across the ridge, and I'll swear I heard the bullets go cracking overhead. "Jesus, Willie," Roley said, "I got to you just in time. If you stand up, they can see you." Our faces were about three inches apart. "Well, this is romantic, isn't it?" he said, looking down at me. "Only I expect you and Alice haven't quite reached this part yet."

He rolled off me, but still held me down with a strong arm, so I wouldn't blunder up again. "Nolan?" he said.

"Gone," I said. "Sanborn was hit." He sighed.

Suddenly, that same confident voice shouted again, from the other side of the ridge. *"Jean, qu'est-ce qui ce passe? Réponds moi!"*
Jean, what's happening? Answer me!

"Now, look, Willie," Roley said. "It would be nice if we could just lie here in the grass until those noisy bastards on the other side of the ridge finally just go home. But it won't work that way. They know now we killed their friend. Sooner or later, they'll get up the nerve to come out of their holes. They can crawl through this grass without our boys up top seeing them." He looked over at the dead man. "They'll come crawling up to the top of the ridge. And they'll kill us. So we've got to go up, and fast."

As if he were a mind-reader, the Frenchman beyond the ridge yelled, *"Arrangez-vous pour qu'ils ne r'viennent pas en un seul morceau!"*

Make sure they don't get back up in one piece!

I nodded. Roley took my arm and pulled me, and we started crawling back toward the slope. When we reached a place where we could see our men, Roley yelled, "Jack! Jack! Willie got the son of a bitch!" There was cheering. "On the count of twenty-five, we're coming up fast! You've got to throw all the God damn lead in the world at them to keep their heads down. You hear me?" I heard Jack shouting that he understood.

"Seventeen, sixteen, fifteen," Roley was saying. We were on our hands and knees. I looked back at the Métis boy. I could see only a blur of grey. It moved slightly, but that was only the dark, glistening, chuckling, mocking branches, swaying in the wind. It had begun to rain a little. "I hope those fellows over there don't understand English," Roley said. "Don't you? Three, two, one, *zero!*" he roared. He pulled me to my feet. "*Go!*"

We went up the hill like sons of bitches. Jack did it perfectly. He had told the men to fire in successive volleys, three in a row. The men knew now where the enemy snipers were. The three Métis sharpshooters had no sooner recovered from one volley than another was hurled at them, then a third. By then the first group was ready to fire again. I doubt very much if in the long ignoble history of the Snider-Enfield rifle, the thing was ever fired and reloaded that fast. The men did indeed seem to be trying to throw all the God damn lead in the world at the Métis.

I tore up that hill right behind Roley, grabbing at rocks, at bushes, at thorns. Once in desperation, as I felt myself going over backward, I grabbed the back belt loop of his pants. Roley yelled and kept on going. The cursing soldiers were firing, whirling the cumbersome Sniders over to eject the spent shell, jamming another into place with reckless speed, slamming the massive gun butts into their shoulders, and firing again, so fast that gunsmoke choked the air. Roley vaulted over the top. I was almost there, swaying, exhausted, weirdly without energy. He reached over and pulled me up and over, and as he did, a bullet spanged off a rock not a foot from where I'd been. We lay there in the wet grass, spent, and the men pulled us away from the edge of the coulee. I looked over at Roley. He was laughing a bit crazily, and I think that at the same time he was crying.

Then he pulled himself up, and pulled me up, too. Jack was there. "How is Sanborn?" Roley said. Jack pointed to a place about ten feet away where men were huddled in a semi-circle. Roley and I pushed through them. Sanborn was lying on his back. The legs of both his trousers were soaked with blood above the knee.

He looked up at Roley. "Jesus, Captain, I'm sorry," he said. "I made a mess of it."

Roley knelt beside Sanborn and squeezed his arm. "No, you didn't," he said, quietly. "You did exactly what you were supposed to do." Two stretcher-bearers were approaching at a run. I was staring at Sanborn's ankles. The bottoms of his pants were pulled well over his socks. The skin of both ankles was almost blue.

The ambulance men loaded Sanborn roughly onto their stretcher. I saw one of them jerk his head toward those blue ankles, and the other nodded. They set off to the rear at a dead run.

Coming from that direction, at a gallop, was an ornately-turned-out officer whom I recognized as Lieutenant Colonel Portman. Now I was scared again. Roley had insulted Portman's emissary an hour or two before, and I knew at once that the colonel was coming to exact his revenge. Jack poked me and pointed toward our left. Evidently, Major Buchan feared for Roley, too, because he was coming at a run from the Winnipeg lines. He had to hold his clattering sword as he ran, giving him a curiously girlish gait, but he was moving fast.

Portman wheeled up his horse with a flourish. "Well, Captain Collison," he said. His face was contorted with anger. "It appears that after cravenly refusing to engage the enemy and sending me an insulting message respecting that dereliction of duty, you've now veered to the other side of the spectrum. You've led an impossibly risky and completely futile raid into the coulee. I understand that one man is dead and another severely wounded. *What do you have to say for yourself?*"

I looked at Roley, and I recognized the terminal signs of him losing his grip on his temper. Sweat was pouring down out of his greying hair. "Say for myself?" he repeated, in a thoughtful voice. "What do I have to say for myself?"

"Precisely!" Portman shouted. "By leading men into the coulee, you have acted in direct contravention of the orders given you. I'll require an explanation; I'll require it now, sir."

I looked at Buchan, who had arrived gasping for breath. I had the feeling that he had long since had enough of Portman, and that the chaos of that day had broken the last of his restraint. That was lucky, because Roley, particularly in his present state, was incapable of doing or saying anything that wouldn't get him into the most serious kind of trouble. But Buchan was going to be doing the talking for our side; that was clear. His little eyes were narrower than usual, and his big chin stuck out. In his agitation, an underlying Scottish accent was showing through. "Orders given to Captain Collison?" he said. "Given by whom, sir? I gave no such orders. I heard General Middleton give no such orders. I have not had the pleasure of seeing you, sir, here at the fighting front any time today to issue any such orders. And I must say, that orders not to engage the enemy would be particularly *eediotic*, if I may say so. Sir."

Both officers looked behind me and stiffened to attention. I turned around, and Middleton was standing there. The old man looked bone-weary. His shoulders were slumped. Like the rest of us, he had mud on his blue uniform. The fur cap with the bullet hole in it was pushed to the back of his head. He had apparently managed to walk up unobserved in the middle of this bizarre confrontation.

The dismay he felt at it was written all over his broad, perspiring face.

"For Christ's sake," he said in a very low voice. "You are having this unseemly brawl in the presence of junior officers and *enlisted men*. I make many allowances for colonial officers who are not professional soldiers—gallant as they are—but I *will not tolerate* unseemly quarreling amongst officers and gentlemen. Not in a British expeditionary force. Now, come with me."

He walked a few paces away from the gawping men of Company Four. Roley, Portman and Buchan followed him. Despite the reference to "junior officers," Jack and I were in no mood to abandon Roley now, and so we trailed along behind. Nor did Middleton gesture us away.

"Now," the general said. "In the first place, Captain Collison, you had no business sending an inexperienced young officer back to the staff area with instructions for Colonel Portman to come and 'stick his fat face' out over the edge of the ravine. Such language is inexcusable. I'll require you to apologize to both me and the colonel for that remark, forthwith."

Jack kicked Roley in the ankle. Roley looked down at it, then at Jack, then at me. Then he said, "I do apologize. I forgot myself."

Portman looked mildly mollified. "Now," said Middleton, "as I have already stated, despite his vulgar and disrespectful language, Captain Collison's hesitation at that point to engage the enemy in the ravine was probably justified." Jack smiled and I did, too, and then as Middleton glared at us, we stopped. "Furthermore, no talk of being 'craven' is justified, given the brave participation of Company Four in our subsequent mass incursion into the coulee. That incursion failed, and we withdrew." He stared down at his muddy boots for a moment and then went on. "Now the question arises, was Captain Collison justified in leading some of his men into the ravine a few minutes ago, to engage the enemy? You spoke, Colonel Portman, of 'orders given,' but it might be more accurate to say that after the failure of the mass incursion, I gave the command that we would cease trying to dislodge the enemy *en masse*. No formal order was given specifically forbidding any officer or man to enter the ravine and engage the enemy."

Portman was swelling up like an indignant toad. "But, sir," he said, "the man has gotten a soldier killed, and another shot in both legs, for nothing."

Middleton looked him up and down without saying a word. I had often read and heard about the capacity of upper-crust Englishmen to express anger and contempt without saying a word. I had not seen it before. "I do not recall inviting your comments at this juncture, Colonel," he said, coldly. Then he turned to me. "Young man," he said, "since you have chosen to ignore my rather broad hint to make yourself scarce, perhaps you can contribute something useful now. I understand that if any successful action against the enemy was taken, you took it. What did you do?"

"I killed one of their sharpshooters," I said.

Middleton reached out and patted my shoulder. "That's a good lad," he said. "That's what we want you to do with them." Then he turned to the others. "Captain Collison did what he is supposed to do. His job is to kill the enemy, and although no one at Sandhurst ever says it, to get his own men killed in the process. That is what war is. If we suffered two casualties to kill one of the enemy, well, such disproportion is typical of war against irregular forces. In warfare against such forces, there are usually more of you than there are of the other fellow." He stopped, and wiped his hand wearily across his mouth. "This incident is closed, do you understand me? It will not be brought up again. It has ceased to be a controversy. And that is all." He turned on his heel, and started walking slowly back toward the rear.

Portman stared into Roley's face. Then he said, "I hope you're happy, Captain. Nolan? Was that the man's name? Or have you forgotten it, already?" Roley simply stared, white-faced now, at Portman. The colonel got back on his horse, without another word, and rode after his general. Despite the forced apology, he had been made to look like a fool. He knew it and we knew it.

"Jesus, Roley," Buchan said. "That man is a dangerous enemy.

Look out for him."

"Oh, hell, Larry," Roley said. "I'm not a professional soldier. What's the bastard going to do to me? Refuse to buy his son's clothes in my store?"

"Probably incapable of reproduction anyway," Jack said. "We can only hope."

Buchan started to laugh. "Christ, you fellows," he said. "You're even battier than my Winnipeg lads. And just look, our friends from across the river have finally made an appearance."

And so they had. There was a sound of cheering. Advancing from the left, the direction of the river, came a wall of red tunics. It was the Royal Grenadiers, with Lord Melgund and the other officers in front of them on fresh-looking, capering horses. The Prussian-style helmets of the Grenadiers shone in the reviving, pale sunlight. It looked like a Sunday parade or an absurd painting. All they needed was a band. They had gotten themselves across the thousand feet of Saskatchewan River, and come to our aid, about three hours too late.

"Dandy," said Buchan. "Perfectly grand. They'll all want to charge into the coulee forthwith. I shall have to tell his Lordship that tactic has been tried and rejected." He looked toward the coulee for a minute. "This will break their backs down there, though. You watch. They have won this battle tactically, but strategically they have completely failed. Because their ambush failed. They'll go home to Batoche now."

He set off toward Lord Melgund, again clutching his sword, again with that slightly comical mincing gait. As so often, he was right. Within minutes, we heard firing breaking out all along the line. Jack came running up to us. "Those three across the ridge have run for it," he said. "We shot at them, might have got one. Anyhow, the word from all down the line is that the whole God damn lot of them are skedaddling."

"Willie," Roley said, "we've got to go back and help Sanborn. See he's being looked after right." Roley's face was deadly pale. He seemed smaller somehow, and older.

We walked quickly back to the ambulance area. The ambulance wagons were drawn up in a semi-circle. Lying everywhere in the wet grass, on stretchers, on sheets and blankets, were dozens of wounded men. Some of them smiled at us through their pain, and some cursed like sailors.

Buchan had been right. The muzzle-loaders and shotguns of the Métis had inflicted jagged, hideous wounds. Everywhere, there were towels and blankets and discarded uniforms soaked with blood. Lying here and there were heaps of blankets and tarpaulins. Unmoving, shapeless things lay under them.

It took us only a minute to find Sanborn. He was still lying on his stretcher. His face was dead-white, and his jaw was clenched with fear, I thought, rather than pain. They had cut his black trousers off of him. They lay in a torn heap nearby. Sanborn's lower half lay under a brown blanket. Bloodstains were coming up through it, somewhere between where his knees and his pecker should be.

"This is a hell of a note, eh, gentlemen?" he said. But his voice caught, and he nearly choked on the words.

"It will all turn out just fine," Roley said. He sat down beside Sanborn and motioned for me to do the same. Roley pulled out his pipe, ignoring Sanborn for a minute, making an even more elaborate ritual than he usually did of lighting it. An instant later, I realized what he was doing. If you are sitting down with a friend for a smoke and a chat, and if the friend's health is perfectly fine, then obviously you won't pay a huge amount of attention to him. You'll light your pipe; you'll pay attention to your own concerns, as people generally do. Only if your friend is possibly dying will you make a big fuss over him. And if there's no fuss, then there can't be much of a problem. I pulled out my own pipe, and ceremoniously lit it.

"You heard that Lieutenant Lorimer got him?" Roley said.

Sanborn grinned through his pain. "I sure did," he said. "Good for you, Willie—I mean, Lieutenant Lorimer."

"Pure luck, I assure you," I said.

A man in a badly stained white coat, thrown on over the dark green Winnipeg uniform, was coming up to us. He gestured peremptorily to Roley and me. "Captain, Lieutenant," he said, and pointed toward a spot between tents where no men lay. We followed him over there. He was a short balding man of perhaps forty, with long black sideburns and a luxuriant handlebar moustache. His eyes were red, and his face seemed crumpled, as if he were ill, or had not slept for days.

"My name is Major Cooke, Doctor Cooke," he said, wearily. "Are you Private Sanborn's commanding officer?"

"Yes," Roley said. "Captain Collison. This is Lieutenant Lorimer."

Cooke nodded to me. "Sanborn's legs have to come off," he said. "Above the knee. Right now."

"Oh God," Roley said. "Are you sure?"

Cooke started to shake with rage. "No," he said, "now that you mention it, you imbecile, I'm just joking. His legs are fine; that's why below the knee they're that dignified shade of bluish-white." He stopped, and looked down. Then he looked up again. It looked like there were tears in his eyes. "I'm sorry," he said. "I had no call to say that. None at all. It's just that I thought I'd finished with all these awful wounds." He stopped and stared off vaguely, toward the rest of Melgund's column from across the river, which was swinging into the camp with much cheering. Roley and I waited. Cooke seemed to have forgotten we were there.

Roley looked uneasily at me. I realized that he expected me to do the talking, as one educated man to another. "Doctor?" I said, tentatively.

Cooke slowly turned and looked at the two of us, as if we had magically emerged from an empty field. I realized that the man was at the end of his wits. "Oh," he finally said. "Oh yes. Regarding Private Sanborn's legs, they do have to come off. Believe me, if it were possible to save them, I'd like nothing better." He sounded almost apologetic. "The enemy must be firing very old-fashioned bullets, very heavy, but with a low muzzle velocity. If he'd been hit by modern bullets, he'd have been dead in minutes."

He seemed to be about to trail off again, but by a supreme effort, he got hold of himself and looked us in the eye again. "Sanborn has been hit in both legs, above the knee. The femur has been shattered hopelessly in both cases. There may or may not be some degree of nicking of the femoral artery. In any case, the shattered femur is blocking the blood flow. Little if any blood is reaching his legs below the knee. That will kill him, by and by. I've palpated around in the wound. The femur is in so many pieces I don't think they could save his legs in the best hospital in London." It had started to drizzle again. He tried to smile, but only grimaced like a man in pain. "And this isn't it."

"What do you want us to do?" I said.

"Yes," Roley said.

Cooke leaned toward us confidingly, and I realized that he was very close to losing all control over himself. He had never been on a battleground in his life, of course, any more than any of us except Middleton. "Well," he said, "this is the shit part of it. Some fool of a teamster overturned one of our ambulance wagons, as we came racing up here after the firing started. Ran it through a rut; it turned over. We had lots of ether and choloroform, lots of it, but most of the bottles were broken when the wagon turned over. The upshot of it is"—he looked almost shamefacedly at Roley and me—"the upshot of it is that we've run out. We have to operate on the lad without anesthetic. The old-fashioned way."

"Jesus," Roley said. "That will kill him."

"It will if I don't," Cooke said. "Lots of men have survived amputation without anesthetics. Tens of thousands in the American Civil War." He was getting his confidence back, as he talked about what he knew. "Here's what you have to do, and it is vital. This boy trusts both of you. Christ, he worships you. For an hour, he has been talking to anyone who would listen to him about these two wonderful officers who, sooner or later, would come back here to help him. He thinks that you, Captain Collison, are the greatest leader in military history, and he thinks that you, Lieutenant Lorimer, are some kind of invincible hero. Well, here is your big chance to live up to his faith in you. You have to be on either side of his head, you have to help hold his arms, you have to reassure him, tell him not to panic, that it will be all right. In amputations of this kind, you see, the patient is thrashing in agony. He can smell his own blood and see it splashing all around him. If he thrashes too much, he can make the operation impossible. If he gets too frightened, he can quite literally *die* of fright. Or of shock, if you prefer medical terms."

"You can do something for the pain, though, can't you, Doc?" Roley asked.

"Oh, *of course* we can," Cooke said. "We can give him all the whiskey he can hold. From my private stock, which was one of the things that didn't break in that God damn wagon. And we can give him a leather razor-strop to bite down on. And we can give him the greatest officers in the world as his cheering section, the heroic figures who got him shot in the first place."

"Doctor," Roley said, "have you performed this operation before?"

Cooke's face twisted with anger again. "Of course I have not," he said. "Nor have any of the other surgeons. Not on both legs. Not under these conditions. Christ, man, do you think any of us have ever seen this kind of butcher's yard before?" Roley said nothing. Cooke gestured. "Come on," he said, and started walking back toward Sanborn.

Cooke knelt on one side of Sanborn's stretcher, and Roley knelt on the other. Sanborn smiled hopefully at Roley. "Going to fix me up good, now, right, Captain?"

Roley said nothing for a few seconds. Then he said, "Jim, Doctor Cooke and I have got some bad news for you. Real awful news, and I'm sorry."

Sanborn looked at him for a moment, and then he turned to look at Major Cooke. He was not a stupid boy. "Part of me has to come off, doesn't it?" he said. "I was afraid of it. I can't move my legs at all, and I can't feel anything down there, either. But that's not so bad. Part of my foot comes off, or I get some scars on my legs. So what, eh? So I won't be able to play third base any more. Hell, I was never any good, anyway. The team'll be glad to see the end of me. They'll…" The words caught in his throat at the look on Cooke's face. Sanborn shut his eyes and waited for the doctor to speak.

"Mr. Sanborn," the doctor said. "Mr. Sanborn, both of your legs have to be amputated above the knee. No blood is getting into your lower legs at all. There's no way it ever can, again. The bones above your knee are all shot to pieces. They are blocking the blood flow. If we don't amputate your legs, right now, you will certainly die."

Sanborn turned his back on Cooke. He smiled at Roley confidently. "This is all shit, right, sir?" he said, brightly. "I mean, I'm sure the doctor here is a good man, but you tell him this just can't be. And you, too, Lieutenant. There's no way I'm giving up my legs. Why, it's ridiculous. Anybody can see it is. There's fifty fellows lying around here, bleeding like stuck pigs, some of them, but nobody's cutting their legs off. I'm not dying. I feel great. Just a little numbness in my legs, that's all. You're in command of me. You tell him."

Roley put his hand on Sanborn's arm. "Jim," he said, unsteadily, "I don't think…"

"*No!*" Sanborn nearly screamed, and I saw how scared he really was. "No, bullshit! You're my C.O.! You led me into that coulee! Now, you tell this butcher to leave off me! You do that, Roley, God damn it!"

He had his hand on the neck of Roley's tunic. Roley did not try to remove it. He hung his head down, and his blue wedge cap fell off and landed on Sanborn's blanket. Roley's sweaty, greying black hair fell down the front of his face. "Aw, God," he said. "What do you want me to say, Jimmy? I only run a little store. I don't know *anything*. If the doctor says you'll die if your legs don't come off, then they…" He stopped. His voice was choked.

"A little *store?*" Sanborn yelled. "What in God's name has your little store got to do with it?" He looked impatiently up at me. "Lieutenant, you go to the college. You're educated. Tell the doctor I'm fine. Hell, I can walk right now. I'll show you." He reared up, his pale face turned crimson with effort, and then he fell helplessly back on to the stretcher. He was still looking at me. I turned away, and after a minute he moaned and turned his face to the ground.

"Right," Cooke said. He was trying to sound confident. He

turned to two ambulance attendants, twins of the one who'd toppled, dying, into the coulee an hour earlier and started all this. I
thought, *Why didn't this God damn doctor keep that one back here
where he belonged, and spare us all?* "Take him into the operating
tent," Cooke said. "Put him on the large table." They picked up Sanborn's stretcher. He refused to look at Roley or me.

Roley and I followed Cooke and the stretcher into a big grey tent
flapping gently nearby in the rainy breeze. As we entered, I heard
Roley's breath catch in his throat, and he muttered "Oh, God," under his breath. There were three big oaken operating tables in the
tent. They had filthy pillows at one end, and the surfaces sloped
gently downward from there toward the foot of the table. Gutters
filled with dark, drying, glistening blood ran down each side of the
tables. At the foot of each table, at either side, under each gutter, was
a shiny white bucket, each about two thirds full.

It was clear that at first, the doctors and attendants had tossed
the blood-soaked sheets and blankets onto the muddy tent floor
and replaced them with clean ones. The muddy ground was awash
in dirtied sheets and blankets. But now they had run out, and so
some attendants were frantically sorting through the soiled linen,
desperately trying to find some which were clean enough to use on
Sanborn.

The attendants put Sanborn on the largest table. One of them
had a full bottle of whiskey in his hand. They started pouring whiskey down Sanborn's throat. "Faster, faster!" one of them said. Sanborn was gagging as he swallowed desperately. The other attendant
had pulled off the blanket which covered Sanborn's bottom half.
The attendants had stripped off the soaked bandages. From two
holes, one in each of his upper thighs, dark veinous blood pumped
slowly and steadily. The whiskey was running down Sanborn's chin,
and one attendant mopped it off his chest and belly, before it ran
down into the wounds. Sanborn seemed to have lost the power to
resist what was happening to him. I kept staring at that awful, re-
morseless flow of dark blood, and the fish-belly white-blueish tinge
of what lay below his knees.

I had just killed a man, and I suppose I had been feeling pretty soldierly. Now, the inside of the tent started revolving around, and I felt my knees giving way. I was going face-forward onto the filthy tent floor. Suddenly, Roley grabbed the soft flesh on the underside of my right arm and squeezed. The pain was terrible, and I shot back into full consciousness again. "Stay awake," Roley hissed. "I need you."

Two other doctors gathered around Cooke. "You take hold of his upper arms," Cooke said to Roley and me. "He'll thrash a lot." The attendants were tying Sanborn's ankles to two wooden posts which stood up on either side at the table's bottom. I had been wondering what they were for. One of the doctors quietly opened a wooden box, in which lay three large knives, and two hand-saws of unequal size. They had been kept unused today; their bright silver steel glittered. He held the box below the table level, so that Cooke could see it, and Jimmy Sanborn could not.

Sanborn was naked now. His sparse brown pubic hair and shrunken penis were not far above the stinking mess that slathered his upper legs. The attendants were inserting a thick, brown leather razor-strop between Sanborn's teeth, shoving it far enough that he could not spit it out. "Watch he don't gag," the older attendant said. Sanborn looked at Roley and me. Tears were running down his face. He was deeply flushed, and he stunk of whiskey.

One of the other doctors leaned over and peered into Sanborn's eyes. "It's taking effect," he said. "And we can't wait, Major Cooke."

Cooke came over and spoke directly into Sanborn's face. Cooke's jaw was working, but he had possession of himself again. "Now, then, son," he said. "If we don't do this, you will die. It's going to hurt bad for a little while. This is where they separate the wheat from the chaff. I know you have it in you to be a brave man. We'll make it as quick as we can."

"Do your best, Jimmy," Roley said, in a quiet voice. "Willie Lorimer and I will be here the whole time."

"Yes," I said. Sanborn's eyes flickered frantically toward me. He may have been as drunk as a lord, but he knew what was happening to him, all right.

The attendants were winding a huge, greyish white canvas tourniquet around the upper part of Sanborn's right thigh. "Pad of it right over the femoral artery," Cooke said. "No, there, there." There was a huge metal screw above the tourniquet pad. One attendant started turning the screw handle, depressing the pad more and more firmly into the flesh of Sanborn's leg. I could not believe how deeply the pad sank. "Damn it," Cooke muttered to one of the doctors. "The incision is going to be too high. The tourniquet's going to interfere with the incision." The other doctor shook his head.

Cooke reached down into the box of surgeon's tools, and brought out a shining butcher knife. It looked a lot like one we had at home. "This is actually the most painful part," he said to Sanborn, almost cheerfully. "So when this is over, and it only takes a moment, the worst is over." Sanborn's eyes were hugely wide. He stared up at the tent roof with desperation, willing for it not to hurt too much. "Hold his shoulders, hard," Cooke said to Roley and me. He gestured to the two attendants, and they grabbed Sanborn's hands.

At a nod from Cooke, suddenly both of the other doctors took hold of Sanborn's right thigh, one on each side of it. With both hands they drew the skin and muscle on either side of his leg upward with great force. Instantly, Cooke in one sweep made a deep, slashing incision right around Sanborn's thigh. The cut was three hundred and sixty degrees around the whole leg, and Cooke accomplished it in less than five seconds.

Sanborn let out a high-pitched scream and began desperately trying to fight his way off the table. He thrashed furiously back and forth like some great white fish. It was all that four men could do to restrain his hands and shoulders. I held on with all my limited strength, but his shoulder on my side kept getting away from me, and the attendant on my side brought one brawny hand up Sanborn's arm to force him down again. The scream went on and on, impossibly long, impossibly loud. I could not stop looking at Sanborn's leg. Bright blood was splattering everywhere, in impossible quantities, over the doctors assisting Cooke, over the attendants, over Cooke himself.

Doctor Cooke had cut all around Sanborn's leg, right down to the muscles. Now he turned back several inches of skin, and folded the skin upward around the top of Sanborn's leg, above the incision, like a mother folding her child's trouser cuffs upward.

To cover the stump.

All through the amputation of Jimmy Sanborn's right leg, Roley held him down by the shoulder. Over and over again, he said loudly into Sanborn's ear, "You can take it, Jim," and "It'll all be over soon, Jim," and "You'll be fine, Jim."

I could not bear to utter a sound. Sanborn never stopped that awful, high-pitched screaming, more like a terrified animal than a human. His face whipped back and forth in agony and panic, back and forth on the pillow, faster and faster. He reminded me of a huge, beached, dying fish. His shock of brown hair beat against my hand and arm as I held his shoulder. Sometimes it whipped against my cheek, as I bent down to reinforce my grip. Sweat from his face flew into mine and Roley's. Sometimes, though, his eyes caught mine. He knew what was happening to him.

And you, Private Sanborn. Think of the fund of stories you'll have after this.

After the initial incision, and the folding-upward of the skin to cover the stump, the muscles had to be divided surgically down to the bone. The arteries had to be tied off. Then the bone was sawed through with a hand-saw. Things went a little awry for Doctor Cooke, though, before the sawing began. The incision *was* too high on the thigh for the tourniquet. The tourniquet just got in the way. It had to be removed, with horrible results. Then one of the two assisting doctors tried pressing down on the arteries in Sanborn's groin with a white, porcelain cylinder rounded at the bottom, like a druggist's pestle. It didn't work very well. I stole a look at Cooke's face. He was crying continuously.

When they had tied off the artery and cut off the right leg, one of the attendants cut the cord binding the ankle to the wooden post. Doctor Cooke pushed the leg off the table. It landed on the ground, with the inner part of the thigh upward. The almost complete leg curved away from us and then, at the knee, curved back again. That finished Roley. With a groan, he fell down to his knees and put his hands over his face.

"Take him out," said one of the doctors. I helped Roley up, and he staggered out of the tent, as other attendants rushed forward to take hold of Sanborn's shoulders. Exhausted, shaking, Doctor Cooke was already commencing the incision on the second leg. Outside, Roley pulled himself away from me. He walked over to a little depression in the ground, perhaps thirty feet from the door of the tent, and sat down on the ground. Sanborn's screaming went on and on. Other wounded men, lying on stretchers or blankets, stared, white-faced and silent, at the tent door.

Roley put his face in his hands and started to cry. I stood a few feet away, and watched him. I had never seen anyone, man or woman, cry like that before. His shoulders shuddered, and he made a low, constant, moaning noise of panic and horror. Tears squirted out of his eyes as if some invisible pump inside him were ejecting them, and then more and more, as if weeping should never stop, as if there were not enough tears in the universe to express what he felt.

I walked over to a little ridge, and put my back against it. I just sat there, watching Roley to make sure that he would be all right. Eventually, he began to get control of himself. His shoulders stopped shaking. "I'm sorry. Aw, God, aw, God, I'm sorry," he kept muttering, his voice quavering. "I'm sorry, Jimmy." He pulled out his handkerchief and carefully wiped the tears and snot off his face. I put my pipe away. Roley got to his feet unsteadily, and looked uneasily around at the wounded men, none of whom looked him in the eye.

Finally Roley saw me. He came over to me, and I got up. I wasn't sure what was going to happen next. Roley put his arm around me, and gave a shaky squeeze, quite unlike his usual bearhug. "Come on," he said in a choked voice, "we're not finished yet. We've got to get Nolan's body up out of the coulee."

Tents were already being put up and fires lit behind us, well to the south of the battlefield. There was no more shooting. Roley and I walked together, wordlessly, back to the coulee. There were redcoats of our company and members of Boulton's Scouts walking around in the ravine where Nolan had died.

Obviously, in that sector, the enemy was gone, although it was feared that to the left, where they had been more numerous, they still lurked. I had been praying that Nolan's body had been picked up, but it was still there. To delay having to touch it, I went down to the left, where the enemy sharpshooters had been before. I saw Sutter, the scout who'd joined us around the fire about twenty hours before. It felt as if a year had passed since I'd last seen him.

Sutter gestured to me, and I walked over to him. He was looking at one of the shallow pits, from where they'd fired at us when we went down into the coulee. "Just look at this," he said. "Just look at it. Didn't I tell you. Didn't I tell you. Over to the left, where the trail to Batoche crosses the coulee, I hear there are dozens and dozens of these. They've improvised them out of game trails, water run-offs, any damn thing you like. The men in them were completely invisible. They would have opened up on us when part of our force was ascending the far side of the coulee, and most of it was fording the stream, or was about to. They'd have been firing at point-blank range, at men in bright coats who didn't even know they were there. Those shotguns would have done murder. Jesus Christ, they'd have killed or wounded most of us in thirty seconds, and those who tried to pull back out of the coulee would have been driven back into it by Dumont and his men who were going to close the trap behind us." He looked up at the rainy sky, and I thought for a moment that there were tears in his eyes. "Thank Christ," he said, with feeling. "Thank Christ there were no leaves on the poplars, and Bill Neilson saw the sons of bitches in the trees. He ought to get a medal from that God damn old Englishman. I 'spect he'll wait till Judgment Day to get it."

Roley had come down the slope behind us. "Willie," he said, wearily, "for God's sake." I went back up the slope with him and then down again, this time to the right of that big ridge of mud. It seemed strange to stroll down the slope of the ravine. There were no bullets now, nothing to be afraid of. The birds were singing gently in the underbrush, now that the senseless human racket had subsided.

Nolan's body still looked absurdly peaceful. His wedge cap was still on. I looked over beyond him, at the big bush where lay the man I'd killed. A couple of our men were looking into the brush at him. I could see the light grey coat still moving in the branches. I realized, now, that I could see the lower part of his face, with its scraggly beard, and one of his thin hands, waving a little as the branches bore him up. Part of me felt that I should first go into that bush and pull out this man whom I had slain, but a saner part of me knew that I would go to pieces if I had to touch him.

"Willie," Roley said again, in that toneless voice. "You take his feet and lead the way. I'll hold his head up." I picked up Nolan's feet. His boots were cold as ice. For just an instant my hand touched the skin of his ankle, and I felt dizzy with nausea. His skin was just a little warmer than his boot. He was starting to get stiff. His stomach and his backside did not droop between Roley and me as much as they would have if he'd been alive, but unconscious.

Take me, Lieutenant. Take me.

I lifted Nolan's feet up above his head, and as I looked back, I saw blood and some colourless fluid fall out of his mouth and onto Roley's leg. Roley gave a little cry and shied away from it like a girl shying away from a bug.

Lieutenant Lorimer's a brave man. I seen it.

We started up the bank with Nolan's body. Last year's wet, yellowed grass and the shining mud were too slippery for us though. Over and over again, one or both of us would start to slip. We'd start to run in place, faster and faster, like clowns, trying to stay upright, and then one or both of us would fall flat on our face, and Nolan would fall back into the ravine. The last time this happened, we almost had him all the way up, when suddenly Roley fell, and Nolan rolled down past him and stopped about halfway down. Roley was pounding his fist over and over again into the wall of the ravine, in the last stages of rage and despair. I walked past him down to Nolan, and looked into his pale face, staring past me upward and at nothing. I had used the eloquence I'd learned in school to inspire this man to follow Roley and me into the coulee. I kept looking at Nolan's face.

Momma, where are you? It's so dark. It hurts. I'm scared.

Finally, some of our men came down and reverently took hold of Nolan, and brought him up. I went back to Roley. He was just sitting on the bank of the coulee, looking across to the other side. He looked up at me and managed a smile. "Sort of pretty, isn't it?" he said. "In a month or so, you could have a nice picnic here."

"Yes, Captain," I said. "Let's go back to the rear. They're putting up tents there and cooking some food." I gave him an arm up. We walked slowly past our men and back to the camp area behind the ambulance wagons. Some of the tents were denominated with little fluttering pennants as being for our company. Roley simply walked into one of these and sat down on the ground. After a few minutes, Jack brought his things over to the tent, and then without a word he went away again, and came back with my gear and Roley's. Jack looked into the tent, and then inquisitively at me. I shook my head.

Later on, Jack and I stood in line at the chuckwagon. All the firing had long since stopped. But Roley, some of our men, and the Scouts and I were the only ones who had been down into the coulee. That was because the Scouts and Company Four were on the right end of our line. Nobody knew if any of the enemy remained to the left, where they had been thickest, where the Batoche trail crossed the creek. Nobody had dared go down to retrieve our dead, or theirs.

The Grenadiers, who had arrived too late for the battle, were excited and elated. They kept slapping our men and the Winnipeggers on the back, and saying how sorry they were that they'd missed the big show. I had no idea how to reply to that. Both Jack and I got huge plates of beef stew. I was dumbfounded at how hungry I was. I took a tin plate of the stew, a knife, fork and spoon, some fresh white bread and a mug of coffee back to the tent, and put it beside

Roley. He did not even look at it.

When I came back outside, Major Cooke was standing there. "I thought you would want to know," he said. "You and Captain Collison. We amputated both of Private Sanborn's legs well above the knee. He will live."

"I'll tell the captain," I said. "Best you go now. He's pretty down about it."

"Is that a fact?" Cooke said. He had his dark tunic on, but his trouser-legs were heavily splattered with blood. He would have a second pair, I thought. These would have to be thrown away. After the second battle, he'd just have to make do.

Cooke looked like a man who has seen his own corpse. His eyes seemed to be staring through me, to a point on the distant horizon. He did not say anything for a minute. Then he said, "Well, I guess he would be. You and he led the boy down there, after all." He looked into my face, a little defiantly, and then turned and walked away.

I went back into the tent. Roley had not moved, nor touched his food. "You should eat, Captain," I said.

"No, thanks, Willie," he said. "You eat it. Shouldn't go to waste." I had some of it. Jack came in. We'd been told that the Grenadiers, having missed the fighting, were going to do all-night guard duty. For once, I could sleep straight through. There was a fire outside our tent, as usual, and Jack set up a coal-oil lamp over the tent entrance. A cold sleet was beginning to fall. Jack looked at me, and I nodded, and he lit the lamp, then rolled himself up in his blankets without saying a word to Roley. I pulled my blankets up over myself, but I did not go to sleep. I watched Roley, who was simply sitting, smoking, staring out at the dying fire and the night.

Finally, I said, "About Sanborn..."

Roley raised his hand a little, to cut me off. "I heard," he said. "I never thought he'd die, anyway." He was silent for a while and then he said, "Did you ever meet Sanborn's girlfriend? Polly? Pretty little thing with yellow hair and a loud laugh?"

"I think I saw her at the railroad station in Toronto," I said.

"I wonder," Roley said, with surprising bitterness, "how she'll like him now."

"Oh, well," I said. "Women will amaze you every time. They're faithful in love, you know, like our moms are."

"Are they?" Roley said. "Are they so?" He turned around to look at me. There were dark blotches under his eyes. His greying hair fell over his forehead. "They must be awful different from men, then, mustn't they?" I did not say anything. "All the same," he finally said. "Little Polly struck me as kind of a fun-loving girl. I wouldn't think she'd be as interested in Jimmy Sanborn as she was before, not now that his pecker hangs down past the bottoms of his legs."

I made a big production of rolling my blankets around me and putting my head down, but I did not go to sleep, at least not for a long while. I was concerned for Roley. Finally, I went to sleep. I awoke a long time later. It had started to snow, and the fire had died. Roley, however, had not moved at all. He was still sitting there, just staring out the door of the tent.

Alice

The wind screamed at my window last night. Like something alive, like a man in mortal pain and fear.

I finally just sat up. I tried to pray, but I have nothing to pray to.

So I just said, Mercy, Mercy, Mercy.

SAINT CRISPIN'S DAY

XI

When I awoke the next morning, the ground was covered with heavy snow. I lay there for a while, listening to our men cursing and expostulating as they fought their way through it to the chuckwagon.

Finally, I got out of my blankets. It was incredibly cold. Jack was smoking his pipe, still rolled up in his blankets like a Bedouin. His thin face was dark with frustration. He had disinterred his fur hat and jammed it back on his bald head. "Back to the past, Willie," he said in a low voice. "Freeze our asses off, all over again." Roley lay as still as a corpse in one corner of the tent. Just before we went to the chuckwagon, Jack and I put our blankets over him.

The food was scanty and bad. Each man got one egg, some bread, and some coffee which would be cold by the time we sat down to drink it. The mess sergeant, after some astonishingly graphic physiological suggestions as to what our men could do with their complaints, became more respectful when Jack and I appeared. Calling us "gentlemen," he explained that the army was already running out of provisions, and it seemed doubtful that any could get through from Clarke's Crossing if the storm continued. We ate out in the cold, so that we would not wake Roley. Theoretically, it was no doubt a court-martial offence for an officer to sleep all day, but Jack and I had both seen the condition he had been in. We were literally afraid to wake him.

Jack and I ate that wretched meal in silence. Then we walked around the camp, and back up to the coulee, where a corporal's guard of men still kept watch in case some suicidal Métis ran up the side of it, and took a shot at us. As we came back to our tent, Major Buchan walked up to us. His red face was even redder in the cold. "How's Roley?" he said.

"All right," Jack said, carefully.

"Look, Lieutenant Price," Buchan said, "I know he sort of caved in after yesterday. Don't blame him, either. But Middleton has called a meeting of all officers for three o'clock. You've got to get Roley up and to that meeting, or the old man will take a shit in his pants."

Jack and I had to get inside anyway before we froze to death. We went into the tent. Roley still lay like a stone. After a minute, Jack went over and shook him, and called his name. Roley shot up immediately, looking uneasily at the two of us. "Jack, Willie," he said. "Christ, how long have I been asleep?"

"It's eleven-thirty in the morning," I said.

"Good God," he said, smiling. "They'll shoot me for dereliction of duty. Anything happening?"

"No," I said. "The enemy are long gone, but we're still too scared to go down in that coulee. There's snow all over the God damn place. It's as cold as January. We're running out of food. And Middleton has called an officers' conference for three o'clock."

"Good," Roley said. "Wonderful. Back to sub-normal, in other words." He got up and got out his razor. I watched him as he peered into the shaving mirror which we had stuck to the centre-pole of our tent. He looked almost like the old Roley. But his face was still very white, his hands shook a little, and there were dark pockets under his eyes.

The officers' meeting was a joke. Middleton was very red in the face. His hands trembled. He called the battle "a minor tactical reverse." And he pompously announced that he had re-thought our entire strategy. Now we would make a wide circuit around Batoche, and link up at Prince Albert with the North-West Mounted Police, whose skills as scouts and light cavalry seemed to have just dawned on him.

Afterward, in our tent, Major Buchan lit a Havana cigar, and looked around at Roley, Jack and me with his expressionless eyes dark in his big, cold face. He blew out a cloud of expensive-smelling smoke. "Middleton's lost his nerve," he said. "He's an old man. He's been working superhuman hours for weeks. He knows he's dealing with men who never fired a shot in anger 'till yesterday. He damn near stumbled into a massacre. He's afraid the men will crack if the enemy attacks us now. We are running out of provisions, and the God damn winter has come back."

He blew out another mouthful of smoke, and looked around the tent again. "Although, to be fair, Middleton's not a bad old duffer. I think he was genuinely shocked at all the bleeding yesterday. He had greatly underestimated the enemy. He still hasn't got up the nerve to send anyone down into the main part of the ravine, but it looks like the enemy's losses were minimal. I've seen one or two dead. And that fellow you shot, Willie, is still hanging around in his bush."

Buchan stayed and had some cold food with us. The snow was still blowing. After he left, we all wrapped ourselves up in all the blankets we had and lay down to sleep. Tonight, our men and the Winnipeg Rifles were back doing their share of picket duty. That meant that every couple of hours Roley would wake me up so that I could stagger around and check each man on sentry duty. In fact, there was no longer any danger of our sentries falling asleep. Yesterday had shown them what the enemy could do. Some of them had realized that but for a lucky chance, all of us would be dead, wounded or captured by now.

Still hanging around in his bush. I did not want to think about the boy I'd killed, hanging in the snow-covered branches. No real soldier should have been thinking of him at all. I kept thinking of how cold *he* was, and then of his mother, wandering all that day from one veteran of the battle to another. Had they seen her Jean? *I am so worried about Jean.* Outside, the wind continued to scream at me. For a long time, I could not go to sleep.

* * *

If ever there was a demoralized army, it was our part of the North-West Field Force, in the days after the Battle of Fish Creek. There was no more nonsense about sending half of what remained of us back across the river. We would stick together from now on.

Not for two days did Middleton get up the nerve to order men down into the coulee to retrieve two of our dead, who still lay frozen and unattended in the snow. Some of the Winnipeg men wept with frustration when they saw their friends finally dragged up from that awful place. Four Métis dead, including the man I had killed, were brought up too, and dumped unceremoniously into an unmarked grave.

On April 27, the burials started, with an impressive show of British-style bugling and drumming, presided over by Middleton and a solemn-looking Lord Melgund. The last man to die was Lieutenant Swinford from Winnipeg, on April 30. The snow melted, and a pale version of spring came back, but the wounded went nowhere.

Every day, Roley, Jack and I went to see our wounded men, all except Sanborn, who refused to talk to Roley or me. When we entered the tent, he turned his head to the wall and would not look at us. Jack talked to him each day. "He blames you both," Jack told us, after the first conversation, "blames you because he thinks you ran out on him during the operation."

"I did," Roley said. "Willie didn't. I did. I ran out on him. Nothing truer in this world." He stared down at his boots, and Jack and I said nothing.

Middleton's nerves were indeed in shreds. He threw the correspondent for the *Toronto Globe* right out of the camp, because the young man had dared to write a dispatch to his paper criticizing Middleton's tactics. I was there when the banished correspondent climbed into a wagon, and angrily shook his fist at Middleton's tent. "Good luck to you, Lieutenant," he yelled, as the wagon clattered away. "You'll need it, with old fuss and feathers in charge of your destiny!"

Our friend Sutter, of Boulton's Scouts, had made several patrols in the direction of Batoche. He and some of his pals had surveyed the place with binoculars, then run like hell when the Métis spotted them and came out in pursuit.

"They've got flags flying all over the place," Sutter said. "The flag Riel used at Winnipeg in '70, with a fleur-de-lis and a shamrock on it. All it needed was a white Yankee star, and it would have had all our enemies, all on one flag. Also, a blue flag, with a thing like an 'eight' lying on its side in white. And a blue battle flag, weird-looking thing, with what looks like a hand and a wolf's head on it. God damn half-breed flags."

"The 'eight' lying on its side is the symbol for infinity," I said. "It's supposed to symbolize the Métis going on forever."

Roley spat angrily on the ground. "Oh, it's the symbol for *infinity,* is it?" he said. "I never even knew there was one. But the '*savages*' apparently do."

"That's not the worst of it," Sutter said. "It gets worse. Am I a prophet or am I not? Now, I ask you. Because they are fortifying Batoche, like I said they would. They are digging trenches, and tunnels and gun pits all around the God damn place. Way more intricate than the improvised gun pits down in the coulee. Beautiful workmanship. There'll be nothing to see. Invisible men, firing at us. No targets for your volleys, no targets for your cannons, except what you can make out of the fog of gunsmoke."

"But," Roley said, "after all, they know we are coming after them, and yes, with cannons. We can surround them. Do they think they can hold us off forever?"

"Well, first of all, we *can't* surround them," Sutter said. "You'll see when you get there. Their position is too huge for this little force to surround. There's villages on both the east and west banks. You'd need thousands of men to surround it. The Métis main body is on the east bank. The old man, with inexperienced troops, will have to go straight at it from the south, right through those rifle pits."

Sutter stretched, and scratched his thigh. "In fact, we're caught in a kind of a trap. Middleton doesn't trust his own men. He knows how green they are. If Middleton tries to overrun their positions, we'll lose a hell of a lot of men. Middleton is afraid the men will crack if the losses get too heavy. So then, he'll proceed with caution. But that way, we probably won't break through. If the 'breeds can hold us off for any length of time, my guess is Middleton will lose his nerve and go back to Qu'Appelle to wait for reinforcements, giving Riel the chance to raise every Indian and half-breed in the North-West against us. Or, if they can cause enough casualties, they may counter-attack from their prepared positions and try to wipe us out. Whatever they do, you won't forget it, of that I'm sure."

The circuitous march to Prince Albert was now off. A steamboat called the *Northcote* was coming on the South Saskatchewan from the west (it had sailed the day before the battle). On it would be men from the Midland Battalion, who had come west after us. And, glory, hallelujah! also on board the *Northcote* would be Second Lieutenant Arthur Howard, of the Connecticut National Guard, and one of his Gatlings. After this, presumably we would march on Batoche.

Day after day, the *Northcote's* arrival was expected, and day after day we were disappointed. The river was low. As soon as the melt-off from the Rockies started flowing through, the *Northcote* would arrive.

The medical officers couldn't properly treat the terrible wounds made by the Métis muzzleloaders and shotguns. Finally, Middleton ordered stretchers made from the hides of slaughtered cattle, and the wounded were loaded into wagons, which set out for Saskatoon. I watched as they left. Some of Boulton's Scouts rode as an escort. The men cursed and groaned as the wagons jounced over the rutted ground. Company Four's Private Shavers reared up in his wagon. He had been hit by buckshot in the side, and his blood-soaked red tunic was gone. In the spring sunshine, he was wearing only his grey under-tunic. Blood had soaked through one side of it. He gave me a resplendent salute, and I returned it. "Good luck, Lieutenant," he shouted. "I'm well out of it." I shouted good luck at him. "Thank you," he yelled, as the wagon jounced away. "If you have a choice between having your nuts blown off or your head, Lieutenant, I'd choose your head. It may spoil your career as a scholar, but you'll still screw like a mink!" There were coughs and snorts of laughter from the wretched men in the wagons.

Roley had gone down to make one last attempt to speak to Sanborn. "I know what happened to him can never be made right," he said, "but I hate to part from him this way." I offered to go with him but he just shook his head silently. So I watched him as he set out for the hospital tents, trailing pipe smoke, with his jaunty, slightly rolling stride. He had almost regained the man he had been. He went into Sanborn's tent and two minutes later came out again.

He came back with a ghastly, dark face, walking very slowly. When he sat down beside me, his face was terrible. He seemed to have shrunken into himself. His features looked crumpled and drained, as if he had been ill or had gone without food for a long time. It occurred to me that I was having a glimpse of what he would look like as an old man. I sat beside him in silence for at least ten minutes. I did not move, nor did he.

During that interval, Roley and I looked out over the camp. Gangs of cursing, sweating men were shoveling drainage ditches for the snow-melt water that still lay everywhere. Other men laboured around the huge pens of horses. The dark riverbank rose in the distance. Men were lying in front of their tents, apparently asleep. On the east side of the encampment, nine men from the Winnipeg Rifles were having a baseball game with nine Grenadiers. There was loud cheering, the dark-coated fielders were falling farther and farther back, and red-coated men were tearing around the bases. Some Grenadier had apparently hit a grand-slam home run.

Roley and I sat for the longest time, looking at this tableau. I carefully avoided glancing in his direction. I could feel his despair. Finally, he turned to look at me. There were tears in his eyes. "He cursed at me," Roley said. "He cursed at me and called me a coward." Then he got up and went into the tent. He did not come out again until almost suppertime.

* * *

The men's attitudes toward their leaders had changed. Before the battle, everybody had said that Middleton was a "seasoned veteran." That was what we wanted to believe. After the battle, the men regarded him as a joke. He was "the old fart," or "General Gasbag." Rumours swept the camp that Middleton and Melgund were going to send for British regulars, to do the job that Canadians could not. This infuriated everybody.

Roley's situation was different. All of our men had witnessed the impetuous charge into the coulee which killed Nolan and maimed Sanborn. Some of our men had seen Roley break down outside the hospital tent, and everyone had heard of it. Nobody but Sanborn questioned his courage. I think that the men all liked Roley even more, after he showed his horror and pity at what had happened to one of them.

After Fish Creek, any room filled with Company Four men would have warmed up like kindling when Roley Collison walked into it. But the attitudes of some of the men had changed. Not all of them. Many still were ready to follow him into hell. Jack Price was one of those, and indeed Colour Sergeant Quinn had to physically restrain Jack from attacking a young private whom he had overheard making slighting comments about Roley's ability to command.

Certainly, I liked him more than ever. But I remembered Arthur Howard's words when we were walking away from that alley in Winnipeg. *Man with Roley's disposition can be a hero, make heroes of others. Or, he can get all his men killed, deader than shit.*

Roley was a sensitive man. He knew that things had changed. One day he asked me to go for a stroll with him down to the riverbank. The sky was a very light shade of blue, like watercolour. The snow was gone, and the weather was almost hot. We walked along the greening riverbank.

"Willie," Roley said at last. He was scuffing at the ground with a long stick he'd picked up. "Willie." I looked at him. Finally he stopped, and with a kind of irresolute gesture threw the stick into the river. Then he turned around and faced me. "Sanborn called me a coward. Is that what the men think?"

"Of course not," I said. "Sanborn was just bitter, that's all."

"No, I know that," Roley said. "Of course he was. Miracle if he wasn't. But what I meant was, will the men still follow me?"

"To hell and back again," I said.

He laughed and clapped me on the shoulder. "Good for you, Willie," he said. "Jesus, what would I do without you and Jack? Sometimes, particularly since the battle, I feel just lost. I feel like resigning the captain's commission, becoming a private. I'd be a pretty good private. Only you can't just quit in the middle of everything." He stared out over the rushing river. "God, God, what did I think I was doing, commanding men to their destruction? I don't know anything about soldiering or tactics or *anything*."

"You know as much as the rest of us," I said.

He smiled. "True," he said. "The fact is, I don't think the men will follow me to hell and back again, not any more. Nice of you to say so, but I don't think it. But I know you and Jack would, and I'd follow you or him to the same destination. You can't know how much that means to me." He looked at me with an odd, sympathetic expression. "I don't have a brother or sister, you know. My little brother Bob died when he was twelve, of diphtheria. My mother never got over it. Sometimes I feel like you and Jack are my brothers." He had turned red. "God, listen to this. Get out the violins."

I said nothing. The truth was that I had followed him down into that coulee out of something akin to love. Now, although I still liked Roley very much, I knew, as the men did, that he knew no more about being a captain than we did. I also was determined that, whatever became of Riel and his rebellion, Willie Lorimer was going to get back to his Alice, with no missing legs or other even more significant body parts. I would do what I had to do, and no more.

Roley abruptly turned and started marching back to the camp, and I had to run fast to catch up to him.

* * *

There was one incident which sticks in my mind. A day or so after May 1, Roley, Jack and I were sitting in dark silence, sullenly blowing out clouds of tobacco smoke, when the tent flap opened and Major Buchan came in. He had something for Four Company to do. North of the coulee, north of the farm which the gunners had reduced to kindling during the battle, were several other farmsteads. They had been reported as deserted. Now, wood smoke was ascending from one of the chimneys. Lieutenant Colonel Portman had ordered Buchan to find out whether the enemy was using that farmstead. "Nine chances out of ten, Roley," Buchan said, his big face perspiring, "it's just the poor bloody Frenchman and his family come back to the only home they've got. But we have to make a patrol and find out. And Portman specified that Company Four was to make the patrol. You, Roley, are to lead the patrol. He wasn't particularly pleasant about you."

"Never stops being a pain in the ass, does he?" Roley said, with a shrug.

We selected thirty men from our company, and set out for the farmstead. As we descended into the ravine and waded through the cold waters of Fish Creek, I looked around at the underbrush and shuddered. A few days earlier, gunsmoke would have blossomed from rifle and shotgun barrels all around us. Most of us would have been dead or wounded before we knew what was happening. We would have been annihilated, if Dumont's battle plan had worked, and it had not worked only because of a fluke.

On the other side of the coulee though, it was spring again. New green grass was coming up. Gophers squeaked and ran around in it. We could see the greyish-white smoke which had alarmed Portman, behind and to the right of the burned farmstead. Two thirds of the way to the wrecked farm, Roley stopped our column and sent ten skirmishers under Colour Sergeant Quinn ahead of us, toward the wood smoke. The rest of us sat down in the middle of the meadow, and smoked, and drank water from our canteens. The sky was immense; a few fluffy clouds chased each other overhead. I lay back in the grass like a boy and looked up at them. I was sweating steadily into the hot scarlet tunic, which was now faded in places from being washed, torn in others. I started to laugh. War was hell, indeed. Up to the day before, I had been freezing to death. Now, I was broiling.

Somebody was shouting. It was Quinn, standing on a rise about five hundred yards away. "I think that means it's safe," Roley said, laughing. "Or else we're in deadly peril of our lives, and he's trying with his last breath to warn us. Anyway, let's go." We got our column up and marched eastward around the burned farmstead. Quinn beckoned us on. When we caught up to him, he pointed down to a little cabin with two smaller buildings around it, set in a small, low meadow of its own, with a minor creek meandering past the rear. Smoke was pouring up from the cabin's chimney.

"Just the settler and his family," Quinn said. "A French 'breed, apparently. They took off in a wagon as soon as they saw us."

Without waiting for orders, Company Four broke ranks and went tumbling down the hill, shouting and laughing. Roley grinned, and we followed our men. Many of them crowded into the little cabin. At last they were going to see how the other half lived, the half that was trying to kill us. "No looting!" Roley roared. "No vandalism!" When the crowd in there had thinned out, Roley, Jack and I went in. We were the only men in the cabin.

The Métis settler's wife had tried hard to brighten up the interior of that little room. The rough floor was spotless, and it had a badly worn red carpet in the kitchen area. The curtains in the front window were bright blue, and they fluttered in the spring breeze. I went over and looked at them. The woman had obviously made them herself. They were rather crudely sewn, but they fitted the little window perfectly. The glass in the window was thick and cloudy. The wife had hung bright-coloured blankets on the rough log walls of the cabin, red on one side, blue on the other, to try to make her home prettier. On one side of the cabin hung a huge Roman Catholic religious picture. The Virgin Mary, rays coming from her haloed head, held the haloed baby Jesus. I thought of Nolan. If I'd known how to cross myself, I'd have done it, for him, even if it made Jack fall dead with an apoplectic fit. On the other wall was a sentimental landscape in lurid colours of red and green. The woman had cut off the back cover of a catalogue, or cut an illustration out of a magazine. Her husband had made a crude frame for it. Beside it was a rough drawing of Jesus at the last supper, which looked like a child might have made it. Jack stalked out.

The wood stove was hot. Beside it were two frying pans in which the woman had been frying pieces of beef and potatoes. They were still sizzling. One of the men had taken the pans off the stove, I suppose because the food was starting to burn. On the kitchen table lay their china, pink and blue, chipped in places, but spotlessly clean. There was a knife, fork and spoon beside four plates.

"Look at this," Roley said. Beside the table was a smaller stand, almost like a lectern. On it lay a very old, worn-looking Bible. Roley had opened it, and was looking at an illustration near the front. I looked over his shoulder and saw a crude drawing of a hulking man, carrying a club, standing over the sprawled, naked body of another. Both men had prodigious beards. At the bottom of the page was a caption: *Cain et Abel.*

"Cain and Abel, is that what that means?" Roley said.

"Yes," I said.

He looked slowly around the little room. "Savages," he said contemplatively. "That's what Lord Melgund called them. I noticed the other day His Lordship is now saying 'semi-civilized people.'" He walked over, and stared down for a minute at the burned slices of beef and potato in the frying pans. His jaw muscles were working a little. Then he said, "You educated men sure have an endless supply of big words." He smiled, and walked back out into the sunshine.

Some of our men, forgetting completely that they were part of a military unit, had started strolling back to the encampment in groups of five or six. Jack and Sergeant Quinn, yelling, were pursuing them and herding them back to the cabin so that we could form into a column.

Some of our men were looking at a plough which lay beside one of the outbuildings. Roley and I walked over to them. "Phil," he said to one of the men, "you came from a farm originally. Is this fellow's equipment any good?"

"Yes," Phil said. "Yes it is, Captain. A little out of date, but he's done a good job of home repairing it. Done some welding, somehow." Roley nodded. Phil hesitated for a minute. Then he said, "Captain? Maybe you and the lieutenant can answer a question some of us have. It looks like these people are just small farmers, mostly. Why in the world would little people like this deliberately start a war with the government?"

Roley turned red. He walked over and poked his finger, hard, into the boy's chest. "Look, Phil," he said. "Shut up that talk and tell your friends to shut it up, too. That kind of talk could get you court-martialled. They *did* start a war, I guess because Riel told them to, and people have died. Now we're here to finish the war. That's all you have to think about, or me either. Got it?"

The boy was bright red with mortification and anger. "Yes, *sir,*" he said.

In a few minutes, the column formed up and started the march back to the encampment. Roley closed the door of the cabin, and then he and I strolled along behind the men. I still hadn't learned to march, anyway. We walked along in silence, like two old friends walking through a park. Roley seemed depressed, and thoughtful. When we were almost at the coulee, he looked up and caught my eye. "There's too much of that kind of talk," he said. "This thing isn't over, for God's sake. It's barely begun. These men are going to be called on to fight a lot more, and some of them are going to die. That kind of talk has to be stopped and stopped cold. Now, you report to me, Willie, any talk you hear of that kind from any of our men, and I'll God damn well deal with it." I said that I would. We went on, but Roley did not seem to be very happy with what he had just said. We walked back the rest of the way to our tent in dead silence.

Alice

I bought a map of the Districts of Assiniboia and Saskatchewan, and pinned it up in my room. I also bought some crayons. I con-

sult the newspapers, and mark down the advances, the battles, where Willie is. The map looks like something that might hang in General Middleton's tent.

I'm not sure why, but it makes me feel closer to my boy. Apparently, though, keeping track of a military campaign is not regarded as a fit occupation for a female. This afternoon, I saw Father coming out of my room. He didn't see me. I went in and found that he had taken my crayons.

Somehow, this idiotic piece of paternalism infuriated me more than anything else he has done. I went down to the library, where he was just sitting down with some men from his firm. He got up, with an uneasy smile on his face, and said, "Well. Here is our little general." They all laughed.

For the first time in my life, I knew exactly what to do with him. I did not say a word. I just held out my hand, palm open. He tried to smile. Then his face turned as red as Willie's coat. The others stopped laughing, and turned a similar hue. Finally, he fished in his pocket and handed the crayons to me.

I went out without a word. And slammed the door.

The newspapers say we got whipped at Fish Creek. The government pretends it's a victory, but no one believes it. Father is positively gloating. So Mother gloats, too. It is fashionable in their circles to say that the militia can never win, not against experienced frontiersmen.

Tonight, at dinner, Father was holding forth on the subject. "Our poor, stumbling little toy soldiers, in their silly uniforms," he said. "Sacrificial lambs, that's all they are. Sacrificed to the manipulative greed of a reactionary government. I feel sorry for them, I really do." Mother simpered.

And I lost my temper with both of them. I threw down my fork and stood up. "Father," I said, "I'm very pleased to hear you say you feel sorry for them. I rather hoped you would, since the only man I care for is out there, stumbling in his silly uniform. If they are all massacred, including Willie, do me a favour, and hold back your gloating in my presence."

And I walked out. Before I got to the door, I turned around. They *both looked like I had hit them in the face with the leg of lamb. "And by the way," I said, "I hate this war, and I was opposed to it from the start. Just so you know."*

Later I heard Father pontificating to Mother. "Young girls," he said, "by virtue of certain physical peculiarities are given to fits of hysteria. That's all it was."

As the Yankees say, oh, brother.

Damn the both of them.

And—almost—damn Willie Lorimer, too. Because his letter after Fish Creek hid more than it disclosed. He's well, he's safe, he's well-fed, everything is wonderful. He was never in the slightest danger, and he never will be. Evidently a war is a lot like a picnic, except with flags and guns.

I know he's lying. Something awful happened to him in that battle. It's clear between every line; it shouts at me from every word.

Oh, Willie, Willie, do you think I'm too foolish to hear the truth?

XII

On the morning of May 5, I woke before reveille to an indescribable racket. Men were cheering, bugles were blowing, one of the cannons went off, and in the distance, some kind of loud tooting noise resounded endlessly. Roley sat up and reached for his pipe and pouch of tobacco. "Jesus Christ," he said. "What now? Riel has surrendered? Queen Victoria has arrived to review the troops? *What*, for God's sake?"

The tent flap opened, and Jack came in, with an uncharacteristic grin on his face. "You'll never guess," he said.

"Grover Cleveland has just appeared and gone to bed with Middleton," I suggested.

"More useful than that," Jack said, still beaming. "The God damn boat has finally come. The *Northcote*. Soldiers hanging all over it like monkeys, so they say. The Midland battalion."

Roley was pulling on his uniform, and motioned impatiently for me to do the same. "And, please, God," he said. "A Gatling gun."

The three of us strolled down the coulee's edge to where Fish Creek flowed into the South Saskatchewan. The men were shouting and laughing like schoolboys on a field day. I wondered if anyone had remembered to keep up a guard as our whole force straggled, unarmed, down to the riverbank, over a distance of a third of a mile. I doubted it.

I think I expected the *Northcote* to look like a Mississippi riverboat. It did too, in the same way that a catfish resembles a whale. The bottom tier of the little steamboat sloshed lopsidedly into the muddy waters of the Saskatchewan. Halfway up was a second tier, a balcony which ran all round the ship. On top, the captain's glassed-in pilothouse reared ponderously into the air. The boat sagged, and it stunk. "Scow" was the most polite expression I ever heard directed at the *Northcote*, particularly by anyone who ever had to ride on the damn thing for more than a few minutes.

The men of the Midland Battalion had been stuck on that bloody boat for two weeks, and they couldn't wait to get off. Shouting and cheering in their scarlet tunics, they poured down the rickety gangplank. Some of them manhandled bulky boxes of ammunition and supplies down onto the riverbank. One lunatic, gesturing exuberantly, jumped, rifle in hand, from the second level. We all waited expectantly for him to come up. He didn't. He'd sunk to his knees in the mud. Some of his pals, roaring with laughter, waded and dived in and dragged him up, choking and spluttering, and a second later one of them retrieved the rifle. Middleton and Lord Melgund, sober and dignified in their immaculate blue uniforms, shook their heads sadly.

There was a roar of applause. Striding down the gangplank came a familiar figure, looking over his shoulder anxiously at his precious Gatling. Canadian gunners were carefully easing it down toward the muddy riverbank.

Arthur Howard jumped with palpable relief onto the grassy shoreline. His blue Union officer's uniform was stained and faded. Middleton and Melgund and the staff officers crowded forward to greet him. Because Arthur had gone straight on to Swift Current from Qu'Appelle, they had not yet met this legendary figure. Salutes and solemn handshakes were exchanged, and then Middleton and Melgund had a long conversation with Arthur. He kept gesturing expansively toward the Gatling. Obviously, his infatuation with the thing had not diminished.

Then he saw us. He waved, and a few minutes later he disentangled himself from the two Englishmen and strode over to us. Arthur had lost weight. Under his tan, his thin boyish face was almost unhealthy-looking. But he grinned and pounded Roley, Jack,

Sergeant Quinn and me on the back and called us "God damn lob-
sterbacks," and "perfidious redcoats." We were glad to see him, too,
and even gladder to see his gun.

* * *

That afternoon, by popular demand, Arthur set the Gatling
up on a bluff overlooking the river and gave a demonstration. We
all crowded around to look at it first. For an instrument of mass
slaughter it certainly was beautiful, with gleaming brass barrels set
high on a massive gun carriage. Arthur was back in his Barnum
and Bailey mode. "Gentlemen!" he roared, as hundreds of us stood
around him in a semi-circle, Middleton and the other brass hats
right up front. "The new and improved Gatling gun is the most important innovation in infantry warfare! As I turn the firing crank
forward, the multiple barrels of this weapon revolve, along with a
lock for each barrel. The forward motion of the lock puts the cartridges in the chambers of the barrel and closes the breech. Each
barrel fires in turn. After the shot is fired, the backward motion of
the lock extracts the spent cartridge case. As the crank is turned,
there are always cartridges going through various phases of being
loaded and more in various phases of being extracted. The process
is continuous. As long as the gun is fed with cartridges, loading,
firing, and extracting of cartridges goes on automatically and continuously. The gun is capable of firing twelve hundred rounds per
minute." There was a sigh of disbelief. Arthur looked proud. "The
weapon can stop an infantry charge cold, and if it fires upward, can
rain down a hail of destruction on men behind fortifications! The
Gatling gun is truly the weapon of the future!"

He aimed the thing at a flock of ducks about two hundred yards
up the river, and opened fire. The racket was incredible. The air
filled with grey gunsmoke. The stretch of water where the ducks sat
turned into a sea of plumes of water shooting upwards. Quacking
with agitation, the ducks took flight, and I actually saw one shot
right out of the sky as the hail of bullets came at them. There was
a roar of applause, and Arthur bowed, like a performer getting a

standing ovation. Middleton was the first to turn away. He did not look elated. As he walked past, he smiled sadly at me. "Not much future for the kind of war they taught me," he said, and walked away.

As we walked back to our tent, Jack was bubbling with enthusiasm. "That'll show the sons of bitches," he said. "That'll show the sharpshooting sons of bitches."

"Yes, I suppose it will," Roley said thoughtfully. "It'll keep their heads down, at the least. At any rate, it'd keep mine down. But let's not get carried away with the damn thing. They'll never charge it. They're much too smart for that. He can rain down bullets all he wants, but when we don't even know where they are, like we didn't know two weeks ago..."

Jack was shaking his head. He wanted to believe in the Gatling. We all did.

* * *

That night we had a feast of roast beef, to celebrate the arrival of Arthur and his gun and the reinforcements from the Midland Battalion. The meat was underdone and as tough as leather, and the potatoes were half-cooked, but they at least had butter on them. There was even a kind of pie, composed mostly of soggy pastry and tinned raspberry jam. It tasted wonderful to us and, I think, even better to Arthur.

He took out his pocket flask and toasted us. "Jesus," he said. "Jesus Christ. Two weeks on that garbage scow, that shit-boat from hell! The food was awful. The thing nearly sank, it was so overloaded. Everybody stank. There was something wrong with the food or the water, and most of us got some kind of dysentery, or the next thing to it. Don't let me get started while you're eating. The scow's captain is an old man named Sheets. Good name for him. *Claims* he was a Mississippi riverboat pilot. More likely the latrine cleaner."

"What's happening in the west?" I said. "We heard yesterday that Colonel Otter fought a pitched battle with the Indians."

"Yes, he did, Willie," Arthur said. "Cut Knife Hill. It was a near-disaster. Otter attacked at dawn, Custer-style, and then it went to hell, Custer-style. One of my Gatlings was there, with my Canadian gunners. Catastrophe. Whole column, lucky to escape with their lives. The Indians have seized the stores and ammunition at Green Lake. Inspector Dickens and his men abandoned Fort Pitt without a fight. His illustrious father could have written a comic novel about it, funnier than *The Pickwick Papers.*"

"So, we have yet to win a battle," I said.

Arthur nodded vigorously. "Unless you call what happened here two weeks ago a victory," he said.

"Ha," Roley said, without any humour at all.

* * *

The next day, there was a general meeting of officers at three p.m. We all filed dolefully into the general's oversized tent. There was a fog of tobacco smoke. Most of the officers stared unenthusiastically at Middleton. They were tired, as tired as total inactivity can make you, and worried. We had sat on our asses for two weeks. How much longer?

At the front of the tent stood the entire crew of senior officers. Portman gave a disdainful glance at Roley, Jack and me. Middleton's red face was suffused with confidence. Beside him stood the newly-arrived Lieutenant Colonel Arthur Williams of the Midland Battalion, his handsome face grave, his moustache impeccably groomed. He looked like a cross between an idealized redcoat officer in *The Illustrated London News*, getting ready to draw his sword, and an artist's model for the most expensive London-made suits.

"Gentlemen," Middleton said, impressively, "our long wait is over. You will be pleased to hear that I have made a personal reconnaissance with Boulton's cavalry, as far as Batoche. I no longer fear the possibility of another ambush. We have restored stocks of food, water, and ammunition, and we are amply reinforced by Colonel Williams and his gallant men. As well as by Lieutenant Howard, and his, ah, remarkable weapon." There was applause. "Gentlemen, inform your men. Our column marches tomorrow at six a.m." There was louder applause.

"We are going to attack frontally," Middleton said, "and destroy Riel's fortifications, then take his capital. Your immediate superiors will give you more detailed instructions. I have also given instructions for the fortification and arming of the *Northcote*. It will become a gunboat, from which Batoche will be shelled from the river." There was a snort from beside me. I looked over at Arthur. He was staring at his boots, and I had the impression that he was trying to keep from bursting out laughing.

After the meeting, outside Middleton's tent, Sutter the Scout caught my eye. "About that reconnaissance of Middleton's," he said. "I was there. On the way back, we came on a half-breed cabin. The poor bugger and his family ran off when they saw us. We went in, and there were all the plates on the table and a huge pot of the most wonderful-smelling beef stew I have smelled since I left my home in Virden. These French women must use some kind of spices in their cooking. Anyway, beef stew with potatoes, carrots, onions and some kind of great big dumplings floating around in it."

"Stop it," Roley said. "This is unnatural cruelty."

"All right, sorry," Sutter laughed. "Anyway, Middleton announced he was going to eat the damn stew. He actually sat down and put one of the serviettes in his shirt front. With a gut like his, he'd have annihilated the whole pot." Sutter started to snort with repressed laughter. His face was turning red. "Middleton had the first spoonful halfway to his mouth. Then one of French's Scouts, Don Parker, said, 'Gosh, General, that's horse meat, you know. That's what that is. Do you really mean to *eat* that?'" Sutter was gasping for breath, holding his side. "Well, Jesus Christ. Our general turned kind of a light green. Then he retreated out of there as fast as if Dumont had personally come in with a shotgun and shoved it up Middleton's ass. Off he rode, lickety-split. Then six of us, who know horse from beef, sat down and ate the whole damn thing. Don Parker ate three helpings. The best meal I'll ever have in this damn war." He burst out into loud guffaws. "None of us ate a crumb of that underdone banquet last night. We didn't need to."

Roley, Jack, Arthur and I strolled down to the river's edge. There was an immense racket of hammering and pounding. Soldiers were swarming all over the sides of the little boat. They were putting up layers of three-inch planks, backed by feed sacks, as armour. Some of the infantry regulars would be going on board, to fire volleys at Batoche, and Middleton intended, somehow, to mount a cannon on the bloody old scow.

"Well, Arthur?" Jack said, on the way back.

"I don't know, I don't know," Arthur said, with a grin. "I know the English love to use gunboats, but I sure never heard of one on the prairies before!"

Outside the newly-erected tents of the Midlanders, a semi-circle of them, and some other troops, too, were standing around. We went over. Lieutenant Colonel Williams was standing on a little table, fixing to make a speech to his men. That was predictable enough. Arthur Trefusis Heneage Williams was a Conservative Member of Parliament from Ontario, Tory Whip in the House, and widely suspected of wanting to be Prime Minister of the Dominion, one of these fine days. He liked to be called "the Squire of Penryn," after his family estate at Port Hope.

I am making him sound like an over-privileged ass. In fact, as some of us knew, he had undergone a lot of misfortune. His wife had been killed in a horrible accident on his estate. He had lost a lot of his money in foolish business transactions. Now he was re-building his life. He had gotten engaged to one of the richest girls in Canada. Whether or not he wanted to be Prime Minister, his flashing eye and dashing, gallant air had already made it clear that he wanted to be a war hero.

The Midlanders loved their colonel. Williams took kind and conscientious care of his men, just as Roley did, and they loved him. He was also a very brave man. Everybody grew to like him. I did too, even if he did look, act, and sound occasionally like a distinguished actor playing an officer. I've always felt really bad about what happened to him.

Now, he was in full oratorical flight. Williams had literally wrapped himself in the flag. He had a huge Union Jack draped over one shoulder, like a cape. He rehearsed the roots of the war ("the fanatical savagery of Riel") and the glories of the Empire ("the greatest Queen of the greatest domain in world history"). He referred glowingly to the United States of America—and few Conservative politicians ever did *that*—and to "the marvelous gun which can fire twelve hundred rounds per minute at our foes." At the end of it, he did something that impressed and astounded me, and convinced me that his future as a politician was unbounded. He got out a book, and quoted *Henry V*:

> *If we are marked to die, we are enough*
> *To do our country loss; and if to live,*
> *The fewer men, the greater share of honour.*

And he skipped over a little of the text, and then he said:

> *And Crispin Crispian shall ne'er go by,*
> *From this day to the ending of the world,*
> *But we in it shall be remembered;*
> *We few, we happy few, we band of brothers,*
> *For he today that sheds his blood with me*
> *Shall be my brother; be he ne'er so vile,*
> *This day shall gentle his condition;*
> *And gentlemen in England now abed*
> *Shall think themselves accursed they were not here,*
> *And hold their manhoods cheap whiles any speaks*
> *That fought with us upon Saint Crispin's day.*

There was a tremendous roar of applause. Williams grinned and brandished the Union Jack with one hand. "God bless you, boys!" he shouted, and I saw that he was as excited as his men. "We march on Batoche tomorrow!" This time, the roar was deafening.

We walked in thoughtful silence back to our tents. Roley was laughing and shaking his head. "Holy cat," Arthur said. "I heard Rutherford B. Hayes give a speech once, but it wasn't even a patch on that." He walked on a little in silence. "Actually," he said, "no one can turn the crank fast enough to fire that many rounds. Two or three hundred a minute is the best I can do. Just so you know." Jack looked crestfallen.

"What was that thing he quoted?" Roley said.

"It's Shakespeare," I said. "The outnumbered English army is about to go into battle against the French. The English king is trying to inspire his men."

"Shakespeare," Roley said, shaking his head. "Did the English win?"

"Of course they did," I said.

We had packing and preparation to do. I was going to write a long letter to Alice. We'd been told that a special post would carry letters back to Clarke's Crossing the next day. I had promised to transcribe letters for three men from the Grenadiers and four Midlanders who couldn't write very well. I doubted that there was a man in the camp who would not write, or arrange to have written, a letter to his sweetheart, his wife or his mother before the ending of the night.

That night in my dreams, Alice came to me again. But this time she did not hold my hand. I did not feel her warm breath on me, in the dream. Her voice was as cold and remote as the sighing prairie wind. "You weren't careful enough, Willie," she said. "You let yourself be careless."

Alice

I had a dream last night. I am never going to forget it.

Not long before I went to bed, my father and mother and I sat in the best parlour and had tea. I think my mother wants to make peace with me, after the scene at the dinner table. In his self-centred fashion, so does Father, if only to make his life more comfortable.

I am beginning to wonder if he has any other motivation.

We almost got through the tea without any trouble. But toward the end, Father enraged me all over again. Or scared me. There isn't much difference. He was actually trying to apologize for the scene at dinner. "It isn't that I don't care for Willie's safety," he said. "You must realize that, Alice."

I said I did.

"But," he said portentously, drawing on his cigar, "it's simply that what one reads of the half-caste people—the enemy, I mean--is so frightening." I started to say something, and he cut me off. "For example, the Sharps rifle. They have it. They used it for buffalo hunting." His voice was rising didactically, as it does whenever he wants to make a point. "The Sharps model 1869 rifle," he said portentously, "can hurl a huge lead cartridge with absolutely impeccable accuracy for nearly a thousand yards. It is said that death is almost instantaneous."

My mother was shaking her head desperately. Finally he got the message and he shut up. But it was too late. We finished our tea in miserable silence, and then I crawled off to bed.

I don't know how long I had been asleep when the dream came. Not long, I think. The dream was very vivid. There was bright light. I was lying in bed, on my back, and I knew that I was naked. Willie was crawling over the bed and rising up above me. He had no shirt on, and probably nothing below. I couldn't see. His arms and his chest were thin. His blond hair was hanging into his eyes and his eyes were shining. I think in any other place I would have laughed at the look on his face—strained, almost as if he were in pain.

But I did not laugh. I knew that Willie was going to make love to me, and that it was for the first time. I knew that his body was ready, the way men get. There was something like music singing in my ears, and it felt as if flames were burning on the surface of my skin. I know I cried out in the dream because his hands were touching me.

And he tried to reassure me. Although what he said makes no sense, I know that in the dream I understood. This is why we are, he said. This is why. And the music in my ears got louder. The flames on my skin burned brighter.

He bent down to kiss me and I cried out again with joy. And then suddenly he rolled violently off me. His elbow struck me hard on my *cheek, and I cried out a third time.*

I turned to look at him. I was starting to cry. You hurt me, Willie, I said. You hurt me.

And, in the way of dreams, he was not naked any more. He had his uniform on, even his boots. For some reason, I was looking at the top of his scarlet tunic. The top button was undone, but it was also just hanging by a thread. I looked and looked at the silver thread which held the button on. I would have to sew it back on. There were dead leaves just beneath it, on his chest.

And then I realized, in the dream, that I was trying to delay looking at his face. So I made myself look. The whole side of his face was covered in blood. It was still sticky, although it was drying. There was blood on the white sheet, lots of it. And I suddenly thought, he is cold. He is completely cold.

I opened my mouth to scream, but instead the voice of my father came to me, shatteringly loud, like the voice of some insane barker at a carnival: "The Sharps Model 1869 rifle can hurl a huge lead cartridge with absolutely impeccable accuracy for nearly a thousand yards. It is said that death is almost instantaneous." Then his voice went down to an insinuating whisper. "They have it," my father whispered. "They used it for buffalo hunting."

And then I did wake up, and then I did scream. I screamed loud and long, but not a soul heard me.

XIII

At six-thirty on the morning of May 7, 1885, the North-West Field Force finally marched north out of our encampment at Fish Creek. At the very beginning, we passed a stone cairn with a tall white-painted cross made of peeled poplar on top of it. That cairn marked the graves of the militiamen who'd died in the battle. As each segment of the column wheeled by, the men gave an "eyes right." Under that cairn were men they'd known, eaten with, traded preposterous jokes with. The officers saluted.

Mounted officers in the vanguard, the column clattered across the meadow toward the farm the artillery had burned, and past it. The day was magnificently warm and bright. Everywhere in the meadows were purple wild crocuses, the jaunty little bloom that the Métis called the Pasque flower.

After the reinforcements from the *Northcote*, we really were starting to look like an army. Middleton had over eight hundred troops, and enough teamsters to bring our numbers to over a thousand. Six hundred horses neighed, whinnied, and heaved through the green grass, hauling one hundred and fifty wagons. Four cannons pounded along, jouncing and glittering, their gunners running ahead to ensure that a wheel didn't fall into a hole in the ground. Arthur's beloved Gatling rattled along with the cannons, its bright brass barrels gleaming in the sunshine, its Yankee owner bounding along beside it like an anxious father teaching his son how to ride a bicycle. His acolytes, the Canadian regular artillerymen, charged along at his heels. They were as solicitous of the God damn Gatling as he was. The irregulars, the mounted Scouts, roamed ahead of us, around us, behind us, peering, sweating, into every grove of trees (leafy now) which might hide the enemy.

In the bright sunshine, our uniforms glowed. Behind Middleton and his staff officers came the Grenadiers, their red coats shining. Some wore their helmets. Some had put on their summer headgear, white kepis with white neck-cloths dangling behind, which made them look like so many French foreign legionaries who'd somehow strayed into Her Majesty's forces. Behind them was the newly-arrived Midland Battalion, in shining red, with their beloved Colonel Williams riding in the van. Then the guns of the regular artillery and the Winnipeg Field Battery, and Arthur and his Gatling. Then our whole train of supply wagons. Then the dark-coated Winnipeg Rifles, and bringing up the rear, good old Company Four, in its faded scarlet, and behind us the red-coated regular infantry.

I swung easily along beside Roley and Jack. All three of us puffed jauntily on pipes. The sound of marching feet, neighing horses, clattering wagons and gun carriages was deafening. The smells of sweat, horseshit, tobacco and hot metal were everywhere. It was a young man's dream of glory, and even my horrible memories of the battle could not keep me from succumbing to the dream all over again.

Middleton and the staff officers had roamed to the back of the column, and now they thundered past us on our right, returning to the column's head. Roley saluted, and one second later, so did Jack and I. Middleton returned our salute, gravely. Lord Melgund saluted us back by touching the brim of his African pith helmet with the tip of his riding crop, and so did white-bearded Lieutenant Colonel van Straubenzee. Van Straubenzee was a British veteran who had arrived on the *Northcote*. He was now commanding officer of the infantry. He also wore the white, shining African explorer's helmet. It evidently was the British notion of appropriate headwear for the prairies, direct, I suspected, from the most select shelves of Lock & Co. of London.

Somebody in the Grenadiers started to sing. It was a measure of the times, and the men, that the only song he could possibly have thought of to start with was somebody else's song. But the men at once joined in the singing, with deafening enthusiasm. Unlike a British column, we had no regimental band, but the familiar tune spread like wildfire, flashing from unit to unit, from man to man, for once perfectly on key:

> *God save our gracious Queen,*
> *Long live our noble Queen,*
> *God save the Queen.*
> *Send her victorious*
> *Happy and glorious,*
> *Long to reign over us,*
> *God save the Queen.*

Now, the songster in the Grenadiers couldn't be repressed. As soon as the singing and cheering had died down, he started roaring out a new song. This time we outdid ourselves. It may have been audible in Dakota, and we all would have hoped it was:

> *In days of yore, from Britain's shore,*
> *Wolfe, the dauntless hero, came*
> *And planted firm Britannia's flag*
> *On Canada's fair domain.*
> *Here may it wave, our boast, our pride*
> *And, joined in love together,*
> *The thistle, shamrock, rose entwine*
> *The Maple Leaf forever!*

At the end, there was a roar of cheering which sounded to me like ten thousand Canucks. Even if the Yankees didn't hear it, it may well have been audible in Batoche. And here came Lord Melgund from the front of the column on his high-stepping black horse. His perfectly waxed moustaches bristled. His grinning face was red with enthusiasm. He waved his preposterous white pith helmet at us, and we cheered louder than ever. When we quieted, he shouted,

"Good lads! Greatly appreciated by us British, if I may say so! Good for morale! Bloody good! However...er...perhaps time to put a lid on it! Need, here, for a certain amount of...er...circumspection!"

The men roared with laughter. Somebody yelled, "Three cheers for His Lordship!" The three cheers thundered into the crystalline blue-and-white sky, and roared back at us from the wooded horizons. Then, having shown in one go our adoration of everything English, and that no mere Englishman could make us do anything, we finally, obediently, shut up.

I found myself thinking of what Lord Melgund would be saying about us in the Carlton Club in London a year from now. There would be leather chairs, oaken paneling, and clouds of fine cigar smoke. A lot of older men with ruddy faces. "Rum lot of fellows," Melgund would say, "these Canadians. Most remarkable chaps. A bit barbaric, one might say. One company had a storekeeper for captain, shoestore clerk for lieutenant." Gales of laughter. "Mind you, fine chaps. Excellent raw material there. Simply the best. Splendid people, the colonials. No concept of discipline, of course, quite untrained, but loyal to a fault. British to the core." Everyone would look serious. Fine chaps, these colonials.

"Yankee officer, along for the ride," Melgund would say. "Even more extraordinary chap than the colonials. Confirmed my prejudices. My uncle Nicky was assigned to Washington during their civil war. Observed on both sides, actually. Quite liked the Southern officers. Rather like us; dashing, you know. Chivalric. But he didn't like the Yankees, the Northerners, that is. Commercial to the core, he said. This Howard chap was like that. Bit of a salesman for this wonderful gun of his. Made a commission on each bullet fired, I shouldn't wonder. Bit cold-blooded, too. Scientific detachment, don't you know. Not fighting for his country or any cause, you see. Just there to test out his bloody gun. Rather gave himself airs too, I thought."

And then they would order three more bottles of port.

In front of us, some of the Winnipeggers were peeling away from both sides of the column. After a while, they began to straggle back. I'd heard no firing; the settlers had run away. But I saw that the militia had looted the cabins they'd searched. They were festooned with furs they'd pilfered from storehouses, and with women's bright scarves they'd taken as a joke. One of them came over to me. He'd stolen three brightly-painted wooden toys which some Métis father had painstakingly made for his kids. There was a tiny, blue wooden cart with two wooden horses, a black-painted wooden pistol, and a little red wooden heart.

In that cabin we'd searched north of Tourond's Coulee, some anonymous trooper of our company had carefully taken some frying pans off the stove to try to prevent the food from burning. I wish that I could say that the whole North-West Field Force continued to live up to that lofty standard. I can't.

As we marched along, two of our Company Four men, shouting with laughter, peeled off and kicked in the door of a cabin to the right of the trail. A few seconds later, they were back. One of them, Private Evans, had a home-made doll he'd stolen from the cabin. The parents of the little Métis girl had painted a brightly-smiling face on the wooden head, and big blue eyes. Someone, probably the mother, had patiently cut out many dozens of strands of bright yellow, frizzy paper which had been carefully glued to the head to make a bright head of blonde hair.

Roley walked over to Evans. "What's that?" he said.

Evans laughed incredulously. "It's a doll, Roley," he said. "For my daughter. What in hell does it look like?"

"It looks," Roley said, and his face was reddening, "like you are taking something that doesn't belong to you." Evans started to say something, and Roley raised his hand, as if quieting an audience. *"God damn it!"* he roared. "We did not come here to steal from these people! *We are Canadian soldiers, not thieves!"* He was sweating profusely, and he hung his head down to get control of himself. Evans looked terrified. Roley looked up at him and, in a lesser but very loud voice, said, "Put it back. And if any man in this company steals anything else, I'll break his arm."

Roley stalked away. Two minutes after Evans replaced the doll, a laughing Winnipegger lagged back from the column, entered the house, and brought the doll out again. I continued to watch Roley, as shouting, laughing men of our column (but not Company Four) returned from pilfering the homes along our route.

Roley's face remained dangerously crimson with rage. He wanted to be Sir Galahad. And knights of the round table did not loot or pillage.

Finally, we reached Gabriel's Crossing, where stood the house of Gabriel Dumont, Riel's general and right-hand man. Middleton gave the order for the house to be razed to the ground. Roaring with laughter, the Midlanders shattered Dumont's furniture and pictures. The civilian teamsters had decided to steal Dumont's gorgeous pool table. Groaning with exertion, they hoisted the massive thing into a huge wagon, which would carry it down to the *Northcote*.

The timbers of the wrecked house were carried down to the riverbank, where they were added to the "armour" plating of the *Northcote*. The men drifted away. Roley and I walked around the ruins of Dumont's big farmhouse. Shattered crockery, smashed-up furniture, and the broken frames of pictures were all that remained of Gabriel Dumont's buildings.

Roley puffed on his pipe and stared wordlessly at the wreckage for a long time. It occurred to me that he had aged a great deal in the few weeks I had known him. There seemed to be more grey in his hair. His face was unhealthily thin, and lined. Then he looked at me. "God, I hate to see that," he said, and then he walked away.

* * *

We were six miles from Batoche along the river road. But that road was thick with brush, and small timber, where the owner of that ruined table might be preparing another ambush for the North-West Field Force. We would have to leave the river and the *Northcote*. One of our cannons was mounted now on that overloaded garbage scow. Thirty-five scarlet-jacketed troopers of the regular infantry filed on to the miserable barge. On board too, was Lieutenant Hugh John Macdonald, the Prime Minister's son, miserably sick with erysipelas. The men were now calling the *Northcote* "Middleton's navy."

Arthur gestured toward the captain of the tub, the American Captain Sheets, who was standing on the shoreline staring at his ship. "Looks a bit pale and sweaty, don't you think?" Arthur said. "Tremulous, like. Not exactly Nelson at Trafalgar. More like my maiden Aunt Fanny being awakened in the night by a mouse's fart. I expect right about now, Captain Sheets is trying to think of a good reason why he should be dying for a Queen and country which aren't even his. 'England expects every man to do his duty.' That's what Horatio Nelson said. Yes, well, Middleton may expect that, but I predict Jim Sheets will have far different ideas at the crucial moment. You'll observe, gentlemen, that the gunners and the regulars are going to be shielded by thick planking. But old Jim Sheets and his pilot are going to be up in that damn fool captain's pilothouse, sticking out the top, *which isn't shielded at all.* So I doubt Her Majesty's Ship *Northcote* is going to be any God damn use to us at all. With due respect to the Royal Navy, of which I guess, technically, it's now part."

We had to avoid that potentially fatal riverbank road, and so, on May 8, the North-West Field Force left the *Northcote*. It marched inland along a prairie trail, and then northward across more open country toward Riel's capital. The weather was still perfect. The settlement cabins were thicker and thicker, all deserted. The Scouts rode busily back and forth. Not a shot was fired. The word was that the Métis and Indians were waiting quietly for us, inside the rows and rows of gun pits which surrounded the village.

On the evening of May 8, we made camp about five miles southeast of Batoche. Now we occasionally saw the enemy. Dark horsemen moved with incredible speed across our field of view and vanished again, into slight coulees, into groves of trees. You saw them for three seconds, or five, and then they were gone from view, as silently as if they had never existed. Twice, the Scouts wheeled out to try to intercept these phantoms and came back, sweating and empty-handed. Once or twice the flash of binoculars or a telescope caught the corner of my eye, but when I whirled, there was nothing there.

Roley, Arthur and I were strolling around the north perimeter of the camp. Lord Melgund was standing there, moustache perfectly waxed, immaculate white pith helmet on his head. He came over to us. "Gentlemen," he said. "The enemy is taunting us."

"Yes, M'Lord," I muttered, like an intimidated barrister. He beamed at me.

Then one of French's Scouts came by, leading a tired-looking grey horse. The Scout's name was McQueen—a thin, balding, black-bearded man with a Dixie accent. He turned around facing us, so that Melgund couldn't see his face, and winked and grinned broadly. Then he turned back to Melgund, the grin disappeared, and McQueen pointed dramatically off to the left.

"Look," he said. "On that little hill there. One of the most interesting examples of local wildlife, Your Lordship."

Melgund stared studiously out. He shaded his eyes, peered some more, and then gave it up. "I don't see anything," he said. "What is it?"

"A side-hill gouger," McQueen said. "Fascinating animal. Dangerous, too. Like a gigantic badger. Their legs are much longer on one side than the other. That's because they live on the sides of hills. That way, they can remain upright. As long as they don't try to go up or down the hill, just around and around it."

Lord Melgund stared at him, fascinated. "Just around and around…" he murmured. I looked in horror at my boots. What would happen when Melgund found out he was being mocked? Suddenly, he got it. He started to roar with laughter. "Wonderful!" he said. "Wonderful!" He clapped McQueen on the back, and then produced two cigars from a case and gave them to the Scout. "Havana," Melgund said. "Bloody good! Bloody wonderful! Side-hill gouger! Splendid! The fellows at my club will fall for it like a thousand of bricks!" He stumbled over to his horse, holding his sides, and rode off, still spluttering with laughter.

Arthur gave McQueen a crisp salute. "Oh, I say. I say, jolly good show, McQueen, old boy," Arthur said, in an affectedly absurd English accent. McQueen's grin grew broader. I had the feeling that I was witnessing some sort of American tribal ritual, from which red-coated soldiers of the Queen were excluded. Arthur's voice rose. "Oh, jolly good! *Rawther* a sticky bloody wicket, eh, old man, old bean, what, *what?*" McQueen winked again, saluted back, and triumphantly waved the cigars at us. Then he turned and led his grey horse away.

"Well, that was as encouraging as hell," Roley said. "We're being led by idiots."

Arthur smiled thinly. "Not to worry," he said. "All armies are."

Arthur was home again. He kept nodding and beaming, almost like a proud father. Here was the enemy he knew, or a version of it. He was stalking around the perimeter of the camp, with Roley and me trotting behind.

The men had taken to calling him "Gat" Howard. They waved, and yelled things like, "That's the stuff, Gat!" at him. They believed his magic gun would make everything easy at Batoche. Or they wanted to.

"There, didn't I tell you?" Arthur suddenly said, as another black horse with a hunched rider flashed past nine hundred yards away and disappeared behind some poplars, before any man could have shouldered a rifle. He gestured with his cigar. His voice was rising. "Better than the Sioux. God *damn* it!" He looked at me and I thought, with amazement, that there were tears in his eyes. "The Indians are beaten, Willie," he said. "Those gentlemen over there in the black coats are almost the last rebels left. If we can beat them, I don't think there'll ever be anyone like that again."

He looked out as another ghostly rider, this one on a huge white horse, flashed into view momentarily, north of the camp. This man, I thought, had circled the encampment. Some of the sentries were kneeling, leveling their cumbersome Sniders. The horseman vanished like a puff of smoke behind the poplars screening the camp to the north. "They say Dumont rides a big white horse," Arthur said. "Maybe that was the great man himself paying us a call. One leader who *isn't* an idiot." He stood for a while, gazing out at the darkening, northern horizon, beyond which lay Batoche. "All the same, your Protestant friend Mr. Price deserves more credit than he's ever going to get. Just look at the way those men ride. It was a sad day for them, and a happy one for Queen Victoria's Canadian subjects, when Jack Price and his merry men slaughtered half the Métis horses at Fish Creek."

* * *

Middleton had called a meeting of officers for nine that night. His big tent smelled of spring, of crocuses and lilacs, under the odours of heavy wool, sweat and tobacco. He stood at the front of the tent beside an easel carrying a gigantic drawing of Batoche and its area. The Métis rifle pits—such of them as we'd identified—were crayoned in with green. The river was blue, and it carried a tiny red rectangle which I supposed was the *Northcote*. Her Majesty's forces were in red, as befitted us. All the red lay far to the south and slightly to the east of Batoche.

"Gentlemen," Middleton said. He looked slowly around the huge tent. An odd half-smile came over his face. "I am proud to have come so far in the company of such brave men. Now, we have to go just a little farther. I am sure your brave Canadian lads can achieve the last lap of this arduous journey and win the victory. It will be the first time a Canadian army has ever done that." He paused and then smiled again. "I know some of the Liberal papers have been calling you 'toy soldiers.' After the next few days—never again." Behind him Lord Melgund nodded and smiled.

"This is the battlefield, gentlemen," Middleton said. "The South Saskatchewan River flows generally northward in this area. But about a mile south of Batoche, it bends abruptly to the west. It continues west for less than a mile, then bends north again, running straight north for a bit less than two miles. As it runs north, one comes to Batoche. The village is located on both the east and west banks of the river, but the main part is on the east. A ferry on a cable connects the two parts of the village. The house of Monsieur Batoche, the ferryman, on the east bank, is what gave this little settlement its name. This east village consists of some houses, some stores, and a large number of tents which house Métis settlers who have taken refuge in Batoche and Indians allied with Riel. North of the enemy settlement, the river turns eastward again briefly and then turns north. The swing of the river to the west, then north, then east, encloses on three sides a little rectangle of land. It is perhaps less than a mile from east to west, and less than two miles from north to south. This is where the enemy's main village stands. This is where many of his farms are. Here is where most of the enemy's rifle pits are located. Here he has chosen to make a stand.

"We will attack frontally," he said, "from the south and east. Here in the rectangle's southwest corner is St. Antoine of Padua's church and rectory. Two hundred yards from them, near the riverbank, is the cemetery. Some hundreds of yards north of the church are the east village and Batoche's house. The whole area is riddled with rifle pits. Not improvised ones, as at Fish Creek, but skillfully made ones, each capable of holding several men, loopholed, proof against everything except direct hits by the artillery.

"There will be no flank attacks, no splitting of forces. That would invite the enemy's flanking us, surrounding our split forces, destroying us piecemeal. Our men will be awakened at four tomorrow morning. It is about five miles to Batoche. We march at five-thirty. Marching with care, we will reach the southeast corner of that rectangle of land at nine o'clock. The *Northcote* will be on the river adjacent to the rebel strongholds at nine, precisely. It carries thirty-five infantry regulars, and a cannon. The ship will stand off the rebel positions and bombard them, and the church and village. If the enemy succumbs to Gallic excitement and emerges into the open to fire back, which I think they will, so much the better. We will attack, *en masse*, at the moment the *Northcote* opens her bombardment. We will, in effect, be coming at the rebels from the land and the river. It is my hope that we can take the enemy positions and the village by storm, very quickly. Now then, gentlemen. My colleague, Lieutenant Colonel van Straubenzee will give more detailed instructions to the infantry. Lord Melgund and I will consult with the cavalry and artillery commanders."

Van Straubenzee gave us our instructions in his quiet English way, his white beard glowing in the firelight. His instructions were general enough. Boulton's Scouts would lead the column the next day. They would advance first into Middleton's precious rectangle of deadly ground. The unblooded Grenadiers had wangled permission to lead the infantry advance. Behind them would come Arthur and his gun. Company Four would march right behind them. Behind us would come the rest of the infantry and the artillery. French's Scouts would guard the rear.

When we got to the rectangle of land, our forces would form a line. The Grenadiers would form the right-most part of the line. We would be just to their left. Other units would extend farther left. This long, flexible line of infantry was supposed to sweep up the rectangle of ground from south to north, enveloping the church and rectory, silencing the enemy in their rifle pits, moving inexorably northward to seize the east village. While this happened, the battleship *Northcote* would be hurling shells and bullets at the enemy from the river. The field guns, and Arthur's Gatling, would be deployed where they were most needed.

That was the theory, anyway.

It looked so reassuring, that thin red line, which would just sweep up the rectangle, and take Batoche. But how many rifle pits, how many clumps of trees, how many cabins, how many gullies, all filled with enemy men and rifles, would be waiting for us? Our enemies at Fish Creek had been all but invisible.

This time, it would be worse.

We walked back to our tents in silence. Before Arthur went off to join the artillerymen, Roley, in a curiously formal gesture, shook his hand, and then Jack's and mine. Nobody said anything. There didn't seem to be much to say. I rolled myself up in my blankets. The early May nights were still very cold. I was beginning to acquire the habits of a real soldier. The night before Fish Creek, I hadn't been able to sleep at all. This time I was asleep in less than five minutes.

I dreamed that Alice and I were walking along the green banks of the Saskatchewan River. The *Northcote* steamed by, but there were no red coats on it, no cannon. The decks were crowded with gaily-dressed young men and women, who were obviously enjoying a holiday. They waved at us, and shouted happily. Some of them toasted us with glasses of wine. I held Alice's hand tight. In front of us were gleaming white little houses arranged near the riverbank, and in the dream I knew that this was the main village of Batoche, on the east bank of the river. We wanted to see the village. We walked straight toward it, along the warm, green bank of the Saskatchewan. We were striding along very quickly, but no matter how long we walked, somehow we never seemed to get any closer to Batoche.

Alice

The wind is howling off the lake. Fingers of cold rain are rattling on my window. As usual, I can't sleep. So I went down to the library, wondering if in this faithless house there was a Bible. And there was: King James' own version. I wanted to look up a passage recommended to me by a religious girl I know:

> *"Thou shalt not be afraid for the terror by night; nor*
> *for the arrow that flieth by day;*
> *Nor for the pestilence that walketh in darkness; nor*
> *for the destruction that wasteth at noonday.*
> *A thousand shall fall at thy side, and ten thousand at*
> *thy right hand; but it shall not come nigh thee."*

You know I don't believe in You. I never did, not even when I was a tiny child. But I'll make a bargain with You. Bring Willie back safe, and I'll believe.

This psalm of Yours better be right.

XIV

The North-West Field Force swung into formation and headed toward Batoche at five-thirty sharp the next morning. The sky was that delicate, watercolour blue. Wispy clouds raced by far overhead. They would reach Lake Manitoba before our stumbling, clattering column fired its first shot that day. Down where we marched, only the softest and most delicate breeze ruffled the heavy folds of the Union Jacks in the forefront of every unit of the column.

We were marching through long, green, tangled blades of grass. There were crocuses in the grass, and we trampled on their purple blossoms, but there were millions more. Ahead of us the dust rose high, but on either side the trees and grass glowed in the morning sunlight, as they must have in Eden.

The ground was getting a little hillier and a little more wooded. I fell in beside Roley. He was puffing on his pipe. He pulled out his watch, at the end of his glittering gold chain. "Just eight-thirty," he said. "One more half hour, Willie."

From ahead of us there came suddenly a thin, feeble tooting, like some decrepit old lady shouting indignantly out the window at kids on her lawn. "Oh, shit," Roley said. "You don't suppose…"

The ludicrous tooting was drowned out by a distant *boom!* which even I knew was the sound of several dozen Sniders being fired in volley. Immediately afterward came a faint, hollow thunder, which was undoubtedly the cannon mounted on the deck of the *Northcote*. Instantly, an ever-louder rattling of small-arms fire answered. I knew now what Métis Winchesters sounded like. The crash of Canadian volley fire came again.

The column stopped and one of the field guns fired a blank round in reply. This was play-acting, to make the men believe that the *Northcote's* bombardment was all going according to plan. But it wasn't.

The racket from ahead of us grew ever louder. The endless, rhythmic crash of the Snider volleys and the booming of the cannon were almost drowned out by the din of the rebel fire. Suddenly I became aware of Arthur, striding along at my elbow. He had fallen back from the Gatling, which was rattling along ahead of us. He was grinning. "There, now," he said. "Didn't I tell you that Captain Jim Sheets was an utter asshole? And it must be contagious. The God damn imbeciles have opened fire a half hour early. Or maybe they're operating on west coast time or something. Anyway, so much for the battleship *Northcote* and the wonderful coordinated attack."

"If they were on west coast time," I said, "they'd have attacked an hour late, not a half hour early."

"Oh for God's sake, professor," Roley said. "Stop showing off. Jesus, we needed all the edge we can get."

"That's war," Arthur said, more seriously. "Everything goes wrong."

Middleton ordered us to advance at the quick step. There *would* be a co-ordinated attack. Fred Middleton had said so. The whole column began jolting forward through the tall grass, the gun carriages jouncing, Arthur's Gatling swaying and banging precariously on its wheels. Sweat poured down our faces; our red tunics started to soak with sweat. Hardened as I was, I started gasping for breath as the column raced toward Batoche. The sound of firing grew ever louder. The rhythmic banging of the infantry volleys and the booming of the cannon from the river became ever fainter. They were drowned out by the incredible din of the enemy's return fire—Winchesters, Martini-Henrys, (both better rifles than most of us had), shotguns, even pistols.

Then we started to hear scattered rifle shots from just ahead of us. The advance guard of Boulton's Scouts had made contact with the enemy's rifle pits. Poor old Boulton and his men were always destined to meet the enemy first. And then, quite suddenly, the tumult of firing from the river stopped.

It was many days later that we found out what had happened. There never was any sensible explanation as to why the *Northcote* had opened fire early. But it had, although they had the audacity to claim we were late. While we were still marching, the boat swung northward, approaching the east village of Batoche. The officers yelled. The regulars bristled up from behind their wooden armour to fire their first volley, and the popgun cannon started blasting away ineffectually at the rebels. Lieutenant Hugh John Macdonald, Sir John A.'s son, his face disfigured by erysipelas, rushed out from his sickbed to join the giant gunfight his father had helped to start.

The Métis and Indians abandoned their rifle pit positions and rushed down to the banks, on both sides of the Saskatchewan. The expression "hail of lead" is much misused, but I gather that's what the enemy threw at the *Northcote*. They blazed away at the old scow with everything they had. It made a splendid target. Enemy marksmen even waded out into the river, ignoring the inaccurate volleys from the chugging, shuddering, bobbing boat, and emptied their pistols at it.

The old tub ploughed past the village, wreathed in clouds of gunsmoke, spluttering rifle and cannon fire, absorbing hundreds of rounds of counter-fire from the riverbank. And the inevitable happened. Arthur had foreseen it. The sharpshooters on the river banks started directing their fire at the totally unprotected, unarmoured pilothouse on top of the ship. Captain Sheets and his pilot found dozens of rounds flying through that tiny space. They shattered the glass, they turned the thin metal walls into Swiss cheese. The poor bastards did what any sane men would do. They threw themselves on the floor and let the boat chug on, unsteered.

Therefore, they did not see what Gabriel Dumont had prepared for the *Northcote*. As usual, old Gabriel was ten miles ahead of the North-West Field Force. He had ordered the Métis to lower Batoche's steel ferry cable, and they had strung it across the river at smokestack height.

The *Northcote* blundered blindly into the cable. Major Smith, the regulars' commander, saw the stretched cable through the fog of smoke and shit swirling around the *Northcote,* a few seconds before it hit. Poor old Smith stood up, puffed out his chest, and roared, *"Stop this God damn boat!"*

Never since Canute tried to command the tides has there been so fruitless an order. With a colossal crash, sparks flying, smoke billowing, the boat's smokestacks and mast were torn off. They came clattering down on the terrified infantry and gunners, sparks setting their hair and uniforms afire, the foul-smelling smoke choking them half to death.

The terrified Captain Sheets still lay on the floor of his riddled pilot-house, beside his pilot. By the time the bewildered, infuriated soldiers had put out the fires, and recovered their presence of mind, the *Northcote* was a mile north of Batoche. Then the comedy deepened. Major Smith stormed up to the pilot-house, and ordered Sheets and the pilot to return to the bombardment of Batoche. They told him to go to hell. They very profanely pointed out that they were American citizens, and that they'd risked their lives enough for the so-called Great White Mother over in London. The enraged Smith relieved them of command. Then Uncle Sam's men played their trump card. The engineer, also an American, told Smith that he'd obey no orders that didn't come from Sheets.

And that ended it. The bullet-riddled, half-decapitated *Northcote* steamed and spluttered northward in the general direction of Hudson's Bay. It never fired another shot. Some of our best men, regulars, were on that scow. The soldiers cursed Sheets, the United States of America, and their fates, in that order. The soldiers couldn't sail the tub. The crew wouldn't. Only two men had been slightly injured on board. There is no evidence that the scow's broadsides hit anybody.

Soon after the decapitated boat headed impotently off to the north, the front of our infantry and artillery column sighted the enemy. As Middleton had said, the river flowed west for a time, then straight north for a couple of miles, then east again, and finally north. The North-West Field Force was crashing headlong, at the quick-step, into a little rectangle of woods, meadows, fields and houses, bounded on the south, the west and the north by the swift-flowing South Saskatchewan.

The green leaves and flowery meadows glowed in the morning sunlight. The flocks of frightened birds driven into the air by the *Northcote's* fusillades were settling back into the heavy trees. The land of the Métis looked like an amusement park, like the site of a field day, like anything but a battlefield.

But ahead of us were thirty or so of Boulton's Scouts, flat on the ground, firing steadily at some unseen enemy ahead of them. Several Scouts were leading groups of horses back to the rear. Boulton himself was running back toward the front of our column, waving us on.

The Grenadiers and our Company Four began to deploy behind the Scouts, as the Grenadier officers and Roley yelled orders. The sweating men were forming up behind Boulton's dismounted cavalry, in long red ranks in the flower-laden, waving grass. The volume of the Scouts' fire rose, briefly. I saw, hundreds of yards away, some Métis skirmishers in their drab coats and slouch hats, running very fast away from us, toward the north. Boulton's men were aiming and firing with care. The Métis were running in serpentine, twisting paths, across the meadow. Not one of them was hit. They vanished into two huts standing in our path, and soon after plumes of smoke blossomed from the windows.

I felt the *crack!* of some unseen thing flying over my head. I realized that the Métis sharpshooters were firing at the long ranks of kneeling men in scarlet, around me in the lazily waving grass. I yelled an order for the men of our company to lie down flat. Seconds later a captain of the Grenadiers roared the same order at his men. It was not until long after that I realized that Roley, Jack and I had remained sitting upright in the grass like the amateurs we still were.

A couple of minutes later, a captain of Grenadiers on horseback came thundering toward our position, a look of grim satisfaction on his face, followed by two of the nine-pounder cannon. Their gunners were teetering precariously on the jolting gun carriages. The guns came to a halt right behind the foremost line of Scouts, just to my left.

The whole column was forming up behind us. Melgund and Middleton galloped on ahead and right past me, binoculars in hand. Both were resplendent in gleaming, white pith helmets. They looked studious, yet noble, grim, yet confident. They brought their capering black horses to a stop and began busily studying the terrain, one hand carelessly holding the reins of the skittish animals, the other steadying the field glasses. This was the Sandhurst look, perfected on a thousand battlefields.

The two of them looked as if they were posing for the heroic painting "The Barrage Begins at Batoche," winner of the Victoria Medal at the Royal Exhibition of Painting of 1886. Middleton and Melgund would, of course, attend the Exhibition. Women would sigh over Lord Melgund. The reporters would cluster around bluff old Fred Middleton, Sir Fred by then, no doubt.

That was what they thought. The only problem, of course, was that Gabriel Dumont had different plans for them and for all of us.

The gunners had set up their field pieces. One of the artillery officers waved his sword and yelled, and the guns went off together with a deafening roar. A huge geyser of mud and grass flew up in front of one of the huts, and beside the other. The officer yelled louder and longer, and the gunners desperately adjusted the sights. The two guns went off in tandem again.

A major from the Grenadiers yelled something at Arthur, and he and his Canadian gunners unharnessed the horses pulling the Gatling. Arthur and his men pushed the gun forward and set it up where Boulton's skirmishers had been lying. The cannons continued to bang. One of the huts had caught fire, and the roof of the other was collapsing. The Métis sharpshooters came out of them in a dead run, heading north toward the village. Firing broke out all along the line, but the range was too great. The Métis hugged the ground as they ran, moving in that same shifting, shimmering, serpentine way. They were hard to see, let alone shoot. It occurred to me how good they were at this and how bad we were.

Melgund had been talking urgently to Arthur. Arthur caught my eye and waved his blue Yankee cap. "U.S. Army leads the way, Willie!" he yelled. "Redcoats to the rear!" Escorted by some of Boulton's men, he and his gunners pulled the Gatling forward.

There was a tremendous storm of yelling and screaming and *God damning* all around us, as officers in the other regiments got their men up and moving. The men of Company Four were lounging in the grass, enjoying the spectacle. Now Roley, Jack and I ran around like monkeys, shouting frantically, getting them to their feet, getting them into some kind of order.

The column pressed forward, to the north, with Arthur and his Scouts at the front. The perfect sky gazed down. The crashing, clattering, clanking column kicked up clouds of dust, and we choked on it. We began to sweat heavily in our heavy red tunics.

Now, ahead of us to the north, we could see the wooden Roman Catholic church of St. Antoine of Padua. It was unpainted, and instead of a steeple, had a small turret with a cross surmounting it. *I'll bet the Protestant boys would love to see Arthur blow that Papist cross to Kingdom come,* I thought.

Just west of the church lay a smaller building, like a big white house: the rectory. Some people were disappearing into the church. Middleton shouted something at Arthur, and Arthur nodded and saluted. His Gatling opened fire on the two buildings. I borrowed Jack's field glasses, and through them I could see the puffs of greyish dust and the splinters of white paint flying, as the bullets thudded into the rectory timbers. A window of the rectory disappeared in a spray of glass fragments. The men cheered. Arthur waved his cap.

Middleton started yelling at Arthur again and pointing. I gazed through the heavy, hot, metal-smelling binoculars, and I saw what the old man was pointing at: a white flag was flying from a small, green-painted house near the church. Arthur saluted again, and the Gatling fire stopped. Then two of Boulton's men rode straight for the church. As they neared it, the doors opened and out piled a crowd of frightened-looking people, shouting frantically, hands in the air. I could see the black habits of priests and nuns and the drab clothing of some Métis. As the Scouts approached, one of the nuns, an old woman, fell to her knees. The priests began trying to help her get up, and one of the Scouts got off his horse and helped to hoist her up again.

The column halted, south-east of the church. The priests, staggering in their heavy cassocks, were brought over the green meadow to our commanders. One of the priests had been grazed in the leg, and Middleton roared at the ambulance attendants to help him. Middleton, Melgund, Arthur, Lieutenant Colonel Williams, our old friend Buchan, and other Canadian officers crowded around the black-coated old men.

Abruptly, Roley banged me on the arm. "Now then, William," he said, with a wink. "I am the commanding officer of Company Four, am I not?"

"You are," I said.

"And so important a person should be part of that conference, should he not?"

"Indubitably," I said.

He started to laugh. "Jesus H. Jeremiah Christ," he said. "Where do you get these words?" And he trotted across the green sward and pushed his way into the conference.

He came back twenty minutes later, his pipe fuming, a big grin on his face. Jack and I were waiting for him. "Interesting stuff, boys," he said, beaming. "Interesting stuff. The R.C. priests are as mad as hell at Riel. Our fearless leaders were not expecting that. Apparently Riel has practically invented a new religion, with himself as high priest. That's likely exaggerated, but that's what the priests think. He's been restricting their movements. So they are talking to Middleton. They say the rebels are short of food and ammunition. Morale is poor. Apparently there are only two hundred Mateys and two hundred Indians, although one of the Scouts said he thinks the Indians are mostly a myth. Anyway, Middleton is cheering up fast. He's going to order the whole column forward at speed." He paused, and clapped Jack affectionately on the back. "Who'da thunk it, Jack?" he said. "You and the Roman Catholic Church on the same side. It's a miracle."

Jack grinned. "Protestants *do* believe in miracles, you know," he said. Then he lit his pipe, and strolled away.

Five minutes later, Lieutenant Colonel Williams rode up to us on his white horse. He was red-faced and grinning. Williams pulled out his sword, and waved it over his head like a Cossack. "Column forward!" he yelled. "Canadians to the fore!" The men cheered. Roley shook his head, almost imperceptibly.

And our clattering, rattling column of men, horses, and guns pushed past the church, heading almost due west. We were marching across the bottom of that river-enclosed rectangle of land which Middleton had said was the enemy's stronghold. To our right, the rise of land which had obscured vision to the north was leveling off. I caught a glimpse of the river. I knew that ahead of us, still invisible, lay a wooded ridge, which Middleton and Melgund called "Mission Ridge." Beyond it was a ravine, full of trees. To our left lay the cemetery and beyond that, and ahead of us, the Saskatchewan, flowing northward.

We pressed forward, sweating in our red, blue, and dark green tunics, horses and men tightly bunched up on the trail. Nobody had seen a single one of the enemy, except for the sharpshooters we'd driven off. The men were excited and optimistic. I wasn't.

We had advanced a few hundred feet, when the men started to cheer again. They were pointing to the right, to the north. I looked and saw that the east village of Batoche had come into view. There were a number of little white buildings—houses and stores—and a great number of tents, which housed Indians and Métis refugees who'd fled as we advanced.

The artillery officers started to yell. The cannons were unlimbered and aimed. "Common shell, percussion fuse, load!" bellowed the lieutenants, and with deafening roars the guns began bombarding the village. I started peering through Jack's field glasses again.

Stinging sweat ran down into my eyes, but I could clearly see the geysers of dirt and mud thrown up as the shells landed among the little houses and the tents. Even at that distance I could see people running from those tents. Some of them were wearing bright, gaudy shirts. I kept pulling the binoculars away and wiping my streaming eyes, but every time I looked, I saw the same thing. Most of the people running were Indian women with their children.

Some of Boulton's Scouts had dismounted. They were advancing past the straining artillerymen. They were leading their tired horses and a host of pack mules. Company Four fell into place and followed them. Nobody told us to do this. It was in the amateur spirit with which the North-West Field Force did everything. Some of the Grenadiers came pressing after us.

Around us, the heavy brush was encroaching ever more thickly on the trail. The ridge loomed in front of us. The sun was getting hotter. Sweat poured down my face. I was getting badly scared. Where in hell was the enemy? I looked at the confident, grinning men around me and tried to suck confidence out of them. It didn't work. I was turning to say something to Jack, who was strolling calmly along beside me, pipe in mouth.

Suddenly, there was a noise like a thunderclap. Puffs of gunsmoke belched out at us from both sides of the trail and from straight ahead. Thank God that the Scouts had all those horses and mules bunched up at the head of the column. Nine of the horses and two of the mules fell over. They must have been riddled with bullets. Nine were dead before they hit the ground; two lay shrieking and shitting, kicking and bleeding.

Two of the Scouts were hit. One of them was right in front of me. I could see blood on his side. He tried to pull himself up on his arms, and another shot scored the side of his head. I actually saw his head whip around, and then it started to bleed in long, spraying dribbles. "Oh, *shit*," he yelled, in a high almost womanish voice. "Oh, *shit! Why now?*" He pulled off his red bandana and pressed it to his head.

Roley ran to him and started dragging him backward. The Scout scrabbled his feet in the dirt, trying to help. "Stop yelling," Roley said to him. "If you can yell, you're alive."

"I believe I bloody am," the Scout said. "Thank you so much." The other wounded Scout had crawled back from the wounded and dead horses. The rest of the Scouts had taken cover behind the dead animals and were returning fire.

Jack was shouting at our men to form two lines and fire by volley. Roley ran over and pushed him aside. "No! Jack!" he screamed. "The men are to take cover!" He looked around, wildly. *"Take cover!"* he roared at our men and the Grenadiers. The men abandoned the straggling line they had started to form in the middle of the trail and sheltered beside it, or lay prone. They started firing; the fire grew ever more deafening as the rest of the column clattered up behind us, cutting us off from retreat.

Our men were not going to stand obediently in rows and have their heads blown off. They *were* taking cover, jammed in behind rocks, lying prone behind logs, throwing themselves behind every hillock of land. They would have dived head-first into water (if there'd been any) if it meant less exposure to the enemy. I saw men almost disappear into the ground, as if they *were* side-hill gougers.

And they were shooting back. They systematically worked the breeches of their Sniders, shaking the clumsy things to get rid of the expended cartridges, directing a heavy fire at either side of the trail.

But what the hell were we shooting at? I peeped out from behind a heavy box which had fallen off one of the dead pack mules. I had my revolver in my hand. From both sides of the trail, and from the ridge ahead of us, puffs of grey gunsmoke constantly blossomed. I could hear the ugly cracking noises of bullets and shot as they sang over my head. But I could not see one human form. The son-of-a-bitch Métis, in their rifle pits, were completely invisible.

More yelling and screaming and whinnying came from behind us. I turned around and saw that the cannons were being moved up to our position. The rest of the troops surrounded them. I crawled over to where Roley and Jack were, in the hollow of a tree. They were rearing up to fire their revolvers at the puffs of gunsmoke. A moment later, a heavy form came crashing down behind us, scaring us all. It was a Grenadier officer, a major, his red face running with sweat, his peaked cap askew on his head. "Captain Collison!" he said. "This is the deployment: French's and Boulton's dismounted Scouts on the right. To their left, the Grenadiers, to their left, your Company Four, and on your left the Winnipeg regiment and Mr. Howard and his gun. The cannons on the left, so that Howard's gun can protect them. The Midlanders are to be kept in reserve, near the church. The church itself will become a field hospital. The men are to stand fast and return fire from cover, until further orders. Any questions?" Roley shook his head, and instantly the man was off and running to the next position.

"Come on," Roley said. Jack and I followed him, and we shouted at our men to take up position to the left of the Grenadiers, who were already pressing into place. The Métis were firing at the crouching, cursing men. I saw a Grenadier captain go down. Our own men crowded behind us and took up positions, prone or crouching. When this laborious, terrifying process was over, our infantry was strung out in a ragged semi-circle facing north, west and south. At least Middleton had the sense not to bunch us up in one mass.

The enemy was still invisible. The bullets flew at us. It was like something supernatural. It made me sick at my stomach; it made me want to hide my head like a child, to beg for mercy. The puffs of grey smoke billowed out of apparently empty ground. Bullets ricocheted off cannons, off trees, off rocks, and occasionally hit screaming militiamen. We tried to concentrate our fire by observing the sources of the gunsmoke, but as soon as an enemy fired, the huge, billowing cloud of smoke was blown away, creating a dense and impenetrable fog.

The cannons were now on the left, firing senselessly at nothing. I saw eruptions of smoke and flame as the shells crashed into the brushy, hilly ground. Branches of trees and bushes drifted down, severed by shrapnel. I saw no dead men. In the middle of the cannons were Arthur Howard and his gun. Arthur was smoking one of his horrible cigars, his blue cap was shoved back on his head, and he was grinning.

There had been a lot of Union Jacks waving on our side. They were lying in the dust now. Suddenly, on the ridge ahead of us, a blue flag was waved defiantly back and forth. It was the Métis battle flag Sutter had described, with a white hand and a glaring wolf's head on it. The men started firing at it, and it was abruptly pulled down.

Right beside me, a bullet struck splinters from the edge of a wagon. There was another man crouching beside me, Private Roylott. The splinters took off a bit of his cheek. *"Prick,"* he said, jamming a handkerchief against his dribbling face. Then he looked uneasily at me. "Not you, Lieutenant," he said.

"I know," I said.

A few minutes later, the enemy's gunfire slackened; then it dropped off almost to nothing. Had they withdrawn? I crawled over to Roley and Jack. I was beginning to feel almost cheerful. Suddenly the oversized Grenadier major scared me almost shitless by appearing out of nowhere and dropping behind me again. "Keep your places," he said. "That's the word from on high. A couple of the Scouts wormed their way forward and took a look. God damn brave men, if you ask me. The rebels have rifle pits all over the God damn place. All over the edge of this hill in front of us. All over the area between it and the river. They're north of us, extending toward the village. One of the Scouts studied one of the pits through binoculars, while the half-breeds in it came up for ammunition. They're every few yards. Loopholed birch logs, camouflaged with brush and dirt, facing us. You won't see a thing until a bullet comes out of one of them and kills you. They knew we were going to come at them from this direction. If we try a charge, we'll get cut to pieces."

"What *are* we going to do?" Roley said.

The Grenadier major laughed, a short mirthless bark. "I don't think Middleton has any damn clue," he said, and then he was off and running again.

"Oh, Christ," Roley said. His face was white. "Look at that."

I looked to the left. About fifty Métis had burst out of the trees. They were making a rush toward the cannon farthest to the left. The gun had gotten jammed in some brush, and the artillerymen were frantically tugging at it, trying to pull it back toward our line. It wouldn't budge.

They were screaming like lunatics. They came at us fast, using cover brilliantly. They ran low to the ground, supple as willows. They dived behind hillocks of land and bushes, as the volume of fire rose from our side. They knelt and fired, then rushed on again. They were coming at us like wraiths, out of a dense cloud of gunsmoke. A Grenadier toppled over, blood pouring down his side. There was a lot of disorganized shooting from our ranks, but the crowd of Métis, twisting like dark shadows in the murk, came on and on.

This was Arthur Howard's finest hour. There were bullets spanging off the gun carriage of the Gatling. The Canadian gunner helping Arthur suddenly threw up his arms, shouted, and fell down. There was bright blood on both his trouser legs.

Arthur did not move an inch. Someone had given him a blue Frenchman's toque with a long tassel on it, and he had it on his head. The tassel blew in the breeze. Arthur stood there like a statue, pouring hundreds of rounds into the dense smoke, at flickering and shadowy enemies that no one could have aimed at. He'd had no chance to adjust his sights, and he told me later he saw nothing at which to shoot. He simply sprayed the cloud of gunsmoke with bullets. The other Canadian gunner had been winged on the arm—I could see the blood running off his hand—but he grimly reloaded the Gatling. Arthur was shouting something and, as I emptied my revolver into the murk, I moved closer to him to see what it was. "Take that, you sons of bitches!" he was yelling. "Take that!"

This steadfast and deliberately showy performance did what Arthur intended. It stopped the militia from falling back. They straightened up and started firing, equally blindly, into the smoke. They even started to cheer.

Suddenly, Arthur stopped firing. He held up his right hand imperiously, like a public speaker silencing an unruly crowd. Most of our men stopped firing at once.

He knew what he was doing, too. The Métis had stopped firing and stopped advancing. The clouds of gunsmoke slowly drifted away. There, facing us, was the green, shining meadow. And despite the snowstorm of bullets Arthur and the Canadians had fired, there wasn't one body on the ground. Not one. Arthur stared at the scene in bewilderment for a few seconds and then remarked, to nobody in particular, "Well, I'll be God damned." As if on cue, a rifle went off from the meadow. A cloud of gunsmoke billowed out. The bullet whanged into the Gatling's barrel. Arthur dived for cover. He knew who was being shot at. Two more rifles went off, and I saw the tassle of Arthur's toque severed, drifting down like snow as its owner vanished into the grass.

"Somebody stand up and show your red coat!" Arthur roared. "These bastards are trying to kill a neutral foreigner!" Some of the men rushed toward him and dragged the Gatling back to cover. Arthur kept low, and I saw that his face was running with sweat and lined with anxiety. He was helping to carry the wounded gunner. "Easy, Jerry," he kept saying. "You'll be right as rain."

A Grenadier captain I did not know came half-slithering and half-running to us. "We're pulling back," he said. "We're going to re-form two hundred yards closer to the church."

"Pulling back?" Jack said. "Why don't we charge?"

The captain lost his temper. "Charge?" he yelled. "Charge what? Do you see one human being that we can charge at, Lieutenant?" He waited for a few moments, with his head hanging down. His brown hair was matted down with dirt and sweat. Then he raised his head, looked at Jack, and said, "Sorry. But we'll be cut to pieces if we charge. Cut to *bloody* pieces. All right?" Then he was off again.

But before we pulled back, something happened. I have said that the enemy's gunfire had slackened almost to nothing. But, periodically, shots were being fired by our men, mingled with a lot of cursing and yelling. I stuck my head up cautiously, to see what the hell they were shooting at.

And I saw. The trail we'd been on stretched ahead of us. About every two minutes, one of the enemy darted across that trail, from side to side. He was always about three hundred yards away. When he crossed the trail heading northward, he was carrying a brown leather bag, which flapped limply against his body. As he appeared from cover, our men started firing, and infuriatingly, they always missed. He fairly shot across that trail. A few minutes later he reappeared, now holding the same bag stuffed full—of ammunition, I thought—and raced southward across the trail again, to supply his friends with bullets and shot. His reappearance was greeted with the same futile, impotent round of shooting and cursing from Company Four.

He was a brave man though. He was tall, with a dark blue shirt and a black hat with a showy red feather on it, clear even from that distance. And now as he reappeared, carrying the full bag, he gave us a jaunty wave as he raced across the trail, and plunged into the bushes on the other side, our men firing as uselessly as ever.

One of his friends rubbed it in. Just as the bugger in the black hat vanished anew into the underbrush, a high clear Métis voice rang out from in front of us. "*Espèces de fous! Trous d'culs d'chiens! Apprenez-donc à tirer!*"

Fools! Assholes! Why don't you learn to shoot straight?

I became aware that Roley was watching from beside me. Apparently he needed no translation. "Shit," he remarked, to no one in particular. Then he reached over and tapped one of our men on the shoulder. "Joe," he said, "loan me your rifle, will you? With three cartridges."

The man did. Roley took off his cap, and shoved it under his epaulette. Then he found a low spot where two heavy logs fitted badly together, and slowly, carefully, eased the rifle barrel out.

"It just so happens," Roley said, "that I took three weeks of training with these useless God damn rifles, five years ago. I wonder if I learned anything."

The men were all watching him now. "Keep your head down, Willie," he said.

But I was incapable of that. I took my cap off too, but I slowly and cautiously raised my head above cover so that I could see.

"Hold your breath," Roley was muttering to himself. "Squeeze the trigger."

The Métis in the red-feathered hat appeared at the south side of the trail, and as he did so, Roley fired. A plume of brightest scarlet flew out of the man's throat, and he dropped like a stone.

I couldn't contain myself. I raised my head a couple of inches, and yelled, "*Est-ce que c'est assez droit pour toi? Et ton ami, comment va-t-il?*"

Was that straight enough for you? And how's your friend feeling?

There were angry yells. I was feeling at that particular moment more or less invincible, or I would not have made the mistake I made. I wheeled around to say some triumphant thing to our applauding men. Roley said something, and grabbed at me, and pulled me to the right, toward him. And then suddenly, somebody hit me with immense force on the left side of my head, just at the temple.

Then I was falling, falling into immensities of space. It was as dark as the void of the Pit there. I did not want to fall into this blackness. I remember thinking, vaguely, *One of the men hit me with his rifle butt. The clumsy bastard. Or was it on purpose?*

Then there was nothing, and then something happened.

I fell into a lake when I was ten. I couldn't swim. I remember thinking that I was going to die, and then I remember being dragged up through the dark choking water. The sunshine kept getting brighter and brighter, and then I was in the air again. I was living after all. That's what this felt like. There was a sudden flash of sunlight, and what sounded like a roar of voices. Somebody was jamming something against my head. My neck was badly twisted. I tried to speak, but for some reason I could only croak.

I heard Roley's voice saying, "He's all right! Thank God! It's just a bad graze." For some reason, the fools were pouring some hot, thick liquid all over me, and I tried to protest this too. Then my vision came back, and I saw that I was bleeding like a stuck pig, all over myself. I must have made some noise of fright, because Roley took hold of the back of my neck and thrust his face into mine. I could smell tobacco on his breath. "Willie! Willie!" he said. "You stuck your head up and they grazed it with a bullet. You're all right. Head wounds bleed like mad, but we'll stop it." He squeezed my arm. "Jesus, Willie, if I'd gotten you killed..."

Then two men were hauling me up and onto a stretcher. They wound a bandage tightly around my head. I kept drifting in and out of full consciousness. I wanted to say something nonchalant to the anxious-looking soldiers crowding around me, but all I could manage was another croak. The two ambulance attendants started to run, carrying me. They were hunched over for fear of sharpshooters. One of them kept muttering, "Shit. Shit. Shit." I sort of fell asleep after that, despite the bumpy ride.

* * *

I woke up to find myself in the church. The pews had been roughly thrown against the wall, and a line of wounded men lay on white sheets spread over the wooden floor. Some of the men on those sheets were moving around, and some lay ominously still. There was a great deal of blood. Officers—surgeons—and ambulance attendants were walking around the room, taking pulses, offering cups of water to the wounded, of whom I was now one.

I was close to the door. By turning my head slightly, I could see out into the beautiful May sunshine. The slant of it looked different somehow, and I guessed that I'd been out cold for several hours. To the west, I could still hear occasional volleys of Canadian rifle fire, and the occasional sharp sound of a Métis Winchester. From time to time, the sharp jabbering of Arthur's Gatling started up again.

I didn't feel too bad. I experimentally touched my head. The bandage was slick with blood, and my hand came away covered in it, but the bleeding had mercifully stopped. Then a young medical officer in a red coat came and knelt by me. "You're awake," he said. "Good. Don't worry, Lieutenant. You're all right. Though if Jean or Jacques or Pierre had shifted an inch to the right before he fired, you'd be talking to Saint Peter right this God damn minute. I'll be a son of a bitch if you wouldn't. The bleeding's stopped, and in a few minutes I'll sew you up. Now just lie there. They're bringing some more wounded men in, and the last thing we need is for you to start heroically trying to get back to the line."

I did not want to say that the line was the last place on earth I wanted to be. I was actually supremely comfortable and sleepy, and indeed I was just beginning to nod off again when I heard a voice I knew, right outside the church.

It was Lieutenant Colonel Williams of the Midland Battalion, and to say that the great man was angry would be an understatement. He was ranting angrily at somebody, probably one of his junior officers.

"Can't charge," Williams snorted. "Mustn't charge the enemy. Best battalion in the Canadian Army, and the Midlanders can't charge, because Colonel bloody van Straubenzee says we can't!" The other man made murmuring, conciliatory noises. The colonel was having none of it. "You heard him," Williams roared. "Van Straubenzee's 'well-acquainted' with my family's 'distinguished service to the colony.' He 'admires the courage and fighting spirit of my men.' But the enemy is 'virtually invisible.' A charge might lead to 'frightful casualties.' So 'discretion is better than valour just now.'"

The other officer muttered something else. "Colony, my ass," Williams said loudly. "Silly old goat. Silly, goat-bearded old English nanny-goat. *Van Straubenzee*, what in hell kind of name is that, for God's sake? I tell you, Charley, I've always been a Tory and a British Empire man, but I have half a mind to resign from the Conservative Party when I get back to Ottawa. I'll sit with the radical Liberals from Quebec, that's what I'll do."

This was too much. In spite of my weakened condition, I started to laugh. I called out Williams' name, and an instant later, he came into the church and saw me.

He really was a very kind man. He dropped his blustering manner at once. He knelt beside me. "Good God, lad," he said. "I didn't know, I'm sorry…"

"I'm all right, sir," I said. "But I couldn't help overhearing what you said. Don't do it, Colonel, don't do it. Don't sit beside Laurier and the rest of the *rouges*. The Empire would collapse. Wolfe would rise from his grave."

Williams started to laugh. "Right you are, Willie," he said. "I can't abandon Queen and country now. Now then, lad, you get some rest."

Before he was out the church door, I went back to sleep. Or passed out. I'm not really sure.

Alice

Something terrible has happened.
I know it has.

X V

I awoke again, and it was dusk. I wasn't in the church any more. I was in some kind of huge tent, surrounded by wounded men on piles of blankets and sheets on the ground. The first thought which came to me was that my head hurt, and that I was fearfully thirsty. The second was that some men were standing, looking down at me. I looked again, and it was Roley, Jack, and Arthur Howard. Except for Arthur, they looked badly scared.

"It's all right," I said, a little feebly. "I'm not dead."

"Thank God for it," Roley said. They all sat down on the ground beside me.

"Where in hell am I?" I said.

"Oh," Jack said, with immense digust, "you're in the hospital tent. In the God damn *zareba*. We all are. In the zareba. The whole army. In case you're wondering, a zareba isn't some animal where you don't know whether it's black with white stripes or vice versa. No. A zareba is some kind of fortification, or some God damn thing."

"It's sort of a glorified giant hole in the ground which we've dug," Roley said. "And Jack is right. The whole army is in here. It's nine o'clock at night. You got hit around eleven this morning. At supper, we abandoned all the ground we took this morning, abandoned the church and the R.C. rectory, and fled hundreds of yards to the south, into this so-called fortification. Where supposedly we'll be safe. While their sharpshooters fire at us."

As if to verify this, a Winchester shot rang out. There was a lot of yelling and cursing, and a couple of our rifles went off in reply.

I appealed to Arthur. "Does this make sense to you?" I said.

"After a manner of speaking," he said. "The old man, Middleton, is being cautious. We can't get badly hurt all coiled up together here. We can't do much to the enemy either."

Arthur looked reflective, and blew out a cloud of awful-smelling cigar smoke. "The enemy actually did not hurt us too much today," he said. "Our casualties are astoundingly low. I have to hand it to these Canadian boys. We have a lot of myths in New England, about redcoats marching at us in well-drilled rows, and the Yankees mowing them down from ambush. Well, these fellows of yours are a different kind of redcoat. The first shot fired at them, they hid themselves better than any Minuteman ever could. And despite all the lead old Gabriel threw at us, damn few of them got shot."

I looked at Jack, whose face had turned bright red. Arthur was not right, of course. At the first shot fired, Jack had tried to bunch the men up in the middle of the trail, to fire in volleys and be annihilated. Roley, thank God, had saved us.

I opened my mouth to change the subject, but Arthur wasn't finished. "No, we can't do much to the enemy from in here," he said. "And I think Middleton is over-estimating the enemy and under-estimating his own troops. And the proof is that…"

He seemed a bit overcome, and Roley finished the sentence for him. "That Lord Melgund has been sent back to Qu'Appelle," he said.

I must have looked totally astounded. "Yes," Arthur said. "And such a man would not leave the field of battle except for one thing."

"To get reinforcements," I said.

"Yes," Arthur said. "Quite possibly British reinforcements. Middleton has been very vocal, more so than he should have been, about wanting a 'solid, experienced force' of British regulars, instead of this ragtag army of colonials and lost Americans. I suspect that's exactly what he has sent Melgund to scare up for him." He brought his fist down on the ground savagely. "Think of it. Jesus H. Christ. It will take months to get a relief force of British troops over here. God, it will take three weeks of band concerts and fancy-dress balls for the officers and their ladies, before they even embark. By the time they get here, every Indian in the West will have joined Riel. And then the damn Limeys will likely get themselves all killed the first day, launching bayonet charges against those gentlemen in black coats over there. Or forming squares, in the middle of a field, as if the Métis were Zulus."

He looked around uneasily. "There's something else, too," he said.

"Your fellow-countrymen?" Roley said.

"Yes," Arthur said. "There's plenty of anti-British and therefore anti-Canadian sentiment down there. The Irish, of course, and the New Englanders still fighting the Revolution, but all kinds of other people who want to annex the Canadian West before it fills up with patriotic Canadians. There'll be people saying Uncle Sam should intervene—to protect the innocent, preserve the peace. You know."

"Will you help us, or them, if the bluecoats come over the border?" Roley said.

"I sure as hell wouldn't help *them*," Arthur said. "Blue coat or not. I don't believe in empires, not the British one nor the American one that so many Americans suddenly seem to want. I'm a Republican, and I want a republic."

Roley smiled and reached over and patted his arm. "Good man," he said. Then Roley brightened. "Willie," he said, "there's vegetable soup and bread out there for the patients. Want some?"

"I thought you'd never ask," I said.

So Roley went out, and came back in two minutes with an enormous bowl of soup and three thick pieces of black bread. The bread was coarse and tasteless, and the soup was watery, with over-sized chunks of potato in it. Somebody had dumped a lot of Worcestershire sauce in it, in an ill-advised attempt to improve the flavour.

And it was the best meal of my lifetime. There's nothing like almost having your head blown off, and losing a vast amount of blood in the process, to work up a terrific appetite.

* * *

The next day I didn't sleep. I ate. The Field Force must have captured at least one hen-house, because they served me an enormous meal of fried eggs, with more coarse bread, and scalding and immensely strong coffee. Halfway through the afternoon, I asked if they had any more eggs, expecting to be ignored or cursed at, and within fifteen minutes another heaping plate arrived.

For dinner they gave me a huge piece of pork with fried potatoes. Blood was running out of the pork. I complained about this. "Nobody else minded, Lieutenant," the ambulance attendant said reproachfully, but he took the plate away anyway. Ten minutes later, he brought it back with everything on it incinerated to a cinder. I gobbled it all down with immense enjoyment.

An hour later, Roley and Jack arrived. They listlessly played a few games of whist with me. Finally, I asked how things were going. "I heard a little firing today," I said. "Not much."

Roley groaned. "Not much," he said. "That about sums up the progress of the God damn North-West Field Force. Not much. It's a God damn disgrace. The old man doesn't have one clue as to what to do. They marched us out and we wasted a lot of bullets firing at an invisible enemy, which hardly even bothered to shoot back. The cannons blasted away at the village and the houses on the other side of the river. And achieved nothing, so far as I could see. The Midlanders spent the day digging useless trenches between here and the river. Then we came back to this stinking hole in the ground, with them jeering at us. Middleton is afraid to try to move ahead. He's buffaloed by their rifle pits, by *them*. Morale could not be lower. The men think we are going to be withdrawn, and then English troops will come."

"Any losses?" I asked.

"A few," Jack said. "One or two dead."

"So we achieved nothing?" I asked, a bit incredulous.

"Well, maybe," Roley said. "French's and Boulton's Scouts found an open space north and east of the church. Middleton may intend to launch an attack from there." Jack snorted. "It's called the Jolly Prairie, or some such thing," Roley said.

"*Jolie prairie,* I suppose," I said. "Pretty meadow."

"Wonderful," Roley said. "We can all have a reunion picnic there, with the enemy, ten years from now, after Riel's established an independent country out here." After a few more minutes of desultory conversation, he and Jack said goodbye, and got up and walked out of the tent.

But a few seconds later Jack came back. I could see Roley waiting for him, standing twenty feet or so from the tent, patiently smoking his pipe. Jack stood looking down at me oddly. "I just thought you should know," he finally said. "Your tunic and pants were all covered in blood. Roley didn't want you to come back to the company looking like a clown. He spent over an hour, up to his knees in a creek in ice-cold water, scrubbing your uniform with a brush and a bar of soap. He washed it over and over again." Jack stared at me. "You know, Willie, Roley sees you as being like a younger brother or a son, almost."

I did not know what to say, so I just nodded. "He's a good man," Jack said. "A really good man. So we shouldn't let him down. We mustn't. Am I right?"

"Of course," I said, a bit irritably. "Why would I let him down?"

"Well, you wouldn't," Jack said. "You wouldn't. I'm just saying, that's all." He stared at me almost defiantly for a few seconds. Then he turned, and walked stiffly out of the tent.

* * *

The next day, I continued to eat prodigious quantities of food. They had apparently decided that I was going to live, so the diet of eggs had been supplanted by huge plates of bully beef, accompanied by what we had learned to call "Government Biscuit," a substance so unchewable and inedible that Arthur Howard had called it "worse than anything the U.S. Army ever knew."

There was intermittent firing all that day, but nobody would tell me what was going on. Probably no one knew. After a colossal supper of bully beef and biscuit, I nodded off, and was awakened by Colonel Williams of the Midland Battalion, shaking me by the shoulder. "Wake up, Willie," he said. "I've got great news for you, lad."

I blinked the sleep out of my eyes and looked at him. His face was almost as red as a soldier's tunic. He looked exhausted. Standing behind him were Roley, Jack and Arthur Howard. Roley looked tired. Jack had an odd look of excitement on his face. The American looked amused.

"The colonel has something to say," Roley said.

"That's right," Williams said. He sat down on the ground beside me. "I came here to say to you, Willie, what I've been saying to a lot of people, including Colonel Grassett of the Grenadiers. And Roley, and Jack, and all the officers, excepting the damned English. You need to hear it too. That's because you're going up to the line tomorrow morning, Willie." Roley grinned at me. I tried to look pleased.

Williams lit a cigarette. "The thing is," he said in a low voice, "that we are fed up. The silly damn old Englishman wasted this whole day, again, farting and bumbling around, pushing men forward and pulling them back again, accomplishing nothing. The men are fed up. We keep getting shot at. We have suffered very light casualties, because we are not *doing* anything. The men can't even see their enemy. We are going nowhere. We haven't taken an inch of ground. And now Middleton has wired Caron, the Militia Minister, I happen to know. The messenger wasn't supposed to show me the telegram, but he disobeyed his orders, like a proper soldier, and showed the God damn telegram to me. In the telegram, bloody Middleton says he's in a ticklish position. He can hold, but no more. He wants more troops."

"The British," Jack said.

Williams looked owlishly at him. "Probably," he said. "Probably. But the thing is, the Indians all over the West are sitting on the fence, waiting to see if we can take Batoche. That's what the Scouts say, and this is their country. We have to take Batoche, and we have to take it now. Even if it's Canadians they send, by the time any force big enough to satisfy that scared old man arrives, every Indian in the West will have risen up against us. We'll have a rebellion which will last for many months, probably for years." He beat his fist furiously into the palm of his other hand. "And there's no reason for it, no God damn reason!" He looked uneasily around him. Other wounded men were staring curiously at us. "So," Williams went on, in a lowered voice, almost a whisper this time, "tomorrow we are going to do something. I am not sure what or when. Unless Middleton comes up with a sensible and aggressive plan of attack, we are going to take the bit between our teeth. We are going to give them hot stuff. You wait and see if we don't. I will give you the signal. I want Company Four right alongside the Midland Battalion. You three men are combat veterans. So is all of Company Four. I need you three, and your company. If we have to act against orders, I will take the responsibility if anything goes wrong. I want you to know that."

He put his hand to his head, and seemed to slump over. "Are you all right, sir?" I said.

Williams shook his head and smiled wearily. "Yes, Willie," he said. "Yes, I am. I just keep getting these damn headaches. And I'm so tired. But this is no time for us to be thinking of ourselves, is it? No, we must think of our country." He looked around at us sternly, impressively. Then he rose to his feet and strode determinedly out of the tent, the very picture of Anglo-Saxon indomitability.

We watched him go in silence. Finally, I said, "Arthur, you're a professional soldier. Does he know what he's doing?"

"Possibly," the American said. "I don't think Middleton has completely lost his nerve, but he's close. I'll give him this: he's got more brains than I expected. He hasn't made the stupid mistake British officers often make, of assuming that 'natives' are cowardly idiots who can be scattered by one British volley. He knows just how good those gentlemen over there really are. But I think he underestimates his own soldiers. And one more thing. The enemy's volume of fire has gone way down. They wasted a lot of ammunition on the first day. Now they save it for effective shots. I think the priests were telling the truth about the ammunition shortage."

"All of which means what?" Jack said.

Arthur looked a bit annoyed. "All of which means, *John*," he said carelessly, "that maybe the gallant Colonel Williams will go down in history as the man who took Batoche. But let's not forget he wanted to charge the afternoon of the first day, when it would have produced a massacre of his own men. So, equally possibly, he may be remembered as the man who got hundreds of troops killed when he lost his head and disobeyed orders. It all remains to be seen." He gave us a grave salute. "But not for long." He turned at the tent door. "I just saw Middleton, van Straubenzee, French and Boulton in Middleton's tent, huddled over a map. I suspect the old man is going to make one last serious attempt to take Batoche."

After he had gone, we chatted a little. Then Jack said goodbye, and got up and left. Roley looked at me speculatively for a minute. "You all right?" I asked.

"No," he said. "I'm not. This whole thing is beginning to make me sick. I killed a man. You saw it. I helped burn down a farmhouse the first day, because van Straubenzee thought sharpshooters might use it. Neatest place I ever saw, that farmhouse. My mother would have approved; it was that clean. The poor bloody Frenchman's wife had made curtains for the windows. On the curtains were printed ridiculous little yellow suns. Little boy suns, with caps on, and little girl suns with bonnets, all smiling. We could have had those curtains in my house in Toronto. We burned the place to ashes, curtains and all." He stopped and stared down for a moment. "Willie, what is going on here? The men are asking me, how could these people have been plotting a revolution, when they don't even have enough ammunition? They aren't stupid, and ammunition is easy to buy. But Lord Melgund said they had it all planned. I can't understand it."

Roley had brought my uniform, and my holster and revolver back. The tunic and trousers were a little faded, but he had done an amazing job of getting the blood out. I said as much. He smiled. "When this insanity is over, William," he said, "I go back to what I used to be. A specialist in retail clothing, including the washing of same."

That night, my new-found soldier's habit of sleeping soundly failed me. I lay awake for a long time, thinking that tomorrow something big was going to happen at Batoche.

Alice

Last night, at dinner, my father began talking about the campaign. I know my mother has asked him not to do this; I heard her.

But I think he could not help himself. He glanced at me before he began, a sidelong glance of anger and malice. I suddenly realized that he wanted to hurt me, that he was determined to at all costs.

"The militia have signally failed," he said, with vast complacency. "The newspapers all report it. They are completely baffled—buffaloed, as our Yankee friends would have it—by the Métis and Indians. Sophisticated thinkers who could see past Macdonald's ignorant militarism predicted it from the start. Our poor, incompetent soldiers, faced by skilled frontiersmen. The Métis have never been defeated on their home ground. They never will be."

He looked at me with palpable self-satisfaction. "The militia have fallen into a quagmire," he said. "There will likely be a great slaughter of them before they get out of it. If they get out of it."

I stood up. I knew that my whole life depended on what I was about to do.

And I did it.

"God damn you, Father," I said. Milly the new Irish maid gasped, and dropped the tray holding the dessert and coffeepot with a tremendous crash. "You knew I hated this war," I said. "And you know I love Willie." My parents were gaping at me, white-faced. "I never want to hear this nonsense from you again."

My father started to get up. He looked as if he were about to have an apoplectic fit. Maybe he was.

"Alice…" he said.

"And don't 'Alice' me," I said, and I walked out the dining room door.

As I reached the second floor, I realized that my mother was charging up right behind me. She grabbed me by the shoulders, and pushed open my bedroom door. She pushed me across the room and onto the bed.

She sat beside me. Her face was working with rage. "How dare you," she said. "How dare you! Your own father!"

"Yes," I said. "My own father. Deliberately goading and hurting me, night after night. What does he care for the Métis? He and his friends want the militia to be slaughtered. That will ruin Macdonald, and prove they were right, after all. And it will get rid of Willie, a man I agreed to marry without his God almighty permission."

"You stupid girl," she said. "You will do what you're told. You will. You are not going to marry that ridiculous little nobody. You are going to marry whoever your father selects. Just as I did."

"Oh, no, I'm not, Mama," I said. "I am leaving this house, even if Father gets his own way and Willie is shot dead."

"Leaving this house?" she said. "Ridiculous. Who ever heard of such a thing?"

"They are going to," I said.

She snorted. "How will you live, you little fool?" she said.

"Oh, Mama," I said. "Don't be so silly. If Willie comes back, and he will, I will live at his parents' place. His mother will have me, and his father does what she tells him. They have a spare bedroom before Willie and I get married, and I will sleep in his after we are." She gasped. "I will help his mother with the cooking and the housework."

"A daughter of mine?" she said. "Doing cooking and housework? Never."

"Willie will go to the teachers' college," I said. "He has already written me that that's what he wants to do. It's only a one-year course, and they would hire him at any collegiate in town, with his marks. And if by any chance you get your heart's desire, and Willie dies out there, I will go to the teachers' college. I have money in my bank account to pay the tuition. They are beginning to hire women as teachers. Or I will work in an office. I know girls who work in an office. Or I will become a nurse." She gaped at me.

"I forbid it," she said. "Your father will forbid it."

"Mama," I said. "I'm twenty-one."

Tears started to pour down her cheeks. "You're crazy!" she shouted. "You're crazy! Nobody ever heard of such a thing! Nobody ever heard of such a thing! What would people say? It's...it's...it's..." Her mouth was working convulsively.

Then she slapped me.

I stared at her in shock. It came to me that it was the first time in my life that she hadn't looked as if she'd stepped out of a bandbox. Her beautiful dark hair was all standing on end, and her beautiful eyes were glazed with tears. Suddenly she clapped her hands to her face and started to cry with a kind of awful desperation. Before she could say or do anything more, I grabbed her, and pulled her into my arms. She doesn't weigh much. I cuddled her, and she cried steadily and inconsolably into my shoulder. I had never realized before how unhappy she must be, every minute of every day of her life.

Finally she made ineffectual attempts to sit up, and I let her. She looked at me timidly. "Will you still love me after you and Willie get married?" she said. "Will you still see me? You're all I've got."

I leaned forward and kissed her. "Mama," I said, "I will love you absolutely until the day I die. You can be in our house every day. We will have a grandchild for you to play with, and he or she will love you too."

"Good!" she said. She looked at me with a slight smile. "I know I'm a silly, useless thing. Your father always says so. You know I will continue to do whatever he wants. I can't imagine living any other way."

I simply hugged her again. She did not make any attempt to resist, nor did she cry any more, and I just held her, for a long, long time.

XVI

The next morning at six o'clock, I put on my uniform. They gave me another colossal breakfast of fried eggs. The weary doctor on duty waved me out of the tent. I briefly surveyed the so-called zareba. It was exactly what Roley kept calling it, a huge hole in the ground with fortified earthen walls. It smelled of excrement and piss, of dirty uniforms, and exhausted, sweaty men.

I walked over to Company Four, which was slumped, exhausted, on the north edge of the zareba. Their heads hung listlessly. Some were flat on their backs or propped up against the zareba wall, with blankets or overcoats pulled over them. It looked like I was the only man in Company Four who had had two decent nights' sleep in a row.

Roley got up and clapped me on the back. He moved slowly; he was pale and haggard from lack of sleep. But he managed a grin. "Welcome back, Sunny Jim," he said. He and I sat down beside the fire. He went through the ritual of lighting his pipe. "Old fuss and feathers has actually come up with a battle plan," he said. "Can you believe it? Middleton, in person, with Arthur's Gatling, one cannon, and Boulton's Scouts are going to advance north and east to this Jolly Prairie meadow. They are going to make a 'feint,' I think they called it. They will open fire, and make a lot of noise. The idea is that the Mateys and Indians will go running over there and abandon the defences in the west.

"Meanwhile, the Grenadiers, Midlanders and Winnipeg Rifles, which are most of the infantry, will take up positions to the south

and west, south of the cemetery and the church. We will be in reserve behind them. Van Straubenzee will be in command. Their
signal will be when they hear old lardass Middleton cutting loose
with his artillery. When they hear Middleton's cannon going *pop!*
and the enemy have all supposedly run over there, our infantry will
move north, past the church, and advance on Batoche. And so will
we, I guess. Or so goes the theory of it, anyway."

"Wonderful," I said. "Positively Wellingtonian."

He smiled at me, and held out his tobacco pouch. "Someday,
young fellow," he said, "I will figure out what in hell you're talking
about."

* * *

At ten o'clock, Middleton, the Scouts, one cannon and its gun-
ners, and Arthur with his Gatling, moved out of the zareba to the
north-east. Arthur waved his Yankee cap to us, and we waved back.
A few minutes later, the Grenadiers, the Winnipeggers and the
Midlanders went crashing out as well, heading north-west. Colonel
Williams rode close by us, and winked at Roley.

We stayed, slouched uselessly against the north wall of that
stinking zareba. It was a cold day. A howling wind blew from the
direction of the river, east and north toward where our intrepid
English commander intended to make his 'feint.' I chatted with
Abercrombie, a skinny Company Four man who was an amateur
astronomer back home.

At one point, I heard a faint distant crackling, and what might
have been a paper bag being exploded about a mile away. I thought,
That can't be firing. Hours went by.

Then a mounted Scout came riding hell-for-leather toward us
from the north-east. He entered the zareba, and rode right past
Company Four. "Middleton's coming back!" he roared. Then he
grinned at me. "The old man is fit to be tied."

About ten minutes later, Middleton's dejected, sagging column
stumbled into the camp. Middleton, however, was not dejected. He
was furious. What I'd heard *had* been firing. And van Straubenzee's

infantry had not attacked.

Middleton immediately sent for van Straubenzee, Williams, Grassett, and the other senior officers. When they arrived, Middleton utterly lost his head. Crimson-faced, choking, spluttering, he roared imprecations at them for their failure to attack. In vain did van Straubenzee protest that nobody had heard any firing from Middleton's column. At the end, his face a kind of rich puce, the old man roared, "This afternoon, van Straubenzee, you can take your Canadians as far as you like. Or as far as you don't like, for all I care!"

He did not salute, he simply turned his back on van Straubenzee and walked into his tent. Van Straubenzee stood there for a minute, looking like someone had spat in his face. I saw Williams come up to him. Williams and Grassett took him aside, and I saw both of them talking very urgently and gesticulating, while van Straubenzee listened without saying a word.

Then Colonel Williams came up to us. "Gentlemen," he said. "Colonel van Straubenzee wants Company Four moved up to the line right now." He looked angry, and also, in some strange way, elated. He walked away, got on his horse, and followed by the rest of the Canadian colonels, headed back toward the firing line.

Roley, Jack, Colour Sergeant Quinn, and I formed the company up, and we marched out of that Godforsaken, littered, stinking stockade. The wind held hard from our left, from the west, from the river. We marched past the ruins of the house which Roley had burned.

It had gotten a lot hotter. The sun shone in an almost cloudless sky from nearly overhead. In two minutes, I was sweating again in my heavy tunic. I marched beside Roley and Jack at the head of the column. Both of them had lit their pipes, and the smell of strong Virginia tobacco mingled with the grassy fragrance of the prairie meadow and the sweet, dank smell of the river only a few hundred yards away. To our right and north of us, there was renewed firing. I guessed that some of Boulton's Scouts had ridden back toward the *Jolie prairie,* and gotten into a gun fight with the Métis rifle pits.

Where in hell was Arthur and his Gatling? I craned my neck around to try to find that reassuring piece of equipment, but it wasn't there.

Colonel Williams' Midlanders were on the extreme left of the line, just south of the little fenced cemetery. Williams gestured Company Four into the position just to his right. To *our* right were the familiar red tunics of the Grenadiers. Some were still wearing their helmets; some had on the white kepis with the white neck-cloths dangling. The dark coats of the Winnipeg Rifles were to their right and slightly behind.

From our left, across the river, there came the occasional sharp reports of Winchesters and puffs of smoke. There were sharpshooters hidden over there. On the far left of the Midlanders, closest the river, our infantry fired back at every puff of smoke. I heard occasional yells of rage from over there, as the Midlanders dived for cover over and over again.

In front of us lay the little cemetery, gleaming in the sunlight. To its right was a grassy slope leading down toward the church and the rectory, perhaps two hundred and fifty yards away. Just before the rectory, the slope went slightly up again. Ahead of us was the forbidding tangle of brush which marked Mission Ridge, the ravine where we'd been stopped cold on the first day. North-east of that, perhaps twelve hundred yards away, invisible on the other side of heavy brush, lay the east village of Batoche. The green meadows and trees shone, they glowed, in the perfect spring sunshine.

But there were rifle pits in front of us, and some more over by the corner of the church. We were solemnly warned by the Midlanders, who'd been there that morning. Our arrival was greeted by a volley of enemy lead. The men threw themselves as flat as pancakes on the ground, and began firing at nothing, at the puffs of smoke from the invisible rifle pits. It was the first day of the battle all over again. It was the second and third days, which I'd missed, but whose futile skirmishes had been described to me. I had the giddy feeling that this would never end: that we and the Métis would indulge forever in this deadly mating dance, sidling up to the perfectly-concealed rifle pits, blasting away at nothing, then dancing back again, always with dead men, or men whose legs or arms spouted blood.

On the Midlanders' extreme left, from across the Saskatchewan, came more shots. Then there was an excited chorus of yelling and cursing. "Shit! Shit!" I could hear someone screaming, probably an angry officer. Somebody had been hit over there and pretty bad. I saw that Roley was looking intently over, toward the left.

Abruptly, he turned to Colour Sergeant Quinn, who was on his right. "Colour Sergeant," he said, "pass the order to fix bayonets." The colour sergeant looked at Roley interrogatively for a few seconds, then did as he was told. The air filled with the clattering of the men pulling out their bayonets and fixing them, while still trying to lie perfectly flat. It was hard to do. Two of the men shifted their position slightly, just to my right. One, Private Wallace, went up on one knee, fumbling with his cumbersome rifle.

As quick as a cat came the *bang!* from the rifle pits and with a shriek, Wallace toppled over. Arterial blood was spouting out of his arm just above the elbow. Cursing, shouting men hauled him backward down a little knoll. They cut long white tourniquets and applied them to his upper arm. Through the crowd of Company Four men and ambulance attendants, I could still see Wallace's white face, covered with a sheen of sweat. His scared brown eyes were desperately rolling like a horse's, as the scarlet splashing from his arm slowed to a slow stream. The blood-spattered attendants started carrying him off to the rear.

Roley was staring fixedly at Wallace as they carried him away. He had not moved a muscle while the man was hit or while he was being treated. Now he continued to stare behind us, into the distance, as the stumbling attendants staggered toward the rear. Sweat poured down Roley's face, down the back of his neck, staining his scarlet tunic. He was muttering something over and over to himself. I strained, and I made it out. "No more," he was saying. "No more."

Suddenly, he hoisted himself to his feet with a fluid motion. He began striding to our right, out in front of Company Four. Jack said, "Oh no! Roley!" and grabbed for his leg. Without looking down, Roley kicked his hand away.

Roley was shouting now. "Do you want to wait for the rest of time while we get murdered?" From a rifle pit between us and the church, two shotguns went off, but the range was too great, and the pellets kicked up dust at his feet. He looked down at this for a moment with a disinterested air. "We don't need any God damn British!" he shouted. "We don't need anybody!" A rifle went off, and I saw the faintest line of scarlet on the left waist of his tunic, as the bullet grazed him. The next one would not. He did not seem to notice it.

I think that this moment was the culmination of Roley's whole life. He waved his revolver, like the British officers he'd no doubt seen in magazine illustrations. *"Come on, boys,"* he roared. *"Charge!"*

I found myself scrambling to my feet, as was Jack, as was the whole company. I looked to my left. Colonel Williams was watching us, and as we struggled up, he started shouting, and waving his sword.

What happened next is still a little hazy in my mind. Company Four started down the slope toward the church at a dead run, shouting like madmen. Roley was leading the way, firing his revolver at the invisible enemy. I looked left again, self-conscious as ever, afraid that we might be charging all by ourselves. We'd look like clowns in a farce. I needn't have worried. The whole Midland Battalion, bellowing like demons, were charging beside us, with Williams running like hell in the forefront, waving that ridiculous sword. To our right, the scarlet tunics of the Grenadiers were pouring down the slope as well. Behind us a cannon went off, and a geyser of mud and grass flew up dismayingly close to our advancing men.

I had my Enfield out and was running half a pace behind Roley. As I ran, my posture was one gigantic flinch. I wanted to turn and run, to throw myself into the grass, to pretend to be wounded, anything at all to avoid the bullet with my name on it. But I didn't die. The avalanche of firing we'd seen the first day would have decimated us. It didn't come.

As we rushed down the slope, one shot went off from a gun pit right in front of us. One of our men fell, and a couple of others stopped to help him. Ahead of me and to the left, two more puffs of grey smoke shot out of a concealed pit. There were shots coming at us from near the church. One of them hit the rifle of a man charging to my right, making a loud whacking noise, and spinning it right out of his hands. He stood bewildered, while his screaming comrades surged past him.

Then we were on top of the pit in front of us. It was deep, with white birch logs surrounding it on three sides. With amazing agility, three Métis vaulted out of the back of it. They were dressed in the unofficial enemy uniform, slouched black hats and black coats. They'd dropped their rifles and shotguns. The men started firing at them on the run, and one of them fell over, clutching his side. The next second, one of our men straddled him, yelled something incoherent, and thrust his bayonet into the back of the man's neck. The Métis screamed, like a terrified girl. Bright red arterial blood spouted from his neck in a steady burst.

I thought, *These are almost the first enemy I've seen since the beginning of the first day.* I was screaming like a demented man. Some of the Métis' blood splashed on my boot as I charged past him. More of them were running ahead of us. I was passing other pits, empty pits. In front of us, at the corner of the church, six or eight men had scrambled out of their holes in the ground. Four or five of them fired, hastily, and from the corner of my eye I saw a Grenadier go sprawling right past his yelling, charging colonel, to roll limply down the hill. There was more disorganized firing from our side, and I saw spouts of dirt kicked up around the Métis at the church. They ran.

To the right, through our yelling and cheering, I could hear the sound of heavy militia firing and the *bang-bang-bang!* of Arthur's Gatling. I didn't know it then, but Middleton had gotten over his pique and was back on the line. Seeing that his left wing had run amok, he had ordered the Winnipeg Rifles, the Scouts and Arthur to form a line to our right and move forward with us, in a scything motion toward the village. This was to avoid the flanking maneuver against us which Roley and Williams had never thought of, but which would have been the first thing to occur to Gabriel Dumont. We were close to the church. Old man Middleton's "feint" had worked in spite of itself. Where were the men who should have been in the empty pits past which we charged? Still over on the right, where the enemy must have expected an attack. And the enemy *was* running out of ammunition. Nowhere on the field, not from in front of us, not to our right, was there the wall of firing which had staggered us on the first day. *Jack, you owe the Catholics an apology,* I thought. *The priests told the redcoats the truth.*

Howling like devils, our men and Williams' surged past the church and rectory and charged straight toward the village. To our right, I could see the Winnipeggers in their dark tunics, pressing forward grimly, bayonets fixed. In the distance, the Gatling blatted. In front of Company Four lay a slight slope downward, some of it meadow, some of it lightly treed with birch. It shone innocently as we poured into it. There were enemies in that sweet-looking meadowland. But they were scared. Their ammunition was low, and charging straight at them came hundreds of men who wanted their blood. A lot of the enemy fired one premature volley and fled. I could see the black-coated forms racing desperately for the village.

Some of them did not run away. They waited until we were on top of them, and then they fired. The thick plumes of grey smoke suddenly shot out in front of our faces, with the thunderclap of collective firing. We did not flinch. Amateur Sunday soldiers that we were, we were running wild now, letting off weeks of anger and fear.

As we hurtled forward, two puffs of gunsmoke belched out of a rifle pit that *couldn't* have been there, a rifle pit invisible in the flat meadow. One of our men fell beside me with an agonized cry. The side of his tunic was instantly sopping with blood. In the next second, a Métis pulled himself out of the back of the pit and headed for the village. Our advance guard fired clumsily and fruitlessly at him. He was fleeing at a dead run, zig-zagging, head held low.

But there'd been *two* rifle shots. Several of us rushed toward the pit. Suddenly, an old man, bare-headed, white-haired, white-bearded, pulled himself laboriously out of the front of the pit. He was intently reloading his muzzle-loader. He didn't look scared, just determined. I wondered for a half-second if we were supposed to kill him or capture him. Then, from my right, a scarlet-coated figure hurled itself at the old man. It was my acquaintance of the morning, Abercrombie, the stargazer. His face was red and contorted, and he was howling like an animal. He slammed his bayonet into the old man's side, with an audible squelching noise, like a cleaver cutting into a watermelon.

We were hurtling forward, yelling, apparently irresistible. I could see more and more of the enemy firing one last round, then streaming toward the village. I had run nearly half a mile, and my head had nearly been blown off three days before. I had never been very strong. I should have folded up like a dishrag. Borne up by sheer excitement, I was not even winded. To our left were the sprawling buildings of the Métis river farms, and then, like magic, we topped a little crest, and there before us was Batoche.

In front of us was a deep slope, shining improbably green and pure. Beyond that was the village, perhaps seven hundred yards away. There were several straggling rows of stores and houses, and a great mass of Indian tents. Some of the buildings were unpainted, others shone white in the afternoon sunlight. There was one big white house, that of Batoche the ferryman.

There were only scattered shots coming at us now. The North-West Field Force had converged, bunched up together in the most idiotic redcoats-up-Bunker-Hill way. Except that we were running downhill, and the opposition had almost ended. With one last roar, hundreds of men charged down that lovely slope and poured into Batoche.

Leaderless, most of the men headed for Batoche's house or the largest of the stores. A few seconds later, there was excited yelling from inside the store. Prisoners had been found, some Métis opponents of Riel, some white.

Now shots came spattering at us again. Some of the rebels had made a stand in rifle pits in brush west of the village near the river-bank. Our men, cooled down from the frenzy they'd been in, dived for cover behind stables and outbuildings. Some of the Scouts made a rush for Batoche's big house, which was close to the river.

Captain French kicked in Batoche's door, and rushed into the house. Seconds later, he leaned out of a second-story window, and threw one leg out so that he straddled the windowsill. He was firing a revolver at something and shouting encouragement to his men. Then a rifle shot cracked, and French simply fell out of the window. His body did a half somersault in the air, and he landed on his back in the dust. A fall like that could have crippled a man for life, but I was becoming more expert in such matters. I knew that he was dead before he hit the ground.

The Métis who had shot him was an older man, still standing in the open near the edge of the village. He began to run with surprising speed toward the river. There was total silence for a few seconds. One of French's men stared at his captain's body and muttered *"Christ!"* The old man hopped and jumped desperately toward the sanctuary of the riverbank. I stared at this, bemused. Under other circumstances, it would have been funny. Then about ten rifles went off together, and the old man crumpled over.

The mass of our men were streaming toward the west part of the village, returning the fire from the brush. Arthur had conveniently appeared, and he started peppering the underbrush with Gatling rounds. Then somebody nearly scared the shit out of me by grabbing my arm. It was Roley. "Come on," he said. "It's not over. Get out of the open, for God's sake."

We darted down a little alleyway between two rows of houses. Roley had his revolver in his hand. I found to my surprise that so did I, although I had no memory of firing it during the charge. As we approached the corner of the last house, Roley carefully pressed himself against the wall. He was breathing hard. He put out his left arm, and pressed me against the side of the house, right behind him.

Roley had his revolver, barrel upward, in his right hand. Very slowly and deliberately, he peered around that corner with one eye. Instantly there was the loud crash of a rifle, and wood splinters flew just above his head. He pulled his head back. "Jesus!" he said. He just stood there for a few seconds. He was still breathing hard. I knew he was trying to get up the nerve to expose himself to the enemy again and fire. "Christ," he said. "Oh, Christ." He took two more deep breaths and let them out. He cocked the revolver. Then he whirled himself partly around the corner, revolver gripped in both hands. Three seconds later, he fired. Then he wheeled back around the corner, so fast his back slammed into the unpainted wall.

"Willie," he said, "I saw him. I think I hit him. There's a kind of loft in the house over there. He's up in the loft. We've got to get over there, before he kills somebody. We'll go in the front door, fast. I'll go first. Keep your finger off the trigger as we run. Don't blow my ass off. When we get in there, you go left, I'll go right. If he's not there, I'll go up the stairs or the ladder. Christ, I hope it's not a ladder. *Come on!*"

He took off around the corner, and I followed at a dead run. The house was only about thirty feet away, but it was the longest thirty feet of my life. The house was two-storeyed, and surprisingly broad. Two wide loft doors sprawled wide on the second floor. As we rushed across the dooryard, I had the now-familiar feeling of waiting for the bullet to slam into my chest.

And once again, it didn't. Roley booted the door in, and wheeled wildly around to his right, the revolver pointed straight ahead of him. The first thing I saw, on the left, was a mass of candles burning. *God,* I thought, *it's a church.* Then I saw that they surrounded a long, pine box supported on a rough wooden trestle. I ran toward it, and my heart nearly leaped out of my chest. There was a man in it. A second look at his waxy skin and open mouth told me that he was dead.

"Come on!" Roley yelled again desperately. The main floor was empty. There *was* a staircase toward the rear of the house. It ran straight up to a landing, then dog-legged to the right. Roley started up the stairs slowly, his back pressed against the right-hand wall of the staircase. His right arm held the revolver, barrel-up. When he reached the top stair just short of the landing, he fluttered his left

hand behind him in a gesture meaning I should halt, and press back against the wall.

He was breathing like a man having a heart attack, and his face was running with sweat. "Holy Christ, holy *Christ!*" he whispered. Then he spun himself around the corner and at once fired. He pulled himself back again, with a doubtful look on his face, then whirled around the corner again. Two or three seconds passed. Then, "Willie," he said. "It's all right. I think he's dead."

He walked deliberately up the two shallow stairs that were in front of him, and his calm manner reassured me enough that I followed. "Why did you fire, just now?" I said.

"How do I know?" he said. He was still gasping for breath. A figure in a black coat lay crumpled up on the floor. We walked over to it, revolvers cocked. But I *was* developing an instinct. I knew he was dead. A long, antiquated rifle was hanging part-way out through the open loft doors. It had not been there as we rushed the house, I knew. Our enemy had been dying as we entered, bleeding, trying to load and fire another round. Roley pulled the rifle back in. "Somebody will shoot at it," he said. With the toe of his boot, he turned the body over.

It was the dead body of a boy. He had pale skin and a lot of jet-black hair, splayed around his face like a halo. He could have been alive, but for the huge blood-stain that covered the front of his ragged shirt. "Oh, God," Roley said. "How old, Willie?"

"Thirteen or so," I said.

Roley stood staring down at the body for a minute or so. His face was unreadable. Then we heard a lot of yelling, coming from the direction from which we'd come. "Come on," he said. "Those idiots will shoot at anybody they see up here, red coats or not."

We clattered down the stairs. I had an odd thought: *Nobody will shoot at me, again, ever in my life.* I walked over to the coffin, and Roley followed. "Oh, oh," he said and pointed.

Tucked in beside the dead man was his hat, with a long red feather on one side.

"It's the man I killed, isn't it?" Roley said. His voice was low.

I looked at the man. A long, narrow sheet of muslin was wound around his neck. There were speckles of blood on it. It probably had been wrapped there to hide the awful wound Roley had made in his neck. I could have looked, but I could never have borne to peel that white wrapping off, and neither, I believe, could Roley.

"I think so," I said.

He did not reply. I turned around, and saw that he had picked up a photograph from the sideboard. It was in a cheap, gaudy frame. The back of the frame was transparent, and you could read stamped on the back of the picture in red ink:

CHAS. MARTIN, PHOTOGRAPHER
Prince Albert, N.W.T.
1883

The photograph had been taken in front of the house. The dead man in the coffin was dressed in an old-fashioned black suit, which I am sure was his Sunday best. He had the hat in his hands. The red feather looked grey in black-and-white. He had his arm around the boy who lay dead up in the loft. The kid looked about eleven. He wore a suit, too, with a white shirt buttoned uncomfortably tight around his throat. The man was smiling proudly. Standing beside them, with a faint, shy smile on her face, half staring downward, was the mother, wearing an absurd bonnet. She looked much more Indian than the man, or the son. Beside her, squinting into the camera and hanging on tight to her mother's hand, was a little girl of about six. She took after the mother.

"Imagine that," I said. "They actually had a formal photograph taken."

He did not say anything. He pulled his tunic up for a second and stuffed a handkerchief against the slight wound he'd gotten when he'd jumped up to order the charge. It wasn't bleeding much. Then he walked out into the street, and I followed him.

All the firing had stopped. We retraced our steps past the corner where the rifle ball had almost hit Roley. In the street beyond it, soldiers were lining each side. A lot of the Métis had surrendered. They were being herded down the middle of the road, women and children after them. The men stumbled, humiliated, down the dusty street. They looked exhausted and half-starved. Their shabby black clothes hung loosely on them. The women glared around them defiantly. The children were afraid; they stared mutely at the ground and did not look at the soldiers. None of our men made a sound.

A heavy, very Indian-looking woman in a dark blue dress caught my eye. She actually shook her fist at me. "*Maudits barbares!*" she yelled. "*R'gardez ce que vous avez fait ! Vous avez tout ruiné!*"

You damn barbarians! Just look what you've done! You've ruined everything!

"Willie," Roley said, "what was that day Williams was making a speech about, before we marched on Batoche? Some special day in Shakespeare, where the out-numbered English had to fight the French."

"Saint Crispin's Day," I said.

"Yeah," he said. "Well, this *was* Saint Crispin's Day, after all. Wasn't it? For these people, not us. Jesus, just *look* at them. Look at their town. They don't have a pot to piss in, or a window to throw it through. There are only a God damn handful of them, and they held off an army with cannons and a Gatling gun. And the day went about as you'd expect, outside of fairy tales. They lost."

Colonel Williams came up to us, grinning like the Cheshire cat. "Gentlemen," he said. He took Roley's arm in one of his arms and mine in the other. We walked down the middle of the street, and the soldiers on either side of it started cheering and kept right on cheering. Some of it was for Colonel Williams. Everybody thought the world of him. Maybe a little bit of it was for me. But the lion's share was for Captain Roland Collison of the Toronto Light Infantry Regiment. I stole a look over at him. He was walking along, staring at the ground, and I don't think he even noticed the cheering.

*   *   *

The village was ours, and the Métis part of the Rebellion—which was most of it—was over. The militia officers shared a general unwillingness to sleep in tents any more, let alone in that infernal zareba. They housed some of us in Letendre's Store, a biggish building (for Batoche) with a false front looming up above the roofline and large plate-glass windows. Roley and I slept in a little room right beside the front door.

About eleven-thirty that night, I woke up. Roley was just coming in the door. He smiled apologetically at me. "Sorry," he said. Then I saw that he had something in his hand. It was the photograph from the house. He looked down at it. "Oh, I'm not stealing it," he said. "For some reason, I just wanted to look at it again for a while. So I went over there and got it. Lucky the sentries didn't shoot me. I got challenged twice. I'll put it back."

I grunted and turned over in my bed. Around one, I woke up again. Roley had lit a candle. He was sitting, exhausted-looking but still wakeful, cross-legged on the floor, smoking his pipe steadily, and occasionally looking at the photograph in its gaudy frame.

THE ARMIES THAT REMAINED

XVII

Reveille the next morning, for officers only, was pushed ahead to a leisurely six o'clock. Roley and I went outside a few minutes later. The rising sun shone.

Nobody was running around looking scared. Nobody was bleeding. A mess tent gleamed beside Batoche's house, and in it I had the most gigantic plate of scrambled eggs I could stuff into myself. "Lots of eggs, gentlemen," the beaming mess sergeant said. "We looted every henhouse for three miles around."

Arthur Howard came and sat beside us on the ground. He was drinking a tin cup of coffee and puffing one of his abominable cigars. "Well," he said, "it's all over, including the shouting. Most of them have come in and peacefully surrendered. A few of them are hiding out in the bush, but we have their homes, their fields, and their women and children. A pretty thorough search has been made for weapons of any kind. It's over."

He looked around him and lowered his voice. "Not to detract from the courage of these men or the quality of the victory," he said. "But I've been talking to some of the enemy who can speak English. They had pretty much had it. They were running out of ammunition, out of food, out of morale. Riel was telling them God would save them. As usual, however, He seems to have been on the side of the big battalions. Jesus, though, you have to admire the fight they put up."

"Riel and Dumont?" I said.

"Skedaddled, both of them," Arthur said. "They won't catch

Dumont. And if Riel's with him, Her Majesty won't get her hands on Louis Riel in this world. Not unless she invades Montana." He grinned. "Better come along and watch the speakin," he said. "Van Straubenzee is going to address the prisoners and the townspeople, in fluent French, apparently. They want me right up there on the platform, too."

At nine o'clock sharp, the militia herded the Métis and Indian prisoners and all the women and children into the big open space between Batoche's house and the village. There must have been several hundred of them. A thick ring of soldiers with fixed bayonets surrounded them, and just to make the lesson clearer, one of the field pieces had been set up, loaded, and aimed right into the middle of the crowd. The gunners looked like they meant business.

The Métis and Indian people looked even worse than they had the day before. They'd been kept overnight in a field, ringed with troops. They had a blank, crumpled, humiliated look. Some of the women were wailing, and some of the men put their arms around them and tried to comfort them. Apart from babies, the children were as mute and terrified as they had been the previous day.

A huge wagon had been turned on its side. Van Straubenzee climbed up on it. His African white pith helmet gleamed in the sunshine. On one side of him was Colonel Williams, peaked cap settled jauntily on his head. On the other was Arthur Howard, in his Yankee officer's uniform. The children looked up timidly at them, then looked straight down in embarrassment and fright if one of the officers seemed to be looking back.

Van Straubenzee pulled out of his tunic a fluttering piece of paper. The crowd made an audible noise, a kind of reluctant sigh. All of a sudden, he started to shout, in a tone quite unlike his usual low and courteous voice. He spoke slowly, for emphasis, and I suspect because he had had to laboriously practice the speech. It gave me time to translate for Roley and Jack:

"Vous êtes maintenant les prisonniers des troupes de Sa Majesté. Toute personne du sexe masculin de seize ans et plus qui persiste sera

tuée."
You are now the prisoners of Her Majesty's troops. Any male over the age of sixteen who continues to resist will be shot.

"Toutes les maisons d'où l'on tire sur les troupes de Sa Majesté seront brûlées, et les personnes de sexe masculin de seize ans et plus qui y habitent seront tuées."
Any house from which shots are fired at Her Majesty's troops will be burned down, and its male inhabitants over the age of sixteen will be shot.

"Tous les adultes qui incitent ou encouragent la résistance seront tués."
Any adult person inciting or abetting resistance will be shot.

"Les ordres des soldats doivent êtres suivis immédiatement."
The orders of the soldiers must be obeyed without question.

"Si vous continuez de résister, cela mènera à la destruction de votre propriété privée, incluant les bâtiments, l'église et le presbytère, les maisons et les bâtiments attenants, ainsi que vos provisions alimentaires, vos chevaux et votre machinerie aratoire."
If you continue to resist, it will be answered by the destruction of all your personal property, including buildings, the church and the rectory, houses and sheds, as well as your stores of food, your horses and your agricultural implements.

"Les soldats surveilleront la distribution de nourriture et d'eau."
The soldiers will supervise the distribution of food and water.

"Un couvre-feu est en effet immédiatement et ceci jusqu'à avis contraire. Toute personne du sexe masculin de plus de seize ans qui est arrêtée dehors entre neuf heures du soir et six heures du matin sera tuée. Ceci comprend ceux qui se rendent aux toilettes."
A curfew is in effect until further notice. Any male person over six-

*teen caught outside between nine p.m. and six a.m. will be shot. This
includes persons using the outhouses to relieve themselves.*

*"Allez chez-vous et ne quittez pas votre maison avant qu'un soldat
vous donne le droit de sortir."*
*Now go to your homes and do not leave them until a soldier gives
you permission to do so.*

"Wow," Roley said. "I guess that's the way you have to talk to
them. Defeated enemies, I mean." He looked at me for confirma-
tion.

"Yeah," Jack said. "I guess it is. I guess so." He did not seem very
sure.

"That's the way they conquered their Empire," I said. "No other
way to do it."

"No," Roley said. "The Empire. Quite right."

*   *   *

About half an hour later, Roley, Arthur, Jack and I were sitting in
one of the abandoned Métis stores, a dry-goods store, from the look
of the merchandise. Jack had been trading with a corporal in the
Midlanders. In exchange for a bottle of whiskey that Jack had liber-
ated from some Métis home, the corporal had turned over a huge
amount of very rich Virginia pipe tobacco. Now we sat in a dense
cloud of white smoke, puffing on our pipes in a kind of communal
ecstasy. Even Arthur had produced a curved briar pipe from one of
the many pockets of his blue uniform.

"What else have you got in there, Arthur?" Roley said. "The Dec-
laration of Independence?"

"A sort of simplified summary or digest of it," Arthur said, grinning. "For God damn red-coated Tories who are too stubborn to
see the virtue of a republic."

I had the feeling that this exchange had irritated Jack. He was
opening his mouth to say something, when suddenly an excited
clamoring and shouting started outside. We sat there for a moment,

bewildered, and then the door was flung open. There stood a gangling soldier in a blue artilleryman's tunic, his red and pimpled face even redder with excitement. "They've got him!" he shouted. "Riel! Come and see! They've caught the son of a bitch!"

So we followed the artilleryman, us and an excited crowd of dozens of other soldiers, through the little village and to a road outside it. Beside the road was a fenced-in field, the field in which the Métis and Indian prisoners had been kept overnight. And now, temporarily at least, they were back in it, pending the decision to actually let them return to their houses. The same mob of soldiers with fixed bayonets ringed the wretched little group of prisoners around; the artilleryman's mates had set up their cannon again, ready to fire point-blank if there was any trouble.

I looked at the crowd of prisoners. Never in my life had I seen human beings in so wretched a state. All the previous night, and now again, they had been ordered to bunch together, in that huddled and pathetic mass, and to remain either sitting or lying prone. If you wanted to go over to the edge of the field to relieve yourself, you had to raise your hand and get permission. If you just stood up, without permission, you might be shot.

Crammed together, exhausted, hungry and thirsty, they squatted on the hard ground of the field. The prisoners had been told to keep quiet, but a kind of humming noise of fatigue and terminal despair seemed to come off them. The children huddled against their exhausted mothers, and the women sat with their backs or sides tightly jammed against other women. This was because they were too tired to sit up. A few worn-looking young women had their shirts open, and were breast-feeding babies, while the guarding militiamen, civilized amateur soldiers that they were, studiously looked the other way. Other infants, neglected and hungry, squalled piteously.

The men were in worse shape. I could hardly believe that these beaten souls were the elusive, terrifying, next-to-invisible light cavalrymen who'd run rings around our Scouts, who'd shot us to pieces at Fish Creek, who'd scared *me*, at least, out of my wits. Now they sat, dishevelled and dirty, crushed with exhaustion, arms limply at their sides, heads hanging almost to the dirt with despair. We stared at them in fascination—the enemy!—but they would not return our glances. I found myself looking for the Métis horseman who'd spared my life that night on the road north. He might have been any one of a hundred beaten men.

A low murmur of excitement, rapidly rising in volume, started up among the militiamen nearest the road. I looked up, and saw that a horseman, followed by ten or more red-coated infantry, carrying bayoneted rifles, was coming down the road. Amidst the redcoats was a single man in civilian clothes.

The horseman was a young, handsome, devil-may-care Métis, although he would probably have rejected that French word. He wore a rakish, broad-brimmed, flat-crowned black hat, and a bright red bandana around his neck. I found out later that this was Tom Hourie, one of the English-speaking ones who were on our side. He had captured Riel. The infantry were Midlanders. The exhausted and almost staggering man they were guarding was Louis Riel.

Riel's hair and beard stood up in comic spikes. He had been hiding out in the bush. He was grey with exhaustion, hardly able to put one foot in front of the other, and indeed from time to time one of the redcoats put an arm around his shoulders and helped him for a while. It occurred to me that British or American regulars would have kicked him instead. As they passed the field, Riel looked in at the huddled and wretched people squatting there, and I thought that he slumped even more.

Then something happened. A boy of about ten, who had been lying propped on an elbow, abruptly and loudly said, *"Louis!"* His mother grabbed at him and said something. The boy pushed her hands away. He got up and stood at attention. After a few seconds, he moved away from the mass of huddled prisoners, toward the road. He took his little black hat off. I think that he wanted Riel to see him. Then he snapped to attention again. The boy just stood there, motionless, his arms rigidly thrust downward at his sides, the tails of his black coat fluttering slightly in the breeze.

Men and women were getting up, and trying to stand straight, although they were staggering with fatigue. Some of the sentries surrounding them were waving their rifles around indecisively, and then an officer yelled something, and the sentries subsided. Every man and woman in the field was getting up, standing straight, silently looking at Riel as he passed by. All the men had taken off their hats. Hourie, the man on horseback, said something to Riel's red-coated guards, and they laughed. The little boys and girls were standing up too. The smaller ones clung to their mothers' hands. Some mothers held their tiny children over their heads, in the style of someone's watching a parade, or as if they wanted them to remember something.

The little procession passed us by, on the way to the camp. Hourie continued to look as elegant as ever. The red-coated Midlanders strolled along, looking as unmilitary as they could. Riel was still stumbling with fatigue, but I thought that he had raised his head a little. The prisoners all remained standing at attention. None of them made a sound, until Riel's guards and their captive started to vanish from sight around a bend in the road. Then a woman among the Métis and Indians shouted his name.

* * *

Roley and I had nothing to do now that the war wasn't on any more. We started wandering around the village and its periphery. Shouting, laughing soldiers were gambolling around everywhere, like puppies. Discipline, never the long-suit of the North-West Field Force, had broken down.

And some of the soldiers and teamsters were stealing from the settlers' homes.

"I complained to van Straubenzee about all this first thing this morning," Roley said. "Do you know what he said? He said, 'I'm afraid it will be the old rule.' Then he said something I didn't understand, something like 'vy victim,' or something like that."

"*Vae victis,*" I said. "Woe to the conquered. It's an old Roman expression."

"Woe to the conquered," he said, thoughtfully. "But what would King Arthur and his knights of the round table have thought of that? They were Christians, like us, weren't they? Sir Lancelot and Sir Galahad would never have said 'woe to the conquered.' They always protected the weak. They looked after women and children, and they were merciful to their enemies once they were defeated. I read up on it in my mom's old books. I happen to know they operated on quite different rules in their time."

I was feeling very apprehensive. "When do you think they lived?" I said.

"Who, King Arthur and his men?" he said. "I don't know, exactly. When Mother gave me all those old books of hers to read, she said they lived in the Middle Ages. You tell *me*, you're the educated one. I always presumed Arthur was king about five hundred years ago."

"Roley," I said, gently, "they never lived at all. They're fictitious people. Invented people, in a story."

He looked incredulously at me. "Come on," he said. "All right, maybe they weren't exactly like what the books said. I mean, the things about magic and swords in stones and wizards were made up, for example. Anyone can see that. But they *were* real people."

"No," I said. "They never existed at all. They are just made-up characters. That's all they are."

He was staggered. He laughed, but his face was bright red. I could see that this really hit him hard. "*No*," he said. "I always knew I was a dunce in school, but I thought all these years that those were real people!" He walked along in silence for a minute. Then he looked at me, clearly ashamed. "You must think I'm incredibly ignorant. And I am, obviously."

"Well," I said, embarrassed. "Those characters were made up, long ago, to point out the right way for men to conduct themselves." I was trying to spare him. "It was a code of conduct, the code of chivalry. Something to aim at. So, if you've modelled yourself on them, that was exactly the right thing to do."

He did not say anything for a while. "Oh, sure," he finally said with a sad smile. "Invented to point out the way to behave. Certainly." We walked along in silence for a while. "All the same," he said, "I *did* think they were real people. It's my belief that Mother did, too."

After a time he said, "I think I'm going to take my uneducated, ignorant head back to the store and give it a nap. I'm still tired, even after a good night's sleep."

He walked away. I knew I had humiliated him, and I cursed myself for doing it. I stood there for a few minutes, irresolute. Then for some reason I decided to walk over to the church.

It was an odd experience to retrace my steps across that broad slope leading from the church down to the village. If I'd come back in twenty years, it would have been an odd experience. To do it less than twenty-four hours after the charge was supremely odd. The rifle pits were empty. The bodies had been hauled away. There was, here and there, still dried blood on the peacefully waving grass, but soon enough it would be covered up. The slope was well on its way to becoming an innocent meadowland again.

In the last five minutes, as I trudged along, I had heard several times the distant sound of a woman screaming. It came from east of the village. It was beginning to alarm me, and so I turned around and started back northward through that almost-pristine meadow. I kept hearing the screaming. Eventually, I saw to my right a crowd of red-coated soldiers around a cabin. They were Company Four men. The shouting was coming from there. At the same moment, I saw Roley walking very fast and purposefully from Batoche toward the cabin, a young private walking beside him. I walked over there.

As I came up, Corporal Sutherland was excitedly addressing Roley. "...the one cabin that hasn't been searched. Woman should have been in custody. Can't put it off forever, sir. Every time we try, she starts acting like this. Why, she's crazy. Look at her. Crazy as a damn bedbug. Like a crazy bird defending its nest."

In the doorway stood a tiny woman of about thirty-five. She was dressed in a kerchief pulled over her hair and a brown dress which seemed to hang askew. If she hadn't obviously been insane, she would have been pretty, in a quiet way. As two soldiers tried to push past her, she started screaming again, spittle flying from her mouth, a mad, cracked yelling that made me want to hide, to turn and run. Her eyes stared, almost as if she were blind. She windmilled her arms at the soldiers, fingers open and tensed, like claws. The soldiers fell back awkwardly. One of them cursed, but they made no attempt to move forward again.

"Willie," Roley said. "Talk to her. In French. See if you can reason with her."

She was running frenziedly back and forth. I did not want to reason with her. I did not even want to go near her. As I approached, I could see her eyes darting frantically from side to side, like a terrified animal's. She showed her teeth at me, like a dog. *Your eyes,* I thought. *They always go for your eyes.* Had I survived everything else only to be blinded by a madwoman? "They always go for your eyes," I said. "If she goes for my eyes, grab her."

"Yes, sir," Sutherland said, dubiously.

I stopped about four feet from her. The woman made a rasping noise in her throat. I stared at her for a minute, thinking. Then I said, "*Soyez raisonnable! Il faut que vous laissiez les soldats entrer!*"

Be sensible. You have to let the soldiers in.

She started sobbing. Of course, part of the trouble was that no one could speak her language. She stopped making noises like a beast. She glared furiously around at the soldiers, then at me. Finally, she opened her mouth. Incessant screaming had ruined her voice. It sounded monstrous, a thick, clabbery, deep, rasping voice like a demon in a nightmare. "*Je vous en prie! Allez-vous en! Ne faites plus mal à ma petite fille!*"

Please! Go away! Don't hurt my little girl any more!

Sutherland had been edging around behind her while she concentrated on me. He grabbed her two arms and pinioned them behind her. She broke free from him like someone breaking a child's grip, turned, and began clawing at his face. Sutherland screamed and hurled himself backward. She flew forward and settled on him, avid, still clawing. One of the soldiers hit her in the back of the head with his rifle butt, and she rolled off, only to start struggling back to her feet again. Two more troopers grabbed her and hurled her face forward onto the ground. One had his knee on her back. Three men managed to manhandle her hands behind her back, and tie them. She was still gabbling in that ghastly, clabbery voice. Sutherland got up, bleeding heavily from a wound under his left eye. "Is my eye all right?" he said.

"Yes," Roley said. He was as shocked as everyone else. Then to the men at large: "Take Sutherland to the surgeon. Get his face fixed. Four of you, take *her* there. Don't let her bite. Keep her hands tied. For God's sake don't let go of her. If we're lucky, they've got a straitjacket. They know everything; they're doctors. Let's see how they handle *her*."

The men led Sutherland, staggering, away. The hissing, snarling woman was frog-marched behind him. Roley pulled his revolver and said, "Come on. Let's find out what's in that house."

He marched in ahead of me. The smell hit us first. It was a sour, vile smell, like curdled milk or rotted cheese. "Oh, Christ," Roley said. There was a green, ragged-looking sofa in the middle of the room. We walked over to it. The smell got worse. Lying on the sofa was a little girl of about eight, in a dark-red dress. She had no shoes on. Her eyes were shut. She had been dead, I think, for several days.

Two little tables had been pulled up beside her. On them lay plates of cookies, a piece of pie, a glass, and some water in a jar. The madwoman had been trying to get the child to eat. Several of her favourite dolls had been put on the sofa beside her, little stuffed cloth dolls with smiling faces. A storybook lay open on the other table. I glanced at it. It seemed to be about a talking pony. The pony smiled upward from the page, in the middle of a golden field. The mother had been reading to the child, talking to her, holding her, anything to make her stop playing the bad game she was playing with *Maman*, anything to get her to open her eyes, look around, speak.

Roley was gazing down at the dead child with a lost expression on his face. "Aw, God," he said.

The door opened, and Arthur Howard came in, with two Company Four men. "You fellows all right?" he asked.

"Yes," I said.

Arthur and the two men came over and stared down at the dead girl. "Poor little thing," one of the men said.

"What happened to her, Arthur?" Roley said. "There's not a mark on her."

Arthur looked at her for a minute. He tied his bandana around his face, and then he gently picked her up by the shoulders. He examined her head and neck. Then, he pointed to some dirt on the back of her neck. He rubbed it. It didn't come away on his finger. It seemed to have been driven into the skin, like sand driven into wood by a high wind.

"Killed by the artillery," he said. "Concussion." He was backing away from the body and removing the bandana. "There's a big shell crater just behind the house. The mother must have been shut up in here with her for days."

Roley continued to stare down at the child's body. Then he turned to me. "Come," he said. "Let's go outside." He walked over to a large birch tree in the front yard of the cabin, and sat down so violently that his head banged against the tree trunk, and his cap fell off. "Ow," he said. He just sat there, staring into space. I finally made some movement, and he looked up at me, and smiled wearily. "Just leave me alone for a while, Willie," he said.

I looked around me. Arthur was quietly telling some of our men that there was a dead child in the cabin, and that she must be buried forthwith in the Métis mass grave. He was telling one of the men to go at once to the surgeons, to tell them the reason for the woman's madness. I looked again at Roley, who was staring into space like a lost child. There was nothing more for Second Lieutenant William Lorimer to do. Perhaps, now that Batoche had been taken, there never would be again.

*   *   *

At eight that night, I was sitting in Roley's and my room in Letendre's store, drinking whiskey with Jack Price. Jack was talking rhapsodically about how great it was going to be to sell a pair of shoes again, and condemning the lack of respect being shown to the Roman Catholic priests by some of our men.

"Jesus Christ, Jack," I said. "I thought you hated the Catholic church."

"Well, I do," Jack said. "I do. But priests, you know. Supposed to respect priests. Aren't we?"

I had opened my mouth to say something, when there was a clattering outside. For a moment, I thought it might be Roley. Then my door opened, and Colonel Williams and Arthur Howard came in. Williams looked utterly exhausted. He held up a finger. "Guess," he said, glumly.

"You've been awarded the V.C. by a grateful sovereign," I said.

He laughed mirthlessly. "No," he said, "although I will look into the matter when next I see the P.M. No, that would be totally good news. My news isn't. We've been interrogating Riel. He doesn't deny a thing."

"Hurrah!" Jack said.

"Well, it's worth half a hurrah at best," Williams said. "The perverse bugger wasn't even captured, not really. He gave himself up to that half-breed scout, Hourie. Of course, he would have been caught. But Riel *wanted* to be in custody, I think. He thinks he will get a big state trial at which he can put the case for his persecuted people to the world. A lofty perch from which to denounce Macdonald and the government. And the worst part of it is, he will certainly get one. I wish he'd escaped."

Jack looked shocked. "I don't understand," he said.

Williams patted him kindly on the shoulder. His hands were shaking. "No, Jack," he said wearily, "I know you don't. Look, this war is political. All wars are."

"Political?" Roley Collison was standing in the doorway. I was shocked by his appearance. He looked forlorn, withered somehow, like a child or an old man. His cap was in his hand. There were leaves and twigs sticking to the side and back of his tunic. He looked at me, and smiled. "I just fell asleep there, sitting leaning against the tree," he said. "When I woke up, I didn't even know where I was, or *who* I was, for a minute. Like a little kid. I haven't felt that confused since I was a little tiny kid."

Jack had gotten up, and was brushing the leaves and dirt off Roley's tunic. "Sit down," he said. "For God's sake, Roley, you have to take care of yourself. Sit down, relax, have some whiskey."

Roley collapsed again rather than sitting down. He looked down, a little bewildered, at the tumbler of whiskey which Jack thrust into his hand. "Just explain it to me," Roley said. "How is this war *political?*"

Williams looked appealingly at Arthur Howard. "Oh, for Christ's sake," Williams said, impatiently. Then he said, "I'm sorry, Roley. But the basic fact to remember is that the only unifying force in this country is the Conservative Party."

He was getting worked up now, despite his obvious exhaustion, his voice rising in the ringing tones of the practised politician. "If Riel can make a convincing case, and he's just the man to make a convincing case, that he had any right, any merit, on his side, we could lose Quebec. If we hang him, we could lose Quebec. That little bugger Laurier will go through Quebec like shit through a tin horn, agitating against the government. I had a telegram from the P.M. this very afternoon. You'd think he'd be happy we took the God damn town. But his telegram was very cold, very cold. He was very categorical about the need to try to avoid alienating Quebec. We're going to have to prevent any kind of further incidents that might anger the Catholics."

Like showing contempt for their priests, I thought. I wondered if he even knew about it. He looked so awful, I decided not to tell him.

"Yes," Williams said, vaguely. He passed a shaking hand over his forehead. He got up, slowly. "My God, why am I so tired? And why do I keep getting these headaches?" He stared slowly from one of us to the other, and I realized that suddenly he scarcely knew what he was saying. "I must get some rest," he said. He paused in the doorway, looking back at us. His handsome face was blank with exhaustion. His mouth seemed to be depressed at one side. Some spittle fell out of it. "Very cold," he said. Then he was gone.

"That man isn't well," Arthur said. "He was his old self again there for a minute, but walking over here, he said a couple of things to me that just didn't make any sense at all. They need to get him back East, to his doctor."

"I'm sorry he's sick," Roley said. "But I still don't know why this is a *political* war." Then he brightened. "I hear you can actually talk to Riel."

"Yes," Arthur said. "I went into his tent. Told him I wanted to talk to him. That I was practically the only other American citizen here, but the bastard just turned his back on me."

I was not really listening to him. I was looking at my captain, who looked sick and desolate. He looked worse than I had ever seen him, except for the amputation of Sanborn's legs.

"Roley," I said. "Colonel Williams's men are going to have to look after him. But *we* look after each other. Are you all right?"

"Yes, I'm all right," Roley said angrily, almost as if I'd insulted him. "I appreciate your and Jack's concern. But my problem isn't sickness. It's that I don't understand what's going on."

He paused, and leaned forward, seemingly almost beseeching Jack, Arthur and me to understand. "I'm a big hero, and they tell me I'll get a medal. Today I saw a tiny little girl, killed by our cannons. There must be a higher purpose, when such things are done. There *has* to be. Don't you see that?" He turned to Jack. "What in hell did Nolan care about the Empire and the Tory Party? What does Sanborn care?"

"Well, Roley," Arthur said, a bit coldly, "you won't be the first soldier to wonder where his war came from. I'm sure books will be written about all this. One of your historians will explain to you in due course the origins of the Second Riel Rebellion."

Roley suddenly looked more purposeful than I'd seen him since the fighting ended. "*No*," he said, with an odd finality. "I've got a much better idea of how to study the origins of the Second Riel Rebellion."

"And what would that be?" Arthur asked.

Roley looked at him and smiled. "I'm going to talk to Riel," he said.

XVIII

The tent holding Louis Riel had been set up right beside Middleton's. Two sentries with fixed bayonets guarded it twenty-four hours a day. A youthful officer named Captain George Young was in command. He was going to transport Riel south to Clarke's Crossing and thence to Regina for trial.

"I wish he *was* a savage," Young said. "The fact is, he's an educated gentleman and would be thought so in any drawing-room in Ottawa or London. He's a much cleverer man than I am. You know, my father was the Methodist minister in Winnipeg in '70, in the first Rebellion. When Riel ordered Thomas Scott executed, my dad comforted Scott as he was being led to the wall. When I introduced myself to Riel last night and told him who I was, he answered with, 'And how is your father, the fine old gentleman?' It's not easy to think of a man like that as an enemy. And that's how I have to think of him, see? I have to get him to Regina. They're going to try him for high treason. And hang him. *He* thinks he can show the judge and the jury how his people were in the right after all, or he pretends he does. It's depressing to talk to him, understand? It's sad. I'd be glad of a break. I'll see if he'll talk to you. He probably will."

He went into the tent and came out again in about two minutes, with the air of a messenger sent by someone more important. "Sure," he said. "Riel will talk to you. In private. Go on in."

It was a small tent, furnished with a cot, a rickety table and two chairs. Riel got up courteously when we entered. I had seen portraits of the man, of course, but I was not prepared for the close-up reality. First of all, he was *big,* almost as tall as Roley, and much more massive. Someone had given him a grey Mounted Police under-tunic and over it he wore a grey tweed vest. He had matching tweed trousers and on his feet, Indian moccasins. Riel had a huge mass of long, auburn hair, and a heavy beard. Above the beard were thin lips, a big, straight nose, and the famous dark, intense, almost mesmerizing eyes.

"Good morning, gentlemen," he said. His voice was low, with a musical quality. His English was excellent, although accented. He looked French to me, although those eyes showed his Indian ancestry. He shook hands with both of us, a gentle handshake. "I wish I had something to offer you," he said. "Tea or coffee. Biscuits. But I am not quite master of my own household any more." He smiled. "Take the chairs."

We both demurred, and he said, quietly, "Then I will sit down, if you don't mind. I am still tired after wandering in the bush." He sat. "How can I help Captain Collison and Lieutenant Lorimer?"

Roley said nothing, so I jumped in. "It is good of you to see us, *Monsieur* Riel," I said.

He smiled at the French word. "My pleasure," he said. "I want to have the chance of speaking to as many English people as I can."

"Although," I said, "you refused to talk to our friend Lieutenant Howard."

"Ah, yes," Riel said, a little bitterly. "My *fellow-American,* Lieutenant Howard. As he reminded me, several times. Yes, he is the one exception I make."

"Why was that?" Roley said.

"Because he doesn't belong here," Riel said. "This is a specifically *Canadian* tragedy. Have you read Sophocles? He would have understood this. I started down the road to all this in 1869, at Red River, and you English started down that road with me. And however much we struggled, we have not been allowed to deviate one inch from our fates. It is entirely fitting, and it was always entirely predictable, that you would be here in your red coats, fighting the French and the Indians."

Roley shook his head, bewildered. "See," Riel said. "*We* are not permitted to escape this. But Lieutenant Howard has no share in this. Why is he here? He is here to test his gun. To interest buyers in the Gatling. Because he craves war." He stopped and rubbed his hand wearily across his face. "Besides," he said. "The Americans are not my fellow countrymen; you are. You just won't admit it.

"I lived there a long while." He smiled again. "I befriended Senator Morton of Indiana, the great abolitionist. He hated racial persecution as much as I did. I met twice with President Grant. He led the army that freed the slaves. I begged him to intervene and help my people."

He looked at me and Roley for a minute. There was great pride in his face. "I will tell you something. Something few people know. It was on a hilltop near Washington, D.C. that the spirit which appeared to Moses in a cloud of flame appeared to me, in the same way, and spoke to me of my destiny. It told me that I must accomplish a mission for humanity."

Roley cleared his throat. "Mr. Riel," he said.

"Yes," Riel said. "I am wandering. I always did love an audience. My wife thinks I talk too much. She's right. What can I do for you?"

"I have been through a lot in this campaign," Roley said slowly. "More than I ever would have thought I could endure. Yesterday I saw a little girl who had been blown up by a cannon. I killed men. I led men to their destruction. We were told you were savages. I can see you are not. *How did this happen*? They tell me you're a madman. Maybe they're right. I'm not a doctor. You were here before I was. Answer my question."

"Well," Riel said, "is that all? It's perfectly simple. The wily half-breed Riel incited his ignorant, illiterate followers to open fire on the Mounted Police. They did, at Duck Lake. They murdered the Queen's police officers and brave private citizens. Canada had to have revenge." He gestured around him. "Look, they have it."

Roley put his hands in his pockets and pulled them out again. He stared at the dirt tent floor and then raised his head. "Sir," he said, "I can understand you not liking me. I played a role in conquering your town. So did Willie. Lieutenant Lorimer. If you want us to leave, we will. But I came here in good faith. I asked you a simple question. I'm not a fool. Don't give me the same answer I keep getting from our senior officers."

Riel sat looking at him for a long time. Then he got up, came around the little table and shook Roley's hand again. "I owe you an apology," he said. "You're that rarest of things. So rare I forgot they existed. A man of scruple. Such a man is entitled to an answer, insofar as I can give one."

He sat down again. "Look," he said, "at what happens in the world. Strong peoples collide with weak ones. Maybe the weak ones are weak because they are few. Maybe because they are ignorant. Maybe because they don't have a Gatling gun. But they are defeated. Worse, they are trampled. They don't get to be themselves again, after the defeat, but with less confidence in their own invincibility than before, like the French after Waterloo. They aren't even absorbed and converted, like your Lowland Scots ancestors were by the English. They are unmanned, they are *disappeared*, if there's any such word. After their defeat, these weak, beaten, supposedly primitive people find their sacred customs being laughed at, their prowess as men becoming a joke, everything they thought was permanent turning to dust before their eyes. I suspect such beaten men look in the mirror and see *themselves* slowly fading away, turning to pale shimmering motes of light in the air. Eventually, if they look long and hard enough, vanishing into thin air. The grandchildren of such beaten people don't know who they are; they don't know who their ancestors ever were. They are utterly lost, lost souls if ever there were such things. That's what happened to every Indian tribe in the East, and it will happen to every Indian tribe in the West. You don't have to murder them, like the Americans. You can just *disappear* them, and it will do just as well. Better. Less messy. Less blood to upset the squeamish. Small price to pay if you destroy their happiness and their sanity in the process."

He sat back in the little chair, and looked Roley in the eye. Roley was leaning forward a little, staring, listening intently, as if his life depended on what Riel would say. "Listen," Riel said. "In 1869, Canada bought the West from the Bay traders. There was chaos. There was no Canadian authority there at all. There were Irish and Yankees who intended to annex the North-West to America. And if they didn't? Then sooner or later the West would fill up with Canadian settlers, and most of them would be English, Protestant, and white. My people have been here a hundred years. They can barely read. They can barely write. They can't speak English. To you, they look like savages. They would have been crushed to powder.

"So, fifteen years ago, we set up a Provisional Government at Winnipeg. We wanted to become a province. We wanted to make sure that the Métis were *not* crushed to powder."

"Scott," I said.

"Yes," he said. "Thomas Scott. A Canadian, a Protestant bigot. A racial bigot. A man who despised my people. A born hater. He beat me up in the street in Winnipeg one time, do you know that? He and his Canadian friends tried over and over to overthrow my government. To introduce chaos into Manitoba, where I had created order. He was tried. He was sentenced to death."

"For what, for Christ's sake?" I said. "For beating you up in the street? For having the temerity to criticize the great Louis Riel, who holds personal conversations with God? He was helpless, in jail. You said it yourself, *Canada* bought the West. *Canada* had the authority, not you. You make the proud boast of all the revolutionary murderers in history. But this is Canada. A *British* country. We believe in loyalty to the law. We don't trade in human blood, not here. Nor in dragging some poor, scared, muddle-headed bugger out and killing him. We're not Yankee barbarians, or Frenchmen. Scott was an obnoxious blockhead, but fifteen years ago at Winnipeg, you and your friends *did* murder him."

Riel did not get angry or throw us out of his prison tent. He simply put up his hands. "Don't you think I have lain awake thinking that I threw everything away? Because I did, you know. It was the death of Scott that made them send the British army against us in 1870. They would not let me take my seat in Parliament. They chased me out of Canada; then they chased me into a mental asylum. And while I rotted in that madhouse, or while I roamed the United States, begging favours, lonely and desperate, the Canadian government took away all that I had won."

"How?" Roley said.

"*The Manitoba Act*," Riel said. "A law of the Parliament of Canada. My representatives negotiated it with them in 1870. I got them to pass it. Sounds impressive, doesn't it? That was my great achievement. It was supposed to guarantee the future of the Métis in Manitoba.

"We had farms along the Red River. Laid out like in Quebec, long, with river frontages. We had been there for seventy years. Long before there was a Canada. *The Manitoba Act* said that no matter how many English-speaking, Protestant, white settlers came in future to Manitoba from Ontario, our titles to our lands were guaranteed in Canadian law. Also, one million, four hundred thousand acres of new, unbroken land were to be distributed to the Métis children."

He raised his head, and looked angrily and defiantly at us. "It was the *law*. Yes, Canadians believe in loyalty to the law. They all say so. You say so. I believed it. And they never, they *never*," --he was shouting now-- "*they never kept a single promise. They didn't obey their own law*." He took out a handkerchief, and wiped his mouth.

"Now wait just a minute," Roley said. "What do you mean? I don't know about this. How could the government of Canada not obey the laws it made itself?"

Riel smiled at him. He didn't seem annoyed. "The Métis of Manitoba never got the legal titles to their land," he said. "In the early '70's, the new settlers from Ontario began to arrive. The government said that the new English-speaking settlers moving in from the East could stake a claim to any 'unoccupied' Manitoba land they found. They could obtain title to this land immediately, from the land titles office. The new English settlers at once laid claim to our land. Though we lived on it.

"When our people found that this was being done, they were

afraid and angry. But they were Canadians. They knew that we were not 'Yankee barbarians.' They knew that here, the law rules. So they went to the land titles office and asserted their claims to the land they lived on. Some of them brought copies of *The Manitoba Act* with them. They could not read it, of course. But they knew the law. You have given an Englishman from Ontario title to my land, they said. The Englishman is saying my family has to move off. You can't do that, they said. The law guarantees my title to my land. This piece of paper, *The Manitoba Act*, says it. It is Canadian law. Our leader, Louis Riel, made the Canadians pass this law.

"And the land titles officers laughed in their faces. 'Oh, yes,' they said, 'we know about *The Manitoba Act*. It does indeed deal with your titles. Now, then. The land titles system is, by law, for people not covered under *The Manitoba Act*. Therefore, since you are covered under the *Act*, you can't register title to your land under the land titles system. Whereas the Englishman from Ontario, who isn't covered under the *Act*, can. Therefore, unless the government otherwise enforces the statute, and it won't, the Englishman from Ontario has title to your land under the land titles system. Therefore, you don't have title. Therefore, you have to get off the land. Next, please.'"

"No," Roley said. "That can't be right. Is it, Willie?"

"Actually, I think it is," I said.

Riel said, "They amended the law over and over. They changed the law, so that the title to Métis land was guaranteed only to Métis men who were actually living on their land on a certain day in 1870. They selected that day carefully. It was a day when almost all the men were at the buffalo hunt. So almost all the men lost the title to their land."

Roley was shaking his head. "But..." he said.

But Riel was inexorable. He was going to tell us the whole story. It occurred to me suddenly that he had given this little speech hundreds of times before. He had given it in the White House— twice—to Ulysses S. Grant. "The Métis children," Riel said. "The children did not get their one million four hundred thousand Manitoba acres. Do I have to tell you this? Isn't it obvious? Don't you already know it? They ensured that the land offered us was on the bald prairie, where my people could not live and would not live. Their lawyers fiddled with the definition of a 'Métis child,' delaying and delaying, until no one knew who was one of us and who wasn't. They issued us with valueless scrip instead of land, and our bewildered, impoverished people sold their birthright to speculators for a song." He sat back in the chair. His face was curiously calm. "So, in the 1870's, while I was in a madhouse, then while I roved the United States, the Métis began to move bag and baggage. To here. To Batoche."

He got up from the little chair, stretched. He sighed. His face was bitter. "I wish I'd been here. It was all wonderful for a while. The buffalo were still plentiful. The people staked out and farmed their river-front farms. They built this village where the main trail came through to Fort Edmonton. The North-West Mounted Police left them alone. The children laughed, and the women sang."

"And then Paradise was lost," I said. I had been attempting sarcasm, but it didn't come out very well.

"Of course," Riel said. "Isn't it always? The buffalo disappeared. And the long arm of Canada was reaching out again. The land surveyors started to turn up again. The whole of the Territory was to be surveyed on the square, in square miles. The Métis said, our farms are the old pattern, the river-front farms, long and narrow. We staked them out when they were vacant. We farmed them. We want our land titles recognized.

"Seven years ago, the Métis petitioned the government for title to our farms here in the Territory. The Territorial Council supported us. When the surveyors came, they surveyed the farms by the square mile. Our farms were not recognized."

Roley had lowered his head, and was staring at the floor of the tent.

Riel raised his voice a little, and Roley looked up. "Can you imagine the desperation of poor men," Riel said, "who could no longer hunt to support their families? In 1882, they petitioned again. Dumont and many others signed it. It pointed out that the Métis had defended their land against the Indians 'at the price of their blood,' and couldn't the government at Ottawa make a tiny exception to their Territorial scheme, so the Métis could keep their farms? They said no."

Riel stared hard at Roley. "Think of it, man," Riel said. "Think of how our people felt. *No land.* The white English settlers would come, and our land would be stolen a second time. In 1883, the government sold a section of land on the west bank of the Saskatchewan to land speculators. The Métis settler who farmed the land knew nothing of it until the Englishmen came to his door and told him to get off his farm. Then everybody saw the handwriting on the wall. They were going to steal everything we had, all over again. The next year the government sent an inspector to investigate. He listened to all the complaints. He said nothing would be done to re-survey the land. He called the Métis 'worthless.'"

Roley pulled out his pipe and looked interrogatively at Riel. Riel nodded. The smell of tobacco filled the little tent. Outside, an angry sergeant was shouting at some men. Far off, someone was singing, a bit off-key. The wind had come up. "By that time," Riel said, "1884, everybody was suffering. The harvests had failed. Grain prices had collapsed. The Indians were starving. The government was not feeding them as it had promised. That's when Gabriel and some other men came to Montana to ask me to come back. They had no one else."

The wind rattled the tent. It was growing cold. I could see the pride in Riel's face. "I came back. I gambled that the government would not molest me for the death of Scott, and they didn't. For just a little while, in 1884, we actually had solidarity. Can you believe that? Whites and Métis. French and English. Protestants and Catholics. We all acted as if we were brothers and sisters. Just for a little while, of course. Such things don't last. But I spoke to huge meetings, *with many white people,* and was cheered to the echo. I wept with joy after some of the meetings."

"Yes, fine," Roley said, impatiently. "Wonderful—or terrible, if you prefer. But the *Rebellion*. The man in my company who lost both his legs. The little dead girl. *All* of it."

Riel looked at him steadily for a few seconds. "Do you think I ever stop thinking about it?" he said. He looked off into space so abstractedly that for an instant I wondered if he had forgotten we were there. Then he spoke. "We decided to petition Ottawa again. Some part of me still believed in the fairness of Canadians. So I wrote yet another petition. I worked on it for weeks. I tried as hard as I could to make it so reasonable, so moderate, that Ottawa could not reject it. I told myself that Macdonald would not want another struggle. The petition asked for food for the Indians. For the Métis, it asked for titles to our farms, so no one could throw us off our own land. For the whites, it asked for reduced tariffs on farm implements. It asked for Saskatchewan and Assiniboia to be made a province, with democracy, with a free ballot for all. And we sent it with pride to Ottawa."

Riel got up and began to stride back and forth inside the little tent. "Even six months ago, we had no thought of fighting. We wanted to be loyal Canadian citizens. All they had to do, *all* they had to do, to avoid this bloodshed, was to say they would consider it." He was almost shouting. "If they had even said they would consider it, if they had even said they would appoint a commission to study whether they should consider it, or any such form of words, *any form of words at all,* I swear to you that *no one would have died.*"

He sat down again in the little chair. He was crying. "They never said it. Then it came to me that when the white settlers came, we would lose all our lands. That God wanted me to lead my people, even into battle, rather than be treated like fools or animals. It was not until March of this year that I spoke to them of taking up arms." He wiped his eyes with his handkerchief.

"I restrained them at Duck Lake," he said. "Gabriel wanted to annihilate all the Mounted Police. They could have done it. I said no. And he wanted to attack the English all over Saskatchewan and Assiniboia. He wanted to destroy the railroad, to destroy your supplies, to harass your column and pick off your men. I said no. The thought of more bloodshed made me sick. We would defend our homes as we always had. I thought God would save us. Even just before you charged the other day, I told the people that God would save us, and God never showed His face."

I opened my mouth to say something. I was afraid of the effect this might be having on Roley. But Riel spoke first.

"This was not the first time I had been so disappointed. No. The other time was in my second meeting with President Grant. That was in 1875. Shortly before going to the White House, I prayed in Saint Patrick's Church. And the Divine Spirit touched me. I knew then that it was given to me to be the prophet of the New World.

"When I went to see Grant, I had prepared so hard. My English was not as good then. I sat up almost until dawn in my room, practising what I would say to the President. I had notes, and maps to show the President. He let me talk a long while. I thought I was convincing him. That an independent Métis nation, protected by the United States, could be established in the North-West. That he could help me protect my lambs.

"He listened. He had a round, crafty face, hard, hard eyes. A little beard. He sipped bourbon whiskey and smoked his cigars while I talked. He kept passing his hand over his mouth. At the end, he suddenly stood up and offered me his hand. He thanked me for coming to the White House. And then he passed his hand over his mouth again, and I knew. He was laughing at me. They all had been laughing at me, all the politicians I had cultivated. I tried to explain to him about the visions, about God, about my destiny. I talked faster and faster. Again he smiled. Of course. The British would have spoken of me to him. They might have spoken of war. Would he risk a war over a lot of worthless half-breeds, and an empty wasteland? English battleships bombarding New York City, to help a lot of half-breeds? No.

"Somehow, they got me out of his office. I don't remember it very well. I think I made quite a scene. He was very nice about it. He even put his arm around my shoulders. He was used to comforting wounded men, of course, broken officers. In the next few days, I broke down. They said I was insane. I know I was not. I was dreadfully tired, dreadfully discouraged, that only. But they shut me up in the asylum for a long while. You can't imagine what it was like. Then I roamed the United States, and then I came back to lead my people, and now I am shut up again. Away from my own kind again." He made an eloquent, Gallic gesture around him. I thought that he was crying.

Roley got up. Riel was obviously spent. Roley shook Riel's hand, and so did I. "Thank you," Roley said. He turned toward the door.

Riel suddenly said, "You see it too? The trap?"

"Trap?" Roley said.

"Yes," Riel said. "One thing we Métis know all about is trapping. Even Sir John A. Macdonald, who thinks us worthless 'breeds, would concede us that. The best trappers of the New World." He smiled. "They taught me how, when I was a boy. Some traps kill the animal outright. Some confine it until the trapper comes and kills it. Many traps catch a limb. The terrified creature gnaws the limb off, trying to escape. The poor stupid animal thinks in its desperation that this will make it free. But of course it bleeds to death, beside the trap." He stood again and looked Roley in the eye with great earnestness. "The trap for human beings is so intricately devised and so large that most people never realize they are in it. Your friend here" (he gestured toward me) "does not believe he is in it. But I tell you that we all are in it. Every one of us. The sad old lady at Windsor, living out her pointless life, with a host of Middletons all over the globe, enlarging her Empire. President Cleveland, in his splendid office. Prime Minister Macdonald, with his whiskey bottles, scheming to hold office forever. You. Me. All of us, all caught in a trap. You are a decent man, Captain Collison. I see in your eyes that you begin to perceive the jaws of the trap. And, of course, the jaws are very close for me. I wish I could help you out of it."

He smiled at us. It was the saddest smile I ever saw. "Or at least, I wish I could give you absolution. But I cannot even give it to myself."

Roley and I walked away from the tent, for a time in silence.

"Well," I finally said, "that lunatic could talk a dead owl out of a tree. We'd *better* hurry up and lock him in a jail, or a hospital, or a grave, because sooner or later he'll precipitate a catastrophe. So he couldn't talk U.S. Grant into an invasion? Must have been having an off day."

"But was it true?" Roley said. "I don't mean the religious talk. What he said about the government?"

"Most of it, I think," I said. "Pretty much all of it. But not important any more, Roley."

I was turning into the front door of Letendre's store. After all that, I needed a rest. I looked back at Roley. He was just staring into space. Suddenly, I felt a chill down my back. I was scared, almost as scared as I'd been in battle, and I didn't know why. "Oh, come *on*," I said. "You're not still worrying about any of this? Look, once they opened fire on the Mounted Police at Duck Lake, none of this could have been avoided. Surely that's clear."

He turned slowly to face me. Usually he took his intellectual cues from me, but I could see from the stubborn look on his face that this was not one of those times. "Yes, that's clear," he said, in a quiet voice. "I'm tired, Willie," and he turned into the store.

* * *

At eight that night, Roley, Jack, Arthur, and I were sitting around a fire we'd built outside Letendre's store. It was too nice to stay inside. Jack had amazed us by cooking us all an excellent meal, beefsteaks he'd fried one by one in a skillet, with fried potatoes done some special way so they were fluffy, with gravy, not the greasy hard chips the army cooks created. He had responded to our praise with a shy smile. "Since Eleanor and I haven't been blessed by any little ones," he had said, "we have time to do everything together. We always cook our Sunday dinner together."

Now the sun was going down. The air was blowing colder. Arthur was holding a whiskey bottle, one of several Roley and I had found in our room and "forgotten" to tell anybody else about. Middleton was turning a blind eye to the Canadian officers' drinking. Probably he had no choice.

We were all drunk. Arthur had gotten very drunk, although as ever it didn't affect his eloquence. He had also been getting angrier and angrier at Roley, ever since we'd all started drinking at five o'clock. Roley kept puffing on his pipe, and recounting our conversation with Riel, almost word-for-word. I had never seen him so dejected, not even after Sanborn's legs had come off. He looked bewildered and cast down. "I can't stop thinking about what he said," he kept saying.

"Look, Roley," Arthur said. "I don't like the way you keep going on about these Métis people. They lost. That's the law of life, that's the law of nations. The strongest and the fittest survive and prosper. The weaker ones go under. That's what war is. That's what it's for."

"I don't doubt it," Roley said reasonably.

"You don't doubt it?" Arthur said. "You *sound* like you doubt it. Look, sooner or later, these people will just be gone."

Roley shook his head slowly.

"Yes," Arthur said. "I know. They're impressive. They're admirable. Sure. Like tigers are. You *know* I admire these people. But sometime in the next century, over in India, some idiot of a British officer is going to shoot the last tiger on earth. I hope after he pulls the trigger, he has the sensitivity to realize the enormity of what he's done. And it's the same with the Indians and the Métis of North America. We want to tame the West. We want to turn the West into a peaceful park, where women can go for nature walks, and children can play. *Don't we?* Well, the politicians will say: you can't have tigers running around where women and children are walking, now can you?"

Arthur half-filled his coffee mug with whiskey and drank half of it at a gulp. "I don't want it to happen. If I could, I'd save them. It's sad. It's tragic, but all war is." He looked at my friend with a kind of exasperated affection. "I tell you, Roley. You're in danger of turning into the kind of bleeding-heart who proliferates back in New England. You don't want to become a bleeding-heart, Roley."

"For Christ's sake," Roley said. "Who said I did? Don't you *see*? I'm not worried about these people at all. I'm worried about *myself*.

I'm worried about my personal honour. I was brought up to think there's nothing more important than a man's honour. That was the last thing my mother said to me. On her deathbed, in her old bedroom of our house. Poor little frail, worn-out birdie. 'Be an honourable man, Roley.' And I told her I would. All those books she gave me, all the dreams I had. I was nineteen, for God's sake. I thought it was the most sacred promise I could ever make.

"I'm worried about my immortal soul. I have to go back to Toronto. I have to go and see Nolan's widow and tell her that her husband died for something important. I have to say it like I mean it. I think he had children. I have to reach down and hold their hands, and look into their faces and tell them how grateful we all should be for their father's sacrifice, how Canada will never forget. Sanborn won't talk to me, ever. I know that. But I'll see him, lots of times, in his wheelchair, in the street. Toronto isn't that big. I wish to God it was. He'll be being pushed down the street by his mother or his father. Not his girlfriend, I don't think. He'll see me. He'll *look* at me. He'll *say* things, about what a coward I am, about what I got him to do." I saw with horror that there were tears in his eyes. "*How am I supposed to bear that?* Sanborn can't walk. He'll never get married. He'll never have a child. He'll never have a job. *I* did that. I talked him into it. I led him into it. It's my fault."

No, I thought. *I talked him into it.*

He was fumbling for his eternal pipe, and I thought that he hoped the familiar ritual would give him comfort. "They stole their farms away from them, did you know that? I didn't. Isn't that pathetic?" He looked over at me. His face was red with anger. "Where in hell does all this leave me? Where in hell does it leave my promise to my mother? I always thought, if you believed in nothing, you were nothing. *Don't you see?* I wanted to make my wife and my son proud."

Arthur was looking seriously concerned. "For God's sake," he said. "Don't talk about honour." He looked Roley and me in the eye. "Look," he said. "Yours is a brand-new country. You'll have to get used to confronting ambiguities, shades of grey. *We* had to learn that. It's painful; I admit it. But nations can't always rely on some simple-minded, medieval code of honour to guide them. This is the first time Canada has had to confront this…this unfortunate reality. You have to get on with it."

Jack said, amazing me, "And lose our souls right off the bat?"

Arthur glanced at him contemptuously. He was very drunk. "Souls," he said. "Oh, Jesus Christ. We're trying to have an adult discussion here."

Jack's bald head turned, in the twilight, as red as his tunic. "Well," he said, with considerable dignity, "I can see that my personal thoughts are not welcome in this discussion. I can see when I'm not wanted." He got up, and walked stiffly into the growing darkness.

"Now that was uncalled for," Roley said.

"Oh, for Christ's sake, Roley," Arthur said. "The man is an idiot."

"Probably he is," Roley said. "But he's my friend. He's a clerk in a shoe store, for God's sake. That's about what I'd be, if my dad hadn't died young and left me a store. We aren't professional soldiers. We aren't educated men. Jack is a nice fellow. He spouts all that crap his friends teach him about Protestantism and the Empire, and he couldn't hurt anybody. Not a Catholic or anybody else. He wouldn't throw a rock through a Catholic church window if you held a gun to his head. If he ever actually hurt anybody, I think it would destroy him. Why do you think I always wanted Willie to back me up? Because I knew Willie was like me. He *is* capable of hurting people."

Thanks a lot, I thought.

"You owe him an apology," Roley said.

"Fine," Arthur said, getting up. "Wonderful. I'll go find him and apologize. This is damn well pointless, anyway." He walked away.

Roley stretched, and turned toward me. The night air was getting genuinely cold. The fire was dying down. It was completely dark now. The night sentries were patrolling, their rifles cradled over one arm. They smiled and waved at Roley and me. "I suppose you also think," Roley said, "that I am just deluded."

"No," I said, "I don't." I was not used to alcohol, and really, there seemed nothing else to say. I went into Letendre's Store and started getting ready for bed.

I glanced out the window once. Roley was still sitting by the dying fire.

XIX

The evening of the next day was reserved for an officers' victory banquet. All officers except those assigned to guard duty were invited. (We drew lots). Apart from a very substantial force of sentries, the enlisted men were to be given their own jamboree at the same time. Middleton *was* getting to understand us. This wasn't the Grenadier Guards, and extreme displays of privilege would be deeply resented.

At breakfast, Major Buchan told me that Company Four was to spend the day re-searching cabins and outbuildings, to ensure that all firearms had been seized. I didn't even think about rousing Roley. When I had gotten up, he'd been rolled in his blankets, dead to the world. I could see how much of the whiskey he'd drunk after I went to bed. He had seemed so dejected and confused the night before that I thought that he needed his sleep. No one would know.

So we spent the day rooting through the poor cabins of the Métis settlers. Even in Roley's absence, none of the men would have been tempted to misbehave. The Prime Minister's cold telegram to Williams had evidently been shared with Middleton. Orders against looting and vandalism *had* gone out after all. There were Canadian and American newspaper correspondents all over the place, and our commander obviously did not want reports of maltreatment of French Catholics to reach the East.

The orders, though, were unnecessary. The men were reverting back at great speed to the civilians they'd always essentially been, though newly shorn of a lot of their respect for authority and awe of the British. Also, they were increasingly sickened by the violence we'd gone through. Proud of their victory, yes. But reluctant to hurt anybody else, and most of all, anxious to go home. Middleton and van Straubenzee were doing a lot of talking about how the rebellion wasn't over and how we'd have to fight the Indians next, but the men weren't buying it. The Scouts knew the West, and they were telling us that almost all the Indians had stayed loyal, and that most of those who had not were determined to surrender. They were telling us that the Rebellion was almost over, and they were right.

The day was uneventful. A couple of Grenadiers claimed that someone had fired on them from an isolated cabin well to the east of the town. Nobody took this seriously. How could you *think* you'd been fired on? Both men had been so badly hung-over after getting into some home-made hooch that a Métis had sold them, that they could barely stand up. No, the Rebellion was over, sure enough.

*   *   *

The banquet started with drinks at five o'clock. The original plan had been to hold it in Batoche's big house, but French's Scouts had complained that this was nothing short of obscene, since their commander had been shot dead out of the front window. Since the night was fine, we drank and ate outdoors, the senior officers sitting in camp chairs, the rest of us sprawled on the grass. There was a huge bonfire in the centre of the gathering. A gigantic beef would be roasted over it in due course.

I had never before seen so much alcohol. I'd read old stories of how British generals went to war with wagonloads of claret and champagne. Evidently we had done little less. I thought, vaguely, that it would have been better for Sanborn if the claret wagon had turned over at Fish Creek instead of the anesthetics wagon. But I did not want to think about Sanborn, and plied by Jack and Arthur with glass after glass of wine, I soon stopped being capable of thinking in any organized way at all.

Everybody was looking around for the two great heroes of the charge at Batoche, Lieutenant Colonel Williams and Roley. Neither was there. The Midland officers were all looking pretty dejected, and one of them told me that Williams was sick. Indeed, the only officers who weren't in seventh heaven were French's Scouts, the Midlanders, and Jack and I. After a while, I became ashamed of how drunk I was getting and I let up on the wine.

From where we sat, I could see Riel's tent, with two sentries, bayonets fixed, standing at the entrance. There was a big fire lit in front of it. One sentry regularly strolled around the tent and then resumed his place beside his friend. I had a brief, drunken, lunatic urge to go over and invite Louis to the party. He probably would have been willing to come (although I'm sure he didn't drink); and, God knows, the upper-crust English are sufficiently weird that Middleton might have welcomed him. The next second, I dismissed the idea as one of those vagrant thoughts we don't even mention in fun.

Middleton was sitting in a camp chair, with van Straubenzee on one side of him and Colonel Portman on the other. I saw how the general deferred to Portman and remembered that Portman had been described to me as a friend of the Prime Minister's. With Lord Melgund gone, in Williams' absence, and with the obvious coldness between Middleton and van Straubenzee which had developed after the general had lost his head in the zareba, I thought that Portman was now our de facto second-in-command. That thought made me very uncomfortable.

Everyone was at least half-drunk, and now the festivities took a new turn. Middleton started indulging in badinage with the lot of us. One or another officer would half-shout out a joking comment, and Middleton, relishing the role he was playing, would, after consideration, reply. His answers were genial and funny; and of course, everyone let him have the last word.

I was just starting to enjoy this, when there was a heavy thud beside me, and I turned to find Roley sitting there. I was shocked by his appearance. His uniform was dishevelled, and he had not shaved. He smelled of whiskey, his face was deeply flushed, and I saw that he was very drunk. He clapped Jack, Arthur, and me on the back, and fumblingly lit his pipe. I saw that other officers were staring at him, and that some of them were making comments behind their hands to their friends.

Jack, Arthur, and I were sitting close to the senior officers in their camp chairs. General Middleton had noticed Roley's arrival, and now he acknowledged it. "Here," he said, "is one of the authentic heroes of the campaign. Captain Collison, we were afraid you would not attend our party. You are most welcome, sir."

Roley half-rose. "Happy to b' here, sir," he said. He was slurring his words badly, and he half-collapsed back onto the ground. Nonetheless, Jack and I gave each other a relieved glance. Hopefully, Roley would sit there and eat and drink, and become indistinguishable from the rest of the boozing officers.

But Middleton would not let it go. I think that he liked Roley, and certainly, like all his class, the old general was a respecter of physical courage. I also suspect that he disliked Portman, and was trying to show what he thought of Portman's unconcealed loathing of Roley. In any case, he did not let it go.

Would it all have gone differently if he had? Perhaps, for sometimes the merest chance shifts the course in which our lives run. Middleton did not let it go. "How have you spent your day, Captain Collison? A happy day, I hope, with thoughts of home and loved ones uppermost, as with us all?"

"Home," Roley said, as if he had not heard the word before. "Yes. I guess I *have* been thinking of them. In a way."

The murmuring and shuffling had died down. It was amazingly quiet. The officers seemed somehow to know that something odd was about to happen, and they did not want to miss a word.

"What do you mean, Captain?" Middleton said, with a smile that was more uneasy than genial. "And what have you got there?" Roley was fumbling with his tunic, unbuttoning it, pulling something out. The something was rectangular. I looked at it for a moment, and saw with horror that it was the family portrait which Roley had taken from the Métis house, after he'd killed the boy who'd shot at us.

"It's a picture," Roley said, carefully. "A photograph, I mean. I took it from a house here in Batoche. I killed the boy in it. I killed his father too, three days before."

"I'm not sure," Middleton said, more gently, "that it's altogether good form to carry about with one a photograph of..."

"Oh, don't worry, sir," Roley said. "I'm not carrying it around out of pride. Nor out of shame, either," he said, hastily. He was starting to slur his words again, and badly. There was absolute silence.

Roley looked down at the photograph. He did not look sad, not exactly, but he looked inexpressibly weary. "I have been looking at it a lot," he said. "There was something about the boy's picture. For the life of me, I couldn't figure out what it was. Then I saw it." He looked up at Middleton. Some of the officers were smiling at Roley's drunkenness, but the old general was not smiling. He looked concerned, and also apprehensive, as if he somehow saw what was coming. Perhaps he did.

"It's the suit he is wearing," Roley said. There was some tittering, and Jack glared around indignantly. "That's what I do," Roley said. He paused, and stared drunkenly around him and then at me, as if asking for help. "I mean, I own a store which sells garments for boys." He shook his head, as if bewildered. "'Our store sells exclusively only the finest garments for boys.' That's what my wife wrote for the newspaper advertisement." The laughter was growing. "Now, this suit this little boy is wearing in the picture, that's what we call a Priason suit. They are made by the Priason Garment Company in Boston, Massachusetts. A very popular garment for boys, highly recommended. My own son has one exactly like it. It wears very well. It..." He was crying now, tears flooding down his cheeks.

The laughter had stopped, as the officers looked in dismay at Roley. But Portman saw his chance. "What one gets," he said, in a high, musing voice, "when one appoints a storekeeper as a captain."

"*Oh, shut up, you filthy son of a bitch!*" Jack said, loudly.

"Yes," Middleton said. "Yes. Lieutenant Price, Lieutenant Lorimer, you must take Captain Collison back to his lodgings now. He is not very well."

We hoisted Roley back onto his feet. Arthur Howard came with us. I expected Roley to try to throw us off, but he let us lead him away very quietly. There was absolute silence as we walked away from the bright firelight into the dark.

We got him back to the room where he and I slept in Letendre's store. "Lied to us," he mumbled. "They lied to us." He slumped down in a chair. Jack looked down at Roley and shook his head. Then, with instinctive gentlemanliness, he walked out without a word.

Arthur had not come in with Jack and me. I went outside. Jack was walking away very quickly toward his lodgings. Arthur had lit a cigar and was standing leaning against the wall of the store. "Willie," he said. "Take care of him. Make sure he gets some sleep. Don't let him drink any more. Jesus. What a mess. Listen. I'm going to come back first thing tomorrow, and we'll talk some sense into him. All right?"

I nodded. "Good," Arthur said. He clapped me on the back, and walked slowly and dejectedly away, trailing cigar smoke.

I went back inside. Roley was still slumped in the chair. I sat in the corner, and watched him. Eventually, he straightened up and looked over at me. His face was wet with sweat. He had lost a lot of weight, and his hair *was* greyer than it had been the day he had walked into Alice's old man's library, six weeks before. "Still with me, Willie?" he said. "I hope so. After that performance, not many others will be."

"Bull," I said. "You're a hero. No one is going to forget that."

"Oh, right," he said, with a smile. "I'm a hero. I almost forgot."

I walked over to him, and put my hand on his shoulder. "Look," I said, "get some rest. Don't be so hard on yourself."

He twisted around under my hand and glared up at me. His face was red. I took a step backward. I'd forgotten about his temper. He was still very drunk.

He came up out of the chair, swaying. "What were you and that Yankee talking about, out there? Thanks for the pity. Thank you so much for the pity." He was standing with his hands dangling at his sides, like a man about to fight. I kept backing away. He came closer.

"You're on my side, aren't you, Willie?" he suddenly shouted. "Of course you are. You *would* be. You're my friend, after all. How often have I said so? But you're on the other side too, aren't you? After that lecture you gave me about how we needed to lock up Riel, you're the one'll get the medal. For literary composition, direct from Macdonald." He moved closer, and he was roaring now. "That's the thing I'm starting to know about you, Willie. The secret of Willie's charm, to man and girl alike. *You're on everybody's God damn side!*"

Roley grabbed me by my shoulder, and his fist shot back. Then he stopped. His face was dead-white. "Jesus. Jesus Christ," he said. "What am I doing?" His fist went down. "Willie, help me," he said. He looked for a moment like a small and frightened child. "Please, I need your help."

He put his arm around my shoulders, and I got him over to his blankets. He collapsed onto them and instantly was asleep.

I felt sick and scared, but it did not take long for me to fall asleep too.

XX

The next morning, reveille blew at six a.m. I ignored it. Nobody was making any demands on the officers any more. All the men of the North-West Field Force were visibly turning back into the civilians we'd once been. Nobody was very punctilious about saluting anyone, except maybe Portman, van Straubenzee, and Middleton. The men frequently "forgot" to carry their rifles. Older men who'd had paunches were cultivating them again. There was a lot of surreptitious drinking. Abercrombie, the stargazer, was compiling a little hand-drawn map of the May evening sky. The previous day, I'd heard two of our Company Four men heatedly debating the merits of term life insurance. Jack could talk of nothing but the new orders of spring men's footwear he expected to see "back at the store." I was now reading the volume of Tennyson which Alice had given me in the station in Toronto. Somehow, I hadn't wanted to until Batoche was taken.

Outside our window, the sky was a deeper shade of blue. The mornings were beginning to become almost too warm. When they went out, many of the men were wearing only their grey under-tunics and leaving the worn green and red uniform tunics behind. Nobody reproved them. Two meadowlarks were having a contest, endlessly repeating the little tune God had given them. Roley was snoring, his head pressed into a rolled-up blanket for a pillow. As far as I knew, I had nothing to do. I had no intention of getting up.

The door opened, and Jack came in. He looked furious. "Get up," he said. "Get up."

Roley surprised me by pulling himself up from his blankets. "What the hell?" he said.

"I'll tell you what the hell," Jack said. "That worthless bastard Portman woke me up thirty minutes ago. He gave me our orders for the day. In person. We have to search that cabin that supposedly fired at those Grenadiers yesterday."

"Oh, for Christ's sake," I said.

"Yes," Jack said. "I know. Nobody fired at those two drunken oafs. That's the point. That's exactly the point. Portman said it, in so many words. 'This is a punishment for Collison. Nothing will humiliate him more in his present state than having to tear some half-breed cabin apart. So that's precisely what he will do, and you and Lorimer, the only friends he's got left, will get to watch.' Roley, I swear I nearly shot the bastard."

Roley was shaking his head and splashing cold water on his face. "No point in shooting him," he said. "A waste of a bullet. Let's get some men."

"Already done," Jack said. "They're waiting at the edge of the village."

As we walked to the edge of town, I studied Roley. He was unshaven, his uniform was stained and dirty, and, although sober, he still smelled of alcohol. But he looked better in some way than he had for days.

We didn't march so much as we strolled toward that little cabin. The men walked in no particular order, their rifles carelessly shouldered, or cradled behind their necks by both hands, or with the barrels dragging perilously close to the grass. Everybody was smoking. Nobody had fixed bayonets. Some of the men smiled at Roley, but others looked at his shabby appearance with open disapproval and dislike.

I walked along beside Roley in silence for nearly ten minutes. He looked terrible, but somehow his mood had utterly changed. He was walking easily, he smiled occasionally, and he seemed at peace. He was more calm than I had seen him since we left Toronto.

"Willie," he said suddenly, "there's something I want to say." My stomach froze. "It's just this," he said. "I did a lot of thinking after I sobered up. I am not going to go on like this any more. It doesn't do anyone any good, does it? I am going to pull myself together and go home. I am going to give my wife and my son the biggest hugs I can manage, and then I am going to be the best husband, father, and storekeeper in Toronto. I am not going to have any more pipe-dreams about adventure and glory and knights that never existed. I am going to resign my commission and never touch another gun so long as I live. I am going to put these *particular* garments into the furthest back closet, and if the country wants any more wars fought, somebody else will have to do it. I just wanted you to know that."

I was feeling better than I had for days. It was all going to work out fine. "Hallelujah," I said.

"Yes!" he said. "And I am going to be a good friend to my friends, too. Speaking of which, here is an idea I had. On Dominion Day, Eatons store in Toronto is having a special event. A friend of mine who works in the men's and boys' clothing department told me about it before we left. They are going to have a big room, and in there they'll have electric lights set up. And they'll have a telephone. And another one set up in a room across the building. You get in a line in one room, and your wife or your friend line up in the other room, and then when your turn comes, you can call them on the telephone in the other room and talk to them."

"Wow," I said.

"Yes," he said. "Isn't that great? I've never seen an electric light or talked on the telephone. But everybody says you'll soon need a telephone in a place of business. I'm thinking of putting one in at the store," he said very seriously, "once I get the hang of using it. And once they're generally available. And Vera will want one at home, too."

"Yes," I said.

"Have you ever seen an electric light?" he asked, "or talked on a telephone?"

"No," I said.

"Anyway," he said, "they are going to have tea and coffee and sandwiches and cakes there. Jack and Eleanor are going to come with Vera, Donald, and me. I'd like you and Alice to come, too. Maybe we could have dinner afterwards. Get real fancy, and have some wine." He smiled.

"Wonderful!" I said. "I could steal a couple of bottles from Alice's old man. It's good stuff."

He started to laugh. "Great," he said. "Keep down the overhead. Old business principle." Then he stopped smiling. "Right," he said. "There's the cabin down there. Let's get this godforsaken business over with. Let's bully some poor woman one last time, and then let's go home."

The tiny Métis cabin stood in a little valley of its own. A profusion of green grass led up to the very doorstep. Flowers rioted in a little flowerbed beside the house. The warm breeze sang through the birches, and the sun bathed the little dell in golden light. I felt immense relief because I could see that Roley was not going to disintegrate when we searched the cabin. He had already in spirit resigned his commission and started to construct the man he would become. Everything was going to be all right.

We gambolled down the little slope toward the tiny shack, like schoolboys on an outing. I found myself whistling. Roley told the men to wait outside. "I don't want these young fellows thinking about this when they think back on what they did," he said. "Let's us officers do this."

He knocked at the door, and when nobody answered it, he turned the handle and went in. Jack and I followed. It was one room, a bare, sparse place, poorer than any I had seen. An exhausted-looking woman of about forty faced us. She was trying to smile, but I could see that she was badly scared. A tiny girl peered at us from behind her mother's skirts. There was also a boy of about nine, barefoot, in a white shirt and much-mended pants. The woman was saying something in French. I couldn't make it out. Sheer terror was making her incoherent.

Roley sighed. "Willie," he said, "talk to her. Tell her we just need to search the place, and we'll leave her in peace."

I thought for a minute. *"On dirait que quelqu'un a tiré un coup d'ici. Qui est-ce qui a tiré?"*

We think a shot was fired from here. Who fired it?

A terrible look of fear and hopelessness came over her face. I wished we could just leave, just walk out, and tell Portman we'd done it. But it had to be done. The frightened little girl was wailing, and clinging to her mother all the harder. The boy was edging away from his mother, toward our left.

Then the woman shouted, *"Allez-vous en! Mon mari a été tué dans le combat. Il n'y a pas de fusils dans la maison ! Il n'y a personne qui a brisé vos règlements!"*

Go away! My husband was killed in the fighting! There are no guns in the house! Nobody broke any of your rules!

I was turning to Roley to translate for him, and I saw the boy reaching into a recess behind the curtain. Something about the look on his thin, pale face stopped me from speaking. In the next second, he was holding, in both hands, a huge revolver. His hands trembling, his arms wavering with the weight of it, he levelled it in our direction. *"Pour mon père,"* he screamed, and he pulled the trigger.

The explosion was deafening. A huge plume of smoke flew out of the barrel. I stood stock still, paralyzed with fear and horror. But Jack was fumbling with the flap of his holster, cursing, scrabbling to get his revolver out. The boy was weeping, and pulling at the huge, clumsy pistol in his hand. It was, I saw, one of the old cap-and-ball varieties. That gave me hope that Jack would be able to fire before the kid did. I was watching like a spectator at some terrible sport. It never occurred to me to act.

"Oh God," Jack muttered, and then he had his pistol out and aimed. He fired, another gigantic noise. At that range, the bullet tore right through the boy's chest, and he dropped like a stone. Screaming, the mother rushed toward her child, and Jack back-handed her in the face with his gun. She fell silently, her face suddenly a mask of blood.

Jack and I looked wordlessly at the boy's body for a moment.

Then we both turned to Roley. His face was white; he tottered on legs that did not seem to work. Then he suddenly sat down, hard. I could see the spreading mass of red on the breast of his tunic.

Jack turned from this to look again at the dead boy and the unconscious woman on the floor. Then he dropped his revolver and clapped his hands to his face in despair.

Roley had fallen over backward, so that he now lay prone on the scarred wooden floor. His arms were splayed out beside him. I knelt to his right. Jack slumped down on his left. Some of the men had started pushing in, and I yelled at one of them to bring the doctor.

But it was too late for that. The splash of scarlet over Roley's heart was not spreading any more. His face was white. He looked at Jack and then at me. I cradled his head on my arm, to raise it a bit. Roley smiled, slightly. He said, "Jack. Willie. Tell my wife and my son." His head was slowly turning to the right, toward me. He was struggling to speak. "That I just wanted to..."

His head stopped turning toward me. His mouth remained slightly open. His eyes were open, too. His face looked like he was determined to finish the sentence.

I got up. Jack was kneeling on the floor, crying like a baby. I looked down at Roley's dead face for a few more seconds. Then I started to push my way through the militiamen who were crowding into the cabin.

I started to walk back to Batoche. The sky was a rich shade of blue. I could see the bright ribbon of the river, off to the north and west. The birds were singing as if nothing had happened.

The war was over.

XXI

General Middleton himself sent for me and asked me to look out for Jack. "Everyone likes Lieutenant Price," he said. "Quite a decent fellow. Some of your officers have told me they are afraid he might make away with himself. Guilt, you see. Over Captain Collison. Not protecting him. I gather Price almost worshipped the man. And the regrettable necessity to kill a child. Anyway, can't let a suicide happen." But I did nothing for Jack, not even when I heard him crying at night in the lodgings we now shared. Riel was taken out of the camp by Captain Young and a small army of guards, heading toward his appointment with the gallows in Regina, and I could not even bestir myself to join the excited crowd that watched him go. Colonel Williams was taken to Battleford, nursed by some of his doting Midlanders, and I could not even be bothered to say goodbye.

I only wrote one more letter home. That was to Alice, the night of the day Roley died. I told her the whole miserable story. She was the only one who knew. I did not write again. I knew that the Ministry of Militia would tell everybody about my date of arrival back home.

A few days after Roley was buried, Arthur Howard, grumbling eloquently, came into my lodgings at Batoche to tell me that the "garbage scow" which old Gabriel's cable had half-demolished had been refitted, and that he, Arthur, must now endure a two-week journey back to the West with the despised Captain Jim Sheets. What little was left of the Riel Rebellion was still going on in north-west Saskatchewan. Arthur, at least, was unchanged, still jaunty, still showy, still chattering about his Gatlings. He saw how bad I was. Of course, he had seen men who had come through battle before. He sat quietly beside me in the stuffy little room for a long time. "You have to let it go, Willie," he finally said. "I know it's hard to lose a friend. But you must mourn Roley, be thankful you got the chance to know him, and go on with your life." I said nothing, just looked at him. Arthur looked hard at me for a few seconds, then shook my hand, said, "Good to have known *you*," and walked out of the door.

* * *

They did not force us to march over that awful terrain between railheads north of Superior, not this time. A boat carried us, and we were eventually deposited upon trains, which would carry us to a heroes' welcome in Toronto.

I sat alone, staring out the train window as we rolled toward home. For months, I'd been dreaming about the euphoria I'd feel if I survived the war, and found myself only a few hours away from my Alice, from my home, from everything I'd ever known. I peered out indifferently at the southern Ontario fields, shining in the lambent light of spring, at the puffy white clouds scudding in a bright blue sky, at the Union Jack-waving crowds shouting on every small town railway platform, and I felt almost nothing.

There was to be a victory parade from the station in Toronto, and only one unit would not be taking part in it—our own Company Four. The reason was simple enough. Our company really didn't have a commanding officer any more, and it would have taken one to arrange our participation in that parade. Jack's manner had become so strained and so odd that the men simply ignored him now. In desperation, the officers from the other regiments came to me to enlist my help in planning the parade.

I had begun to learn that if I just ignored people, they would give up and go away. The officers loomed over me as I slumped in my seat, talking louder and louder, laughing uneasily, clapping me on the back, blowing tobacco smoke around, offering me nips from flasks, trying to arouse some response. I said nothing; I betrayed no reaction. It was bad to do those things, because then people persisted in trying to make a connection with you. I stared into space, and I found an interesting thing: if you tried, you could fix it so that even what people said was unintelligible. It just became a meaningless roar of noise, somehow almost comforting. Eventually, they *did* just give up and go away, casting frightened glances at me which I ignored. The only one who remained was Colour Sergeant Quinn. He leaned over me and stared right into my face. He had lost a lot of weight, and he looked ill under his suntan. His Burnside whiskers needed trimming. "Willie," he said, in a hopeless way, and pressed my shoulder. I shook my head slightly, and turned to look out the window until I was sure he'd walked away.

The train stopped at a village just outside Toronto. A crowd of pompous, overweight old men in frock coats, top hats and striped pants clambered onto the train. They were, I knew, federal, provincial and civic politicians. They knew that in the cacophony which would accompany our arrival, they wouldn't get the chance to say anything to the men. They were taking this chance to talk to the returning heroes, pat them on the back, tell them how noble they were, and of course, sew up some votes in the process. As I looked dully at them, I wondered if *they* might get into a fight, Liberals socking Conservatives and vice versa, as they struggled to fawn on the victorious men of the North-West Field Force.

I wouldn't have gotten out of my chair for them, but shortly after the train headed toward the city, a fat old man in a black coat approached me. He turned out to be the deputy mayor of Toronto. "I wanted," he said, "to meet the celebrated Lieutenant Lorimer, the hero who went into the ravine and killed an enemy sharpshooter at Fish Creek."

I had not felt stirred or even interested by anything for weeks, but this caught my attention. I finally shook his outstretched hand. "Hero?" I said.

"Oh, of course, all heroes," he said. He looked thoughtfully at me for a minute. "That's not to say that there isn't a certain amount of re-thinking going on about the war. A certain amount of remorse, even in English-speaking circles. That is, among the people who enjoy wallowing delicately in remorse and guilt. The only one who hasn't been heard from in *that* crowd, is that tiresome windbag, your radical father-in-law-to-be, who will now, because you're a hero, have to keep his mouth shut in perpetuity about the outrages we all supposedly perpetrated in the North-West." He winked. "You should be aware, though, that we in government have found it useful to let some of the public unease about our role in the uprising devolve upon that officer in your company who died. Collinson, was that his name? His death really didn't look very good. He'd already killed some young child in taking Batoche, and then, dirty and half-drunk, being killed by some other little boy who was only defending his home. Not good in the public perception. I mean to say, it can't really hurt Collinson or whatever his name was, now, can it? It's been found expedient that he be in some ways a sort of scapegoat. To satisfy the radicals, and of course the bloody French. The government and militia are not saying anything in defence of this Captain Collinson."

I was so weary I could hardly speak. I did not *want* to speak. But I thought I should say something. "He had a wife and a son," I said.

He looked at me with amusement. "Oh, *come* now," he said. "I had you marked down as a promising young man. A man cold-blooded enough to descend into a coulee and shoot some half-breed dead shouldn't dabble in such sentimentalities. *Come* now. The wife and son will receive a pension. In the long run, they'll have nothing to complain about." He stared out the window for a moment. His face was impassive. "We are trying as much as possible to arrange things so that it will be as if this Collinson never really lived at all. That's the best way."

I thought for a minute, and then I said the only thing I could say. "Toy soldiers," I said.

"What? *What* did you say?" he said. He was getting angry. I did not reply, and after a few moments he wandered away.

The train was in the outskirts of the city now. Alongside the track on both sides were immense crowds, roaring applause. I have never seen so many Union Jacks in my life. Everybody had signs: WELCOME BACK, and WELL DONE, and WE ARE PROUD. As well, of course, as HANG RIEL, and THREE CHEERS FOR MAC-DONALD, and GOD SAVE THE QUEEN. I ignored them.

The train pulled into the station. If there had been a cacophony of patriotic noise when we left, now there was a Bedlam. A dozen bands seemed to be playing. A wall of cheering came at the train; the windows seemed to bend in under it, and the men looked a little scared as they shouldered their packs and started filing off the car. I could see excited, gesticulating people outside. I didn't really want to get out of my seat, but I knew I had to, and so I finally got up and approached the exit. Jack was there. For some reason, I said his name. He stiffened and darted an angry look at me. Then he got off, and I saw him pushing his way through the crowd, to find his wife I guess. He was moving in an absurdly stiff, awkward way. He looked like a little old man.

I got off and started pressing through the crowd. It occurred to me that it would take me hours to find Alice and my parents, who I was sure would be there. In fact, they found me, and in less than five minutes.

It wasn't at all as I'd imagined it would be during those long nights on the prairies. I didn't fall into Alice's arms and then my mother's. In fact, my mother started to cry as soon as she saw me. My father actually managed a look of patriarchal concern. Alice was standing between them. She was wearing the same military-looking little blue cap, although no overcoat in the June heat. She did not say my name, she did not reach for me. She stared intently and very sadly into my face, and took my hand in hers.

Behind her loomed Mr. Niven, beaming fraudulently. Alice's willowy, decorative, dark-haired mother wore a light blue dress ten times more elaborate than her daughter's. She gave me her usual creamy smile and took my other hand, rubbing her finger insinuatingly against my wrist, a mannerism I had seen her use with her husband.

However, for the first time, her heart did not seem to be in the performance. She glanced uneasily at Alice, and then at her husband. "Willie, *dear*," she finally said, "how brave you are. All our friends are waiting for you at our house. A huge reception, just for you, Willie dear. We are going to take you and Alice, and...of course your parents, straight over there. They are all *so* anxious to hear all about the uprising, from the soldier's point of view. You'll have to convert some of them; they're great supporters of Riel." She flashed the seductive smile again, and again it didn't quite come off. I had the vague idea that she was somehow ashamed of herself. In my utter weariness, I glanced at Alice. She was staring at me and her mother, and there was a lot of pain in her face.

Then one of the most astounding events of the entire Riel Rebellion occurred. My mother said, "*No!*" in the loudest voice I had ever heard her employ.

"No?" Mrs. Niven said.

"Certainly not," my mother said, firmly. "Willie is *my* son. Willie and Alice are coming to *our* house for one hour. One hour, only. Then we shall all come to your reception. And thank you very much, I'm sure."

Mr. Niven's face had turned red, and his mouth was opening and closing without audible sound. "We're going," my mother said. She started hauling me along by one arm, and Alice tugged with even greater strength on the other. I felt as distanced from all this as I had from everything else that had happened to me in the last few weeks. I said nothing.

My mother and Alice pushed their way through the crowd with remarkable tenacity. My dad brought up the rear. The throng outside the station was gigantic, and deafening. People waved to me, saluted me, beamed at me. However, the police had created corridors through the crowd for anybody in a uniform, and it was down one of these and to a waiting cab rank that my family dragged me.

The cab rattled off down a relatively empty side street. "You can have more than one hour, Alice," my mother said. "You can have as long as you like."

"I know," Alice said. She was pressing my hand so hard the blood flow was almost cut off. She pressed one gloved hand against my cheek. I still did not speak, and I did not cuddle against her hand. It was intriguing. In the cab with me were the only people for whom I really cared in the world. Yet I found myself nestling down even more comfortably into that cold sense of isolation. Nothing would get too close to me, not even here. I was busy looking at the familiar Toronto streets. They looked the same, yet somehow completely different. That was interesting, too.

We arrived at my house. My mom and Alice got me out of the cab and into the front hall. "That poor woman," my mother said grimly, to no one in particular. She pushed open the sliding doors to the front parlour, and waved Alice and me in. "As long as you like, as long as you need," she said to Alice, and kissed her.

We sat side by side on the red Chesterfield sofa my mother loved so much. "Alice," I finally said, touching her shoulder, "I..."

"I read your letter," she said. "I know Roley's gone, and you think you're responsible. I see how it is with you, sweetheart."

Here at last was something that I could get my teeth into. "Well, Alice," I said, "I *am* responsible. I as good as killed him." I felt suddenly that there was some huge thing inside my chest, pressing against my lungs, against my voicebox. It was hard to breathe or to speak. "I let him down, Alice. My best friend. He trusted me. I just stood there like a fool. I did nothing. It's all my fault."

She reached out both hands, and put one against either side of my face. She was a very strong girl. It felt as if I were in a vise.

She put her face very close to mine and stared into my eyes as if she were trying to mesmerize me. "Listen to me, Willie," she said. "You didn't kill your friend. Roley wanted to be Saint George fighting the dragon, and there aren't any dragons, and there aren't any saints, either. It's not your fault. Not one bit of it. Roley didn't die because of you. He died because the gods are as cruel as hell."

She tightened the grip on my face. "*Willie*," she said, "you have to come back to me. This is killing you—I can see it—and it will kill me too. *Come back to me.*"

I opened my mouth to rebut what she'd said. To my horror, what came out was an awful, braying sob of shame, defeat, grief and pain, a noise I'd never dreamed any human could make. At the same moment, my eyes filled so much with tears that I was utterly blinded. I started to fall forward. Alice pulled me over and held my face against her shoulder. I lay there for an eternity, sobbing convulsively, my whole body shaking. I was still a little outside myself, at least at first, and I remember being astounded that the whole neighbourhood could not hear me. Perhaps they could. I wailed, I howled. I was crying for Roley, for Jack, for the boy I'd killed, and for all the rest. Perhaps, most of all, I was crying for the Willie Lorimer I'd always been, who was now gone forever.

Alice held me tight. She held on to my shoulder with one hand, and with the other one she caressed the back of my neck. She kept kissing me as I lay there and sobbed. "It's all right," she kept saying, "it's all right," and after a long while the suffocating thing came out of my chest, and I stopped crying; and that was how I came home.

* * *

I went to see Roley's wife and son after I got back. I was a little shocked by what a humble home he had had. The woman's nervous face was thinner than ever in grief. She was full of rage, too, I could feel that. The little boy, perched on a chair too high for him, looked utterly lost. It was a very tense and unpleasant visit. To my vast relief, neither of them asked how he had died. I got away as soon as I decently could, knowing that I would never return.

One thing happened, though, just as I was leaving. "Just a minute," Vera Collison said. "You seem to be one of the few people who will even admit to knowing Roley, and he was certainly very fond of you. I have the letters around here somewhere. He was always writing about how brilliant you were, how much he relied on you, and what a good friend you were. Would you like to have something that belonged to him?"

"Yes," I said.

She went away for a few seconds, and came back with a worn,

thick, blue book. *Tales From Shakespeare* was printed on the cover. "I found this in his things," she said, her voice tightening up a little. "It's the stories of all those plays, done in a simple style. I expect his parents bought it for him, when he was young. To help him study. He was never very good in school, you know."

I thanked her and left. A few months later, I heard that she had sold the store, and that she and the boy had left the city. I never heard of either of them again.

One day, about ten years later, I found the book on some neglected shelf, and I ruffled through it. Sparse stuff it was, indeed. But then I noticed some writing on one of the blank pages at the back of the book. Roley had been idly jotting on it, in pencil. It looked like it had started with his trying to practice an adult signature. Two of the signatures were slanted forward, one backward, as if he were trying to see what looked best:

Roland Hewitt Collison
Roland H. Collison
R.H. Collison

July 5, 1867, ten p.m. Sitting in bed, thinking about great day I had. Mom, Dad, and Aunt Kate downstairs, playing cards. Bob crawled in here and went to sleep. Charlie [a dog?] asleep on bottom of bed.

My first day in the store. Dad said I did great. We took in $41.98. I can't wait for tomorrow.

Roley

XXII

June 2, 1941

Alice died four years ago, and our only child, John, was killed in 1916, in the Great War. So I have a lot of time on my hands. I suppose I have been thinking that at seventy-seven, if I didn't write down what happened now, I never would.

Yes, Roley was a remarkable man. He wasn't a well-educated or even a particularly thoughtful man. Yet he saw through the thing. *They lied to us.* Yes, they lied, they lied; perhaps they always have, perhaps they always will.

Yet he also said, *A man is nothing if he believes in nothing.* And I believe that too. So, old, alone, I still try to move toward the light. And more and more, my thoughts turn toward that distant past when every morning glowed with hope, when every new day promised to bring me all the wonder, and all the glory, of the world.